M000232452

OPHELIA

ALSO BY NORMAN BACAL

BREAKDOWN: THE INSIDE STORY OF THE
RISE AND FALL OF HEENAN BLAIKIE
(non-fiction)

ODELL'S FALL
(fiction)

OPHELIA

A NOVEL

BY
NORMAN BACAL

BARLOW BOOKS
fine books for enterprising authors

Copyright © Norman Bacal, 2021

All rights reserved. No part of this publication may be reproduced, stored in a retrieval system or transmitted, in any form or by any means, without prior written consent of the publisher.

This is a work of fiction. Names, characters, places, and incidents are either the product of the author's imagination or are used fictitiously, and any resemblance to actual persons, living or dead, events, or locales is entirely coincidental.

Library and Archives Canada Cataloguing in Publication data available upon request.

978-1-988025-65-0 (paperback)

Printed in Canada

Publisher: Sarah Scott
Book producer: Tracy Bordian/At Large Editorial Services
Cover design: Lena Yang
Cover art: Sharon Bacal
Interior design and layout: Liz Harasymczuk
Copy editing: Wendy Thomas
Proofreading: Joel Gladstone

For more information, **visit www.barlowbooks.com**

Barlow Book Publishing Inc.
96 Elm Avenue, Toronto, ON
Canada M4W 1P2

*For my wife and life partner, Sharon,
whose art adorns this cover and
who has taught me so much about
the meaning of love and friendship*

This novel was originally intended to be a study in the relationships between fathers and their children. To that end I dedicate this book to the memory of my two fathers, Michael Bacal and Max Westelman.

∼

May their memories be a blessing.

"Who knows three? I know three.
Three are the fathers
and two are the tablets that Moses brought.
One is the God, One is the God, One is the God,
in the heaven and the earth.
Umpa Lumpa, Umpa Lumpa, Umpa Lumpa.

BACAL FAMILY TRADITIONAL HAGGADIC POEM

PROLOGUE

Gerhard Neilson stood at the kitchen window facing out over Snekkersten harbor. He could barely make out the fishing boats, dormant until dawn, bobbing in the light impatient chop. A dense mist that had descended just after sunset hid the stars on the moonless night. Or maybe it was the veil of secrecy that had descended on the village ever since the Nazis imposed martial law at the end of August, a month ago. The older kids had been whispering in the schoolyard just this morning about the strange comings and goings.

He recognized Father's familiar silhouette, the bill of his oilskin cap, hands thrust into the deep pockets of his raincoat. The village might be sleeping but the tides were always at work, whispering secrets that only Father could decipher. But why would he be out so late in this weather? He was usually asleep before Gerhard.

Gerhard threw on a navy woolen sweater, overalls, and a waterproof coat and tiptoed out the front door, wary of waking Mother. Father was standing just in front of the stone retaining wall that for generations had kept the turbulent waves away from the house.

The harbor smelled like rotten fish. And salt. Like it did every day. Like it always would.

"Why are you out here, little navigator?" Father asked without bothering to look over in Gerhard's direction.

Gerhard winced. When was Father finally going to drop the childish nickname?

1

"Are you judging tomorrow's weather?" Gerhard asked. As generations of Neilsons had learned to do since the Vikings arrived. As Gerhard was certain he would never be able to learn.

"Tonight I am waiting."

Gerhard heard the faint cry of a child from a distance. Father broke off and looked over Gerhard's head.

Gerhard turned. Three adults and two children were struggling against the wind along the harbor wall. The woman in the lead was dressed sensibly and warmly, like Mother would be dressed on a night like this: a dark heavy coat with a thickened hood and rain boots. Father took a few steps forward to greet them.

A man and a boy stood a few paces behind the woman. The man wore a fancy coat with a gold star sewn on the lapel. He was carrying a small bag, tethered to his wrist. The boy looked to be about Gerhard's age. Twelve or thirteen at the most. His leather shoes would not last very long in the soaked, salty air. Just behind them, the mother struggled to hold onto her head-scarf in one hand and the screeching girl in the other. Their ankle-length dresses flapped wildly from under their coats. She lifted the girl to her chest and began to soothe her.

Father nodded at the woman in the lead in a familiar way. She began shouting over the wind. "Twenty-six were taken by Aksel, but there was no room for these four. Can you take them, Thalem?"

Father's eyes turned grim. "There is nowhere to hide them until tomorrow night?"

"You know the answer."

Father studied the boat, rocking against the rubber tires moored to the dock. It was simple but rugged, recently painted white with a small sturdy helm in the center and a polished wooden cover over the bow. Gerhard doubted it was built for the open sea, except maybe on a calm night. And how would they navigate without any visible stars or landmarks? Gerhard was a master of calculating time of arrival to their regular fishing locations, though occasionally Father lost patience with all the chatter. Gerhard enjoyed working out latitude and longitude to the last second — the only thing Gerhard liked about fishing. Father had no idea how much Gerhard could calculate in his head, beyond his simple navigational problems, like the speed of the rotation of the earth or the amount of time it took sunlight to reach the earth.

Father finally turned to Gerhard. "If we are traveling four and a half kilometers at our usual speed, heading due west, given this breeze and currents being double what they usually are, how long would it take?"

Distance and direction meant Sweden, Gerhard thought. Out of the Øresund and into open seas. In this boat? And in this weather? To help complete strangers? Was Father going crazy? Gerhard closed his eyes and forced the thoughts out of his head. "Heading out into this wind? All in, three and a half hours, maybe four — unless there are other variables you haven't factored in. Like a change in the weather or the winds once we leave the harbor."

"Bring the woman and child to the kitchen to stay warm," Father ordered. "Wake your mother. Then get the boat ready." Looking over to the man with the bag he added, "Perhaps your boy can give mine a hand." The men walked away to begin a discussion.

Gerhard studied the boy and made a quick evaluation. He was about Gerhard's size, but his shoes and clothing would make him completely worthless tonight. "Come along, you need a pair of boots and a warm coat." The boys exchanged names, a love of soccer, and a few minutes later, Paul was proving himself not so worthless as a boat hand.

"What's with the yellow star your father wears on his coat?"

"The Nazis require it in the countries he travels to. And that bag he's carrying? He calls it his inventory. Takes it with him everywhere. Like the star."

"What kind of inventory fits in such a bag?"

"He calls it my future." Paul added, "Though it won't mean much if we all drown. Diamonds at the bottom of the sea."

"Diamonds?" For a trip to save their lives, the diamond merchant should be prepared to pay a lot. Enough to allow Father to send Gerhard away from this stupid village. Away from the stink. The first Neilson to attend university. Better to drown tonight than come back to this dead-end life.

■ ■ ■

Once they left the protection of the harbor, the wind blew up in the Øresund. The lights from the shoreline, what few there were to start with, were now invisible. There was still no star to navigate by, just Father's instincts, and unforgiving gusts buffeting the boat. Mother and daughter sat huddled along with Paul's father in the stern. The girl was already sick to her stomach and the mother was not in any better shape.

After about an hour, the swell increased and water began pouring into the boat.

"Bail," came the order from Father, and Gerhard reached under the cover for a pail. He crouched and filled it halfway, then tossed the water over the side. At least the saltwater washed away the vomit and the sickening odor.

After a couple of minutes, he felt pressure on his back. Paul had taken the second pail and was bailing furiously, though he was having trouble getting his sea legs. Back to back they worked in unison, the waves continually bringing more of the sea into the boat, saltwater stinging his eyes. They were too far out to go back. Besides, Father's honor would sooner they all drown than give in.

Gerhard heard a scream from Father's direction but could not hear a word. A wall of water overcame him and tossed him toward the gunwale. Then nothing but blackness.

■ ■ ■

Dawn broke on a new day. The sunlight filtered in from the horizon warming his eyelids, returning him to life. He woke with a gasp and a choke, vomiting a rush of seawater onto the deck. After a few moments he pushed his prone body from the deck to a sitting position. Paul was beside him, right leg askew at an impossible angle, face ashen. His pant leg was torn and bloodstained. Paul's fingers were squeezing the gunwale; his teeth were clenched.

Paul forced a thin smile. "I won't be playing much football this year."

Gerhard rose slowly. His breathing had settled back to normal, though his head ached, but otherwise nothing felt broken. The two fathers were standing together on the pier. In the light of day, the distinction between the two men was more apparent. Father's ruddy cheeks had been toughened by years of sun and wind. Paul's father's face was pale and soft. In his hand he was holding the brown felt bag. The moment of reckoning had arrived. "Bless you, Father," Gerhard thought. Paul's father poured a bunch of clear stones into his free hand.

"Take these, Mr. Neilson," he said to Father. "I know you refused earlier but you have risked your lives. And surely your boat has suffered some damage."

Father turned his head away to look at the mother and daughter. "What makes you think I'm about to change my mind? Go tend to your family. God's thanks are all I need."

Paul's father tried once more to force the stones into Father's hand, which was now closed into an unyielding fist. The same way he kept it closed to any form of temptation from the devil. "Keep them. Your journey is only beginning. Go. We must be heading back now."

"In my community it is said that he who saves a life saves the world. Our families are linked forever by your act of selflessness. You have my vow that as long as any member of my family lives and breathes, your kindness will be rewarded. God be with you."

"And you."

Gerhard shook his head in disbelief.

The man stepped back into the boat and lifted Paul into his arms in one smooth motion. Paul screamed at the sudden movement and passed out. His father stepped off the fishing boat and did not cast his eyes backward.

"You've had a long night," Father said. "Let's get ourselves some bread and a little herring. Then we can head home. Never forget this lesson, little navigator. Serving God is of far greater value than all the diamonds on earth."

Gerhard's face burned. He felt a fever racing through him. A fever reminding him his life was ruined. Father, the village fool who had cheated himself out of a secure life for his family. God's thanks was all Father needed? How selfish and shortsighted. Gerhard made his own vow that would serve him the rest of his life.

PART I

CHAPTER 1

Sixty years later
October 2003

———

Geri Neilson paced outside the Manhattan brownstone, fixated on his watch, boiling with each passing moment. The black stretch limousine pulled up at the curb, and the driver came racing around to open the passenger door.

"You're six minutes late," he fumed.

"Sorry, sir. It took a little longer than expected to collect the passengers."

"Tell Mr. King to get out here for a moment."

A moment later Red King emerged from the car, smiling. He stood a good half foot taller than Geri.

"Ready for a great weekend?" Red asked. His South African inflection had softened over the years, along with his belly.

"We need to speak. Now."

"Geri, I've got our investors in the car and this is supposed to be a long weekend. Fun. No work. Remember?"

"I was up half the night. And the only reason I didn't cancel is because we have to talk. It can't wait. And I'm not getting in."

Red didn't rise to the bait. "You can't back out now, Geri." His tone had hardened. Geri crossed his arms. They stood facing each other for a moment. "Just get in the car, Geri." His tone was a little softer. "I promise you we'll talk. Tomorrow morning before the golf. The boys are inside waiting. If we're going to keep our stock price moving up, I need you to help schmooze them."

Geri's shoulders relaxed. "All right," he grumbled, following Red into the car.

Tomorrow morning they'd finally have it out. Geri took his seat on the dark leather back seat, beside Red, facing four passengers in golf attire who were laughing at the punchline of some joke. Geri recognized them all: the key fund managers who between them owned close to twenty percent of Danmark's stock.

"Atlantic City, look out!" Red yelled over the din.

Atlantic City, my ass, Geri thought. What could be more pathetic than adults wagering their fates when the probability of winning was rigged against them? That was not the way to amass a fortune. Calculating statistical probability for success and acting on it, combining ingenuity and uncompromising standards, that is what created wealth in America. Measure the risk and exact the reward. He and Red had built Danmark from the ground up on that premise.

He'd never set foot in Atlantic City before, but he had a pretty good idea what to expect. Golf, gambling, alcohol, and servicing any other whims of these investors. Air Jordan was flying in tomorrow to join them at the country club. Red admitted that at last year's weekend in Vegas he'd been taken for $150,000. "Well worth it," he insisted. "You'll never understand. I didn't lose it to just anyone."

■ ■ ■

Geri restrained himself through dinner, allowing Red to regale the boys with anecdotes about the world leaders he and Geri had met.

"Remember that night in Berlin with the Clintons and that Austrian couple? What were their names again? Some famous count, I think."

Geri nodded. Faked a smile. Red didn't really need him to keep the story going. Geri was just a prop tonight. A façade. Like what Red had set up in Ireland. If what Geri discovered yesterday proved out, it was a sham that could destroy everything they'd built.

Just after midnight Geri begged off and headed to his room. Enough of the sham.

A few minutes later he sat down at the desk in the suite and opened up his notebook, picked up the fountain pen and began to write.

Well over an hour later, after numerous scratches and corrections, Geri looked down at his work:

Chapter 2: The Exodus and my ten commandments

I navigated Father home from Sweden on calm seas in a little over an hour and a half, but it was too late. Well into the morning, a gang of men in black coats and jackboots were waiting. Nazis. The barking was louder than any dog I ever heard. The leader with the lightning bolts on his shoulders ordered them to take Father away.

He didn't return for three days, and when he did, just as Mother was serving dinner, his face was drawn and bruised. His upper lip was split and blood was caked on his cheeks. I'll never forget his eyes. Defiant. Maybe that's where I get it from. Mother attended to him and once she finished, Father, never one to use more words than necessary, looked up at her and said, "They'll be back. Midnight. We go."

That night we repeated the crossing, this time the three of us and whatever clothing and possessions I could squeeze into the boat.

What did I take from that? Father was a hero to the Jewish family, but had made us refugees. The rest of his life was struggle and failure, but I have to admit everything worked out for me. Maybe not the mythical Moses and his mythical Yahweh or God, but close, what with the crossing of the sea, wandering through Sweden and on to the promised land ... America ... but we'll get to that later. It took a lifetime to realize that my stunning success was driven as much by reward as by risk.

His thoughts were interrupted by a persistent knocking at the door. He looked over at the clock. One-thirty a.m. Are you kidding me, he thought. "Go away, Red," he shouted. "I'm in bed."

The knocking persisted. Red did not shout anything back through the door, but realistically who else could it be at this hour? Nothing was impossible, but certain eventualities were far more likely than others. In this case, statistically speaking the person at the door was more likely to be Red than anyone else.

The pace of the banging accelerated with an impatience that matched Geri's heartbeat. "Haven't I done enough for you tonight? Go to bed. We agreed on tomorrow. Not tonight!" he shouted, to no avail. They had stayed in enough hotels over too many years and Red had interrupted too many nights of sleep.

"Enough already," he muttered, slamming shut the notebook and sliding his blue reading glasses up onto his forehead. Geri was left with no alternative but to consider the possibility that it might be someone else, before opening the door.

In the time it took him to rise from the bed, adjust the tie on the plush white hotel robe, cross the suite, and approach the peephole, he had already run through the various permutations of potential outcomes. Game theory at play. Assume for a moment that it's not Red. If it was an evacuation, the fire alarm would have sounded, and if the person in the next room was choking, they'd be better off calling the front desk or 911 than knocking on the door of a complete stranger who likely had no training in dealing with emergencies. Which left open the possibility of robbery — or worse.

Geri laughed. His philosophy put to the test. Measure the risk and exact the appropriate reward. There was some risk of opening the door. What reward should he exact?

"Honey, I know you're standing on other side of door, but it's not polite to keep a girl waiting." There was the slightest inflection, and she stood far enough back from the peephole to allow him to identify her as a blonde in a low-cut red dress. Low enough to tell the story. This was not her first late-night appointment.

"Who sent you?" Geri asked.

"Room service."

Geri laughed and opened the door all the way. "I must be the first?" He couldn't trust Red, but after forty years he had become all too predictable.

"Nice suite," she said, scanning the living room. "Call me Angel. You Geri?" He nodded. He wasn't born Geri, but Gerhard was not a name that would allow an immigrant high-school kid any chance of survival.

"Do I know you, Angel?" There was an air of familiarity to her. He recalled some sociological theory about cross-race bias he'd read about before his last trip to China, suggesting most Asians looked the same to Caucasians. Geri had to stop reading mid-way through. Like most theories, it was worth nothing until proved through scientific method. All theories had to be carefully tested and retested, then analyzed and criticized by a broad community of experts. The essence of science. The core of a great pharma business.

She laughed. "You'll get to know me really well, Geri." She did not need directions to the bedroom.

Angel looked surprisingly muscular for a girl in this line of work. She carried a large handbag, and as she passed Geri on the way to the bedroom, the hem of her skirt swayed a good eighteen inches above the knee. No doubt about the length and tone of those thighs and what they may be capable of achieving. The view was spectacular when she bent over the bed to unzip the bag in preparation for whatever was coming. The pink thong left nothing to the imagination, except for what might transpire in the next half hour.

Geri looked over at the prescription bottle on the night table. Maybe he should grab the heart medication in advance. Except that would be a sign of weakness and his rapid heartbeat was beginning to slow. To hell with the idiot cardiologist who doled out warnings about self-restraint like someone who wasn't getting it anymore. Geri made a mental note to get to the pills later. She laid her own small bottle and a couple of condoms at the foot of the bed.

"Come. Lie down, honey," she said without turning around.

Geri propped himself up on the silk-lined pillows at the head of the bed and crossed his ankles.

"Close your eyes, honey. Relax. You're so tense. Like you think too much." She laughed. Geri sighed. He closed his eyes. She uncrossed his legs and began to massage his feet. The lotion was warming.

The shuffling of thoughts in his brain resumed, accompanied by a crackling from the foot of the bed. She was probably preparing the condom.

"You need a little help, honey. Keep your eyes closed. I'll get you ready."

Relax, Geri. The reward is coming. Keep your eyes closed, he thought. Something just wasn't working. Her annoying inflection. Or was it something else? His tenth commandment. Never close your eyes to risk.

Never close your eyes. Fuck, the voice screamed in his head. His eyes bulged open. The syringe in her hand was poised to enter between his toes. His leg jerked upward, sending it twirling like a majorette's baton. The follow-through caught her flush on the jaw. She howled in pain while his other heel kicked her in the chest and off the bed.

That's when he felt the constriction in his chest, the paralyzing pain in his left arm, the feeling he was drowning. He collapsed back on the bed as she rose off the floor, rubbing her jaw with one hand, grabbing her purse with the other, momentarily studying him. Hesitating. If she had worked for him, she would know what she had to do immediately. If you start a job, you finish it. He closed his eyes.

■ ■ ■

Angel closed the bathroom door behind her, reached for the burner phone, and dialed a number.

"Needle broke. But he's having the heart attack anyway."

"Did you administer the drug?"

"No."

"Did you leave any residue?"

"Hold on." She left the bathroom and got down on hands and knees, crawling across the room, phone in hand, tamping on the beige carpet with the other for traces of moisture. "Carpet's dry. No stain."

"Is that him moaning?"

"More like choking."

"Collect everything and leave him there. You delivered the message. Perhaps this is a better result. Return to Shannon on the next flight."

Angel gathered her things, the plastic syringe, and the broken needle and stuffed them in the handbag. Geri was gasping as she eased the door closed behind her. She measured her pace to the elevator. When the car arrived empty, she let the door close behind her, then hit the stop button, moved to the corner underneath the camera, then commenced her methodical transformation: she carefully removed the wig and red dress and placed them at her feet, then appraised her face in the compact mirror. The bruising at the jawline wasn't too bad, but would be in about an hour. She applied the cover-up in coats until she was satisfied, opened the bag and reached for the folded full-length black dress, slipped it over her head, then rolled the wig into the red dress and placed it in the bag; scanned the elevator floor for any traces of blond hair. Finally, she restarted the elevator and emerged in the lobby as Li Shan.

■ ■ ■

The moment the door had clicked shut, Geri picked up the house phone, dialed 0, and called for help. It takes more than an ordinary assassin to kill Geri Neilson, he gloated. I'll deal with Red in the morning. Then he fainted.

The house was full to capacity at the Holy Trinity Lutheran Church, across from Central Park. Standing room only. Who but Geri Neilson could pack them in like this on an angry Thursday morning in late October? Tal Neilson turned his head to catch a glimpse of the sea of heads filling the pews behind him. The *Who's Who* of Manhattan business and political elite were in attendance, coats in their laps, wearing their Sunday best. Tal faced forward to resume his bird's-eye view of the polished casket from his front row seat.

The organist churned away at the final bars of the Bach cantata, the last bars lingering in the air, inevitably slipping away, perhaps imitating the departure from this world of Father's dominating spirit. Pastor Bernard Marcellus had kept his speech short, finishing with words that would surely have annoyed Father. "May the soul of the departed, through the mercy of God, rest in peace." Mythical God, Father was wont to say. An invention for the masses.

Red King left his pew, from the other side of Mother, ponderously making his way up the carpeted staircase to the podium and waiting patiently for the silence to fill the room. Jesus and the apostles looked on from above.

"Geri Neilson was as close to a mythological figure as a mortal can become in seventy-two years. Let me start by addressing the legend of his nickname."

Leave it to Red, opening with the story of how President Clinton chatted with them at a cocktail party during his first term. Clinton kept insisting that Father call him Bill. By the fourth time that Bill referred to Father as Gerhard, as Red told it, Father's face turned bright purple until he practically exploded. "Do me a favor, Bill. Call me Geri?" Father recounted a different version of that story, but Red's became the company lore, and CallMeGeri was no longer around to defend himself.

Red the crowd pleaser. The crowd teaser. Always the grand storyteller, leading everyone along with anecdotes from the good old days. How he and CallMeGeri built the business, the daring and bravado, the court battles with drug conglomerates who put up every possible roadblock to prevent them from accessing the market with their cheaper generics. Red and Geri together — the unstoppable force.

Mild-mannered business school graduates in '63, soon to become superheroes. Tal had heard it so many times it made him nauseous.

Tal felt an icy hand land on top of his. Mother. As cold as her heart. Trudi Darrow playing the role of grieving widow. He looked over. A couple of tears that she refused to wipe set the right tone for the occasion. Her eyes the right amount of pink. Enough so that even a cynic would accept she was a widow in mourning, though not distraught. That wouldn't suit Trudi Darrow. She didn't have an ounce of distraught in her. Right now, she was completely focused on Red. Screw them both. Tal didn't buy the act for a second.

The seat to the other side of Tal was the only empty seat in the house. He'd kept it reserved just in case she changed her mind. This morning he'd begged her to join him in the front, but when he and Mother had entered the chapel, there she was in the back row, eyes refusing to make contact. Dark defiant hair flowing over the black dress, suitable for the occasion. No makeup or lipstick. Her. Ophelia.

The only other family in the chapel were sitting right behind them. Mother's two brain-dead cousins. At least that's how CallMeGeri always referred to them. To Mother they were Wilder and Stinky; she never called them Walter and Steve. Wilder was tall, slim, and bald on top, with the pale coloring of an undertaker. Stinky had a full head of curly salt and pepper hair and a stomach that stuck out so far, it could launch airplanes at sea. They'd nodded greetings when Mother had taken her seat. Tal was not sure if she was deliberately ignoring them or was simply oblivious to everything but the show of her grief. Tal could hear them just before Red began speaking.

"I just wish he would have listened to us. Just once," Stinky whined. "What we were asking for wasn't outrageous." Exactly the adjective Father would have used. Father had said he'd rather be lying in a box than speaking to either of them again. *The brain-dead cousins and their outrageous demands.* The only thing Tal could be certain about today was that there was nothing in the will for them. They had been litigating with Father for at least ten years, claiming he owed them a hundred million, or some such number. More likely, they were hoping that Tal or Mother would be more amenable to a settlement of the litigation than Father.

Tal slouched and extended his legs, closing his eyes. Red might go on forever.

"Geri came from humble beginnings. He immigrated to the United States in 1946, the son of a Danish fisherman."

"Not his story to tell," came a male voice from behind.

Tal pulled himself up in his pew. He turned to glare at the brain-dead cousins, though no one else noticed.

"Geri was that one in a million. A true genius. Could have been the next Einstein. Won a full scholarship to MIT. He wanted to get into the space program in the early sixties. I was the corrupting influence. Geri had never even heard of generics."

Red paused for the appropriate time to acknowledge the polite laughter.

"I had the business plan and Geri had the brain. Then the lightning struck."

"BAM." The jolt came from within Tal's head. *"A one in fourteen million chance that a lightning bolt would strike a twin prop carrying Trudi's father and her uncle."* A familiar voice. *"Another one in ten million or so that it would explode the fuel tank."*

"Father?" Tal mumbled.

"Some might say it was fate that drove us to Bethlehem, Pennsylvania, to meet the widows of the founders of Darrowpharm in '63. Trudi's mother and aunt. The widows put their faith in two university grads who promised to carry on the family legacy. I'll confess we needed a fair amount of luck for the first few years."

"It's never about luck. I found the money for the down payment. I worked day and night. I took advantage of every opportunity. I even taught myself how to pick the best drugs. Then I made the calculations to engineer the Danmark version. I trained the team of scientists to expand the business."

Each of Father's emphatic I's shooting through Tal's lower molar, piercing the nerve. He brought his thumb to his jaw and pressed hard to counter the shocks.

"But we didn't have a plug nickel to pay the million-dollar down payment. I bluffed and Geri delivered a miracle. He found the money."

"It was Thomas Leiden and his Smol Foundation, connected with MIT. Originally they funded my scholarship, based on need and academic brilliance. I was an orphan, after all. On a hunch I called him after our first meeting with the widows. He made us a loan, few questions asked. Your mother, the cynic, was suspicious, insisting his accent was German. Hundreds of millions in Nazi loot was being moved through Switzerland at the time. If she was right, my father's been rolling over in his grave for forty years. Me on the other hand — I figured the Nazis owed me."

Tal turned around. Leiden, the lead director of the company, sitting two rows back on the aisle, beside Drew Torrance, the chair of the board, both appropriately dressed in a black suit, starched white dress shirt, and narrow black necktie, crisply folded handkerchief poking out of the breast pocket. As if there was a uniform to mourn the CEO. Their hair had whitened though Leiden's face bore the scars of aging, suggesting stress, perhaps from the past secrets he guarded, while Drew's face radiated a halo of success. Aside from his chair duties he was renowned as a political heavyweight in the Republican party and the head of a major law firm. For years Father's personal lawyer and adviser. They were perhaps the only two men in the world who Father never maligned, though in the days before all the facework, the mention of either name caused Mother to grimace.

"We covered the rest of that purchase by way of royalty, an idea I devised. Geri called it my specialty."

"He specialized at what he's good at. Lying. Telling the widows what they needed to hear when we couldn't pay them the first few royalty payments when they came due. Telling them stories to keep them from suing. Buying us time. We needed the cash we owed them to reinvest in the business. That was my partner's expertise. Get people to trust him. Then betray them." The word "betray" rang loudly, as if Geri had shouted it from beside Jesus on the ceiling over the altar, for everyone in the audience to hear, shaking Tal's brain. He covered his ears.

Trudi yanked at his left elbow. "What's the matter?" she whispered. Then she fumbled around in her purse, pulled out a tissue, and handed it to Tal. "Your nose is running again. Take this, lovey."

Tal shook his head and bit on his bottom lip. Lovey had grown up to become the son with the perpetual runny nose and the childish nickname. Of course something was the matter. CallMeGeri was going ballistic and Tal couldn't turn down the volume.

"Paying for our acquisitions through future royalties from the business became our model," Red said.

"A model built on deception." Another voice, this time from behind.

"Yeah, they swindled us for twenty-five years on that royalty," Stinky chimed in.

"Swindled them? Are those clowns serious? Once we caught up with our payments to the widows, we made every subsequent payment promptly. Fifty million we've paid out to those ingrates since the widows died. Worst business deal Red ever negotiated. The agreement left open a loophole for their lawyers to argue that we owed far more. Thieves, all of them."

"The rest, as they say, is history," Red intoned.

"Cliché."

"Touché," Tal said to Geri's voice, and then laughed.

"Shhhh." Trudi pinched Tal's arm.

"Geri was always spending too much time looking after the business to take care of his health. The sudden heart attack was just so tragic."

A moment passed. Finally, a break from Father. Maybe Red had hit a nerve.

Father had been in great spirits a couple of months ago, celebrating his birthday at Alfredo's, his favorite Italian place around the corner from the apartment. It had been just the three of them at their regular corner table at the back of the restaurant, far from the kitchen. Green and white checked tablecloths, fake candles, red wine glasses kept filled by the wait staff. The place was packed. Tal had flown in from Evanston for the occasion. CallMeGeri was in one of his better moods. Made it much easier to put up with them. That and the couple of lines he snorted in the bathroom. Not enough for either of them to notice.

"Promise me, the two of you, regardless of whatever happens to me that you'll never settle with your brain-dead cousins," Geri said, just before taking a forkful of the pasta rolled to an inch thickness on his fork. "Nothing like a good carbonara," he added with a smile.

"What do you mean 'whatever happens to me'?" Tal asked. Who talked like that? "Your blood pressure again?"

"Nothing like that. Blood pressure under control, fifty push-ups every day. Not bad for a guy my age. They say I could run this company 'til I'm a hundred and ten. Nothing would give me more pleasure as far as your mother's family is concerned."

"And look what you're eating," Trudi said with disgust. "Nothing but fat and carbs." Trudi shook her head and looked at Tal. "His heart is beating a little funny lately," Trudi added matter-of-factly. She nibbled on the mozzarella spread over a morsel of pancetta. "The cardiologist says it's some rare arrhythmia that should be treatable with a heart medication." She glared at Geri. "He also says that you should stop doing those goddamned push-ups. Something's going to burst."

"Eight hundred and fifty bucks a pill, if you can believe that," Father said, ignoring Mother. "The brand companies are running a racket. Only the rich can afford the medications their cartel is manipulating. But I'm still here to keep them honest." He reached into his pocket and pulled out the bottle of tiny pink pills. "When this drug the doc's making me take comes off patent protection in a few years, I'll be selling the Danmark version for a quarter the price and we'll still make a two hundred percent profit. They'll do anything they can to stop me in court but they'd be smarter to hire someone to kill me," Geri laughed.

"Is someone threatening you?" Tal said, having completely lost his appetite. Not that he'd had one to start.

"Don't worry, son. I know how to take care of myself. Been doing it all my life."

"You have no respect for your body, Gerhard." Trudi was clutching her knife, pointing it in Father's direction, tapping it out to the beat of her words.

"Do not use that name on me," Geri snarled. "Or that tone."

"Or what? Or you'll stop taking your pills and kill yourself? Have you been taking them every day?"

"You know the answer to that."

"If I knew the answer, would I be asking?"

"Will you ever let up? It's my body. My life."

"Okay, then go ahead. You want to tempt fate. Be my guest." Trudi spat the words out.

"And I don't want either of you talking about my heart condition," Father sputtered. "You get it? If this gets out to my board, Red will manipulate them to put me out on sick leave. Whatever Red asks them for, Red gets. I'd rather be dead than home in bed."

"Go ahead. Kill yourself, Geri. Maybe when you're gone, I'll rejoin Red at Danmark. Take my old job back. Better yet, I'll take on your role. The job you screwed me out of. Literally."

Father blanched. "And you had no hand in leaving the company? It takes two, Trudi." He turned to Tal. "She helped us with the negotiations with her family. Practically talked them into it singlehandedly. I'll give her that much. Came to work with us every day for five years. Until she was big as a house. Past her due date."

"Until the day you and Torrance pushed me out."

Father's volleys followed by Mother's vicious returns. Inevitably the child became the ball. Were they the couple arguing over the son they invented? Or the son who was never really there? His teenage best friend Cornelius had a better description: the "maculate" conception in the manger of cornstalks. Nine months later Tal was born in Bethlehem, Pennsylvania, a few miles from the Darrowpharm plant.

Tal reached for his wine glass, empty again. The waiter dutifully refilled the glass. Geri rolled his eyes, as he continued his rant, his voice getting louder until he was almost yelling. "At that point *something* in your mother's life had to be more important than Darrowpharm. Like you."

Father was staring directly at Tal. The heightened intensity preceding the final serve in front of a huge audience.

"Maybe if she'd paid as much attention to you as she did to Darrowpharm before you came along, I wouldn't have had to fork out thousands in legal fees to bail you out of the DUI, the shoplifting, the possession charges. Even worse, all the time you had me waste making your problems disappear. Then in and out of rehab." Game, set, match, Dr. Neilson. Father raised his arm and slammed it on the table.

A hush fell over the entire restaurant.

Tal stood and faced the diners, raising his glass high. "Let's all wish CallMeGeri happy birthday." Tal began to sing at the top of his voice. The crowd joined in. The glass was swishing back and forth, toward the rim. Toward Father. Toward Mother, until the final chorus when the wave of ruby wine broke out of the glass on a perfect arc in its journey toward the table, coating Trudi's dress, her perfectly coiffed blond updo, and down her cheeks. The waiters came rushing over with a pile of white linens.

They sat there in silence while the table was cleared. Another perfect Neilson family dinner.

■ ■ ■

Red had finally advanced the narrative to the nineties, the years when Tal entered the Danmark picture. When there was still a possibility of earning Father's respect. After the uncontrollable teenage years and the antics with Cornelius. No more arrests. College graduation without formal incident. Following Father's design that Tal work at Danmark — as long as Tal remained clean.

In typical fashion he got shunted into the marketing department, an entry-level position, under Red's direction. Out of Father's sight. He might as well have had an office with the janitorial staff in the basement, for all the attention he got. After the second year, Red transferred Tal to the international division based in Orly, just outside Paris, where he could go on completely unnoticed. Tal wondered whether Father even knew.

Screw them both. He resolved to pay his dues, learn about the international market. Enjoy Paris. Maybe even meet someone. Learn enough to crawl out from under Red's thumb. Finally get Father to take notice, then climb the corporate ladder. Paris was the opportunity to clean up and get serious. To study the processes of marketing and distribution and the sales chain. After a few months he began to catch the hidden inefficiencies in the business that were becoming obvious.

He was alone in his office at three in the morning when the epiphany struck. A revolutionary idea for the international sales of their drugs. A realization that had to be proved out. He began work on a computer program to prove his theory. Do it Father's way. Do the math. Make him proud. Once he had worked out the bugs, he began to test the hypotheses, running and rerunning the computer models. Day and night, the bennies kept him going.

Danmark's panoply of drugs became my life, Father, Tal thought. Exactly what you wanted. Three years at the company and Tal was addressing the secrets of the universe that mattered: how Danmark could triple market share in Europe; quadruple it in Asia; the algorithms were perfection. The underlying idea would put Danmark miles ahead of the competition. He could implement the plan from here. Stay in Paris, far from Red. He just needed a little authority for now. Let the improved sales numbers speak for Tal. Father always noticed the numbers. He did the quarterly math and fanatically analyzed the results.

Then and only then could Tal return to Manhattan to make his move up the corporate ladder. The prodigal son returning home. Sure it was a leap, but in three years he'd accumulated ten years of knowledge by anyone's standards. By Father's standards. A ticket to the executive suite. He sent two copies of the business plan back to the New Jersey head office. One for Red. A second for Father. Then he waited.

He heard nothing for three months, until Danmark issued a press release announcing its new joint venture with Cunzhuang Pharmacies to distribute their drugs internationally. An insane decision. Why share the profits with some Chinese mail order company, headquartered in Ireland, when he had modelled out how to do it on their own? A kick to the gut.

He'd stewed on the betrayal for days until finally getting on a plane to confront Father in his office. He barged in unannounced, without an appointment. The bald spot on Father's head poked out from the top of the leather desk chair. His back was to the door, and he was screaming. His finger was pointed at a spot on his computer screen. From where Tal stood he could make out that it was some compound, but he was too far away to recognize it.

"The molecular chain is different!" CallMeGeri shouted. "That's what I want you to hammer home at trial."

Tal hammered on the desk until Geri's chair finally swiveled.

"Hold on," Geri said, then removed the headset and laid it beside the computer screen on the desk. He peered out over the top of his bifocals.

"Aren't you supposed to be in Paris? What are you doing here?"

"Why don't you guess?" Tal tasted bitter acid in his mouth.

"I don't have time for games, Tal. I've been preparing the lawyers for the Lanoximine trial for months. The case begins tomorrow. You know how patent infringement cases go. Day and night. No rest."

Tal knew all too well from teenage summers. Mother hosting charity functions for the Neilson Foundation. A bone Father had thrown her to keep her busy. Father busy preparing for the next case. Tal spending most of his time toking with the only person who would listen, his best friend, Cornelius. "Did you read the business plan I sent?"

"You know I don't have time. That's why you're working for Red. Go see him." Geri began to turn his chair back toward the computer screen.

Tal's neck tensed along with his fists. "Don't turn your back on me. Not again!" he yelled.

CallMeGeri turned back to face Tal. "Do you have any idea how much time I've spent stepping in for you? Trying to get you to stand on your own two feet? You have an idea? Go fight over it with Red. Like I do. Be a man. That's how it's done around here."

"Bullshit. Never the time of day for me. Not even when I've come up with something for your beloved Danmark—"

"Tal, I have eight lawyers on hold. It's costing me five thousand dollars an hour. They're preparing opening statements. It's my life right now. Ten million dollars. That's what we're losing for every day that those thieves at Canray run this patent infringement suit to keep Lanoximine off the market."

"Cunzhuang is a huge mistake." Tal's temperature was rising with his voice. "A catastrophe. It'll take you no more than thirty minutes to go through my work. You don't understand—"

"No. *You* don't understand," Geri interrupted, shouting over Tal's voice. "I've got more important things I have to deal with."

Geri slid the headset back up onto his head and turned his chair back to the computer.

"This is what I want you to start with!" he shouted.

"Thanks!" Tal shouted back, slamming Father's door behind him.

He stood in the hallway for a few moments allowing the tension in his wrists to subside, unclenching his fists. Waiting for his control to return. Red's office was next door. He knocked firmly waiting for the acknowledgment, before entering. Framed blown-up photos of custom sports cars filled every inch of wall space to the right. The desk straight ahead under the window was perfectly clear, but for a Tiffany lamp on one side and a neat stack of white folders off to the other, a trace of maroon sticking out from the very bottom. Red jumped out of his dark leather chair, came around the desk, and extended his hand.

Tal accepted the empty gesture.

"I was expecting you." The prick was smiling. Retain composure, Tal thought.

"You never responded to my proposal," Tal said, keeping his tone measured.

Red laughed. "No small talk first? No matter." Red turned and pulled out the maroon folder. "This one?" he asked, holding it up to eye level. "The Transformation of Danmark's International Business," front and center in bold caps on the cover.

"Did you read it?"

Red laughed. "Did I read it? Why would I?"

"It's transformative— "

"You think I sent you to Paris to produce *this*?" He held the file out toward Tal, as if to return it, then as Tal reached for it, he dropped it to the floor, splattering pages at Tal's feet. "It doesn't matter what's in this *thing* and I don't care."

The blood and the adrenaline hurried to Tal's defence. "It's a hundred times better for Danmark than what you've just announced," he yelled.

Red looked off toward the window and the forest outside. As if he were admiring nature. No longer part of this conversation.

Tal could feel the heat prickling his back. The tension in his neck. The itch in his fingers. If he'd had a gun… He didn't move.

Red turned back, crossing his arms.

"Lovey," he mocked. "Let me give you a little free advice." Red's voice had turned harsh. "Fuck off and get out. Go back to Paris."

Tal stood there for a moment, his head pounding, his eyes burning. Then he slowly turned and retreated, head down, one foot ahead of the other, one step at a time, out the doorway.

One foot in front of the other, back to the cab. Back to the airport. Onto the flight; one drink after another until any memory of the flight disappeared. Back to Paris, one step backward at a time.

"Lovey, pick yourself up." Mother's voice dragged him back to the endless eulogy.

"How old do you have to be before you stand up to her? Be a man."

Mother reached into her purse for another tissue and dabbed her eyes. The consummate actor. Red paused up on stage. The widow was breaking down.

When Red looked down at them from the podium, it was obvious what he was thinking. He'd manipulated Father on the deal with Cunzhuang and maneuvered Tal out of the company. It was all too easy. Then he witnessed what Tal had become. Exactly what he had predicted. An assortment of degrees, the latest from Northwestern, along with the bachelor's in amphetamines and a master's in addiction. Tal Neilson BA, MA, MBA. No longer any threat to his ascendancy to the corporate throne.

"I'm sorry, son. I should have given you the time. If I'd listened maybe I'd still be here. Most important, you were right about Cunzhuang. Mea culpa."

"In closing," Red continued.

"It's about fucking time," Tal yelled.

Red stopped. The silence in the room was deafening. Mother shot him a hate stare that could kill a baby. Red continued.

"All that's left for me is revenge." The voice was now screaming the words. *"Deliver justice for me, son."*

"Revenge," Tal whispered. "Justice for the two of us."

"Read the will, then do the math, Tal. The math never lies. Watch what Red does next. It is so bloody obvious."

What was "the math" supposed to mean? Tal wondered.

Red was reaching his crescendo. "He was recognized as a true leader in his industry, a king among men, a dreamer and a shining beacon for the rest of us to follow. Geri was not only my best friend but a role model who affected thousands of lives. I would like to think that the world that Dr. Nielson left behind was a little better than the world that he entered in no small measure as a result of all of his contributions. Geri was one of the great ones."

"You've gotta clean up and figure this out or you'll be lying beside me, and the two of them will be dancing on our graves."

"The two of them?" Tal repeated under his breath.

All eyes in the cathedral were focused on Red King as he stepped away from the podium and made his way down the stairs to the grieving family. Everyone in the front row jumped up to greet him. Even the brain-dead cousins were on their feet. They needed to curry favor now, but with whom? Trudi put her arms around Red, holding him close and openly crying on his shoulder for a few moments longer than was appropriate in the circumstances. Tal cringed. The two of them.

Trudi turned to Tal, now standing, reaching for his hand. She stepped in closer to Tal, touching him. The perfect image of the grieving family. The mother who wants to share in the grief, reaching for her son. For her lovey. He gently pulled away from her touch extending his arm to touch her shoulder: the dutiful son, giving his mother comfort. He kept his arm at length, gently kneading her shoulder, keeping her from advancing any closer. Two could play this game.

"He was not a happy man. Never was," she said. How could Mother fail to understand? Father thrived on controversy and mayhem. He never settled a legal case. The papers were reporting there were some two hundred cases outstanding on an assortment of matters. He took every opportunity to ensure that anyone who crossed his path the wrong way felt miserable. That is what made Father happy.

So why was Father reaching out? It was obvious. Living in my head is making him happy, he thought. Driving me insane is making him happy. Even the apology. There were always strings attached to Father's words. It was only a matter of time before he tripped over them. There was no pleasing Father. In life or in death.

Tal led the procession, following the coffin which was shepherded by the pall bearers, all the members of the board. As he reached the final row, he glanced to the right and made eye contact. Ophelia's eyes held onto his, absorbing his pain. Ophelia.

CHAPTER 3

Ophelia Einbreier checked her wristwatch for the fourth time in the past half hour. Twenty-seven minutes after nine. Six minutes since the last time she looked and another three before she was due to carry out Paul Farber's instructions. She reached into her knapsack and pulled out a pair of well-worn sneakers. Comfortable and silent on the hardwood floors and the concrete stairwell. She sat on the tall-back swivel chair and eased off her two-inch heels, sliding them under her workstation alongside her purse, then slipping on the sneakers without having to untie the laces.

Tight-fitting blue jeans that accented her hips, comfortable beige blouse, tan leather jacket, her North American standard uniform. A long way from battle fatigues. A long way from what she'd left behind.

She adjusted the knapsack onto her shoulders. It contained all the tools for tonight's mission, most of them compact and lightweight. The cleaning staff would have finished their tasks on the second floor about ten minutes ago, and the floor security guard was due to make his rounds at ten. Plenty of time to get in and out. The energy-saving lighting system in the building was about to shut off any remaining office lights, and any stragglers who'd been working late would have to get out from behind their office desks to turn them back on. It made for an easy way to tell whether anyone was left working at this hour.

On most nights virtually all the staff in the suburban New Jersey drug plant were gone by six-thirty. Only the truly dedicated Danmark employees would be around at this hour and she knew who they were — never anyone in the executive suites upstairs and only a few on this ground-floor level, and they would congregate in their doorways to complain about having to turn the lights back on. One male researcher, around her age, in the office down the hall had started a week ago and had not yet left before her. The first few times they saw one another in the doorway, he had stared at her but had never spoken; on one occasion he smiled a little too long. She didn't reciprocate. Some of the drug-patent agents were too weird for words. Was that the idiom the Americans used? Too shy to flirt unless they were talking about a drug compound they were working on and then they would not shut up. There were other things in life besides drugs. He was cute but she had other responsibilities that didn't allow time for another relationship. Last night he'd thrown her an angry eye. And this morning the comb she kept on her desk was missing.

The staff had all left early tonight, eager to party. They had come to work in costumes and makeup this morning. She had no idea that Halloween came eleven days early in America. A holiday not even recognized in Israel. Here, it was an excuse for merriment in the workplace. Americans and their odd traditions. Like pouring cold milk into hot coffee. What civilized European would do that? She could hear the wind pelting the raindrops against the office windows. This was the way she remembered Amsterdam nights as a child, though she had not been back in years.

Her office was steps from the well-lit stairwell, and it took no more than a few moments to reach the second floor, wait for the shutoff, then count twenty heartbeats. The pace was regular and slow. A dull fluorescent emergency light buzzed softly, providing enough illumination to make her way down the hallway. All the blinds had been lowered. Likely an accommodation for the birds in the neighboring forest.

It was time to begin Paul's work. Corporate espionage was a child's game compared to her Israeli missions. Get in, get the information, and get out. No one to kill, no risk of violence, and no one to cry over. She stopped at her destination, studying the nameplate outside the office. *Red King: Vice Chairman.* The letters were embossed in blood red, though it all looked black in the dull light. She pulled a pair of latex gloves from her pocket, then took her time rolling them on. She tested the door handle. Unlocked. Likely a convenience for the cleaning staff. She could hear her breath in the deathly quiet as she eased the oak door open a crack. Spring loaded, unlike downstairs. It resisted her efforts. No light emerged from inside. She removed the knapsack and leaned her shoulder into the door, holding it wide enough to slide her thin frame through the opening, an old habit. The door eased shut behind her.

She stopped for a moment to observe. All the blinds but one to her left had been closed, leaving a trickle of moonlight refracted by the water sheeting on the windows. Just enough light to make out the shadows of the sports cars framed on the wall to the right. Probably the same ones that rotated through the vice chairman's reserved parking spot. On the back wall, his imposing mahogany desk with a Tiffany lamp and a comfortable leather chair left askew. Classy little touches that distinguished this suite at the end of the sprawling two-story building. She imagined that Dr. Geri Neilson's office next door had been equally opulent. She wondered if they had bothered clearing it, though there was no indication as to who might be moving in. The nameplate had not been removed. People downstairs were behaving as if Geri were still around, stalking the hallways, his spirit keeping a close eye on those who might be breaking his commandments. The president and vice chair, side by side, just as they were on the plaque in the reception area downstairs. Underneath the plaque was a photo of the two founders, back to back, posed with their arms crossed, taken when they renovated the facility in the late eighties.

According to Thomas, Paul's source on the board, Geri's death was unexpected. The fights between the founders over the direction of the company had been legendary, but lately had turned ugly after Geri convinced the board to terminate King's Cunzhuang deal. Thomas had been anticipating a showdown. He believed Red was working on something big for the company. Nothing had been shared with the board yet, and if Geri had been aware, he would have discussed it with Thomas.

Paul had called from Amsterdam late last night. The one-bedroom apartment on the Lower East Side was a little cramped since Tal had moved in, but he was fast asleep on the living room couch when the phone rang. She shut the bedroom door and spoke in a whisper. It had to be five a.m. in Amsterdam.

"Why are you so suspicious of Red?" Ophelia had asked.

Paul said, "Thomas sat down with King after the last board meeting, before Geri's death. The two of them were in the middle of a conversation but King cut him off three times to take calls on his BlackBerry."

"Since when is that unusual? You've told me King has the attention span of a gnat."

"Since the BlackBerry is not the company smartphone. It had to be something private."

"So what? There are a hundred reasons why Red could be using a private phone," Ophelia said.

"Your job is not to question. If Thomas is concerned, we all need to be concerned." There was a harshness in his tone. She had crossed a line. It happened often.

"Ophelia, I want you to search the office," Paul ordered.

"What am I looking for?"

"If he's working on a deal, find out what it is, then report to Thomas. You worked Intelligence. Did they teach you nothing in the navy?" She smiled to herself. She'd told them she was in Intelligence, because she could not tell them about Shayetet 18, the secretive unit spoken of only in rumors. Like the one that suggested that the special ops unit did not accept women. Little did Paul know what she'd learned in Shayetet 18, things she could not talk about with another living soul.

She reached into her knapsack, removed a penlight, and put it in her mouth to use as a head beam. She tested the desk drawers, one by one, until she found the drawer that would not yield. The locking mechanism was primitive. No need to remove the sophisticated tools from her bag. Americans and their inefficient security. She picked the lock in under fifteen seconds and slid the thin drawer open. A few trifles. Her fingers felt along the rear wall of the drawer until she found the slot. A false back. She pried it open with her forefinger and thumb and felt a flash drive. She stopped for a moment. Not a sound coming from the corridors. Plenty of time before the next security sweep.

Paul had been very clear. Copy the contents of any disk. He still thought in terms of floppies. Then transfer the information to Thomas as soon as practical.

She took her laptop out of her knapsack and inserted the flash drive. Nine forty-eight, plenty of time to return the desk to its original config-uration and get back to her office before the next security sweep.

■ ■ ■

There was no light from the office down the hall. The creep must have finally gone home. At the doorway of her office, Ophelia stopped dead in the darkness. The hairs on her arm began to tingle. The door was slightly ajar. She always closed the door on the way out. First priority: check for the ambush. She reached for the handle and edged the door open slowly until she felt the resistance of the doorstop.

She surveyed the room; not large enough to hide anyone waiting to strike. Her desk was covered with a few files neatly stacked to the right. Three nondescript empty bookshelves and a hook holding her sweater. Her purse and pumps were where she'd left them under the desk. No stalker.

Except the swivel desk chair. Out of position, pointed backward toward the window. Rely on training. Release the tense shoulders. Breathe. Don't give in to the fear. Review the details of the operation before you left, Ophelia. She had sat to change into the sneakers. The trash can on the left wall had been emptied. She had stood and placed the knapsack on the chair, then loaded the knapsack on her back. The chair had pointed left — not back. Definitely.

The chair began to turn.

"Don't move," she ordered. A bluff to buy a moment. Too close to retreat and too far to defend against a pistol. She advanced to within a meter, crouched and coiled. Arms raised — high enough to protect the head and low enough to cover the vital organs. Strike and disarm.

The chair continued to rotate. The silhouette of a male figure in profile. Curly hair falling over his ears, dark sunglasses, leather jacket. About her age. His empty hands rested on the arms of the chair. Palms down. As his profile came into view, he reached for the desk lamp.

"I came to apologize," a familiar voice exhaled.

"*Mijn god,* Tal, don't do that to me," she pleaded. How long had he been sitting and waiting?

"I need to talk to you. You keep hanging up on me."

"Go back to the apartment. I have another hour of work."

"I'll wait. I rented a car. This way you won't have to get into a cab at midnight again."

Ophelia shook her head and sighed.

"What do I have to do to make it up to you?" he asked.

"You can start by accepting there was no way I was sitting beside you at the funeral. Instead of throwing these shots that I wasn't there for you. I *was* there."

"In the back row."

"I was there. And you can't let it go. Even now. I told you twenty times. That was not the time and place to meet your mother for the first time. I don't even know what this relationship is. I'm not allowing myself to relive what I went through in Paris. Not again."

"My father died. It was shocking. I slipped. I keep telling you. I'm sorry."

"Are you always going to be giving me meaningless apologies? You know what you have to do, Tal." Her open hand extended toward him. Slowly, he reached into his pocket and withdrew the plastic container. Reluctantly he handed it to her. She gave it a small shake. It sounded about half-full. "That's a start."

He looked up with an earnestness in his eyes that she recognized. "I swear." His voice was firm, almost determined.

"Your vows are worthless." She knew all about vows and the costs they exacted. She was also professionally trained to weed out the lies; to understand it took only a momentary lapse in judgment to lose a life.

Tal rose from the chair. He walked around the desk and took her in his arms. "I was wrong. Again, I'm sorry."

"No, Tal. Not here, not now," she protested.

He stepped back immediately. Finally, a show of some respect for her feelings.

"Hand over the car keys," she ordered. "I'm driving."

CHAPTER 4

The private room at the back of the pool hall in Soho was dimly lit. The beer mugs and shot glasses littered the table, and it was only a matter of time until the next showdown. Stavros Micolonides, known to everyone as Mac, was holding a couple of pairs. Enough to win most hands with these jokers. Actually, that wasn't a fair description of the boys he'd been playing poker with every Wednesday. Cops and firemen. You could tell who they were by how they bet. The detectives held back, gathering all the information at their disposal before leaning in with the pressure bets. The firemen rushed in, like first responders, betting heavily early on, attracted to the danger of the unknown. They all tried to hide their proclivities, but if you studied carefully, human nature trumped the efforts they made to disguise who they were.

Kelly, the fireman sitting across the table, had just made a considerable raise. With a huge pile of poker chips in the center of the table, Mac was considering whether to go all in when his cell phone vibrated.

"Mac, don't touch that phone!" Kelly warned.

The four others at the table, who had already folded, chuckled as the drama played out.

Mac figured it was time to let Kelly stew a little. He scanned the number on the screen and waited until the fourth buzz. "Sorry, Kelly," he said, hitting the green button. "Mac here," he said into the phone.

"Mac, you ripping off those idiots again?" Bernard Obront said. Obie the reliable partner, the man who taught Mac everything he knew. "Why do you waste your time with cards when you could be putting money on the horsies? How many times have I tried to teach you? Ya can't trust people."

"I know," said Mac. "Can it wait half an hour? I can be there by ten."

"You running a bluff?" Obie asked.

Kelly tapped his fingers on the table. "Now, Mac!" Kelly turned toward the room. "Your wife want you to pick up the milk?" Another laugh.

"Sorry to bug you," Obie said, "but that rich kid keeps calling the lieutenant. Convinced his father's been murdered. Wants to come in tonight. Won't wait."

"Has the coroner arrived yet?" Mac asked, returning Kelly's hate stare.

"Lieutenant says you gotta hear him out. Get here before eleven. Should give you time to finish your game."

"I get it. ASAP."

Mac put the phone away. "Sorry for the interruption, boys. Duty calls."

Kelly scowled. "You know the house rules, Mac. We finish the hand. Then we deal with the emergencies. Priorities, Mac. Priorities. If you must leave immediately, you have to fold. Nobody walks away from the table."

The poker table was always good practice for the interrogation room. Keep the person across the table off balance and wait for him to make a mistake. Mac stood up and pushed his chair back from the table. He started to put on his suit jacket.

"You know what they say, Kelly. Homicide detectives never rest."

Kelly stood up as well and locked eyes with Mac. "Not with money on the table, Mac. You're not leaving until you bet or fold. I don't know what your big rush is. Another homicide in Manhattan? The stiff's already dead. Does anyone give a crap how cold he gets?"

Laughter exploded around the table.

"It's not my decision, Kelly. Sorry to upset the game. I have to leave now."

"Bet or fold, Mac. Those are your only two options right now. You're not leaving."

Mac was now certain he had set the hook. Time to reel in Kelly. He pushed his chips into the mound in the center of the table. "Okay, then. I'm all in. I've really gotta go."

Kelly leaned back into the table and pushed in his remaining pile of chips. "I call. Red kings and queens, the color of blood. How's that for homicide?" He tabled the cards with a flourish, to a chorus of *oohs* and *ahhs*.

Mac slowly turned his cards over. An eight, a four, a black ace. He waited. Then a second eight. He hesitated before turning over the last card. Another black ace.

"Isn't that the—"

"Yeah," Mac interrupted Johansson, one of the newcomers to the group, "aces and eights. The Dead Man's Hand. I've obviously fared a lot better than Wild Bill Hickok tonight. It's Kelly's stack that just got killed." Kelly's face was now the color of cooked beets. Appropriately red. "I only bluff in the interrogation room."

He probably shouldn't have rubbed it in like that. Bad sportsmanship and all. Mac was better than that. He made a mental note to call Kelly and apologize tomorrow. Maybe throw in a bottle. He had plenty of home-made Greek liqueurs sitting on the shelf in the pantry at home.

"Would one of you guys count these up and pay me in the morning?" he called as he headed for the door. "I've got to go listen to a story."

■ ■ ■

The man pacing in front of Desk Sergeant Vishinski had both hands thrust in the pockets of his tailored blue jeans. Under his designer tweed jacket, he wore a white button-down shirt, dark curls hanging over the collar. Masculine face, strong jaw, full lips, face with a growth that looked to be about two days old. Handsome by any standards. Yet all of it marred by the shades. Might work at a poker table late at night, but not in a police station. The man might have been over six feet standing straight, but that did not seem to be his habit. His shoulders were slightly hunched, and he walked like a man who had no idea where he was going. Funny how first impressions worked. Obie had drilled it into him: begin the profile-building immediately, but don't be taken in by appearances. First impressions could be deceiving. As the man turned toward the front door of the station to catch the source of the draft, Mac rubbed his chafed hands together to create a little warmth. He pulled his own shorter, squatter frame to attention, though that still left him a good five or six inches shorter than the younger visitor.

Vishinski gave him the nod from behind the desk. "Mac, this is Mr. Neilson. He's been waiting for about an hour to speak to you."

Mac held out his hand. "Detective Micolonides. Please call me Mac."

"Talem Neilson." His grip was firm enough. First surprise. "Thank you so much for coming in, and I apologize for interrupting your evening but this could not wait. Every moment lost is critical."

Neilson followed Mac up the protesting wood staircase, a reminder of how long crime had been a fixture in central Manhattan. Mac led him to a small interrogation room. Most people found it intimidating. Might as well test Mr. Neilson. They sat opposite one another at a wooden table. Brown cigarette burns stained the yellowed top, from the old days when Obie used to smoke a pack a day. Mac was willing to bet these jeans and this sports jacket had never been acquainted with a chair and table reserved for suspects. Neilson's hands fidgeted on the table. The fingernails nubby, as if he'd been biting them.

"How can I help you, sir? I'd offer you some coffee but by this hour it's usually burnt."

"Thanks anyway. I'll get straight to it. My father. He's dead." Neilson stopped and put his hand to his right ear and shifted in his chair as if that might relieve the pressure.

Who in Manhattan hadn't followed the funeral of Geri Neilson? Natural death according to the mainstream press. The *New York Enquirer*, at the grocery store checkout line, had a huge cover shot of Trudi Darrow, outside the church, with a headline reading, "Black Widow? Find Out the Real Story."

Neilson finally continued. "I'm convinced he was murdered."

The story did cite a family source. Otherwise it was standard conspiracy theory nonsense that sells papers. A guilty pleasure. Still Mac tossed it out before he got home. Jennifer would never let him forget it if "that rag," as she called it, entered the house, then she'd probably insist on using it for weeks to wrap kitchen waste, her idea of humor. Marriage.

"What is it that convinces you, sir?"

"If someone were to take a careful look, it would be obvious."

If only every investigation was obvious. Mac could go home and get into bed with Jennifer every night at a normal hour. He followed up with the checklist of questions, eliciting from Neilson that his father had suffered a coronary, was rushed immediately to hospital where he died a few hours later. Neilson knew his father had an arrhythmia and was taking medication. That could explain the heart attack. Autopsy refused by the widow, no surprise there. Neilson had no idea about the medical certificate, but there was probably nothing unusual in it. Otherwise the New Jersey M.E. would have insisted on the autopsy.

"Sounds like natural causes, sir."

"You don't understand." He was clasping his hands now. A little too tightly. "Someone is hiding the real story."

"What is the real story?"

"How can I tell the story when you're shouting?" Neilson said, his voice rising in pitch.

"Sorry?" Didn't matter how rich they were, not if they were suffering some mental illness. Best to let them rant; there was no minimizing the agitation. Mac was now convinced that indeed the young man across from him was suffering some kind of delusion.

"Not you, detective. Something happened in his hotel room or in the hospital. I'm convinced. There's no way he would go like that." He snapped his fingers. Then he paused and leaned in on his elbows. "We know who did it."

"We? Who else knows, Mr. Neilson?"

"Never mind. It's enough that I know."

Neilson sat there, looking left and right. Anywhere but straight at him. As if he were taking instructions from a voice in his head.

"All I can tell you … right now," continued Neilson in a whisper, "… is.that death by natural causes is a subterfuge … part of a plot." Neilson stood up. Began to pace. Rubbing his hands together, then holding his ears, this time with both hands. His eyes closed. He was fighting an intense pain and bent over until the spasm passed. He removed his glasses. His eyes were bloodshot. Maybe he hadn't been sleeping. More likely drugs. Or both.

"I have a jurisdiction problem, sir. The death took place in Atlantic City. It's up to the New Jersey police to decide whether to launch an investigation."

"My father lives … lived in Manhattan for years. The murderer is in Manhattan. You must be able to investigate that? Go to his house? Ask him some questions?"

"You know who did it?"

"Claude King," Tal shouted. "My father's business partner… I don't know who else is in on it besides King. Possibly my mother… No. I don't really believe it's Mother… She's just a pawn in King's game…" Short little blasts of thought that made perfect sense to Neilson. Only to Neilson. "There must be some grounds to take action. At least go talk to him. Someone needs to look into this before it's too late."

Lieutenant's orders were plain. Give the man a full hearing. The Neilsons were plugged into the power structure at City Hall. Money. The lieutenant clearly didn't know that young Neilson was a nut job. It might be a long night. If Mac was lucky, the lieutenant would make the problem someone else's tomorrow.

Mac removed the notepad and pen from his breast pocket. Failed to conceal the sigh.

"All right, sir. Let's start at the beginning."

CHAPTER 5

Tal arrived for his appointment in midtown Manhattan a few minutes early. Father had drilled into him for as long as he could remember that people form early impressions about a person based on when they show up for meetings. Geri applied some simple Lutheran good sense to his personal and business affairs. He insisted on arriving on time for every appointment and kept his watch precisely six minutes ahead of standard time, running his life as if his clock was the only accurate measuring device in the world. In short, Geri was always six minutes early for everything. His ninth commandment.

Tal had been ushered into the main law firm boardroom, long and deep with a lush area rug and a huge mahogany table. A meeting room suitable for a large crowd. Made sense for the reading of a will with potentially numerous beneficiaries; who knew what surprises CallMeGeri had left in the document?

The first impression on the estate lawyer today was critical. He had made sure to shower this morning and had thrown on the black suit he'd worn to the funeral. He had to project control. He stood studying the portraits of the founders of TGO. Torrance, Gottlieb, and Overton. Catching sight of his reflection in the glass of the portraits, he buttoned his shirt collar and centered his sober necktie, which had gone askew.

Unlike most founders' photos, these had been taken recently; the firm was only about ten years old. All Father ever talked about was Drew Torrance, whose photo was in the center of the trio and who had been with him and Red King from the very beginning. "He always had my back" was the way Geri described him. He used to say that about Red. Not anymore.

The clicking of a woman's heels on the hardwood interrupted his reverie. An altogether different redhead faced him — one with long flowing curls and deep green eyes. She was wearing a white blouse and dark green skirt cut just above the knees. Besides her hair, one thing stood out: the smile of someone accustomed to dealing with another's grief.

"Mr. Neilson. Lucinda Horat." She held out her free hand. A maroon accordion folder was tucked under her other arm. "Do you mind if I call you Talem?"

"Tal. That's the name I go by."

"Please call me Lucinda. I am so sorry for your loss." No doubt she'd used those words on countless occasions, but she managed to make them sound sincere.

"May I offer you some tea? Please take a seat," she said, pointing to a tan leather chair near the head of the long table, across from where she had just placed the folder. She headed over to the matching mahogany credenza along the wall facing him. Sitting on it was a silver tray with a white china tea service, a pitcher of ice water, and a number of tall glasses.

"Don't get distracted. Remember why you're here."

Tal straightened his back. "Nothing, thank you. Tell me how this is all going to work," he said, staring down the vast table.

Lucinda stopped suddenly. "It's frightening," she said. "The voice."

She heard it too?

"No question you're Geri's son. I could have sworn it was him talking. You sound just like him. Your father was quite a man. My first trip out to meet him five years ago, he insisted on giving me the plant tour."

"You can't understand me until you understand Danmark?" Tal interrupted.

Lucinda laughed. "Did he use that line on everyone? He took me back to the reception area—"

"Ordered you to read his Ten Commandments." CallMeGeri wanted to make sure anyone who worked for him knew them cold. The framed poster was in the shape of stone tablets. The staff couldn't get in the front door without looking at them. "I didn't realize his lawyers needed to memorize them, too."

"I worked with him on the will for over four years until he was certain it was perfect. Right up to the end."

"Keep working on it until you get it right," Tal said without thinking.

"The seventh commandment he insisted on repeating at the start of every meeting."

"So did you?"

"Did I what?"

"Did you get it right?"

Lucinda's lips pursed tightly for a brief moment. Then she broke eye contact and glanced to the side, before she resumed her consoling smile.

"Are you ready to hear the reading of the will?" she asked.

"Is anyone else coming?"

"She should have invited Red and your mother. That would be dramatic. Allow us to confront Red face to face."

Lucinda stood up and poured herself a cup. "It's not like the movies, Tal, where they gather all the family members to hear the reading." Lucinda chuckled.

It wasn't funny. Though just as well. Tal was in no state to confront anyone.

Lucinda put her grave face back on. "In my experience, it's preferable to deal with the beneficiaries or their attorneys individually. I have mailed out a copy of the will to your mother and other pertinent beneficiaries."

"But you didn't mail one to me?"

"There's a lot we need to process together. Particularly since your father's death was so unexpected."

"There's a reason it was unexpected. Share the truth with her."

He'd made a fool of himself at the police station last night. The detective had to think he was crazy. He was not about to share Father's murder theory with anyone else.

"I think it's time to review the provisions of the will." Lucinda opened up the document that she had just taken out of its file folder. The document had a pale blue cardboard cover and a red seal on the cover page, shrouding it in formality.

"This is your father's last will and testament. If it's okay, I'll give you a summary of the key terms."

He nodded.

"Your father appointed me as executor of the estate." She paused.

"You and your mother are the two principal beneficiaries of the estate, other than what has been left to charity. There is a proviso in respect of your mother. If she remarries within sixty days of the death of your father, she will not inherit anything." She looked up from the will and made eye contact.

"Did Father suspect something?"

"These types of clauses are not unusual," she continued. "Some of our clients are very concerned about appearances and propriety. Others worry that their spouses may need a dose of reality before rushing off and remarrying because they can't adjust to the loneliness.

"Your father has left the homes in New York and Lake Como, Italy, and all the contents to your mother. There is one exception. He has specifically bequeathed to you the globe in the study as well as any papers or books that you select.

Tal felt a piercing jolt in his chest right beside his heart. He gasped and waited for the spasm to pass. Father's study with its death machine.

"Are you okay, Tal?" she asked, looking up suddenly from her papers.

He drew a deep breath and nodded.

"He's also left both you and your mother twenty million dollars. There is a further twenty million dollars left to Pastor Marcellus, in trust." She scrutinized him, refusing to break eye contact. Maybe she was expecting an angry reaction to the gift to the pastor.

Tal couldn't have cared less. "Father made the fortune; it's not for me to judge how he's spending it." Maybe he'd found religion late in life.

Lucinda sipped her tea, then stared over Tal's head for a moment. Her face had turned pale. Could it be CallMeGeri, reaching out to her as well? She inhaled audibly, then took a breath. Her eyes had narrowed. There was some other news about to be delivered. Geri was probably standing on Tal's shoulder, arms crossed, bifocals riding down his nose, studying her, worrying that she didn't have the balls to deliver the news.

She finally looked down at the will. "There is a caveat, however. You must attend a live-in rehab program for twelve consecutive months followed by a certificate from an expert that you are clean of drugs after a series of monthly tests." She did not look up.

The rip tore through his chest. Father had briefed her on the drug situation. Lucinda returned her focus to the document. His son, the drug addict who would fritter it all away. The surgeon, having made the first precise incision in the intercostals with her scalpel, hesitated before cutting through the muscle to remove the organ. Was she expecting a scream of pain or shock? A gush of Tal's blood? A pound of flesh?

Tal took a few deep breaths, letting the shock wave pass through him. "Just like Father," he said. Finding a way from the grave to inflict the pain. "Father's death. I needed something to get through the funeral. I'm done with the pills."

Lucinda kept her head down and continued reading from her notes. "I am authorized—"

Tal interrupted. "I'm over thirty years old and my father didn't trust me to let me have *any* money outright? None of it?" Tal drummed his fingers on the table in time with his racing heart. The message was clear enough. Talk about a meaningless apology at the funeral.

"May I continue?"

"How about I bring my own medical report stating I'm clean?" Tal shifted in his chair and smoothed his tie.

"I'm bound by the precise provisions in the will."

"And if I disagree?" His neck was chafing under his tightly buttoned shirt collar.

"The terms of the will are unambiguous. They leave me no discretion as to procedure. If you disagree, your only recourse is to take action in court." Now her tone was curt, as if he'd offended her by even asking.

"I have to hire a lawyer and sue you?"

"Tal, the will states that if any beneficiary unsuccessfully challenges the provisions of the will, they forfeit their inheritance. It's a fairly standard clause in major estates. It creates real jeopardy for anyone thinking of attacking the will. Regardless, litigation might take five years, perhaps longer."

"All or nothing. Risk and reward." Father's philosophy revealing its temptations like the snake in the Garden of Eden. Wrapping itself around his throat. Tal coughed.

Lucinda rose and stepped toward the credenza, returning with a tall glass of water. "Take this." She waited a few moments while Tal took a few gulps. "May I continue?" Tal nodded.

"I am authorized to pay you a living allowance. In that period if there are any emergencies, the will permits me to advance funds on your behalf." As if that might soften the pain of the first cut. "The allowance will run until we find the right program." She looked up and made direct eye contact. "He assumed you would not want to move back in with your mother."

Tal looked off into space. "CallMeGeri had something right." In reality, though, this was no different than the way he'd been living right through the MBA. Every month funds showed up in his account and he always found the money to get what he needed. The odd month he had to borrow from friends to get him over the hump, but he'd never gotten in over his head. "So, you'll advance me money every month. The way it's always worked."

"No." Lucinda paused a moment to let the jab sink in. "Each month you will submit an expense report to me. I'll pay the rent directly and everything else must be charged to your bank card and verified by me. No cash reimbursements. No exceptions. Those are the rules."

"Father's thought of everything. Hasn't he?" Tal bared his teeth. Lucinda was not watching. Probably reading her next scripted line.

"Then there is the matter of his shareholdings in Danmark. He has left two-thirds of the stock to you and the balance to your mother."

"I suppose that's also subject to the get-clean edict? And what forms do I need to fill out to sell them?" He made no attempt to mask the sarcasm. "So, some time in the next century—"

"Hopefully in a little over a year," she interrupted a little too cheerfully.

"You're talking to a three-time rehab loser, Lucinda. Let me rephrase the question. Isn't that what you lawyers say?" She did not bother with a response. "One day I'll get out of rehab and I'm worth how much?"

"All I can tell you is that today his founder's stock represents around fifteen percent of the company."

Tal interrupted. "And the market cap of the company this morning is just over two billion. Two point zero three to be more precise. Making his stock worth just under $304.5 million, which translates to my two-thirds being worth $203.01 million."

"You worked that out in your head? I had it at two hundred."

"Isn't that a hoot? I'm so rich on paper that a rounding error alone is worth over three million." But that's all he was. Rich on paper. He began rubbing his forehead.

"There must be a loophole here somewhere," he said. "Help me through this. How do I sell some shares?" he barked.

Lucinda did not respond. His head began to throb.

"Geri went to great lengths under his will to preserve his legacy."

"You're not answering my question. I need money. I'm not interested in living on the dole from you. How do I sell the shares?"

Lucinda nodded carefully. Like she knew where the money would end up. If she had followed all of Father's commandments, there would be no loopholes. Though Father always liked tricks and mazes. Questions with hidden answers. With Father there was always more than what met the eye.

"We're not through with this yet, are we?" he asked.

"There are other agreements involved in assessing the legal picture."

"I don't want to hear about legal pictures today," Tal continued, unable to control the irritation or the headache. "I just want a straight answer." His hands began to shake. He drew a deep breath, then exhaled slowly. "Please just explain to me how I sell some shares."

"I've told you. You can't sell your shares." Lucinda's voice was calm but decisive. A slap across the face, but delivered without anger or frustration. More of a wake-up slap. As if she had prepared for this moment.

Tal jumped out of his chair and began to pace. "I can't believe he did this to me," he said hotly.

"He wanted you back in rehab. Once and for all. There are a couple of world-renowned programs. He acknowledged he couldn't make you do anything, except by cutting you off. He mentioned something about a birthday dinner in our last meeting when he made the final adjustments to the will. He was about to let you know just before he died."

"He wants to control me."

"A year passes quickly, Tal. Then you'll be on your way back."

"That's how little he thinks of me." Tal jammed his hands into his pockets.

"That's what he decided."

"Always what he wants. It's always about CallMeGeri. Anything else?" He made no attempt to disguise his bitterness.

"Why don't we take a break, Tal? I know this is a lot to digest. Go take a walk. Get something to eat. I've booked the day for this, so whenever you're ready we can resume. If not today, then when you're ready."

"Sure. While you run up a huge bill."

"You do sound like your father."

■ ■ ■

Lucinda rejoined Tal when he returned. She thought about how much more she needed to cover today and how painful Tal was going to make it. Just get through it, she thought, like you always do. He had removed the tie, and the top button of his shirt was undone, the way Geri usually dressed, though Tal's suit was form fitting, showing off a build that could stand to gain a few pounds. His face was a little too thin, his hair a little too long, running over his collar, but it suited him. She guessed that Geri must have been quite attractive in his youth.

"Before we begin, Lucinda," he said, just after taking his seat across from her, "I apologize. I was out of line this morning. A little shocked by what I heard and what I must face. But none of that is your fault. I'm feeling better now."

This was not the same Tal she'd faced this morning. That man was tentative, defensive, almost defeated from the start. His objections were easily put down. The worst kind of client. Completely reliant and negative. Bitter. In her experience, it was a toxic combination.

This Tal was ready and raring. There was an edge, yet he was speaking a little too fast, with a little too much enthusiasm for an heir who had been boxed into a corner from which there was only one exit, with a woman, a stranger, holding the key to unlock his life. He had either reassessed his views on rehab or, more likely, taken some pill or other as his lunch. If so, the clarity might be short lived.

"The last thing you told me was that I couldn't sell my shares," Tal said. "Let's approach this a little differently. What are the obstacles?"

"That is the right question to be asking. Your father and Mr. King each own about fifteen percent of the company, representing in total thirty percent of the outstanding shares. Almost a third. In most public companies, that is more than enough stock to control appointments to the board of directors. So you need to understand a few things."

"Educate me." Tal smiled. It was Geri's smile. The one he used whenever he wanted something from her, usually at the end of an argument. When Geri was about to play her. The charm might have worked on others. It worked on her the first couple of times. She'd smile back then give in. Lucinda looked down at her notes. "To understand the situation, we have to go back to the beginning of the company when there were just three founding shareholders who had bought the company from the Darrow family."

"Father, his partner, and Mother."

"You're probably quite familiar with this but please bear with me."

"This was how we spent dinners. Most kids were learning about baseball. I was hearing about the good old days. Mother had ten percent and the balance was split equally between my father and the … if you don't mind let's call him the bastard."

Geri had told her that the two men did not get along, but this was beyond what she had been expecting. There was obviously some story Geri had not shared. Or perhaps he wasn't aware of the depth of Tal's animosity. She recalled family abuse cases where the adult child came apart at the seams when having to confront the childhood abuser. Perhaps it was a stretch here, but she couldn't be certain.

"The three of them signed a shareholder agreement," she continued. "Mr. Torrance drafted it in the early seventies and it's been amended from time to time."

"It required the three shareholders to agree on major decisions like mergers, acquisitions, and sales of Darrowpharm divisions. It also prevented any of the three from selling or borrowing against their original shares without the consent of two-thirds of the shares."

"So two of the three shareholders could override the wishes of the third?"

"It's a little more complicated than that, because it is based on the number of shares, not the number of shareholders. Let me fast-forward a little so I can explain it better." Lucinda pointed to a thickly bound document in front of her with a baby-blue cardboard cover. "When the company merged with Danmark and became public, most of the agreement became obsolete. All that was left is a single restriction applicable to the original shares that went into a pool called a voting trust. There is a single trustee, Mr. Torrance. He votes those shares on behalf of the three shareholders when a two-thirds majority instructs him to do so. Those shares cannot be transferred, sold, or used as collateral for a loan, without a written instruction to Mr. Torrance by the two-thirds majority of shares."

"So this applies to the original shares of Mother, Father, and the bastard. How does that translate today?"

"I checked the public record and Trudi's original shares represent slightly more than one and a half percent of the company. Geri and Red—"

"I asked you not to use his name in front of me."

"I'm sorry. The two each owned fifteen percent when your father died."

"So essentially the bastard and CallMeGeri each had a veto right on share transfers."

"Correct. There was no way for any two of the three to get the two-thirds majority of shares. The term 'veto' would be a good way to describe it."

"How does this apply now that Father is dead?"

"The estate steps into his shoes. His shares and with them his voting rights are divided between you and your mother. Once the shares are distributed after the two-month waiting period, your mother will own six and a half percent, while you will own ten percent."

"Leaving the bastard with fifteen percent." Tal paused and rubbed his chin. Drew a deep breath and sighed. "So, you're telling me that I can't do anything with my stock unless I get permission from— ?"

"Yes. From ... essentially."

Tal's face turned a deep shade of purple. "That bastard killed my career. Anything that crosses his path dies." Tal's voice was getting louder. "He's the reason Father had to do all this to me. That ... that thing is the devil. I can't even call him a man. The wildebeest. Evil incarnate. I'd rather be lying on the street, strung out and bleeding to death, than asking that bastard for anything." He smashed his fist on the table.

No question this was abuse, she thought. But what kind and when? She would have to tread carefully around the subject of Red King. No point mentioning that the board vote to appoint him as CEO was scheduled for tomorrow.

"Fine then," he said. "I'll just sell some stock to Mother. That will get me a little liquidity."

"Also a non-starter I'm afraid. The will is clear. Geri left you each particular percentages of stock and he didn't want that to change. You and she cannot trade shares with one another."

"That's ridiculous. And it's completely arbitrary." His face had turned beet-red. His tone was bitter.

"Geri spent months working this out. He didn't explain his motivations to me. In the end he simply told me that this was what he wanted. What he intended."

"He intended to put me in this hell? Sounds just like him."

Bitter Tal had returned. It was time to leave the sensitive topic. "Your life isn't over, Tal. Get yourself clean then we can consider other options."

"We?"

"You might think of me as the enemy but I'm here to assist however I can."

"I'll go to rehab. I swear. Father's forcing me to disappear for a year. And even after that I have to come in here once a month, drop my pants, and pee in a bottle until you're satisfied?"

How was she going to respond to that? Lucinda sat silently for a moment.

"I'm too pissed to think right now," Tal said. "I'm angry … at them. My parents. I tried to play it Father's way. He trusted the bastard over me and look where that's got him."

"Pardon me? Where did it get him?"

"Never mind." Tal got up and walked past Lucinda toward the door. "This has nothing to do with you."

The boardroom door slammed shut behind him.

CHAPTER 6

Tal stood on the street outside Ophelia's apartment waiting for the taxi that would take him to the Neilson family house. Just a short visit, he'd told Mother over the phone this morning. He might have asked her if he could crash there until he found an apartment of his own. Except he wasn't yet that desperate. That was an option he would not consider unless the alternative was a park bench or a homeless shelter. After all, isn't that what he was? Homeless. As of an hour ago, that was his status.

It had been his unofficial status the night he'd returned from Northwestern, a month ago, to attend the Danmark anniversary party. Mother booked a hotel room for him at the Ritz for a few nights. She never even thought to offer him his bedroom. He had given up the apartment in Evanston, packed a bag and his brand-new diploma, and abandoned the rest. Mother had insisted he show up, if only for appearance. He'd finally consented, on the understanding that with five hundred people in attendance he would keep his distance from the bastard. Five hundred faces milling about, sipping their drinks, engaged in their fatuous small talk. An inconsequential evening — until one face caught his attention.

She was standing off to the side of the bar in the reception room, wearing a strapless hot-pink tube dress, tight at the waist, showing off her bust, her tanned legs and unruly auburn hair hanging over her shoulders. Wild. Unmanageable. Ophelia. His heart beat a little harder.

Her eyes scanned the room, like a hawk. Tal waited, trying to figure out an opening line, swirling the ice cubes in his bourbon. He did not move until she finally locked onto his eyes. He approached slowly, carefully, wondering if she saw him as prey, until he had encroached on the edge of her personal space. She had good reason to devour him. She didn't break eye contact.

"I never said sorry," he said, mustering a contrite tone.

"It's never too late," she replied.

Tal smiled. She stood impassively. A few uncomfortable moments passed.

"You still haven't said it," she said. Ophelia pursed her lips. A sign Tal recognized all too well.

"I've been sorry for years. I was a miserable human being. You deserved better than what I gave you at the end."

"That's a start." Her mouth began to relax. "You can wipe the shock off your face now."

"So you know my first question."

"The one that begins with 'of all the gin joints'?" She laughed. The irresistible laugh.

"Yeah, something like that."

"Shall we pick it up from the moment after you walked out on me in Paris?" No forgetting that the irresistible laugh was often followed by a slap across the face. He reached up involuntarily and rubbed his cheek. That was one version of the Paris story. He had walked out, but his last memory was returning a few hours later to find a note she had left taped to her bathroom toilet. Then days, weeks, months waiting for her to return. Then giving up.

"How about if we get out of here so we can talk?" he asked.

"Don't you have a speech to make tonight? Heir to the throne and all that?"

Tal laughed. "After Paris? I don't think so. I've put in my obligatory time. No one's going to notice I'm gone."

They meandered the perimeter of Central Park heading north. He took a turn, she took a turn, filling in the dates and details that covered the passage of years, both carefully avoiding the feelings. She spoke of years in naval intelligence, but she spoke of it in a manner he had come to recognize. A manner that suggested that half of her statements were true, the other half convenient fiction to mask the reality. His expertise. Probably something she had learned in Israel.

When they reached the Museum of Natural History, he stopped and extended his arm upwards toward the imposing entrance. The columns stood tall like a Roman cathedral. "Somewhere on the other side of this wall stands the elephant in the room."

Ophelia looked perplexed. "Sorry, another of my American idioms," he said just before pulling back the hair on the right side of his forehead. He ran his finger over the scar and felt the tingle.

■ ■ ■

Neither of them spoke for a while. Ophelia was deciding whether to step through the doorway Tal had just opened.

"Elephants never forget, do they?" she said. That night had been tucked away. The night she took a time-out from the life Paul had been directing. Her relationship with Tal might have ended with a crash that night, but it had begun two years earlier with an innocent hello at the Danmark office in Orly.

The instructions were clear. "Find him, keep an eye on him, and let us know if he needs assistance. Part of your work at the company." It never occurred to Paul or to Thomas, her handlers, that it would become personal. An unthinkable breach of protocol. So she never told them. Just filed her periodic reports on how the "Neilson heir," as Paul referred to Tal, was progressing. She began her research work, planned the excuse to bump into him on a lunchtime break, then found ongoing excuses to talk. Doing her job. All by the book. Except it was never by the book. Not since he smiled at her in their first encounter. He had a natural charm. Brief conversations led to more: a coffee, a drink after work, a bowl of mussels and a bottle of wine to share, a walk along the river in the moonlight, a clandestine meeting at her apartment four nights a week, wildfire. Was she "in love"? A question best not answered, given her obligations to Paul and Thomas.

The fire consumed them until it had burned away the fuel. Until he began working day and night on his "plan to transform the company." He was completely consumed by his new love, this one a child of his own conception, a child she had no part in parenting. Cut off. Isolated. Spending more time at his own apartment nurturing his baby. Or sleeping at the office, judging by his appearance some mornings. For a few weeks after he'd sent the brainchild off to New York, he improved and began to show interest in her once again.

By now, it was shortly before their second anniversary. She planned a simple celebration. A night out on the town. They walked the Left Bank, shared a platter of *moules* and a bottle of Chablis at Les Deux Magots. He began complaining that he still had not heard from Red.

"Happy anniversary, Tal. It's about us tonight. Let's give Danmark and Red a break." She handed him a tiny white box with a brown bow.

His face reddened. "I'm sorry, Ophelia. I didn't … you must understand why this has consumed me. How important this is to my career at the company and my chance to impress Father. Red still hasn't responded."

"I understand more than you know, Tal. But sometimes it has to be about us. I'm worried about you."

"There's nothing to worry about. I've never been more directed in my life."

"You're very edgy. You're not—"

"I promised you months ago. No drugs. I needed a little boost while I was finishing the spreadsheet, but I swear I'm clean. I'm just tense is all."

"Stop talking and open the box, Tal. I don't need a gift." His smile would be enough.

He fiddled with the bow then lifted the lid. Underneath a layer of snowy cotton was a thin gold chain. He lifted it out, opened the clasp, and hung it around his neck.

"I won't take it off. I promise. I love it."

The night ended the way she had hoped. Without thoughts. Without concerns. The way things were the night he first stayed over. She fell into a deep sleep until she heard footsteps on the floor. She reached for Tal but he wasn't in the bed. A light slivered from under the bathroom door. She got up to check if there was a problem. Rubbed the kinks out of her bed head and the concern for him into her sleepy eyes. Perhaps he'd eaten a bad mussel. What she saw made her sick. His back was to her. The lid to the toilet tank sat on the floor. On top of it she saw a roll of silver duct tape and several pill bottles. Tal was bent over the toilet, one arm in the tank. Caught.

"How could you? You swore to me. Liar!" she yelled. She shoved him hard. The crack of his forehead against the tank barely registered while she grabbed the stash and flushed it down the toilet.

She stood over his body on the floor. Blood was pouring down his forehead over his lips and onto the yellowed tile floor. Tal made no effort to stem the flow from the gash over his eye. He stood up to face her, hands balled into fists. Like a tough guy ready to fight it out. "That was eight hundred euros," he screamed at her. His voice then went quiet and cold. "How dare you."

The stream poured, like blood, from her eyes, down her own cheeks and into her mouth. They stood silently, neither moving. The taste of salt and bitterness lingered. But she was ready for a fight. They were way past due. Instead Tal took off. The apartment door slammed behind him.

Action — reaction. When the light suddenly shines into darkness the vermin don't fight — they scurry. He had turned on the bathroom light, she had responded. He had turned off the light within her, she had flashed her temper— Tal didn't stay to fight it out. He scurried. Action — reaction.

She might have waited for him to cool off. She might have taken time to calm herself down, to ignore the actions. The abuse of her trust. Instead she threw on a pair of jeans and a T-shirt, penned a note telling him not to expect her back any time soon and taped it to the toilet seat, shoved a few days' worth of clothes into her backpack, and walked out into the Paris night. A half-moon sat above a haze, casting a glow over the pre-dawn streets. She had no direction, no destination. She watched the sun rise over the Seine until she'd had enough. Enough playing spy on the dysfunctional boyfriend, enough of this life. She knew exactly what she had to do immediately. She flagged a cab to De Gaulle and bought a one-way airline ticket to Israel.

A turning point in her life, now represented by a scar on Tal's head that had mostly healed, barely visible behind a hairline. A turning point that would lead her on a dangerous path to her own scars that would never heal. That she could never share. The curtain on her past lowered once more. She stared at Tal under the streetlights at the foot of the steps to the museum.

"I've regretted my behavior that night more than you can imagine," he said. "I spent two months in Paris waiting for you to return. I didn't expect you to ever forgive me, but I owed you an apology. Finally, I gave up, though I never forgot you." He kneeled down to tie his shoe and Ophelia could make out the quick sparkle of a thin gold chain around his neck. She shivered. He'd never forgotten!

Ophelia linked her arm in his as they headed west then turned down Broadway, eventually passing through the bustle and gaudiness of Times Square, which she barely noticed while he recounted his story of the past three years, taking it all the way through to the party, while she fed him what she was permitted to say about Israel and her move to Danmark's office in New Jersey. Eventually they sat down for eggs, toast, and coffee at a greasy spoon in the Village at five in the morning and finished outside her apartment as the sun was rising.

He slept on her bed with his clothes on. The deep sleep of a child, while she rested on her elbow, just watching, touching his scar. Paris was so far in the past. She had left Tal so that she wouldn't drown in him. The blood gushing from his forehead was somehow a symbol of what her life with him had become. What it might always be. She'd lived an entire life since then. A life filled with lessons of survival. A life followed by a death and now a return to her old life complete with her obligations to Paul and Thomas. Obligations she abandoned when she escaped from him in Paris. The Danmark party was no coincidental meeting. Thomas had ordered her to be there. She sighed then rested her head on Tal's chest. Paris was far in the past.

They woke ravenous in the mid-afternoon. He ran out to the local market and returned an hour later with a bag of mussels, a package of crostini, and a bottle of white wine. A few hours later she steamed them with garlic, a little wine, and her own stash of Mediterranean herbs. The aromas filled the air with whispers of Paris. They feasted. Then he followed her into the bedroom and took her in his arms. The next morning, when she opened her eyes at dawn, he was spooned into her. She had forgotten how much she loved his bare skin against hers.

A few days later, when he had joked that he was homeless, she agreed to let him stay for a few days while he looked for his own apartment. Just as night claims the day, the moon claims the sun, the tides claim the beaches, death claims life. Except death changes everything about you. She had learned that. She had faced that. But could Tal?

Just a brief cell phone call from his mother to start. Geri was dead. He took off immediately for Atlantic City. Returned on the corporate jet and slowly began to shut down. A few days later she was studying herself in the mirror. Making the final adjustments. The morning of the funeral.

"You'll sit beside me," he ordered, putting on his black suit jacket.

"Your family doesn't know I exist," she said. "Besides we've only just restarted, Tal. If that's even what we're doing. I'm not sure yet. I want to go slow. You're telling me this is going to be the equivalent of a state funeral. We don't need the pressure of the scrutiny. The media. The circus."

"I don't give a damn about anyone or anything. I just know I can't get through this alone."

"I'll be there in the back of the chapel."

"I can't face the bastard on my own." He pulled the pill bottle out of his pocket involuntarily and popped a couple in his mouth. Swallowed. Caught the look in her eyes, the pursing of her lips. "I just need this to get through the day."

Her body tensed. She fought to keep her tone measured. "Today's not the day to get into this. But it's also not a day I'm going to be arm in arm with you in *that* state. I'll get there on my own."

Those had been her final words to him before the limo arrived to collect him. Just a few hours before Father had moved into his new home: Tal's head. Father joined him for a drink after the funeral. He and Father.

Just a quick one. Doing what they hadn't been able to do while Father was alive. Just be out without an agenda. Father and son. Two guys drinking. They didn't return from the funeral until the middle of the night. When Tal finally stumbled in, she jumped him at the door.

"You're out of control! Where have you been?"

"With Father, of course," he slurred. "Where did you think I'd be?" He didn't need to ask in order to know where he'd be sleeping that night. They hadn't spoken until he'd finally driven to the office to apologize. That was last night. He had not touched another pill since the funeral — at least he couldn't remember doing so, but how could he be certain of anything? He'd heard a voice in the middle of the night a few nights ago. Thankfully it was Ophelia's voice, but who would she be talking to at that hour? This morning she'd discovered the pill bottle with a pair of remaining pills in plain sight beside his pillow, just before leaving for work.

"What you desperately need, Tal Neilson, is a pair of ruby slippers," Ophelia shouted at him this morning on her way out the door. "I don't want you here when I get back. Go click your heels. Go home, you irresponsible child. I mean it. I swear I'll never learn."

CHAPTER 7

Had she thrown him out this time? Tal wondered. Or had she once again run out on him, when she left for work this morning with the reference to the ruby slippers? In Paris she'd never returned. This time he expected she would return but he had no plans of being there when she arrived. "Go home," she'd shouted, then slammed the door so hard the entire apartment shook. Except once he walked out the door, he was homeless.

There was no place like home because home was a fictional place in novels, films, or other people's lives. CallMeGeri's three-story brownstone was a once-upon-a-time, something to fill the space between one boarding school and another. Little more than a prison from the time Baby Jeffrey *left* the family over twenty years ago. The euphemism Mother insisted upon. Mother would never face the truth. Jeffrey didn't *leave*. He died. Fact of life. Fact of death. Tal's friend Cornelius, who knew of the whole sordid affair, rationalized it for him in the way that children make sense of the world: the death machine killed Jeffrey.

■ ■ ■

A few hours after Ophelia took off, Tal left her apartment, carrying the same bag he'd arrived with. The first expense reimbursement check from Lucinda had arrived in his account that morning. The apartment hunting could commence shortly. He'd find somewhere to crash for a few nights until he had it figured out. There was only one item on today's agenda. The visit required by the will to Father's study. Perhaps he'd left something of value among the papers. Something Tal could pawn.

Mother was her usual indifferent self on this morning's courtesy call. "If you insist on going to the house, you'll have to do it on your own — I have plans for the day." As if he could spend another moment in her presence.

■ ■ ■

The study lay in wait at the far end of the second floor, just on the other side of the living room, beside the grandfather clock that Father so hated. A birthday gift from Mother. He stood beside the clock and stared from a safe distance at the door that once separated Tal the child from Father. The study had been off limits unless Father issued an invitation, which was rare. "Enter the study without permission on pain of death" was Father's edict. Prophetic words. Tal turned around, facing the bay window that cantilevered onto the street. An intermittent late autumn drizzle dripped off the umbrellas passing by below. The last of the sun fought to poke through the clouds.

The weather reminded him of his final authorized visit one Saturday afternoon in the late summer, so many years ago. Jeffrey was napping. Just a few weeks before he *left*. The streets were awash in rain, driven relentlessly by an easterly wind that was breaking the midsummer humidity.

Father beckoned him inside the study to take a seat on the desk chair. Tal remembered swiveling on the rotating base as a much younger child. There would be no swiveling today. Father had that expression on his face, the one he usually got when he was explaining something important. The desk was cleared but for an open notebook and Father's fountain pen and blue bifocals. The paper was lined and filled with blue-black doodles with letters and octagons all over the pages, connected by straight lines.

"Tal," Father began, "I want you to take a look around."

Books from floor to ceiling. Thousands of hardcovers. One shelf where every title had the word chemistry in it.

"I'm trying to build an empire that will help the lives of millions of people around the world."

"An empire, Father? Like the Romans or the Greeks? My history teacher says those didn't end very well."

"You may be right," Geri laughed. "I mean more like we're an extremely large business. Have you learned yet about Alexander Fleming in school?"

Tal nodded. What middle school child hadn't heard of him? "The man who invented penicillin."

"He didn't invent it, Son," Geri corrected. "He discovered it. It was already there. He just figured out what to do with it and got all the credit for changing the world. That's a myth. The real story is that he lost focus and a couple of other guys did all the work to turn it into a drug that the world could use. Ever hear of Flory and Chain?"

Tal shook his head.

"They shared the Nobel Prize with Fleming, but only hard-core scientists know that. Funny, isn't it. You can do something that changes the entire world and almost no one will remember who you are. Not me. The world is going to remember that Geri Neilson did something with his life. Just like Fleming. One day they're going to say that I built a drug empire that changed the world. That would never collapse."

Father reached for the notebook on the desk. "Here is where I work out the formulations for the drugs that interest me. It involves a lot of math and chemistry."

"Math's my favorite subject. But the teachers baby us way too much."

"I know what you mean. They don't push you nearly as hard as I do." The calculus books had begun arriving at school last year followed by Einstein's theories. Tal had listened to the stories of Father's childhood and felt obliged to follow Father's private lesson plans.

Father could not possibly understand that math was currency Tal could trade for favors in the private schools he rotated through. Math homework for the boys in exchange for protection. It may not have earned him friends but it did earn him survival. Even a grudging measure of respect from the older boys who needed him.

"Listen to me, follow my example, learn my commandments, study hard, work hard. You need to toughen up to lead. One day you'll be taking over all this for me."

Tal nodded wordlessly.

He listened once more to Father recounting the story of his childhood survival. How he used to wake up while it was still dark outside and get together with all the other fishermen in the village to get the boats ready to leave the harbor at daybreak and begin the day of work. How life changed so dramatically. How Father adapted to that change.

Father walked Tal over to the globe perched on a three-legged brass stand under the window on the back wall of the study.

"I just had this custom made by an artisan upstate." Father sounded very proud. "Cost me a lot. But it's worth it. Look at the craftsmanship. Go ahead. Touch it, son." The mountains were bumpy, the forests were various shades of green and the oceans much bluer than in the school geography books.

"This is not an ordinary globe, Tal." Tal would learn that lesson shortly and carry it for the rest of his life. Sometimes a globe is not just a globe. Maybe Father saw it as art. He rotated it until the European continent was front and center.

Tal reached down to slide his fingers along the edge of the brass axis holding the globe in place.

"Careful," Father said sharply, just as the skin on the inside of Tal's pointer finger split open. Father grabbed a tissue, folded it, and squeezed the fresh wound. "It's only blood," he said in an indifferent tone. "Hold your hand above your heart and press the tissue like I'm doing. We don't want the blood spilling on the carpet. It will never come out."

Father pointed to a spot on the coast of Europe, to some barely visible writing. "I had the artist put Elsinore on the map. The place where my life philosophy began to evolve. One day we'll visit, so you can measure how far we've come, though it's probably still just a poor fishing village. What I'm trying to tell you is that you can make something of your life regardless of where you start. Regardless of the odds against you. I may not have liked growing up there, but Elsinore holds the secrets of my life."

"Yes, Father, you've told me the story, so it's not a secret. The boy named Paul and his family that you and Grandfather saved."

"Why do I tell you this story, Tal?"

"Something about the diamonds that Grandfather refused to take."

"You're old enough to understand now. My father could have used those diamonds to make a new life for us when we were forced to abandon Elsinore and his life as a fisherman. Sweden was not for us. America, he insisted. The land of opportunity. He got that wrong. Instead of opportunity, he struggled and worked hard at menial jobs in Wisconsin. He fixed toilets. That's how far the proud fisherman sank. The Dane, they all called him. No one even bothered to learn his name. Your name. My mother died of pneumonia in her bed. Never even got to the hospital. We couldn't afford it. By the time I turned fifteen, I knew better than my father. He was a peasant in America." Father spat out the word "peasant" as if it were a crime.

"He didn't have to," Father continued. "He could have taken those diamonds. At night in my bedroom I cursed him for having made our lives so difficult, for being such a proud fool."

"Would you have taken those diamonds?"

"Without a thought. I would have taken care of my own. Family comes first. He let his pride come before his family. He traded a life of security for a worthless blessing from a family of strangers he'd never hear from again, if they even survived. For the rewards of Jesus."

"How would they even find him?"

"Good point. Unlike my father, I would find that land of opportunity. I began by learning to speak English like an American, so the kids in school would stop teasing me. I learned how to fight, how to defend myself. I discovered that bullies don't like to take on people who fight back, who'll bloody their noses and aren't afraid to shed a little blood themselves. No one was going to push me around."

"Nobody teases me in school," Tal said in a defensive tone. Father didn't react. Maybe he knew it was a bald-faced lie.

"I was embarrassed for my father. I was so angry with him. He died before I graduated college. He died broke, had no idea who he was at the end. No less delusional than before he lost his mind to dementia, believing his reward for what he did for that family was coming in the next life.

"If something is owed to you, take it. I've worked hard for everything I've earned, and I've protected my family, made sure you didn't suffer as I did as a boy. Family first. You got that, Tal?"

Tal shrugged.

"Something doesn't make sense to you?"

"All the charities. Everything Mother supports. The foundation she's always talking about."

Father smiled. "Once I made my fortune, I set money aside in a foundation so your mother could take care of strangers. It makes her happy. Gives her purpose. *My* job is to keep an eye out for danger. Someone is always trying to take advantage of me. Trying to destroy the empire I'm building. That's exactly what they'll do to you once I'm gone if you let them. It's the way of the world. When someone tries to take what is rightfully yours, will you fight for it or give in? What kind of man will you be?"

■ ■ ■

What kind of man? So many years had passed and Tal felt no further ahead. Four paces separated Tal from the oak door, protecting the uninvited from Father's edict. Enter the study without permission on pain of death. Tal raised his pointer finger. The faint childhood scar could never be erased. He drew a breath and exhaled, counting down the moments, each step closing the distance between present and past. Between reality and fantasy. Between life and death. The blood coursed through his veins, his heart pounding, his ears beating. His fingertips twitched on the cold antique door handle. He drew another breath. This one he held on to tightly, like his grip on the handle, his connection to the present, then closed his eyes and waited. The fear of so many things that ruined the lives of two children riveted him to the spot. The death machine, the faint dotted shadows on the Persian carpet that could never be erased, the coppery-iron smell of fresh blood, and the ghost lurking in the room.

"Open the damned door."

The handle clicked and the hinges protested the invasion with a squeal. A final glint of sun filtered through the window facing him, revealing a swirl of particles that immediately disappeared. Perhaps it, or they, melted into the faint carpet stains just in front of the brass legs of the stand under the window. Stains visible only to Tal. Stains no one could ever erase. The last tangible proof of Jeffrey's existence. Tal walked over to Father's prized artisan globe. Now his globe. A gift he could barely look at.

The day Jeffrey left, Tal was babysitting while Mother escaped Jeffrey's screaming in the crib to do some errands. Tal lifted him up and carried him piggy-back down the stairs. That usually got him to stop. There had to be a distraction in the house. They stopped at the grandfather clock. Tal pointed out the pendulum swinging. Still no end to the crying. Maybe if they played with Father's colorful globe, Jeffrey would calm down. They were about to enter without permission.

He'd be careful to keep Jeffrey away from the desk and chair, so Father would never know. He pushed open the study door and put Jeffrey down on the carpet. He raced to the globe. Tal gave it a hard slap. Jeffrey squealed and clapped his hands. Then Jeffrey reached out to touch it and lost his balance. Grabbed for the bottom of the stand as he was falling. The inside of his wrist was trapped between the sharp edge of the stand and the spinning globe. The blood gushed out a short moment before the pain registered and Jeffrey's shrieks pierced his ears.

After that the memories came in pieces. Were they real or reinvented by the retelling to Cornelius? A jumbled order of sounds, smells, and horrors: yanking Jeffrey's arm out while the skin on the inside of his wrist tore away; the gash deep and wide; Jeffrey's wrist, a ripe plum split wide open; the coppery smell; the scratch of the label of Tal's T-shirt against his neck as he pulled it over his head and jammed it into the wound; holding Jeffrey's arm upward; slowing down time; watching it turn from white to bright red; front door closing; feet racing up the staircase; Mother in the doorway, then more screaming; grabbing for Jeffrey; everyone hysterical; Tal naked from the waist up, soaked T-shirt falling to the carpet.

Did he see Jeffrey after that? Never again as far as he recalled. Jeffrey had left forever.

Jeffrey now reduced to imagined stains on the carpet. Still there for Tal. The death machine sat ignorantly, completely unaffected. Unrepentant. Unpunished. He smacked at it with his right hand. The crack of a whip sending the globe into a wild spin of aquamarine, mountainous browns, and forest greens. A world out of control.

He shoved his index finger between the globe and the brass axis, jolting the globe to a sudden halt. Then waited patiently for the moment to recur, the pain to register, and the blood to ooze out of the transverse slice. This time the room was silent, but for the memory of the curdling screams that displaced any presence of Father in his head. Tal sank to his knees, allowing fresh drops of blood to drip onto the carpet, before bringing his finger up to his lips and licking it clean.

"You belong in hell," he shouted.

Tal reached into his jacket pocket and pulled out a small plastic container. Prying off the top, he shook out a couple of tabs and swallowed. It would be a few minutes before the edge would ease off and the dulling euphoria set in. He turned back to look at the globe, then at yet another bloodstain soaking its way into Tal's history. Dropping his head to his knees, he began to cry.

"*Pull yourself together.*" The voice was stern. Admonishing.

Why did he make me come for the death machine? Tal wondered. Then the words in his mind, but not spoken by Father this time. "*Elsinore holds the secrets of my life.*" The words he'd used so many years ago. The words he'd reinforced the countless times he'd retold the story of saving the Jewish family.

Tal picked himself off the rug and turned on the overhead light, then walked up to the death machine. Rotated it slowly until the coast of Denmark came into view. He bent over and ran his finger over the word Elsinore. Under the dot a circular indentation in the middle of the word. "Elsinore holds the secrets," he said out loud. "Of course," he shouted. Father never made it easy but there always had to be a trick. Tal pressed on the indentation with his middle finger and heard a click. The top of the globe split slightly. Enough to insert a finger and pry the rounded panels apart. His heart began to pound. There was a thick blue file inside the globe.

Tal reached in and removed it, felt around carefully inside to make sure it was the only item, then carefully slid the panels back together. Another click, then the only sounds were the waves pulsing in his ears. What was in this file that was so important?

He brought the file over to Father's desk and flipped open the cover. Tal's spreadsheet was on the top, ignored. It had none of Father's fountain pen hatches and scratchings; beneath it were other notepapers, colored white on the top and frayed and yellowed on the bottom. Some kind of collection of memorabilia? But why his spreadsheet? It looked untouched. There was nothing of value here. Just another let-down. A worthless dead end.

The pills had set in and Tal no longer had the patience to make any sense of it. He jammed the file under his arm, squeezing it between the sleeve and torso of his leather bomber jacket, and made his way out.

CHAPTER 8

Ophelia stood with her back to the window, in the living room of the apartment on West Fifty-Ninth. The neighborhood was upper class, but she would never have guessed that from the inside. The place was devoid of the accumulation of *things* that people collected to mark the passage of their lives. Uncle Thomas had been accustomed early in life to living with nothing, to relying on no one. He lived conservatively, making no-show to the outside world of the wealth he had accumulated.

She knew little of her uncle's early years. He refused to speak about them. The story she knew began when he was adopted by her grandfather, a diamond merchant turned investment banker. Now Thomas was a respected member of the Danmark board, a man who could wield power and wealth, yet never showed any outward affectation. The walls were barely adorned, the fireplace mantle empty, but for a single family photo. It was intended to be his *pied à terre*, far from the home in Milan where he'd raised his son and lost his wife just last year. High enough up to have a view of the river. A view Ophelia avoided.

A simple couch with a few bland throw pillows, a couple of love seats, and a low rectangular teak coffee table defined the living area. Thomas perched on the edge of a plain wooden chair, the kind she remembered from her high-school auditorium. He was caressing the centerpiece of the room, working his fingers with eyes closed shut. The cello was whispering. Was it love or pain? Were love and pain inseparable?

"I've never heard you play so well," she said, turning to face him. She envied his fingers, sliding up and down the fingerboard, as if he were connecting with the spirit of the woman he loved.

He didn't miss a beat or open his eyes. "It's the Montagnana, not me. Richer than a Stradivarius. A little wider, a centimeter or two shorter. Makes all the difference."

The *kippenvel* rose on her arms underneath her white blouse. Tiny little bumps that made the dark hairs stand on end.

"Eliza was the shopper," he continued without stopping. "What she bought was what we owned. For years she had been urging me to splurge. To buy one *thing* for myself. I really should have listened. I denied her the pleasure. Just after my month of mourning I gave in." Thomas's voice betrayed little emotion. "His cellos come up for sale so rarely. I picked it up at a Sotheby's auction last year. This one was built in 1702. Almost plays itself."

His Dutch accent was so much softer than her own, his tone unreadable, like the thoughts in his head or the pain he must be harboring in his heart. They had grown up on the same street, in the same home in Amsterdam, a generation apart. A generation that separated the destroyers of the world from the rebuilders. Thomas and his sublime talent had survived that destruction.

"Is that Clara Schumann?" Ophelia asked absently.

Thomas opened his eyes to answer without putting down the bow. "Impressive. Most people only know her husband Robert's compositions. She wrote this for the piano. I worked out a variation for the cello." He closed his eyes once again and continued playing. His head bobbed, his abundant white hair waving in the air currents, the only sign that revealed the passion he kept well hidden.

Was it a deliberate choice? Almost no one played the music of Clara Schumann. She'd made the mistake of rushing into a marriage her father opposed, the father who dominated every moment of her young life to the point of editing her diary entries, the man who sued her husband Robert after they married. Perhaps Thomas was sending her a reminder that her voice might be heard over the domination of a relentless father.

She stood at the far end of the room, trying to make sense of the artwork hanging on the wall. The first was a signed print; beside it hung a poem in black ink, also framed. It was curious that Thomas had displayed the English translation of the poem rather than the original German. Perhaps it was the product of assimilation into American life.

Black milk of daybreak we drink it at nightfall
we drink it at noon in the morning we drink it at night
drink it and drink it
we are digging a grave in the sky it is ample to lie there

She quietly repeated the opening words, then played them over in her head. "Black milk of daybreak." Why those words? "We drink it and drink it," repeating the words, over and over until silence filled the room.

"What does the poem mean?" she asked.

"The opening stanza to the 'Death Fugue' by Paul Celan," he said. "Goes well with the music, doesn't it?"

"I don't understand," she said.

"You know, my dear, they would have cremated me, too, were it not for my musical ability. My mother unwittingly saved me. The music lessons she insisted upon when I turned five. By ten I was somewhat of a prodigy. My father was fortunate to have been shot on the street the day before we were rounded up. I had this talent, and the Nazis separated me when we stepped off the cattle car. They were building an orchestra for the commandant. That's how I survived."

Thomas closed his eyes once more. "They didn't bother with graves for my three sisters and my mother. Their ashes rose to the sky and rained down on us. At least that's what I imagined. Black milk that fell from the sky. The desecration of the women and children that we gathered on our tongues as our memory, so we could carry their memories within us forever. "

Ophelia felt the shudder building from deep within. "You've never spoken about them."

"I carried them with me, but until recently, it was not something I was prepared to discuss. I buried them deep inside along with the memories. Eliza never pushed. Yakov... Well, you know Yakov. It was not easy for him growing up. Another child of a survivor."

Thomas stood and walked over to the window. Ophelia wasn't certain if he was lost in thought or admiring the splinters of light bouncing off the Hudson River, which she caught out of the corner of her eye. Ophelia turned her back to him.

"I always preferred Italy to America," he said. "For years I commuted. But with Eliza gone and Yakov back in Israel, there's nothing for me in Milan. Yakov probably feels about me the way you feel about Paul."

"What do you mean, the way I feel about Paul?" The embers of anger were stoked. "I love my father. I honor my father."

The corner of Thomas's mouth curled upward. "Of course you do. But you don't always like him. You're not obliged to like him, just to honor him. Like Yakov and me."

"Yakov has his own demons."

"Who among us are exempt from demons?"

Thomas had no idea where her demons were hiding. They sent her to Paris to keep tabs on Tal. She filed her work reports. The rest she kept secret. Until the night she bolted, not as a result of any demon, just a relationship turned sour. She ran out on her family obligations. That was all he and Paul understood.

She'd sent Thomas an email from the barracks in the Negev letting him know she was done with Paris. Then she buried the phone in the desert sand. Defying Paul over the vow was the equivalent of family treason. Thomas's wisdom and patience evidently triumphed. They let her alone until she'd completed her service of her own will.

In Israel she discovered what Paul and Thomas had both learned. Life was timing. Timing was life. Demons had an odd way of appearing in the water and impacting your life choices. Demons that shooed her out of Israel and returned her to family and its obligations. They sent her back to work in New York.

She reached into her purse and withdrew the flash drive. "As you requested. The information from Red King's computer."

"I'll have it analyzed — thank you. I just need to fit together the pieces of whatever it is Red has been working on. This is as much as you can do to assist. You'll continue to monitor the heir."

"Can I ask you a question that's always bothered me?" she asked.

Thomas nodded.

"Why have you always treated the vow like it's yours?" she asked. "The fisherman saved my father and his family but he didn't save *your* life. You survived the war without their help."

"If he doesn't save your grandfather Lazar, there is no one to rescue me. Who knows what becomes of a Dutch orphan wasting away from typhus in a Belgian refugee camp? I am bound by the vow as much as if I had been sitting with Paul on the fishing boat. So are you."

"I don't accept that." Ophelia felt a measure of control returning. "I've given what I've given out of a sense of duty to my father. I am obliged to honor him. But the Neilsons are multimillionaires. Geri built a drug empire. He was living a fairy tale that you and Paul helped him build. What can I add? Why keep sending me on these missions to watch the heir to the empire? It serves no purpose."

"It serves a purpose. Your grandfather called it God's purpose. Paul's life has been shaped by it and it must continue. One day you too will understand that it is the purpose of your life as well."

"As if Paul owes his life to Geri? Isn't Paul's damaged leg absolute proof that it's the reverse?" This was part of the story Paul rarely spoke about. Two twelve-year-olds bailing in the stern of the fishing boat. A wall of water knocked them both over, smashing Paul against the side of the boat. Geri was halfway into the sea, Paul fighting to hold onto Geri for dear life, practically destroying his own leg in the process. Paul pulling Geri's limp body back into the boat, while in excruciating pain.

"When you think about it, Geri's father saved our family, but *Paul* saved Geri from drowning. Paul was the hero. Never Geri." Thoughts she'd nurtured in a special box in her head.

His eyes flashed with an anger he made no effort to hide. "They risked their lives to save Paul, your aunt, and your grandparents from incineration."

Ophelia's box incinerated along with her argument. Poof.

"And if Paul had not been saved, your life would not exist." Thomas said the words as if it was a simplistic high-school conditional statement. If A then B. If Tal's grandfather and his son Geri save Lazar and his son Paul, then Paul must take care of Geri, and Paul's daughter must take care of Geri's son. A simplistic, irritating logical proposition. They were often flawed.

"Haven't we done enough?" she said, barely hiding her irritation. "Doesn't it ever end? How much do we have to continue before our debt is repaid?" Lazar had financed Geri's education. He had loaned Geri the money to buy Darrowpharm. He had installed Thomas on Geri's board for forty years. Paul continued the loans and investments, putting up the money every time Geri needed it to expand. Had they not repaid the debt twenty times over? A hundred times? "When is enough?"

"It's not a debt that can be repaid in dollars, Ophelia. How do you value a life? How do you value the lives of an entire family that would never exist but for the fisherman and his son? Lazar made the vow. A vow he repeated every Friday night until he died. As long as any member of our family lives and breathes, their kindness will be rewarded. Paul added his own condition. He insisted we all work behind a veil to preserve their dignity."

Ophelia swallowed hard. "What about my life?"

Thomas sat there without responding, cello at his side, giving her time to listen to her own voice. She had the sudden sense that she was pleading. They had accepted her play of the escape-from-the-vow card when she left Paris. He was allowing her to come to her own conclusion about the appropriateness of begging for any more leeway.

"We are at a crossroads, Ophelia. Geri is gone, Red King cannot be trusted, and your job is to find out what Talem wants."

CHAPTER 9

Trudi Darrow stood in front of the mirror, applying a final coat of mascara and took a half step back to do an appraisal. "Not a day over forty-five," she whispered with satisfaction into the reflection. Thank god for the plastic surgeon. In about an hour she would head out for a French manicure and hair salon appointment, then to the lawyers to discuss her legal situation. It was the sixtieth day of mourning in her sixty-fourth year. Time to move on. Tomorrow she would begin to reclaim her life.

The task at hand was to hear out the guest downstairs and stick to her schedule. Had it been anyone else asking to meet with her today she would have put them off, but Pastor Marcellus was making his first visit since the funeral and hopefully his last. No doubt he would be on his best behavior so she might as well get it over with.

Pastor Marcellus rose to greet her as she entered the living room. The neatly trimmed black goatee, streaked with gray, matched his sport jacket. The black horn-rimmed glasses gave him a look of erudition. Funny how he'd looked so much taller when he spoke from the podium at the funeral. On equal footing he was an inch or two shorter than Trudi.

"I really appreciate that you made the time for me," he said with his most charming smile.

"Did Esmeralda offer you some tea?" she asked.

"I passed, thanks." She ushered him to the love seat beside the baby grand, where he could have a direct view of the study door. She sat opposite him on the colonial chair. The stage was set to begin the conversation on safe ground.

"You know you were the exception in Geri's life?" she asked.

"I'm sorry?"

"The study. No one was allowed in that room. Geri invited me to visit twice in all the time I can remember. Even Esmerelda had to make an appointment to get in there to dust and vacuum. You should consider yourself quite honored." Pastor Marcellus used to show up at all hours of the night to meet with Geri. The last visit had been a week before Geri… No point dwelling on it. She knew full well what the pastor wanted from him. What he always got. Geri never spoke about it. He just took the meetings and wrote the checks. He thought she didn't know about the account, but he was sloppy with the checkbook, leaving it in the breast pocket of his pinstripe suit in his bedroom closet. Esmerelda brought it to her when she noticed a stain on the lapel and added it to the dry cleaning pile. Easily a hundred checks over many years. The notations were always the same. *Re: the project.* Probably something for the building fund.

"We spent hours debating life philosophies," he said. "I'll miss that."

"You mean *he* lectured *you* about *his* philosophies?" It was unlikely they were discussing religion. Geri made no time for God, never even showed up at the church until the funeral. Geri didn't believe in God, not at all. The only thing Geri believed in was Geri and his stupid ten commandments. He also had very little time for people. He wasn't comfortable with them. Preferred to fight them. So why did he take the pastor's calls and visits? And why in heaven did he leave him twenty million? That had to be more than any building project. What was Geri thinking? But really. Why should she care? It was just another twenty million that wasn't going to the foundation.

The pastor laughed. "There was only one Geri." His face turned serious. "I just wanted to check in on you," he said.

"I appreciate that, pastor, but it's really not necessary."

"There's often a delayed reaction that sets in."

He was right about that. Red had called her to break the news at four-thirty in the morning from the emergency room of the Atlantic City hospital. "It's serious so just get here. The driver is on his way," he said. "The flight crew will meet you at the jet." No time to put herself together. No time to even make a written checklist. Get dressed. Pack an overnight bag. Throw the makeup in her purse. Find the number of Dr. Simons from the Sinai Hospital board to get a bed ready in the cardio unit as soon as she could transfer Geri. Red could take care of the medevac flight. She'd negotiate the foundation endowment to Sinai once Geri recovered. Throw on the overcoat.

The keys were in the front door lock when she had the flash. Geri's drug. She ran back up the stairs and pushed on the study door. It wouldn't yield. She pushed harder until it popped open. Why didn't Geri get the damn thing fixed? She ran past the desk to the bookcase. Where was it? With the philosophy books. On the top shelf. The yellow spine. *ETHICS*, Spinoza. Geri's idea of humor to pick that title for his hiding place. She pulled it out and dropped it on the desk. Opened the false cover. Reached for one of the vials and a syringe and dropped it in her purse. Closed the book. Replaced it on the shelf.

She put herself together in the back seat, though there was not much time. At Teterboro, the night security checked her off a list and opened the gate. The floodlights reflected off the fuselage and she mounted the small staircase, careful not to catch her heels in between the metal slats. Fifty minutes in the air and two Bloody Marys later, she'd had just enough time to work through all the scenarios she'd be fighting over with Geri, which in a way was both sad and funny. He was sleeping when she walked into the private room. Although he was hooked up to all kinds of monitors, he looked almost peaceful. An hour later he was dead. That *was* a shock she couldn't process until returning home that night.

How many nights had she lain awake in her bedroom, wondering what it would be like to be free of this marriage without the public humiliation of divorce? It was nothing like she had imagined. It was a hundred times better. Pure joy. The delayed reaction, but not the one the pastor was imagining.

That was a sentiment best masked.

"When I arrived, the resident said he was in stable condition. I walked to the lounge to call Tal. Red joined me a few moments later. We heard the 'code blue' and ran back to the room. He was dead before we got back. So sudden." She pulled out a handkerchief and dabbed her eyes.

"I'm so sorry."

"The doctor said that sometimes the heart gives up."

"I can't see Geri ever giving up," the pastor said.

"No, me neither," Trudi agreed. "You don't have to worry about me, pastor. Geri would have wanted me to get back to my life quickly. I'm beginning to do that."

"I hesitate to mention it," said the pastor, "but this death must bring up some difficult memories for you. Do you want to talk about them?"

It took her a moment to realize what the pastor was talking about. Of course, he was around when Baby Jeffrey left. He knew she had fallen apart. Maybe he really was concerned about her.

"Those were also tragic times," she said. "The loss of Baby Jeffrey hit us all hard." What she couldn't tell the pastor was that it wasn't the death that had driven Trudi to depression. It was his conception and birth. "It took me a while to accept that I couldn't recover my baby." How could the pastor possibly understand she was on the verge of recovering the only "baby" she'd ever cared about?

Geri's death had opened a door that had been slammed in her face many years ago. She had all but given up any hopes of returning to Danmark in any capacity, but step one toward reopening that door was set for tomorrow, day sixty-one of the post-Geri era. Joining the board was step two. After that there was still an ascension to consider. Step three.

"You've been through a lot, Trudi. These situations are always hardest on the surviving spouse. If you ever have a need to talk, you know where you can find me," Marcellus said, standing up and heading to the door. Trudi waited for the door to click before reaching for her purse to pull out her checklist. This time she would not forget anything.

Step one was sure to shake up New York high society. They'd crucify her on the gossip pages, painting her as the weakling widow. Or worse, the conniving widow. That she had breached the unwritten rules for high society mourning. Her close friends would understand immediately. The announcement would be made just before she left the country. Let them all wait for her to return before explaining. Keep an air of mystery.

It was finally time to begin her comeback. One more day.

CHAPTER 10

The last meeting in person with Tal was two months ago. Lucinda had lost track of how many times she'd called Tal since then, just to touch base. The first few times he'd taken the calls, discussed the various documents she requested he sign, agreed to the rehab program she had found for him. It was rated as one of the best in the world and came highly recommended by Drew Torrance. One of the Danmark board members had a son who had been through it. Tal was placed on a waiting list two to six months long. They agreed it was worth the wait. He had not responded to her in the last month, though there was no news to share with him. She just wanted to make sure he was managing before she disappeared for the week. One last shopping day to Christmas eve and the trip to Boston for a well-earned week with her sister Bea and family. She'd head to Fifth Avenue right after this meeting with Tal.

Yesterday morning Tal had called out of the blue. "I need to meet with you," he said without even a hello.

"I'm glad to finally hear from you," she said.

"I wanted you to know I'm not frittering away my time waiting for rehab. I needed time to think. Time alone. So I shut myself up in a hotel room. A place where they know my credit's good. I'll eventually get you the bill."

"Don't worry about that, Tal. What are you working on?"

"The math... The math had something to do with the veto. I couldn't figure out the connection."

"Sorry, Tal, where does math come into this? We never discussed math."

"You're not the only one he communicated with. He insisted I do the math."

"Your father?"

"Who else? The math has everything to do with my shares and the restrictions he placed on me. I finally get it." He stopped a moment as if to let it sink in. "Maybe I can't sell my shares, but for the next year I don't need any money. I'll be in rehab. It's the *wrong* starting point. CallMeGeri would *never* be selling his shares. He'd rather die. And if he did die, he'd want me to step into his shoes. But Father never asks for anything directly. He either ignores me or he sends me puzzles to solve. Always higher math. Did that right through school. It was always the same. Do the math. Solve the puzzle."

She wasn't sure how to respond. Manic Tal was at the other end of the line, making sense only to himself. "This is a little complicated for me, Tal. Tell me how doing the math fits in."

"It's mostly game theory. Sophisticated mathematical analysis of alternatives."

"I'm a lawyer, Tal. I freeze up over math problems. Please go slow."

"Imagine calculating the risk to two decimal points of opening your front door to find a trained assassin sent to kill you. Or that you'll die of a mysterious virus next month if you go to a crowded restaurant tonight."

"I have no idea how to do that but continue."

"So I apply it to my situation. Instead of being me and reacting to a situation I can't control, I turn the problem on its head. Analyze the alternatives. Since Father died, I've been living in the world as Tal Neilson. Instead of being like Tal, thinking like Tal, I have to think like CallMeGeri. Perform the game theory like he would. Do the math, but do it his way. What are his options and what is his best percentage move? That's what I did. But that takes time and analysis. Days, nights. Like the days and nights I spent in Paris working on the transformation of Danmark… Never mind that. It's history." Tal paused.

He was already off in too many directions. Hotel rooms, Paris, game theory, assassins, reincarnation. What was he on right now?

"I just had to perceive the world through the eyes of the greatest sonofabitch in history. *What will the bastard do next?* is what Geri would be asking. Not what would Tal do. To be or not to be Geri. Get it?"

She pulled the receiver away from her head and rolled her eyes. Fortunately, this was a phone call. "Go on, Tal."

"I have the veto. It's useful for only two purposes. I can prevent the bastard from selling the company and I can stop him from selling any of his shares. The bastard is a profligate spender. Have you seen his cars?" Tal paused, as if to switch gears. "He's three years older than Father, about to turn seventy-five, diabetic, stepping in as CEO. What does game theory predict as his next move? He's going to be selling out. Except he needs my approval. I can't get rid of him as CEO, but there's only one way to get rid of me... Actually given recent history there are two ways... Never mind."

"It's beginning to make sense. I'm following."

"I go into rehab and you become my mouthpiece. Get it? After a few months you let him believe I might sell my stock at a premium."

"But you told me you'd never sell your shares to him. I don't get it."

The exasperation at the other end of the line could probably be heard in the TGO office in Chicago. "This is a game, Lucinda," Tal shouted. Then she heard him take a breath, breathe out slowly. His voice calmed. "A game with rules. Rules of my design. Of CallMeGeri's design. Of course, I'm not selling to the bastard. But in this game you keep telling him it's only a matter of price. Let him keep telling the board he's close to solving the Tal problem. An entire year to make him miserable while you haggle on my behalf. Every time he thinks he's about to close the deal, I change my mind. Ask for more money. Change my mind again.

"Then I get out of rehab and have the twenty million to play with. Money to bide my time. Wait him out until the board finally figures out they need *me* to get anything important done. That's when they fire his ass. Except in the corporate world they call it retirement. Almost mid-seventies. They throw him a big party. Give him a Cartier watch."

"So how does doing all this tie in with you or your future?"

"Can't you see? If the bastard leaves the company, I can make my comeback. I'm not crazy, Lucinda. I wouldn't expect the board to install me as CEO. But with my father and the bastard both gone, I can start making my way back up the ladder. As a ten percent shareholder there's a path for me to return. They'll have to listen to me this time. My ideas weren't just good when I worked in Paris. They were capable of taking Danmark to a whole new future. I'll do it again. That is Geri's math all worked out. I had to disappear for a month to get here.

"This can't wait any longer. I want to get into rehab. I need to get to rehab. Except I have one legal question. Once I'm in rehab, do I lose any of my rights as a shareholder?"

"No, Tal. A voluntary decision to go into rehab has no impact on your rights. The voting trust imposes no special conditions of that nature. It would be different if you were committed for psychiatric purposes, but that is clearly not the case here."

"So to confirm, even while I'm in rehab I have the veto attached to the stock in the voting trust. The bastard can't do anything without my approval while I'm away for a year?"

"No one can take away any rights attaching to your shares." She paused to make sure there were no further questions. "Why don't we meet tomorrow? In the meantime I'll double-check on how quickly I can get you into a spot."

"Okay, but not in the office. Do you know where the Boathouse is in Central Park?"

"Yes."

"Meet me there at two-thirty tomorrow."

■ ■ ■

She enjoyed the crunch of the snow under her leather boots as she ambled on the path through Central Park. The first storm of the season had passed through town a couple of days ago, leaving a residue on the path that combined with the flakes of rusted deadened leaves. Not quite a white Christmas, but enough to raise her spirits. The sunlight poked through the naked tree branches and felt warm on her back, neutralizing the chill in the air. When she'd left the office just after lunch, she let her tightly curled hair out of the ponytail. It felt good to be alive and out walking, an escape from the sterile environment at TGO, where life was an endless cycle of paper, computer screens, and gray-tinted Manhattan views.

The bleak season suited the nature of the practice. Divorce, child custody battles, parents meting out retribution to ungrateful children through last-minute will alterations, children plotting to institutionalize sick parents to get at the fortunes earlier. The darkness enveloping the souls of dysfunctional families.

She was trained to retain an air of detachment, to radiate empathy but not get sucked into the drama of family disputes. Inevitably she succeeded in restoring balance. The women sent thank you cards or floral arrangements; the CEOs delivered rare bottles of wine, to recognize Lucinda's efforts in restoring the normalcy, radiating light back into their lives.

Geri had been unlike any other client she'd ever encountered. Maybe that's why Torrance had handed Geri into her care. She never lost an important firm client. She never lost control. Except once with Geri. The day after he returned from his trip to Ireland.

Just before leaving on the trip, he'd changed his mind for the umpteenth time over whether to leave Trudi any stock and how to protect Tal from himself. She finally thought she had it right. At least according to her last set of notes. She'd walked into his office and laid the revisions in front of him. He pushed the blue bifocals down his nose and began reading. A few seconds in, he picked up the fountain pen and began slashing at the work.

"No... No... No... No... Not what I asked for... I said two-thirds, one-third. Not the right provision ... wrong, wrong, wrong, wrong." He stopped reading and threw the document back to her. The blue-black crucifixes, or hatchets, as Geri called them, marked the death of this draft.

"The math in this is all wrong." He threw his arms up in the air. "I'm gonna die, and this still won't be finished. You're completely screwing up." He was yelling. Someone eased his office door shut.

She was accustomed to the bursts of anger but this was a whole new Geri. He rotated his body away from her to look at something on his computer. "How much time did you waste on this?"

"It took me about a dozen hours."

"No effing way that was a dozen hours. You didn't do anything I asked. I could have done it myself in half an hour. That's all I'd pay for. If you'd gotten it right."

There was nothing to apologize for. Her notes were clear. But it might buy some peace. He usually calmed down. "I'm sorry."

He turned back toward her. "Sorry? How can I trust you after this? And twelve hours to produce this drivel? I don't believe it." The door was shaking in the frame.

Her hands were also shaking, but it wasn't fear. Her voice was breaking but it wasn't tears. It was more like a sudden adrenaline boost lifting her to her feet and almost out of her shoes. The monster was slipping out of confinement to play with Geri.

The burning began in her roiling stomach and built upwards. In a matter of seconds it had built to an inferno in her heart, then into her head. Until the monster had taken control. She was screaming back, louder than she'd ever done. The monster's voice had taken over.

"You know what, Geri? I was wrong. I'm not sorry. I can't read your mind and you change it every meeting. Only an idiot apologizes for nothing. You know who I learned that from?"

The monster made eye contact and held it. Geri could go screw himself.

"I was wondering whether there was anything lurking inside you," he said quietly. "Now I know. Please just finish the will ASAP."

Probably as close to an apology as it would ever get from Geri. It slipped back inside and Lucinda resumed her seat.

It took five hours to recover from the adrenaline crash and three days until the laryngitis cleared. Four days until the will was signed and just a few more until it became relevant. Did Geri understand some-where deep inside, where his monsters resided, that his death was immi-nent? He took that secret to the grave. How dramatically death changes life!

■ ■ ■

Snow crunching, sun drenching, Lucinda marching toward the restau-rant. Death had altered Tal's life and her role was to get him back on solid footing. Yesterday on the call he'd been focused, convinced of a course of action, even if it sounded a little bizarre. He had a long way to go from whatever state he was in to resuming a role at Danmark, but that was more than a year into the future. At least he was focused on recovery. Did it really matter how he came to it? As long as he came to it.

There had to be a person in there behind the good looks. In a year she would find out. While in rehab she would become his voice to the out-side world. Clients had always looked back at how she stood by them in their darkest moments. That was how she built client loyalty, taking them toward the next phase in their relationship.

Tal was seated at a table for two by the window, gazing off into space, tapping his finger on the table, shaking his leg to some rhythm in his head. His shoulders were rounded underneath the unzipped brown bomber jacket. His gray T-shirt fit tightly, though he did not have much definition around the chest. Nothing like those men she couldn't help but notice in the gym. His sunglasses reflected the glare, making it impossible to read the dilation of his pupils and the state of the whites of his eyes. Tal finally took notice and rose slowly and with effort to greet her. A far cry from yesterday's Tal.

"Thank you, Tal. Are you all right?"

"Exhausted. I can barely keep my head up."

He removed the shades and rubbed his glassy eyes.

A waiter dressed in an angel-white apron approached. Lucinda ordered an espresso.

"Just water for me," Tal said. "No ice." The waiter scurried away. "I need to take a couple of pills for the pain. Everything aches. Don't worry. Just two painkillers."

"Perhaps you overdid it working on your math problem," she said.

Tal shook his head tentatively, as if his neck were strained. "As usual Father was two steps in front of me. My math was bad."

Strange, she thought. While she was not any good at it herself, she had learned enough to know that math was neither good nor bad. Just right or wrong. She read that math could be used to prove or disprove theories, could be used to discover the principles of the universe or to destroy cities in Japan, or to launch airplanes at innocent civilians, but it was never the math that was bad. It was the people who used it and their motivations.

Tal continued. "The right math is tied to knowing that the bastard was just smart enough to figure out how to neutralize the veto. Sweet-talk the widow, manipulate her, promise her fidelity *ad infinitum*, in sickness and in health, 'til death do us part."

The drinks arrived. Tal reached immediately for the water glass and emptied a few pills out of a plastic container and into his fist, then threw them to the back of his throat. Chugged half the glass. It took her a few moments to notice the espresso cup. The pungent scent, filling the moment, erasing a bad mood. Then the first sip, always the best, rejuvenating her spirit. She would need every bit of positive spirit to steer him through the conversation.

"What are you saying, Tal?" she asked but she knew what had to be coming next.

"They're married. It's a done deal. A merger. Mother finally informed me last night. They were at the airport, about to take off for Italy. Not even a visit. A phone call. If I hadn't picked up, I would have found out by voice mail." He was shaking his head slowly once again.

"She married him in a private ceremony before a justice of the peace almost a week ago. All hush-hush. No notice, no warning, no invitation, no nothing."

"The snub must have been hurtful."

"Don't be ridiculous, Lucinda. My phone was off for a month. Maybe she tried. Anyway not the point. The point is that together they own more than two-thirds of the stock in the trust."

"But just because they're married doesn't necessarily mean they vote together as a unit."

Tal sat there staring at Lucinda. Was she always going to be this dense, he wondered. "That's incredibly insightful," he said, not bothering to hold back on the look reserved for the dunce who had stood up to let the class know that it was gravity that caused the apple to drop on Newton's head. "Why the hell else do you think they got married? My father's body has barely begun to decompose. Two months is all it took the bastard to manipulate Mother."

He slumped back in his chair. What was the point of rehab? What was the point of anything?

"I'm screwed. He doesn't need my approval. Doesn't need to buy any of my stock. If they vote together they control my vote and they can prevent me from selling to anyone. I'm now his prisoner. Father warned me. Do the math, he kept telling me. He'd already figured this out."

"Telling you, Tal? When? Why would Geri be talking about this when he was still alive?"

No sense holding back from her anymore. What was the point? "He began talking to me at the funeral. He's been living with me at the hotel for the last month. Will not leave my head."

She downed the rest of her espresso, then gave him an inquisitive look.

Tal paused. "Father warned me and I was still completely blindsided. I'll never be him."

"Perhaps that's not a bad thing, Tal. Focus on rehab," she argued. "The world will look entirely different when you come out. Put the stock aside. You'll have twenty million dollars. If they sell the company, you don't have to resist. You'll have hundreds of millions."

She didn't get it. He'd been rich for years. CallMeGeri's rich and screwed-up kid. Rich and hearing voices. A three-time dropout from rehab. Why was the fourth time going to be magic? Game theory suggested the chance of relapsing, even after completion of the program, was seventy percent. All the money was going to lead to one place. A spot next to Father in the cemetery. Exactly as Father predicted at the funeral. *"The two of them will be dancing on our graves."*

"You take the money. Use my name, give it all to charity. I had all the warnings. Father's head is shaking. I've had enough of his disapproval. I've had ... enough."

"Tal, I have no authority to spend your money. And you can't give up on rehab. Not when you're so close to being admitted. The place I've been in contact with has an incredible track record."

"Stop lying to me about rehab. I know what you won't tell me. It's in your eyes. Father's look. Another Tal failure to be financed. But there's a bright side. At least you'll get paid for it. All those hours checking up on me."

"I'm sorry if you think that, Tal, but that's not at all true." There was a slight edge to her voice. As if maybe he'd provoked her a little. It felt better. Her flash of anger replaced the pain in his head. Maybe a little adrenaline was helping more than the pills.

He decided to press on. "You think I don't get it? Lucinda has a fat juicy client. She has to get him healthy to keep him going. That was your hope and you see it slipping like the leaves falling from the trees. The ones you crushed on your walk over here. You try to mask it but your eyes give it away." Her cheeks turned deep red. Maybe she was finally ready to slap his face. Revive him.

■ ■ ■

How dare he? After all the hours she'd spent researching rehab programs, completing the paperwork, the logistics, calling him, calling him, texting him for the last month, worrying about him. And this was his reaction? Questioning her integrity? What he needed was a good smack. Just once. Like the one she'd delivered to Geri to bring him back to reality. It worked that time. This time she decided to let her control abandon her like those leaves from the trees surrounding them outside. Just an act to shock him. Of course there was always a risk when you let the monster out to play. Game theory.

"Grow up, Tal," she barked. The restaurant suddenly went quiet. "You've been offered every advantage in life. But now you're speaking nonsense. Wasting your life!" The yell was liberating, like a banshee scream.

His head jerked upright. She saw the look of shock registering on his face. He put his shades back on. But the monster was out of the cage, about to rake Tal with a swing of its claw. "You think you're talking to another cynical lawyer. You're not. You think you're the only one with an abusive father? You're not. Try growing up in the projects in Hoboken. I put in the hard work to get here today. I earned every inch of my crawl from the slums. Be a man, Tal. Show me you can crawl and pick yourself up. And stop treating your life like it's a slide to oblivion. It's goddamned precious."

She covered her mouth. No way to reverse time. No way to swallow up the monster's words. As the adrenaline died down, she knew she had crossed a line.

"I'm s... so ... sorry, Tal," she blurted. "I don't know what came over me."

He didn't flush. There was no sign of any anger. Just a gaping void where his emotions should be. Except for the thin smile. He didn't say a word. He readjusted his shades, pushed both hands on the arms of the chair, and raised himself up, wobbling at the knees. Once erect, he turned. She watched his legs, tentative at first, then picking up speed and with resolve to get away from her. She didn't break her gaze until he rounded the bend and disappeared out the door into the park.

Girl, kiss your client goodbye.

CHAPTER 11

The sun peeked over white-capped Alps in the far distance, leaving a streak of gold along the lake right to the tip of the shoreline, just below the balcony. Trudi sat erect at the breakfast table, her breath a floating cloud in the morning chill, sipping from a tall glass of juice, which could not be called orange, at least not the American version of orange. This was sharper, brighter, and richer in texture — like the egg yolks that were floating over her breakfast toast. Who knew what the Italians fed their chickens, but whatever it was it made the yolks so much more vibrant — just like her mood this morning at Casa Bellagio. Geri had called it their getaway when he'd bought and renovated it fifteen years ago. She'd given it the name. Everything in the villa was bleached white, modern yet simple, tasteful but not lavish. But Geri had never been short on excuses for why this week or that week was not the right time to take the flight to Milan, then the transfer by limo to the lake house. Summer was too short. Too many meetings and conferences, lawsuit discoveries. Too complicated ... too much time away from the office.

For the last ten years of their marriage, Trudi had resigned herself to making the annual trip on her own. She enjoyed the tranquility. There was nothing to argue about without Geri around.

She grew to accept her life as the charitable matron. The host of hosts. Geri's representative to the world of charitable endeavors. What choice did she have? As long as she accepted the role and played the part, he would never turn on her. She was the queen and he was the king. Good enough for Elizabeth and Philip for all those years that they probably hated one another's guts. Good enough for Trudi. Not that she hadn't thought long and hard about divorce. Though there was no reason to believe Geri would be any less harsh with her than with any of his other lawsuits. She'd tested it out once about five years ago. He got very quiet. The only things more dangerous than Geri ranting were his prolonged silences. They usually preceded war. Divorce would have been scorched earth. A personal attack unless Geri instigated the proceedings. It would have required millions to fund her own lawyers. She backed off and toughed it out. But she also began to prepare for the worst, just in case. A business partnership with Red that allowed her to build a secret fund. Her insurance.

She felt a hand gently smooth the cashmere sweater that she'd thrown over her negligee. A stubbly chin rubbed against her cheek followed by a soft kiss.

"If I had owned this, I don't think I ever would have come back to work afterward," Red said.

"You were always too busy with your cars," Trudi said. Like the brand-new trophy sitting in the driveway. A car meant to be noticed. "How many do you own? Ten? Twenty?"

"I'm down to half a dozen. Forget generic drugs. I should have gone into the warehouse business. Those guys make a fortune." Red eased himself into a chair and poured himself a cup of coffee from the silver carafe on the table.

"How long have you been out here?" he asked.

"Since before daybreak. I always loved the peacefulness out here."

"I'm having trouble adjusting to the peace and quiet." Red smiled.

It was too early for tourist traffic at this hour. Just the flapping of the birds nesting around the lake, the rustle in the bush, probably the feral cats. A lone fisherman in hip waders, fighting to reel in a gray speckled trout dancing at the end of his line, disturbing the surface of the water.

A family of ducks waded in single formation from the shoreline just in front of them and swam out slowly onto the lake, the mother leading the ducklings. What mother duck had babies at this time of year? The fall had been unusually warm, but hatching eggs in December was beyond explanation. The problem when a female loses sight of her priorities and responds to natural urges at unnatural times. Trudi walked to the edge of the balcony to watch. One duckling trailed the pack and was having trouble keeping pace. The mother paddled back until she was alone with her baby. Probably to teach it to keep up. Mother reached for the baby with her beak and dragged its head under the surface of the lake, holding it down for a moment, then released. The baby poked its head back up and began to swim toward the brood. Mother circled round and grabbed for the baby's neck once more, this time holding it down, while Trudi held her breath. The duckling's head did not resurface.

Trudi sighed. "Story of my life," she said.

"Pardon me," Red said.

"Just thinking out loud," she said.

"I wanted to talk to you about my retirement plan," Red said. He dipped a spoon into a small jar of strawberry preserves and turned it over onto a corner of toast. "Doc keeps telling me the stress combined with the diabetes is going to kill me. Besides, the board knows I'm an interim measure."

"Do what you like, Red. I'm going back on the Danmark board as soon as we get back. I want Geri's seat. We had a deal."

"You've made that abundantly clear, but…"

"No buts," she interrupted. "We agreed on a plan. First I get back on the board. Then you recommend to them that I join the executive. You work for two more years, then I succeed you. That was our agreement. With control of the voting trust, no one can stop us."

"Work," he said as if it was another disgusting four-letter word. "My insulin levels are flying up and down like a yoyo. They don't understand why. I'm thinking… " He stopped and slid the edge of toast into his mouth.

"You're thinking what exactly?"

He finally swallowed the mouthful. "I have a better idea. I want to enjoy these moments, Trudi. I know you didn't want to marry me, but we could both use the company. I've waited for you for thirty-five years. You may just find that this relationship surprises you."

No more surprises, she thought to herself. If the cost of getting back to an influential role at Danmark was marrying Red, it was well worth the price. She had years of experience at loveless marriage. "I've given you what you wanted. That will have to be enough for now."

"I only wanted it because I knew that over time we'd find what you once had with Geri."

"Maybe I once loved him. Maybe I didn't. All I know is that ever since that one mistake with you … anyway that's history. Now it's about what I want if you don't mind."

It was hard to compare any love to her lifelong attachment to Darrowpharm, her father's business. It intertwined with her existence like the strands of a rope. The love affair began with visits to the Bethlehem plant with her father on the weekends, sitting in his old rotating oak chair, secretly studying the drug inventory of the company during her summers as a college student. She was about to approach her father to begin work full time when the plane went down. Her mother and aunt had different ideas. Men built Darrowpharm and men needed to run it. "Not proper work for a young woman," they said the day before Geri and Red showed up, caps in hand, with the audacious offer to buy the company. Trudi made it all happen. Became the third partner in the new business. She had kept her legs closed to Red despite all his advances in those first five years together building the business. She paid dearly for opening them to Geri.

"It's time to sell the company," Red said.

"What?" Trudi choked at the shock. She glared at him. "And you wait for our honeymoon to drop this bomb? That was never the deal."

It was finally all in reach, except for whatever it was Red was doing to double-cross her. Like Geri and Torrance had done to oust her in her ninth month, many years ago.

"It's all arranged if you'll just take a few minutes to consider it. I have a buyer for our block." He took a sip of his coffee, making it almost impossible to read his face.

"Who?"

"Sterling Yildirim. He's been slowly increasing his stake in the company. At one point he asked Geri for a seat on the board."

"The Turk? Geri considered him nothing more than a pirate... Not a chance. I don't have to think about it. I'm not selling. Which means you're not selling either."

"You mean you'll exercise Geri's veto."

"This isn't about the veto. We're partners. We've been partners. I did the wedding, but that's where I draw the line. We're keeping our stock."

"Fine. I'll drop it. I'll make you a deal. I'll stay two years as promised. Less, if I can talk the board into making the transition quicker..."

Trudi smiled. Everything was falling into place. She could even forgive him for the splurge on the Ferrari the day after the wedding. Red and his Paul Newman fantasy. For the life of her she could not figure why he needed—

"... But I need something else from you... The point is, darling, I'm strapped for cash."

"How is that possible?" Her fingertips suddenly felt numb. "I've got twenty-five million in my account. Don't you have the same?"

"My account is empty. A few poor decisions at the tables in Macao. I owe about twenty-five million."

"Owe? To whom?"

"People who are running out of patience."

"And against this you went out and spent how much on *that* car?" Her voice rose with each syllable.

"Not a car, my dear. *The* Ferrari of all Ferraris and it was only two million. You never should have bought me the Paul Newman Rolex. Think of the car as an investment. It's going to double in value in the next few years."

"How long has this been going on?"

"A few years. Money comes in, money goes out. Like my Danmark annual bonuses."

"A few years... Since you set up the Cunzhuang deal in Ireland?"

"Since *we* set up the Cunzhuang deal," he corrected.

Their Cunzhuang deal. The beginning of their partnership. Red had the connections, Trudi had the clever idea. Set up a drug distribution deal between Danmark and Cunzhuang for mail order sales outside North

America. Perfectly legitimate on its face. The side business they set up with Red to distribute back into the U.S. was not. The scheme required thoughtful planning and organization, which Trudi provided behind the scenes. Red took care of the flow of their share of the profits, depositing the money to his account on some European island and to her account on the other side of the border in Switzerland, a forty-five-minute drive from the chalet. Red had his reasons. She had hers: insurance against the day that Geri might decide to divorce her and leave her with nothing. Geri's death put an end to that issue.

"The people who own Cunzhuang run the casino in Macao. That's how I met them."

"We've made well over fifty million," Trudi said, her tone acerbic. "Tax-free."

"Need I remind you that half went to your account, dear?"

"And you're telling me your share is all gone and you owe twenty-five on top of that?"

The gambling in Macao. Red was always prepared to throw the dice and take a risk. It would have taken just a couple of wins to double it and repay them. "So sell your cars."

"Darling, they're in a big hurry and these cars never fetch much when you need to sell them. The market sniffs out a desperate seller."

"Your houses, other investments, then."

"All conventionally leveraged to the hilt. Let me put it succinctly. Aside from my stock in the company and my annual salary, I am broke. They threatened me. Never would have happened if Geri hadn't run over to Ireland. I tried to talk him out of going. It was just a few weeks before he died."

"He was hotter than all hell when he left New York," Trudi said, though she had to guess why he was so upset. Just one more day in the life of Geri Neilson. Another day, another lawsuit… "I thought you had the support of the board for the Irish deal. How did you screw that up?"

"You know Geri whenever he decided he knew better. He wouldn't back down. We had a huge fight. Once again the board kowtowed to his wishes."

Red crossed his legs, lowered the coffee cup to the table, and sighed.

"Geri told them that he was cancelling the agreement immediately. These are people who don't bother with court to get what they want. Instead I got a call. Pay them seventy-five million or fix it."

"I thought you owed twenty-five?"

"Since Geri killed the deal they want an additional fifty to compensate for the loss of revenue from their legitimate deal with Danmark."

Trudi shook her head. This couldn't be happening.

"Once Geri began to fight me over the deal, I began to look for alternatives. They began to get antsy. I stalled them to a point. Told them I was planning to sell shares."

Trudi sat quietly, the shock of the series of revelations sinking in, slowly evolving into a sense of caution. The Turk wouldn't just call Red one day and offer to buy a huge stake in a multi-billion-dollar company. He must have been looking at this for months, having his minions go through every bit of information on Danmark, speaking to Red regularly to answer a thousand questions. That's how the leading American shareholder activist behaved. How he'd made his fortune. If he liked management after he stepped in, he'd work with them. If he didn't, then it wasn't long before he was breaking the company apart.

It might be a risk Trudi would take if she were CEO and needed to make a move to protect the company from scavengers. The short sellers were always out there ready to drive down the price of your stock if you were experiencing problems. The Turk sometimes proved to be a good partner while defending his investment. But Geri would never accept that risk. He would never have agreed. For Red it was a simple choice. He would rather sell the company than die. Geri would rather be dead than retired. He was dead. Trudi felt a shiver run up her spine. Then it hit her.

"You've left something out of the story."

"I might have mentioned to them that Geri would never let me sell the company or my stock for that matter. That he had a veto."

The chill was suddenly unbearable. That was not all that Red had left out of his story.

"When you called me from Atlantic City, in the middle of the night, you told me Geri'd had a serious heart attack. That there was likely a stroke as well. That he might wake up a vegetable. You told me to bring the drug." The last item she had almost forgotten. The vial hidden in the bookcase. "When I arrived in Geri's hospital room, I dropped it in the bedside table."

Geri was emphatic about the arrangement. Each of them had a vial. For the just-in-case scenario. Geri was petrified of the dementia that took his father. It was the only thing in his life that scared him. None of them were ever to end up vegetables. She and Red played along. She was certain Red did not have the courage to end his own life voluntarily.

The drug didn't leave a trace, as long as it was administered through an IV line, so there would never be embarrassing questions to answer, but the deal they'd agreed to was assisted suicide. Never murder.

"The code blue happened so fast," she said. "I had left you and Geri so I could call Tal. You were alone with Geri for a couple of minutes before you joined me in the lounge. You owed money to gangsters. You found Yildirim to solve your problem. You knew Geri would never let you do it." The flash exploded in her head. "You didn't leave any of Atlantic City to chance, did you?"

Red smiled. His charming smile. "They were supposed to finish Geri themselves in the hotel room. I don't know who and I don't know how. They're quite secretive about these things. I've only ever met the head of the organization, if she's even the real head. Anyway, they failed. Geri's heart attack presented itself despite the screw-up. At first the doctor told me it wasn't too bad. He'd need surgery for the ruptured artery, back to normal in six months. So I did what I had to. I confess. I knew you'd understand, dear. What was the point of telling you before the honeymoon? Oh yes, I remember now. Something about the confidentiality of confessions to spouses."

Red's face hardened.

"Let's not play games, Trudi. You brought it. I injected it. I may have overstated his condition to you over the phone. Did you really want to be involved in what I had to do for you? That you could never contemplate. Did you want to spend the rest of your life worrying about when Geri was finally going to turn on you like he'd turned on Cunzhuang and countless others? You didn't have the will to do what had to be done. I had the opportunity. I took it… I realize that makes you look like an accessory…" He left those final words hanging in the air.

Partners in embezzlement, she thought. Partners in murder.

"Last week they told me if I couldn't repay them, they'd show me how they collect. I could really use your twenty-five million to stall them."

"You've overwhelmed me, Red. I need to give all this some careful thought."

"You don't play around with these people. If you're not ready to say yes, darling, then I must be off to Ireland. If I don't go to them and stall, they'll come to me. And now that we're married… All I'm saying is that we don't have much time."

We don't have much time, she thought. The immense responsibility attached to two simple words: "I do." *I* becomes *we*, 'til death do us part.

"Stop pushing so hard." Every instinct was pushing her to run back to New York and annul this marriage. Like it never happened. Except responding to the emotion was counter-productive. Breaking up their partnership would cost her the CEO position. Then there was the prenup. Red had insisted on a penalty clause payable by the one who walked away. Bastard. He'd covered the angles. The press in New York were probably clamoring for their return to fill in the gaps of all the stories they'd been writing about their marriage for the past few days. Backing out would be a fiasco of major proportions. In any event the Asians would never accept it.

Trudi turned toward the calm waters of Lake Como. The ducks were gone. Was the brood going to sense anything missing in their lives? Mother duck set her priority — survival of the babies she cared about. Exactly what Trudi's priority needed to be. Protect Danmark. No sense punishing Red for opening the door for her, even if he had done the unthinkable to Geri. Don't give in to the panic. Focus on the goal. Solve the immediate problem. Be Mother. Give the appearance of calm while beneath the surface, the webbed feet are madly driving forward.

Staring at the scene beyond the balcony but not really taking it in, she began to consider some alternatives. No way was she selling the company to pay off this debt, but there was an option.

"Tell them you're reinstating the agreement. That fixes everything."

"The board has authorized the cancellation. At this point I'll never convince Torrance and Leiden to change their minds. They'll figure out immediately that I have an agenda. The two of them pretty much control the board opinion."

"Then let the Asians know that you're going to sell your shares to cover their demands but it's going to take some time. We still have enough stock left to control the board."

"Would that it were so simple."

"It *is* simple. We'll call a couple of the institutions and place a few block trades."

"Doesn't work, sweetheart. Do the math."

Trudi's irritation built. "You want to sell the stock. You want to pay off the debt. Just goddamned sell it and be done with them."

"The veto, Trudi."

"We have enough stock to control the voting trust and nullify Tal's veto."

"Unfortunately not. If I try to sell seventy-five million worth of stock, we drop well below two-thirds, so Tal's veto rights kick back in. Given the current stock price, even thirty million worth of stock would be too much. He can block the sale. You saw him at the funeral. You heard the way he interrupted my eulogy. He hates me. When I signed the Cunzhuang deal years ago, I had to screw Tal. He had developed a business plan in Paris. He sent it to me and Geri for validation."

"Geri never mentioned it."

"It landed on his desk during one of his big cases. It was a pretty good plan for Danmark's future. But I was worried about *my* future."

"Go to Shannon," she said. "Buy us some time. I have to think."

Red headed inside the chalet.

Trudi sighed. The twenty-five million in her Swiss account might be a start to buy them time. Then there was the twenty million she'd just inherited, but society living was expensive. She could sell the Manhattan house and, if necessary, this house, but all of that could take time and leave her with nothing. An impoverished millionaire. They could eventually sell a small percentage of stock, to keep control of the voting trust. They could live on Red's salary, and then hers once she got back to Danmark, but there had to be a better solution to the seventy-five-million-dollar problem.

All this would also mean going into the Swiss account and transferring funds. It was not supposed to leave a trace but American regulators were putting incredible pressure on the world of secret banking to open up. If the regulators ever got hold of that information it would not take much imagination to tie her to Red's embezzlement... She needed to make a list of all the issues, develop the plan, eliminate loose ends.

Perhaps she'd cross to Lugano once Red left. Leave them wire transfer instructions so that if she had to get hold of the money on short notice, she could do it by phone.

She grabbed her note pad and began to write out a checklist of issues. Halfway through the list, the words jumped back off the page and into her head. The solution.

Tal's veto. The roadblock to Red selling shares, getting Red out of debt, take the death threats off their heads, and returning her to the executive suite with the minimum of risk. Mother had taken care of the lagging duckling. Now that the honeymoon had abruptly ended, it was time to deal with the lagging son. She would head back to Manhattan and play the role of mother duck. She couldn't just grab Tal by the neck. She would need finesse.

■ ■ ■

The fisherman stood quietly with his listening device planted in his ear, about to cast his line once more, hoping he would not get any action. The conversation between the couple had ended five minutes ago and he could hear the distinctive engine revving from the edge of the lake over a hundred yards away. Ferrari GTZ. A car he could never afford in a hundred lifetimes, just something he dreamed about.

No upside in sending this man to his death. Then he could never repay the debt. Perhaps his boss, Lingdao, had something else in mind. The new wife might be an inroad to other options. There were so many ways to frighten when family was involved. His job was not to consider strategy, though. Lingdao would make the decisions about how best to enforce repayment of the debt. His job was to surveil, Li Shan's to execute, but only when the order was given. That meant keeping a close watch on the widow for now. There was no disobeying an order from Lingdao, with her fierce temper, especially once she lost her patience.

He caught himself and cast the line back in the water.

CHAPTER 12

Tal had retreated to the brownstone a few days after Mother had cleared out and moved in with the bastard. He was still too embarrassed to go back to Lucinda after the debacle at the Boathouse and it beat crashing with dealers, though it had irked him to ask Mother's permission, an acknowledgment that the house was now hers. He swallowed his pride and Mother was surprisingly accommodating. No strings.

Father's voice had calmed somewhat. Perhaps he'd also given up. Father's notes were spread over the kitchen table, still unintelligible. Tal couldn't concentrate. Besides, what difference would deciphering the code and doing the math make at this point? Too little too late.

Mother had made a surprise visit last night. The first time as Mrs. Bastard. "I'm worried about you, lovey," she had said.

"And I'm worried about your sanity," he shot back. "How could you do it?"

"Do what?"

"Marry him. Share Father's villa with him."

"Tal, you have to accept your father is gone. It is my villa now. This is my house now."

Tal's back went up. "He murdered Father. He's playing you for the fool. The weak-kneed widow. Don't think I'm going to sit by idly and allow him to manipulate you."

"It's just not true, Tal." She refused to raise her voice.

"That's not what I've been told. He stole from Father." He caught a moment of panic in her eyes.

"Not what you've been told? By whom?" Her voice sounded shaky. Her fists clenched for just a moment. He'd struck a nerve. Maybe he was getting through.

"He stole Father's life. How could you marry the man who killed your husband? Haven't we been through enough?" Tal yelled.

He expected a blowback, indignation, defensiveness. Instead her shoulders relaxed. Her hands loosened. The façade was slipping back into place.

"Tal, rather than looking at me maybe you need to focus on yourself." Her tone was motherly once again. He'd lost the momentum. The fight in him was ebbing away. "I know a specialist who's been a friend of the family for years. Your father trusted him. Dr. Rosen's clinic is among the most exclusive in the northeast and had great success with adults dealing with drug abuse."

Mother had no idea that the anger kept him afloat. Like a buoy. Counterbalancing the thousand-pound anchor of guilt chained to his waist. "You and I know what destroyed this family," he said in a half-whisper.

She stood up and walked over to the cupboard, pulling down an old mug. A Mother's Day gift that Tal and Jeffrey painted. "World's Best M m." The "o" had washed off over time. She put on the kettle.

"I'm sorry about what happened to Jeffrey, I should never have left you alone with a Down's child," she said.

"Why are you apologizing, Mother? It was my fault." How many times were they going to retread this thorny path? She would begin with the apology as if that might help. He would admit to the guilt that was never going to subside.

"Don't say that. Don't ever say that," Mother said. Her eye muscles were frozen by the Botox but she managed to muster a few tears. "It's just that you haven't been the same since we lost him. There's not a day that goes by when I don't think about your brother. Such a tragedy. It was not your fault, Tal. It was never your fault."

Of course it was. He hadn't just caused Jeffrey's death; he'd destroyed the entire family. By the time he'd arrived home from the new school for summer vacation, Father and Mother were living in separate bedrooms as if it were the most natural thing in the world. They never bothered to hide it. She refused to use the word "died." Jeffrey *left*. That was as far as she could ever go; Father wouldn't talk about it at all.

Mother stood up, walked across the kitchen, and hugged him. She rested her head on his shoulder. The subject of Jeffrey always seemed to break her down. He didn't buy the crocodile tears over Father's death, and with good reason, but there was something about Jeffrey's death that always moved her. Perhaps guilt that she had left Tal in a position where he had failed in his responsibility to his brother. He felt all her bones. There wasn't much to her anymore. Was she eating? Was he now on her list of issues driving her to starvation?

"Just promise me you'll come with me to Dr. Rosen tomorrow," she said.

"I have an appointment with the lawyer."

"Cancel it. This is more important."

■ ■ ■

The consultation at Dr. Rosen's clinic was scheduled for ten that morning. Tal figured it wasn't going to be more than a couple of hours. Except he hadn't cancelled the appointment at TGO. Instead he had sent Lucinda a quick text, asking if he could come by in the late afternoon instead. He owed her an apology for his behavior at the Boathouse. Lucinda had touched a nerve. He was tethered to nothing in his life, had no connection to anyone. He'd screwed up royally with Ophelia again. Maybe it was nothing but chemistry, or maybe she'd responded to something in him that he was blind to. Or maybe he had to reject anyone who was attracted to him. Regardless, he needed to get on his knees and crawl back to Ophelia, to Lucinda, to himself. To himself first.

The evergreens along the side of the curving roads reminded him of New Hampshire in the winter. Interesting how as an adult Tal still enjoyed riding shotgun, staring out the window, lost in his head, while the scenery rushed past. White-capped pines, the way they were meant to stand. Predictably. Forever. Fascinating how each tree was its own life, with its own story. Sitting in a forest, they blended into something that might be mistaken for monotony. But the patterns were all there, just waiting to be discovered by anyone with the patience to find them. He needed to figure out the patterns of his own life. Nothing was fitting together. Perhaps a consultation with a shrink was exactly what he needed. Get him back on track for rehab.

"Maybe Dr. Rosen can help, lovey." The voice from behind the steering wheel pierced the daydream. The scenery blurred and a wave of nausea doubled him over as the car dipped down a short hill. No one could help. He raised his head and took a couple of deep breaths. In through the nose, out through the mouth. The wave subsided. They began the climb up the next hill. Open sky out the front windshield, lined with trees on both sides, as if they were about to drive up and over the end of the world. This must be what heaven looks like, he thought.

"How do I get there?"

"Are you okay?"

"Talking to myself." There was no point in responding. Did it matter?

Half a minute passed before Mother's eyes cast a glance in his direction. Barely long enough to verify that Tal was still alive. After all, she was driving. She couldn't take her eyes off the road. The story of his life. Just enough attention from Mother to make sure Tal was not dead. Otherwise focused on where she was heading.

Just like the car ride home from the Midland Academy over twenty years ago. The day he was expelled for leading the student insurrection. At least that's what the headmaster had called it while the three of them sat in his office. Braverman behind the desk, Geri across from him on one side, Mother on the other, holding a pacifier jammed into Jeffrey's mouth.

"Your son might have great abilities," Dr. Braverman told them after he had explained the situation. "But this is not the right venue for him."

"Come on, sir," Geri had bristled. "The boy has incredible potential. You're going to want him as an alumnus one day. Tal, tell Dr. Braverman. The square root of the speed of light."

"The common presumption is 432 hertz, but that result is not accurate. If you want it to four decimal places, it's actually 431.6044."

"Exactly!" Geri shouted triumphantly.

Tal wasn't quite twelve at the time, but he caught the smirk on Father's face. Was it pride? Then Tal cast a glance at Mother and Jeffrey. Was she studying his forehead or was her head bowed in shame? He could not be certain. Braverman stood, signaling an end to the meeting and led them out of his office, out of the facility and to the car, as if meaning to let Father know there would be no change of heart. Tal turned his head to look back at the school as the car drove away. Braverman was still standing there, hands on hips, needing to be certain that Tal was off the property.

Mother and Father had been arguing in the front seat from the moment they hit the highway. Mother was holding the baby on her lap. Jeffrey had spit out the pacifier. He was crying. Not a normal kind of cry. More like bursts of shrieking. As if he understood that Mother did not want to be holding him. It was a gray day, but Mother was wearing the large hoop sunglasses that covered half her face. She had worn them day and night ever since Jeffrey was born. Close to a year and a half.

"I keep telling you, Geri, there's something wrong with Jeffrey."

"It's too early to tell."

"How the hell would you know? You left the first one entirely to me and you're doing it again."

"I was building the business," he snarled.

Jeffrey screeched.

"This is all a result of your stupidity. Live with it, Trudi."

■ ■ ■

The car pulled up to a ten-foot-high brick wall with an iron gate. A security guard in the small guardhouse asked Trudi for identification and checked her name against a list on his clipboard. The iron gate opened slowly, and the car headed toward the long circular driveway. The grounds were lush and forested. Tal could barely make out the chain-link fence running from the end of the brick wall, presumably all the way around the perimeter of the manicured lawns.

Nice-looking resort, Tal thought, a couple of hours from the city, but that Rosen didn't have a consulting office in midtown Manhattan was a bit of a surprise. You would think he could bill a lot more patients that way.

They were greeted at the sliding glass doorway by a matronly woman, her shiny platinum hair rolled into a tight bun. The perfectly starched smile suited the old-fashioned nurse's outfit, which showed off her wide hips.

"Good morning. You must be Mr. Nielson. The doctor's been expecting you and your mother. My name is Mariana Guilden, the chief nurse at the facility." Each word spoken with a precise German authority. A woman not to be trifled with. "Please follow me, sir, and do us the courtesy of leaving your cellular phone with your mother," she ordered. Military in her style.

Tal felt his shoulders slump, swallowed up in her authority. His head dropped and he followed her efficient shoes.

She stopped momentarily, casting a glance back, and Tal barely avoided bumping into her ample backside. "Ms. Darrow, perhaps you can take a seat in the reception. My colleagues will set you up with the paperwork."

"Paperwork?" Tal asked, turning back toward his mother.

"Required by the state," Nurse Guilden snapped. Like a soda biscuit. Her demeanor had changed considerably.

"Don't worry, lovey, I'll take care of it. Billing information for the consult. Just follow the nurse. I'll catch up with you later."

Nurse Guilden escorted him down a long antiseptic corridor toward a set of swinging doors, which folded open in response to her swinging hips. He shuddered as he heard the doors slap shut behind him with a surprising finality.

■ ■ ■

Trudi got back into the car and flipped open her pocket notebook. Put a checkmark beside today's mission. Next on the list was set for two months from today. The unopposed court motion to extend Tal's stay and appoint her guardian of his medical decisions. More important she would become guardian of his property, including his Danmark stock. That would give her control of his veto just long enough to allow Red to sell his stock and pay off the debt. Red had negotiated the extension, but it would be the last. After that maybe Dr. Rosen would let Tal out, though that decision was really tied to how long she wanted to continue paying the monthly costs of this exclusive resort.

CHAPTER 13

Lucinda Horat blasted away at the document on her computer screen, the only light source shining in her office in the winter darkness. At least spring was just around the corner. The overhead fluorescent lights had automatically turned off a few moments ago, conserving energy in the building on a dark Manhattan Monday night. After a long and frosty weekend visit in Boston with her sister Beatrice and her husband, she was back to work, trying to catch up, following the lives of her wealthy clients. She could not protect them from trouble, but she could plan for it and for the passage of their riches. The days were lengthening but so had the long nights of work.

The files on her desk were neatly organized, each one bearing the name of someone who would eventually die. Years from now some survivors would be gladdened, others horrified at the legacies she was drafting tonight. They were all theoretical but for one exception that had been dogging her in the past few weeks.

Tal invaded her thoughts at every turn. Ever since he had been a no-show for the appointment over a month ago, she had found herself wondering about him at all hours of the day and night. At first she was angry. It was beyond rude rescheduling a meeting from the morning to the afternoon and then not showing up at all. No message. Once again she replayed the sequence of events. After their meeting in Central Park, she had penned a handwritten note of apology, then figured she would let a few days slide before calling. He responded with a request for the meeting, though she had no idea if it was to fire her in person or to forgive and move on.

Regardless, things would never be the same between them. Was he really suicidal or did he just need a little attention? Maybe he just wanted a shoulder to cry on. Instead she had chastised him. Accused his father of abuse. You couldn't cross that kind of personal line and then pretend to be impersonal and objective. At first she wondered whether she should be passing him off to another lawyer. The problem was, she was the firm's expert and sending him out meant risking a loss of the client file. She sucked it up, then waited for him for a couple of hours. Her assistant had tried to track him down. Nothing. Nothing for weeks.

It was all the more worrying because Tal didn't seem the spiteful type, the type who would go to the trouble of confirming an appointment and then leave her hanging.

Maybe if she had not attacked Tal like that none of this would have happened. The firm represented numerous second- and third-generation emotional cripples who had no idea of their place in lives dominated by a patriarch. She handled them all. Never a problem. Tal might be frail and in need of a steady adviser, but so were most of her clients who had experienced loss, whether it was a death in the family that required estate work or a messy separation or divorce. She was used to meeting them at their worst and helping them to regain the legal footing of their lives and eventually their personal relationships. Usually they were angry and acting out. Tal had been detached, floating, even needy to the point of not recognizing it.

She'd mentioned it to Bea. More than once.

"Maybe there's more to this guy than you're letting on," Bea had suggested.

"Don't be ridiculous. I know how to separate personal from professional."

"There's knowing and then there's doing, Lucy. Is there anyone in his life right now?"

She had to admit that she hoped not.

"How did you describe him again?"

"Attractive. That's all I remember saying." The brooding eyes, broad shoulders, square-cut jaw. The looks of a man who could be very powerful if he could just step out of the shadow and find it in himself. The confidence and strength had to be in there somewhere waiting to be found by the right person. Was that the attraction she was fighting? There should not be an attraction. It was not professional. But it was human.

Typical of her to be so analytical. She had begun packing up her briefcase, loading up a couple of eighty-page trust agreements that had to be reviewed tonight — after a late dinner and before she opened the red wine — when the phone rang. She didn't recognize the number. It looked like an upstate New York area code. She was suddenly very hungry and decided to apply the rule of the last call. Once she'd made the decision to leave, whether at eight or ten p.m. or two in the morning, it was a mistake to take a call. Inevitably it was some work question that could wait until the morning. The partners all had her cell number in case it was a real emergency. She let it ring through six times and then picked up once the red message light began to glow.

"Hello, hello. Hello. Are you there, miss? Are you there? It's urgent, or at least Tal says it is. This is Roscoe. They kept me locked up but I just got out. He's in there, too. But they had to let me go. He told me I had to call you. I should trust only you. Nobody else. They're out to get us both but they had to let me out today. It's about Rosen. I'm not Rosen. I'm Roscoe so don't confuse us. He says you've got to check out Rosen. I've just finished my sixty days and they released me tonight. I'm calling from a phone booth at the convenience store a mile down the road. But Tal's only halfway through his sixty days and he begged me to call you. I think Rosen's okay. It's Nurse Guilden you have to look out for. Tal says he needs you to get him out of here. He says you're the only one I can trust. Did I say that already? Gotta go. My lift is here. I couldn't call my parents because they'd send me right back for another sixty. I swear I'm not nuts. Just need to stay on my meds. That's what they keep telling me. But the pills muddle my head so much I can't think straight. Did I say my name is Roscoe?"

The recording cut off. She slumped in her chair. She tapped the hashtag button on the phone to replay the message a couple of times. What was it about "sixty days" that sounded familiar? She tried to call back the number. An automated female voice told her she was calling a number that did not accept incoming calls. Perhaps Rosen was a doctor since he mentioned Nurse Guilden. She made a note of their names, along with the telephone area code and number. Roscoe mentioned that he was about a mile from the facility. Hopefully that was enough to go on.

One thing was clear: Tal was in trouble. Roscoe had said, "They had to let me out." Something about "sixty days." She replayed it once more. "I've just finished my sixty days but Tal's just halfway..." Could Tal be halfway through a sixty-day hold?

Of course. It had to be. Two years ago. Elyssa Kalinos. Her father, Theo, was the CEO and principal shareholder of Body-Sculpta, the network of over a thousand workout facilities around the world. Elyssa was a fashion model. She wore a confident Sculpta smile, a halter cut at the midriff to show off the tight abs, red shorty shorts to highlight the tanned legs, and pink sneakers. The Sculpta image, plastered on billboards, television commercials, and internet ads. Except Elyssa was bulimic. Starving. Worry about her was consuming Theo and his wife. The family doctor had given up, and Elyssa was refusing treatment. The couple were desperate, looking for some solution to save their daughter, even against her will if necessary. Lucinda discovered that two professional consult medical opinions could have her committed to a medical facility for sixty days, after which a court would have to approve an extension. Once she had the extension, she made a further application so that her parents could manage Elyssa's assets while in treatment. She was slowly recovering, but when they'd forcibly marched her through the doors of the hospital, she'd weighed seventy-five pounds.

Once committed, if no one advocated for the mental patient, he could be stuck in there indefinitely. Had Tal's mother done that to him? Maybe he should accept it and not fight. How different was this from Elyssa?

She shut her computer and rested her hands on the desk. Maybe this *was* different from Elyssa. Tal's cynicism about his mother. His question about losing rights as a shareholder if he went into rehab. Could his mother be doing this to control the voting rights attached to his shares?

Lucinda thought for a moment. Roscoe sounded disturbed. Hardly a trustworthy source. But why would he have made this call if Tal had not begged him? And it was not for her to question her client. Just to act on his wishes. And to do so immediately.

She certainly owed it to Tal to find out what was going on. She also owed it to herself. Here was the opportunity to rebuild trust with him. There was nothing she could do tonight but she would have the firm's investigators look into it first thing in the morning. She would also have to consult with one of the litigation partners about the legal remedies. She knew how to get someone into an institution against their will, but she had no idea how to break them out, even if they were worth millions. She left a message for her assistant asking her to clear her daytime agenda for tomorrow. She knew how she would be spending the day.

CHAPTER 14

The three-story brownstone had stood empty ever since Tal entered the care of Rosen and Guilden, just over a month ago. "Maybe you were right about this place, Geri," Trudi had whispered, as she let herself in the front door earlier that morning. He could not afford it when he bought it twenty-eight years ago. It was not their first argument, nor was it their last. They had just arrived from Bethlehem to the big city or what Geri quipped was "New Jerusalem."

"Geri, we could get by, renting a two-bedroom apartment in the Village," she'd complained.

"It doesn't matter that I can't afford it today," he screamed at her. "We're getting the biggest house in Manhattan that we can't afford. One day we will."

"Who knows whether Danmark is ever going to turn a profit? All we have is worthless stock right now. Tal's not even five. Let's wait a couple of years."

"The real estate market's in a slump. Now is the time. This is a great investment."

"Great, Geri. You're going to bankrupt us. Please wait. I'm begging you."

"Too late, Trudi. I made the down payment this morning. One day you'll thank me for it."

She had to admit he'd been right, but the time had arrived to dispose of it. Let someone else deep-clean the final remnants of Geri Neilson lurking in this place. It would go on the market shortly, at about thirty times what Geri paid. The cash reserves would be comforting. But there was one final task to be accomplished in Geri's house.

Today was a special occasion for special family, who needed the presence of Geri more than she needed to avoid him. Thank you, Geri, she thought, for making the last few years such a misery for me. Now work your magic on my guests.

The first thing she did when she reached the second level was to restart the pendulum on the grandfather clock just outside Geri's study. Trudi had been at a loss as to what to get Geri for his fiftieth birthday. He owned every watch she could imagine; he had been collecting them as antiques since before they could afford them. Beyond watches and work, there was nothing in his life. What do you get for a man who cares for nothing but work? She decided that it needed to be unique yet stately, something that would mark the continued passage of time. She must have spent six weeks working with a specialist on grandfather clocks until she found exactly the right one. It was a Bornholm built in the mid-1800s on a small island in the Baltic, not all that far from where Geri grew up. She'd hoped he would find it symbolic. Tall and stately, painted beige with gold trim. An acknowledgment of how far he'd come.

She'd covered it with a bedsheet and unveiled it with a flourish after they returned from a birthday dinner out with Tal. Geri had opened the box and checked the back of the movement until he found the manufacturer's plate. Nodded his head, then looked back to Trudi. She searched for any sign of gratitude. Did he like it?

"Reminds me of my father," he said. "Tall, proud, stubborn." Then he whispered at the clock, as if his father were in the room. "It needs a name. *Triste lille ø*," he said. The words lilted off his tongue, the first Danish words he'd ever spoken in her presence. At least she assumed it was Danish. She knew there had to be more coming, so she waited. Geri did not have patience for long pregnant pauses.

"Sad little island, in case you were wondering."

"Meaning what?"

"The place it was built. Bornholm. Like this clock. Like my life in Denmark. And don't ever start it up if I'm around. The ticking will drive me mad. Not a bad piece of furniture, though."

A classic Geri thank-you. At least the clock now had a name. The last time it had ticked, Trudi was leaving the house for Atlantic City. She found it comforting, but only when Geri was away on road trips. After he died, it became a morbid reminder of the lonely life she wanted to leave behind. Today was different. Today she felt at one with Triste lille ø, beating out its comforting rhythm. The rhythm of time inching inexorably forward, steady and predictable in its pace, a framework for the unpredictable rhythm of life.

Walter and Steve, or Wilder and Stinky as she always referred to them when they weren't around, the brain-dead cousins, had arrived a few minutes ago. At Geri's funeral they had been in the row behind her, the snake and the lizard, repressing their victorious smiles. Their boots might be painted with the muck of their litigation with Geri, but today they'd probably brought their tap shoes along.

Geri could be crude but she felt his characterization of Aunt Emily's boys more than hit the mark. Wilder understood only one thing in life — how to slither around his prey and choke every last dollar out of the sweat and labor that Geri and Red had put into Danmark.

"Let the numbskulls dream on," Geri had said right up to his trip to Ireland. "Neither of those pea brains is getting another dime as long as I'm alive. Never." Geri never responded well to anyone who reached for his wallet. He wouldn't lose a moment of sleep by cutting off their limbs. That was Geri's view of anyone who wanted a penny more than he believed they were entitled to. "Keep their slimy hands off," he repeatedly told the lawyers.

The cousins had been in and out of court with Geri for years, claiming they'd been cheated out of their royalties under the 1964 agreement between Geri, Red, and the family. Their lawyers had filed a claim for over a hundred million and claimed punitive damages for fraud. In his last appearance before a court-appointed mediator, Geri told them flat out, "It would be cheaper for you to hire someone to kill me, because this case will never settle. Not as long as I'm alive." If she didn't know better, she might have guessed they'd taken Geri at his word. Together they had a penchant for trouble and had earned their nicknames, though it had been years since Wilder and Stinky had last tried to kill someone.

She couldn't have been more than nine years old. Wilder had been fourteen, Stinky eleven, dressed in identical navy shorts, red T-shirts, and shiny new white kicks. The adults were downstairs, still sitting around the Sunday lunch table with the pastor engaged in some discussion, probably about church business. She and the boys were in the upstairs guest bathroom.

Wilder had smiled at her. "Toady, come in here," he said. "Steve's got something to show you."

She hated the nickname. Every time she heard it she wanted to punch him. But she followed them into the bathroom, no more than a toilet, a pedestal sink, and a pale green matching tub. Steve eased the door shut, leaning back against it. Wilder held out a glass candy bowl containing a mound of little white balls just out of her reach. They looked like mints. The kind that would fizz up if you dropped them into a glass of Coke.

"They're for me and Steve. Toads can't have them. Too spicy."

She reached to grab one of the candies, and Wilder held the bowl over his head, at least a foot above her reach.

"But I want one," she said all too predictably.

"Only if you promise not to tell. We could get in trouble for sharing with a toad. Specially a girl toad," Steve said. The boys each grabbed a candy and smiled as she greedily reached for a couple. "First, ya gotta suck on 'em slowly, 'til you get used to the taste," Wilder said.

She popped one in her mouth, rolling it over her tongue. It tasted vile. Like gasoline ready to be ignited. Like the raucous laughter that was splitting her ears. She fell to her knees and gagged. The fire rose from within her, searing her throat, before exploding all over the tiled floor. The mothball was lodged in the stench of half-digested salad and lasagna. Underneath the foul-smelling pile were Steve's brand-new white sneakers.

Tears of laughter ran down Wilder's cheeks at the calamity that had befallen his brother. "Stinky shoes, stinky shoes," he sang. Wilder never let Stinky or Toady forget the moment.

Toady now set herself up on one side of the living room coffee table, a bowl of white mints in the center, separating her from her two guests shifting uncomfortably opposite her, their backs to the clock.

"To what do I owe the honor of the visit, cousins?" she asked, wondering whether Wilder would be the spokesman for the brothers. She guessed wrong.

"We're truly sorry for your loss, Trudi. Isn't that so, Walter?" Stinky began.

Wilder blinked three times and nodded. "We come in peace. It's been too many years since we've tried to sit down and resolve the misunderstandings between us. After all we're Darrows. Our fathers would have wanted us to work this all out. There has to be a way to finally settle all this outstanding litigation."

"I'm listening," Trudi said.

"I am truly remorseful about having to involve lawyers in our family disagreement. All I ever asked from Geri was equitable restitution in accordance with the agreement our late mother signed."

"Yes, Walter, but the agreement had a particular stipulation, didn't it? The royalty due to your mother was based on drugs manufactured at the Bethlehem plant. Geri shut that down ten years ago."

"True indeed, cousin," Wilder persisted. "However our attorneys advise us that by closing the plant, your dear departed frustrated the contract, as it were, making it impossible to earn the royalty. He basically transferred the manufacturing operation elsewhere in a shameful attempt to defraud us. I tried on so many occasions to make overtures to Geri, to no avail. His ears were shut to reason. So tragic that he died." Wilder took a long sip of tea, pointing his pinky finger outwards. "I was hoping more reasonable minds could prevail with Geri no longer in the picture, so to speak."

Wilder playing the reasonable man. "Not how the contract reads, cousin." Trudi smiled. "But let's assume for the moment I'm prepared to be generous."

Stinky smiled a little too quickly. Trudi continued, "There's just the matter of the reports in the tabloids that were circulating just before the funeral that we need to clear up first."

Stinky dropped his head and took a deep breath.

"Look at me, Steve," Trudi ordered. He raised his head slowly. "So you weren't one of the 'sources from within the family'?" Trudi paused and glanced over at Wilder. He was not ready to make eye contact yet. She continued, "As I recall those were the words the *New York Enquirer* used." She flipped over the tabloid to the headline and her picture that filled the front page. She smiled. She must have had her hair done shortly before.

"You know better than to believe what those ... those rags produce," Stinky sputtered. "They hounded me for comments after Geri's death. But... but... but..."

"But what?" Trudi asked.

"I don't recall telling anyone that you killed Geri. They must have jumped to that conclusion on their own," Stinky said.

"Can we get back to the matter at hand," Wilder interjected. "My brother's memory is questionable at the best of times, Trudi. You know that."

"I can f— f— fight my own battles, Walter." Steve's tone was harsh. His brow furrowed and his eyes narrowed. Wilder's barb cut him deeper than her accusation. "It wasn't me, Trudi. I swear."

"Thanks for clearing that up for me, cousin. I really didn't give it much credence." She reached for the candy bowl. "Would either of you like a sweet?" Stinky's mouth puckered like a dead fish. Now Trudi was smiling. They both declined the little white balls. "You did come here to discuss a settlement to the litigation?"

"We hoped to work out some kind of arrangement," Wilder said.

"I think you'll find me to be a very reasonable person. I always like to start with a little Bible study. Do you recall the Old Testament's thirteen attributes of the Lord that we are to follow?"

"Sure. We learned them together in Sunday school at the church. God is merciful and forgiving. Full of compassion," Stinky said. A hopeful beginning to the class. "And we're created in his image."

"Exactly. What does it go on to say, cousin?" she asked.

"I don't remember," Stinky said. Wilder began to nod, though the snake was now on its back, its mouth in the form of a frown. The serpent in the garden, wiser than all other animals and condemned to slither for eternity. He understood all the lessons without having to be told.

"It goes on to say that the Lord remembers the sins of the fathers and visits them upon four generations," Wilder whispered.

Trudi smiled. "Blood is thicker than water, cousins, but the Lord is the Lord."

Trudi sat silently, letting Triste lille ø do the talking. Tick, tick, tick, as the pendulum swung and would continue swinging for the next hundred years. "Perhaps my great-grandchildren will pardon yours. Now if you will both excuse me, I have an important appointment to attend to."

"Wait a minute," Stinky said. "The Danmark financial statements still note the lawsuit. There must be some value in cleaning that up?"

Predictable as Triste lille ø. "Cousins, Geri would probably strike me down from the grave but I'll make you a one-time offer good until the bell tolls."

The two men strained their necks to the right. One minute to the hour.

"If you'll drop all the litigation, I'll convince Red and the estate to grant you a three-day option to buy one million shares at ten dollars a share."

"The stock is trading at twenty today," Walter said. "You're offering us ten million in value to give up a claim for a hundred fifty million?"

"Well done, Walter. You cut me a check for ten million, you get stock worth twenty, and you can sell them any time." At this point a little extra pocket change might come in handy given Red's proclivities. The house might not sell for months.

"Come on, Trudi. We can't possibly make a decision like that in forty-five seconds," Wilder said.

"I'll be dead before another opportunity comes along. Geri made Tal vow never to settle. Just so you know. The clock is ticking, cousins. Thirty seconds."

CHAPTER 15

Lucinda prided herself on remaining calm and in control. People occasionally read it as weakness. Nurse Mariana Guilden might have underestimated her when Lucinda had showed up at the clinic three days ago asking to meet with her client. At first the nurse was not prepared to confirm whether he was even a patient.

"I'm terribly sorry, miss, but I'm sure you understand that our clients expect complete confidentiality."

"Are you refusing to allow me access to my client?"

"The facility does not permit visits during the treatment period. It is part of our operating procedures to protect our patients."

"So he is here? That's all I've come to ask."

"I am not confirming or denying. I am not authorized to disclose that information."

The trace of a smirk formed at the corner of Guilden's mouth. Perhaps this was a game the head nurse was familiar with. No visitors permitted other than those who were footing the bills. Round one to Guilden.

This morning's frost nipped at Lucinda as she marched toward the clinic. Today she was armed with her brown leather briefcase and accompanied by a couple of reinforcements. A strong scent of pine hung in the early spring air; the final vestiges of winter snow sat in tiny clumps on branches that were poised to grow.

Lucinda once more asked Guilden to produce Tal. When she refused, Lucinda made a show of clicking open the briefcase and removing an official-looking document.

"This is a writ of *habeas corpus*. In accordance with the decision of Judge Villasignales, you are ordered to release Mr. Talem Neilson to my custody. You may have a moment to review it. Then you *will* release Mr. Neilson."

Nothing like relying on Article 1 of the Constitution every once in a while. Judges had been issuing these writs for centuries to produce the bodies of people detained unlawfully and against their will. Yesterday the judge was intrigued by her description of Tal's detention: that he'd never shown up for a legal appointment; that he'd dropped off the face of the earth; and that a phone call to her office from a patient, recently released, had suggested Tal was being held against his will. She and her litigator were in and out of the judge's office on the uncontested motion in under fifteen minutes.

Guilden clearly had not faced a *habeas corpus* before. For good measure Lucinda beckoned to the state troopers on either side to step forward, then politely asked the bitch if she was prepared to produce her client.

"Dr. Rosen cannot be found right now, and he is the only person authorized to discharge patients at this facility," she said.

Lucinda turned to the trooper on her left.

"Produce Mr. Nielson now or you will be held in contempt," the officer said.

Twenty minutes later a patient was rolled out by an orderly pushing the wheelchair. His face was pasty and his eyes glassy. His head was tilted forward, making it difficult to verify his features behind a thick growth that covered his face. He looked about aimlessly. Nurse Guilden went through the process of confirming his wrist bracelet identification with the officers, who spent a few moments comparing what they were observing to a recent photo. "You sure this is your client?" one of the officers asked. She nodded. He looked like hell but there was no question.

Finally Tal caught sight of her. "I love you, Lucinda" was all he said before he slumped forward and almost fell out of the chair.

Lucinda signed the discharge papers, masking her panic. She had planned every moment of the escape but had not prepared for a client who was barely conscious. She also had to act before word of Tal's release reached Dr. Rosen. Lucinda was lucky she had been able to secure Tal's release in front of a judge with no opposition in the room. This version of Tal would be recommitted on sight if she had to litigate against an opponent. If she couldn't get Tal looking human quickly, this would all be for naught.

The officers helped load Tal into the back seat of the black limousine.

"You sure you don't want us to call for an ambulance?" the taller cop asked.

She could not afford to leave a trail that could be followed quickly. "Just lay him down across the back seat. I'll be beside him. I have medical help on call to assist." That last line was a bluff, but she did have the number of a local doctor, whom she immediately called to confirm the rendezvous.

An hour later the doctor and someone who looked like he was a nurse arrived at the motel room Lucinda had reserved. He hooked Tal up to a portable EKG machine, took some blood, and monitored his heart rate and breathing.

"They haven't taken bad care of him."

"Will he be able to travel?"

"The heart and lungs sound normal, and the EKG shows no irregularities, but I want to check his toxicity levels before I give an okay."

"When will you know?"

"I should have results first thing in the morning."

That should be sufficient to pull this off. "Good timing," she murmured.

"From what I can tell he's somewhat dehydrated," the doctor said. "I've put him on an IV drip and I'll stay to monitor him. Whatever sedative they've loaded into his system should wear off in about twelve hours. We'll have a much better idea in about three hours whether I'm right. The good news is that he's unlikely to be suffering from immediate withdrawal. He's drugged up, but just enough so that he won't resist treatment."

■ ■ ■

All went well, as the doctor had predicted, and the next day Lucinda was able to move Tal to a hotel in Manhattan under an assumed name. Once the IVs had flushed the drugs out of his system, his charm began to return, and Lucinda found that she kind of liked him with the beard. After two days she cancelled the round-the-clock nurses, or "police" as he called them.

The next day, she paid him a visit on the way to her office.

He greeted her at the door, still dressed in the white hotel robe, his hair unruly.

"Do you want to come in?"

She hesitated for a moment, then followed him through the door.

"Would you like some coffee? I can order room service."

"No thanks, Tal. This is just a short check-in. To see if you're ready for tonight."

He took a seat on the edge of the bed. She remained standing.

"I get it you can't stay long," he said.

He was alert. Perceptive. Thank goodness.

"Can I tell you a really short story about the best day of my life?"

"Sure."

"The day my baby brother came home from the hospital, Father placed him in a rocking cradle, inside my room. Then he left to help Mother into bed. I was almost eleven. I talked to Jeffrey for an hour. Every so often I'd kiss him on the forehead. I was hoping maybe he'd remember my smell. I still remember his." Tal closed his eyes. "Every time I smell baby powder I think of Jeffrey. He was everything I'd ever dreamed of." Tal opened his eyes. "The next day I was shipped back to boarding school."

"That's a beautiful memory, Tal. Thank you for sharing." His eyes were glassy. Moist. The first sign of tenderness she'd noticed.

He grabbed a tissue from the night table and dabbed his eyes. Then he collected himself and stood in front of her.

"You're here to triple-check the plan for tonight?" he asked.

"Midnight at the check-in line at JFK. Got it?" she said.

Tal nodded.

"I'll send a limo to pick you up here."

"No. There are some things I need to take care of," he said, playing with the wisps of his mustache. "Also a visit I have to pay before I disappear for who knows how long. Something my father would want. Don't worry. I'll use cash. No credit cards. Nothing traceable."

"A few days out of the hospital and you're focused on your father?" Her eyes narrowed. Was he back in his revenge fantasy?

"Sounds noble, doesn't it? Eventually CallMeGeri will be proud of me. Even if it's from up there." He glanced up, then laughed and pointed his finger to the floor. "More likely from down there."

"See you tonight." She needed to show some trust in him, but she turned and left with an uncomfortable premonition. A lot can happen in a day, she thought.

CHAPTER 16

This was going to be one very long night. Officer Rachel Brodinsky was on the Manhattan side of the Brooklyn Bridge hunched over in a coughing spasm, which was beginning to subside. She'd been the first officer to respond to the call almost two hours ago, securing the scene, directing foot traffic away from the crash site while the fire was raging, and now waiting for the detectives to arrive. Plumes of heavy black smoke, smelling of burnt rubber, had gusted in her direction for twenty minutes, burning at her lungs, which were already struggling from the head cold that had dogged her for over a week.

Four fire trucks had rumbled to the scene a while ago, and a captain was still barking out instructions over a megaphone to a bevy of NYFD's finest. The fire had lit up the south end of the island briefly, like a Fourth of July display, and the news helicopters, which had been hovering for about fifteen minutes, had already taken off in search of the next bit of breaking news.

The red convertible sports car was still smoking, crushed like a Dr. Pepper soda can up against a concrete barrier running across all lanes of the bridge. A couple of fire trucks were just pulling away from the scene, tires kicking streams of water toward her. Rachel stood at the edge of the yellow tape and took a few shallow breaths before waving to the CSI people who had arrived about five minutes ago.

A couple of guys approached, sauntering along like detectives, in no rush, unperturbed by the goings-on behind her. The portly fellow, around five foot seven, brown hair, widow's peak, probably in his late thirties, flashed his credentials. He looked to be about three inches shorter than his older partner, bringing up the rear with the slightest limp. The older detective looked right through Rachel to the accident scene behind her. She guessed he wasn't long from retirement. His eyes were unreadable, as if he was just cataloguing this scene among the countless horrors he'd visited.

"I'm Mac," the younger one said. "My partner is Obie. Looks like the sight speaks for itself."

"Rachel Brodinsky. You should've been here an hour ago. Who would have thought such a small sports car could create such an inferno?"

"Imports," Obie quipped.

"Certainly got a lot of radio coverage," Mac said. "And traffic was backed up forever."

They walked about thirty yards to the crash site. "The bridge was closed tonight," Rachel said. "Overnight construction. And thank God, otherwise who knows how many fatalities would have resulted. There were plastic pylons at both ends of the bridge. The driver plowed right through them. I don't know how fast he was going when he hit the concrete barrier, but it made one hell of a boom. I heard it from a mile off. As I pulled up, the car was flaming. Vic never had a chance."

Mac headed over to the wreckage. Obie was already way ahead, taking his time to bend over the crushed door to the vehicle, poking around the soaking interior.

"Do you mind if I follow?" Rachel asked. "I'll fill you in on what I know." Mac didn't bother responding. Rachel took it as an invitation.

Mac made a slow tour of the exterior from front to back, then whistled softly. "Do you understand the importance of what happened tonight?" He was standing at the rear of the car, fixated just above where the bumper used to sit. The front end was crushed and burned, but the rear end was still somewhat intact though the fender was lying askew. Possibly a result of the explosion.

Rachel said, "Besides the body? The guy behind the wheel was bagged immediately. They cut him out of the car half an hour ago. Third-degree burns to more than half of his body, unrecognizable face."

"Forget about the guy. Do you know what this car is?" Mac looked up and shouted. "Obie, you have any idea what this car is?"

"Also dead?"

"Very funny. It's a Ferrari GTZ 550. Only five like this in the entire world."

"I guess only four now," Obie said without hesitation.

"It had to be worth over a mil and a half."

Men and their toys, Rachel thought. "You a car buff?"

"I don't know the first thing about cars," Mac said. "Just a fluke that I could recognize this one. I was reading the Sunday *Times* a few weeks ago. This car was plastered on the front page of the Lifestyle section. The logo is quite unique. A big shot New York businessman bought it at auction in Italy, picked it up on his honeymoon, then had it shipped here."

"I've run the plates through the system," Rachel said. "Car is registered to a Claude King. Address on the Upper West Side. Might make the identification of the body a little easier?"

Obie put his left hand on his lower back, his right hand on the wreck, and hauled his body erect. His exhale sounded more like a grunt. "We can't be certain the owner was driving the car tonight."

"Gives us a place to start," Mac said. "Might not have to wait for the dental records."

"Probably alcohol — or drug-related?" Rachel asked.

"Not much to do until the tox screen comes back from the lab," Obie said. "Good thing the bridge was closed. No other cars, no other bodies. Just one dead son of a bitch. Must have really wanted it."

"So you figure suicide?" Rachel said.

"Could be," Obie replied.

Mac scratched his chin. "Claude King. Name rings a bell. If I'm not confusing him, his nickname is Red."

"Name goes well with the car," Rachel said.

"Went well," Obie corrected.

"The papers will be all over this," Mac said. "His business partner died suddenly a while ago. He married the widow. It was a big story."

"You mean the drug company guy who runs Danmark?" Obie said.

"Ran Danmark," Rachel corrected.

"Yeah, pretty sure. If it's him, we got two dead drug guys in a very short period." Mac hesitated and scratched his head. "Hey, y'know I met the widow's son once. A real whack job. He came into the station to rant about his father's death. Claimed this guy King murdered him. Doesn't look like a homicide, but I guess we can't rule out the possibility," Mac said.

"Death by Brooklyn Bridge construction. There are a thousand ways to die in the Naked City," Rachel said.

Neither detective laughed.

■ ■ ■

Lucinda paced just outside the check-in line at the airport for thirty minutes until Tal finally trotted in with his bag. A little out of breath.

"Sorry," he said. "You were probably worrying."

She studied his eyes for a moment. No sign of drugs. He was shifting his weight back and forth like he had to pee.

"You're over half an hour late," she said. "We agreed on midnight the latest."

"No need to admonish me. The flight doesn't depart for another two hours."

"Where have you been?"

"I had a few things to take care of. One particular farewell."

Lucinda wondered if there was another woman.

"I did what I promised myself I'd do tonight. Now I can disappear from the radar for a year."

They were second in line to check in at the airline counter. Lucinda reached deep into her purse to find the reservation. He dug into the back pocket of his jeans for his passport. They hadn't said anything to one another for the last few minutes. As if talking about it was going to jinx the plan.

"Thanks for getting me out of there," he said. "You saved my life. You don't think I'm—"

"Crazy?" she interrupted. "Tal, you have a drug dependency problem. This program is among the best in the world. It's a one-year commitment on your part."

He took the boarding pass from the clerk and headed to security. She watched until he disappeared and then stayed another five minutes to make sure he hadn't changed his mind. She still had no idea what Tal was capable of doing in this state of mind.

CHAPTER 17

Mac hated visiting the family in the middle of the night, but these meetings never went well if you waited until you knew everything. Usually he did this with Obie. In fact, Obie had always taken the lead. You wouldn't expect that someone that crusty could handle a death notification with class, but Obie managed it. He sized up the family members on the way in the door and knew exactly who he had to make eye contact with at the precise moment, especially if the family hadn't yet figured out why two cops would be at the door without being called. More often the family members were already beside themselves with worry about a loved one who had been missing for half the night or longer. And if they had already filed the missing person report, they often broke down before Obie could get the words out of his mouth.

Obie had complained of stomach pain again. He left at one in the morning writhing like a dog attack victim. Mac wished he would just visit the doctor already. For a shrewd detective, Obie had a way of avoiding the truth when it came to himself. Might explain the two divorces and the estrangement from his daughter.

This was a very fancy neighborhood. Expensive brownstones, most of them three stories. Mac was wondering whether Mrs. Neilson (or was it Mrs. King now, given this was Mr. King's residence?) had been up all night.

Six-thirty in the morning. The first slivers of daylight had done nothing to remove the damp chill from the air. A woman in a long silk housecoat and fluffed white slippers greeted him after he'd identified himself over the intercom and held up his badge to the video camera over the front door. She looked to be in her late fifties, brunette, tough eyes, no makeup

of grief out the door. Someone else from the department would have to set up the meeting for her to come down to the station.

■ ■ ■

Trudi paced the living room, then checked the window to make sure the detective's car was gone. Tal's escape had destroyed her plan. It was all so simple. So elegant. At the end of his sixty-day commitment she planned to apply to the court to extend his stay in the clinic indefinitely and apply for control of Tal's assets, which would allow her to eliminate his veto. Red could then sell enough shares to pay back the Chinese. Tal cost Red his life. But how could they know that Red was no longer in a position to sell the shares? No one yet knew Tal had been released. Unless the idiot let it slip. That might explain the note, sitting in an envelope in the drawer of the coffee table. Or else… She made a mental note to have the house immediately swept for listening devices.

There was no more time to waste. No more stalling. Message received. She looked at her watch and did a quick calculation in her head. Six hours ahead. Lunchtime. She reopened the envelope that had arrived mysteriously sometime between midnight and when the detective arrived this morning. Reread the threat that now made perfect sense. "Pay us what we are owed, or suffer the fate of your two husbands."

She reached for the phone and dialed, waited, then asked for the private accounts department. A long hold, while she paced again, until she heard a voice.

"Account number, please."

A number committed to memory for this moment. "12486572."

"How can I help you today."

"Please execute the wire instructions on file."

"Thank you madame."

What was the likelihood that the authorities would ever discover the transfer? No doubt they had the forensic skills, but first they would need reason to be looking. She couldn't imagine any reason. It didn't really matter. The message from the Chinese was clear. Either make the transfer and take the risk inherent in being tied to Red's embezzlement and money laundering scheme in Ireland, or perish. Perhaps not by heart attack or fiery car crash. Perhaps by something unimaginably worse.

The twenty-five million she had just wired to the Chinese to pay off Red's debt was a first step. They had insisted on an additional fifty for terminating the contract. No doubt she was now responsible for that as well, but no need for panic. It was time for rational thought and a plan. She reached for her pen and pad and neatly jotted a few notes.

> *Brain-dead cousins $10 million*
> *Inheritance from Geri $20 million*
> *Find financiers willing to lend the rest against my houses, Red's house and cars.*
> *Check insurance claim on the Ferrari.*
> *Check life insurance on Red. He mentioned something about 10 million?*

Ironic that Red was worth more dead than alive. She could probably have this all turned around within the month. The silver lining in all this was with Red gone, she could execute her plan to return to Danmark without distraction. She would need the salary to live on. Perhaps when all was said and done, things were working out quite well.

■ ■ ■

Mac returned to the station at around noon. Obie was sitting at his desk reading from a thin file.

He looked up. "So? How'd it go?"

"As bad as ever. How's your stomach?"

"You mean the ulcer? As bad as ever."

Mac took a seat behind his desk. The wooden desks faced one another as they probably had for the last fifty years. Scratched up, sturdy, built to endure, with a lot more class than the stainless-steel rectangles in the interrogation rooms. Mac reached for the New York Giants mug on the corner of his desk.

"Have you been eating my pistachios again?" he said to Obie. "I filled it just before I left yesterday. It's half empty."

"Also half-full, you pessimist. I've told you a hundred times. I don't ever touch those pistachios."

Mac stood up and looked down at the floor on the other side of Obie's desk. "So why is there a pile of shells at your feet?"

"Shrewd detective work, partner." Obie's mouth turned up slightly but there was not the slightest sign of remorse for the crime.

"I met with the widow," Mac said. "She showed genuine shock."

"Did you let her know how serious the burns were?" Obie asked.

"No, but she's no idiot."

"And she must have read the morning papers by now. The objects found on the body are probably all that's left to make an I.D. Not perfect, but I want her to come in anyway. Watch how she reacts to some photos. We'll know for certain when we check the dental records."

"She told me her husband dropped her off at about ten and left for the country. He liked to go driving when there wasn't much traffic and let it cut loose."

"No kidding. I checked the plates. Then I ran his name through the system. He had a few thousand dollars in speeding tickets. All outside the city. Some of them on the squashed can."

"You mean the Ferrari."

"I'll bet it's half of what it should have been," Obie said.

"You figure the cops sometimes let him off with a warning if he gave them a tour of the car?"

Obie smiled. "Here're the forensics." Obie passed the file across the desks.

Mac began reading. No real surprises. The fire in the car had burned the victim beyond recognition. Tribeca wasn't too far from the bridge, so unless King was carjacked or kidnapped last night, the body was most probably his. The contents of the car had been analyzed as well. All that was discernible from the front end of the car were a few tiny pieces of residual metal that might have been syringe needles. Between the fire and the water damage, there was little expectation of recovering anything from the remnants of the cell phone.

One point caught his eye: according to the report, the victim had been dead behind the wheel before the fire started. There was no smoke inhalation in the lungs. That would make the meeting with Trudi Darrow a little easier to manage. He always hated the first question the family always asked. "Did he suffer?"

CHAPTER 18

Mac prepared for Trudi Darrow's arrival at the station. He went through the stack of photos, showing the body on the M.E.'s gurney, taken at various angles, separating the shots of the head and body. The extensive burns to the head area left nothing of what might have been Red King. Just charred remnants and exposed bone and teeth. Mac tucked those photos back into the file. That left a half dozen close-up shots of the victim's wristwatch and wedding ring, but did not show any of the severely burned skin surrounding the pieces. Mac had them laid out face-down on the table. You could never predict how people were going to react, but the goal was to be as respectful as possible and flip them one at a time. The preliminary notes from the M.E. matched the victim's body length with the information in his state driver's license, and the shape of his skull matched the photo in the system. Identifying King's jewelry was one more piece of corroboration. For the family it was a step on the path to acceptance; for the detective it was a chance to learn more. They would eventually match the dental records for final confirmation.

Early this morning there had been no point admitting to her that he'd already met her crazy son. The one who heard voices in his head. The one who had blamed her now-dead second husband for the death of her first husband, Geri Neilson. After Tal's late-night visit to the police station back in October, Mac had checked with the Atlantic City police and they'd done it all by the book. There was no evidence of foul play. Now, with the second husband dead, the son's accusations were academic. Or were they? There was no way he and Obie could assume King's death was accidental with the son's accusations out there. If that wasn't motive for a revenge killing, what was? Finding Tal Neilson had become a priority. There was still plenty of time to wait for the M.E. report, run down alibis, delve into the story of the two-time widow. Obie might not be exactly by the book, but he had a nose that Mac was beginning to acquire for the stench of fishy deaths.

Trudi Darrow arrived fifteen minutes late for the three o'clock appointment, wearing oversized dark sunglasses and a conservative dark gray dress. They never wore black until they were certain.

"Facework up the wazoo," Obie whispered as she approached. "Look at that kisser."

Her brunette hair, likely dyed, was tastefully rolled in a bun under a small matching pillbox hat. The look was a little retrospective of Jackie O, perhaps a role model in Darrow's life. He was also impressed by the fact that she still went by her maiden name. Perhaps she was one of the pioneers of the women's lib movement. For a serial widow she looked very put together — by now she had plenty of experience. Mac always wanted to give immediate family the benefit of the doubt, but two dead husbands in quick succession demanded a little skepticism. After six years working homicide investigations with Obie, he had come to accept that anyone was capable of doing anything; it didn't matter how much money or education they had, his job was to root them out.

Mac ushered her into the interrogation room and offered coffee, which she politely declined. He didn't blame her.

"Detective, I'm very sorry about this morning. It was not directed at you. I was just…"

"It's all right, Ms. Darrow. I am so sorry to have to make you go through this, but we have to be certain. Please take a seat." The room was cramped and lit with a dull fluorescent bulb. It was never intended to be cheery for anyone they were interrogating, or in this case confirming death. She said nothing. Wise enough to understand they were not going to the morgue.

Ms. Darrow took her seat at the rectangular metal table without removing the shades. Mac hated playing poker with guys who wore sunglasses at night. Most of the regulars in the Wednesday night game didn't take it so seriously, but every once in a while, a replacement fireman showed up who acted like he belonged on the world tour. Mac studied the eyes as part of his baseline, so he'd be ready for the deviation. The tell that spelled out a bluff. He could not read anything at all behind Darrow's shades.

"Ms. Darrow, we have a series of photographs showing the jewelry that the victim was wearing at the time of the car accident last night. We were hoping you might recognize it."

He flipped over the first couple of photos. The glass cover on the wristwatch was smashed but the steel head and the three screws on the Rolex were quite distinctive. There were three internal smaller circles on the face, set up like a speedometer.

"It's the Paul Newman," she said.

"I'm sorry?"

"The Daytona model Rolex. I got it for Red as a wedding gift, just before our honeymoon in Italy. Maybe that's what caused him to run out and buy the car at auction."

A car to go with a watch? A whole level of rich Mac would never understand.

"He put it on whenever he took the car out. See the remaining outline of red paint on the back of the facing? There are a number of different Daytona models, but only one Paul Newman."

Mac was actually touched. His wife, Jennifer had gotten him a fly fishing rod for his fortieth birthday a few months ago. It was the exact model he had been looking at in the sporting goods store, but it was a little out of his price range. He didn't want to splurge on himself, not when she was still walking around in a pilly winter coat. He supposed money was no object but Darrow obviously cared about her husband.

"I'm sorry for your loss, ma'am."

"I may have been married to Red for a short time, but I knew the man my entire adult life. I met him when he barely had the means to buy lunch at the diner where I was waitressing. We grew up together. Paul Newman was Red's hero."

Except Newman knew how to handle a race car, Mac thought. Best not to mention it.

"The watch could measure his speed and acceleration. Maybe it was a distraction. They say speed kills."

Mac was unsurprised by the bitterness in her tone. Grieving wives often exuded anger, particularly when they felt the death could have been avoided. But there was still no explaining why King would have been driving so recklessly.

"Was Mr. King on any medication?"

"Nothing to speak of, except for the diabetes."

"There were a couple of needles found in the car, and some melted plastic — likely a syringe."

"To deal with his blood sugar levels."

"Would he do it while driving?"

"Maybe at a stoplight. He kept a syringe with him at all times. It would only take a few seconds to inject. I suppose he could have done it in the Ferrari as well."

"Did you usually accompany him in that car?"

"No, he took me with him on a road trip only once. That was enough for me. As soon as he saw some open road, look out. Red drove like a madman. At his age I wasn't going to change his life habits, but I was not ever going for a joy ride with him again."

"But you did get in the car with him."

"Pardon me?"

"Last night. You told me he dropped you in Tribeca."

"On the island he was fine. Obeyed the rules."

"Anything unusual about the drive?"

"Not really, but I never should have let him go. This is all my fault." She began to cry, just a few tears running down her cheeks. He handed her a tissue.

"Why do you say that?"

She dabbed at the corner of her eyes. "I had this sense we were being followed. Just some headlights in the rear-view mirror. One of the lights was burned out. Every few blocks it reappeared behind us. Sometimes I saw him in the side view mirror."

"You know it was a male?"

"No. I never saw the driver. Just a sixth sense. Know what I mean? And now he's dead. I should have said something to Red. Warned him."

"Was Mr. King upset about anything recently? Any special stress in his life?"

"You're not insinuating—" Darrow's eyes narrowed. She almost spat out the words. They never liked it when you touched on the possibility of mental health issues or suicide.

"I'm sorry, Ms. Darrow. I know this is difficult and I don't mean to anger you, but I have to ask the questions."

"Red would never take his own life. Yes, the adjustment to becoming the CEO after Geri died was a responsibility that weighed heavily on him. He took his job very seriously."

"That was a job your first husband held, wasn't it?"

"Until he died. But you can't compare them at all. When Red and Geri took over Danmark in the eighties, it was a small underperforming company. They turned it around. Red was there every step of the way.

"They each had their area of expertise and it worked. But the company today is a hundred times the size of what we began with. And Red no longer had Geri there beside him. There were moments when Red felt overwhelmed. But depressed or suicidal. Absolutely not. Or … I just don't know." She began to cry. He handed her another tissue and waited a minute for her to calm down.

"Did he have any enemies? Anyone with a grievance?"

She hesitated. "Not that I can think of." Mac had heard the response before. He'd have to come back to that question later. Maybe it was tied to the car she thought was following them. She was holding something back.

"Any possible business enemies?"

"If there were, I wouldn't know. I've been out of the loop for so many years."

"Were you ever in the loop?"

"Red, Geri, and I bought the forerunner of Danmark from my family. That was all before my son was born. I left the business and became a mother. After my second child died tragically, I got involved in charitable endeavors."

"The Neilson Foundation?"

"Yes."

"And how is your son handling all this?"

Ms. Darrow dropped her eyes. Lowered her voice as if she were embarrassed. She probably did not want to ever discuss the crazy son. "We've not been in communication." She said the words stiffly.

Clearly major issues with the son and not too surprising. Except something else was nagging at Mac. He could not put his finger on it. Something to do with her controlled grief. Too much of a turnaround from this morning? He was not certain.

"He was being treated for serious drug addiction problems. The problem got worse after Geri died. That weighed heavily on Tal. He idolized his father. I tried talking to him about it but he just could not get over Geri's death. He became convinced that Red had murdered his father. He was desperately in need of professional help."

This was consistent with what Mac remembered about that evening with Talem Neilson. Mac pulled out his pad and began jotting down notes. "I hope you don't mind."

Trudi nodded. "He was hearing voices."

"What type of voices?"

"He kept telling me his father was demanding that he seek revenge."

"That must have been very frightening."

She looked him in the eye. Her entire demeanor hardened. "You don't know me. I don't scare easily. I was more worried about my Tal. He was behaving like a madman." Her voice began to shake ever so slightly. "And

I was … am … his mother. He couldn't cope and I made a decision. I drove him up to a well-respected clinic, hoping that once he got all those drugs out of his system, he might begin to function normally."

So she took care of the problem. Darrow might be one hell of a tough cookie. Obie would probably call her a rich bitch. The type who did whatever she had to do. "You said he made threats against your husband."

"You don't mean to suggest … ?"

She shook her head. "Not possible. Tal might have been delusional but he would never hurt anyone, especially not a family member. Red was an uncle to him."

"Were any of his threats specific?"

"Just what I already told you. He kept talking about revenge."

"And he's still a patient at the clinic?"

"He was released without my knowledge."

"When?"

"Just a few days ago. His lawyers got him out. I'm sure you can understand why I didn't go public."

He understood too well. News of a rich society heir being locked up might create a media circus. As it turned out, however, she'd got one anyway. Rich second husband dies in a car crash, destroying a luxury car. If the news got out about the death threats, this story would never end. Maybe this was a tragic accident but there were just too many coincidences to rule out homicide. Lab results might shed some light.

After Darrow left, Mac walked over to Obie's desk and took a seat on the far edge.

"She's pointing fingers at the son," Mac said.

"But you don't buy it. I can tell from your tone of voice."

"The whole story is off. Married just two months after she buried the first, then widowed again shortly after that?" Mac said.

"Let me ask you something, partner. If Trudi Darrow was a man and remarried two months after his wife died, would anyone even notice? Men do these things all the time. Afraid to live alone. Has no idea how to feed himself after so many years of marriage. He's resigned to eating takeout for the rest of his life if he has to. But does he have to? A woman sweeps in, even a friend of his late wife, who knows how to make a good chicken soup. Do we blame him? Do we immediately think the best friend killed the wife? No. Men think with their peckers and their stomachs. A woman does the same thing and we call her a black widow. Is that not a double standard?"

"Obie, have you been getting sensitivity training?"

"Don't joke about such important insights," he sniffed.

Maybe Obie was right. It was time to find Talem Nielson. If he was hiding anywhere within reach, they would ferret him out. Rich families had their dysfunctions ... just like everyone else.

CHAPTER 19

Paul Farber led the small contingent of American businessmen and their wives on a walk along the Prinsengracht. One was a banker from Houston, the other two real estate magnates from Dallas who had made their fortunes in oil. All of them were partners in Paul's recent American real estate developments. He'd brought them all over on the family jet, for this special bonding experience. Not one of them was Jewish, but that never mattered. In his experience, the southern Christians were even more moved by the experience than the Jews.

Last night they had shared a sumptuous *rijsttafel* dinner. The Indonesian dishes were vastly superior to Dutch domestic fare, and Paul doubted the Americans would appreciate a plate of schnitzel. The restaurant he chose rolled out twenty-five small bowls of the finest cuisine; the men raved about the satays, and the women loved the vegetarian options.

Today was another chilly, damp day in Amsterdam, fairly standard for mid-April. He had found lately that the dampness sank deeper into his bones than it used to. His limp had become more noticeable in the last couple of years, and he had finally taken to using a wooden cane. At seventy-two he had nothing to be embarrassed about. The arthritis in the knee was nothing new — a souvenir from the boat crossing so many years ago — but he found he could no longer travel at the same pace as he had when he was in his sixties. The price of living a long life. That was a price he was more than prepared to pay. When your existence hinged on a miracle, you learned to appreciate every moment.

It was ironic that he had chosen to remain in a city surrounded by water. On more than one occasion he'd thought about picking up and resettling his family. His American friends kept insisting that Colorado might be a nice place to slip into retirement. "The Alps have nothing on the Rockies," the woman from Dallas kept repeating at dinner last night. Other friends had pushed him toward Munich, particularly after reunification. The real estate development deals in Poland and Austria were incredibly lucrative, but those were no places to live, and he had a team on the ground who could handle the work.

He still could not help spitting on the ground every time he thought of anything German. Childhood memories of black Gestapo uniforms stalking the streets of Copenhagen never faded. Just a few months before his thirteenth birthday, his coming of age. Instead of planning a celebration, his father was hurriedly plotting their escape from the country that had been home to five generations of diamond merchants. The entire local Jewish community were hustled to the coast of Denmark, set to escape around the Jewish new year on any vessel that could transport them to Sweden. The alternative was a transport to German work camps. No one could yet imagine what took place in those camps.

These thoughts did not recede with the passage of time. They burned more brightly. Paul was one of the lucky ones. He had an obligation to remember, like the vow to protect the family of the righteous gentile who had saved his family.

For the past week Paul had woken up in the middle of every night, gasping for air. The same dream. A wave had thrown him viciously against the gunwale of the small fishing boat. The anguish to his knee was instant and overpowering, waking him with an agony as real as it was on that night in the Øresund. In his dream Gerhard fell overboard. Paul reached out but Gerhard disappeared into the night. Dead.

The dream had begun six months ago, after Gerhard's tragic death. Perhaps the dream was a symbol that Paul no longer had the power to save and protect. It was time to turn the responsibilities of the vow to the next generation.

The canal was to his right, and a long white tour boat was navigating in the opposite direction. He could hear the loudspeaker as the guide switched from Dutch to English. That was the beauty of Amsterdam. A wonderful mix of peoples and cultures who had understood tolerance. Christians, Muslims, Jews, and others from all over Europe and Asia. It began with Dutch trading dominance, and after the war it was a great place to assimilate as Europe was rebuilding. It had been a resting place for his family after the chaos of being displaced from Denmark to Sweden and finally to the Netherlands.

He could not understand the recent wave of hatred and intolerance sweeping Europe. The Party for Freedom, which espoused values having nothing to do with freedom, had won a surprising number of seats in the last election. This time around it was all directed at the Muslims. Intolerance always started with one target group. Then it spread. He knew that from the hard experience of his parents. The daring escape from Denmark, just ahead of the Nazi extermination, was a story Paul's father insisted on retelling every Friday night before the Sabbath. Just after the blessing for his wife, the woman of valor, but before he said the blessing over the children. A story his father made Paul and his cousin Thomas vow to continue when he was on his deathbed twenty years ago. The story came with a vow. And the vow required action and vigilance. So far Paul had been good to his word and he was teaching Ophelia to continue the tradition. No, *tradition* was the wrong word. There was an *obligation* to fulfill the vow.

The walk took them past a series of four-story, uniformly drab brick buildings. Here he stopped.

"We have reached our destination. The symbol of Dutch resistance and Jewish hope. Anne Frank *Huise* or House, as you Americans would say. You will excuse me if I leave you here. I cannot manage the stairs as well as I used to."

"Paul, this was very kind of you to arrange," one of the women said. "It's all we've been talking about for the past month. My church group read the diary together to prepare."

"They say no one departs from here without leaving some tears behind," Paul said.

A moment after he saw the guests make their way in, Paul's cell phone buzzed for the third time since he left the office. This time he answered it.

"Paul, I've been trying to get hold of you for an hour."

"Sorry, Ophelia. I had guests to host."

"He's disappeared," she said, her tone brittle. "I've no idea where he's gone and he responds to nothing."

"Who, my dear?"

"Tal."

"The boy is gone, you're saying?"

"He's not a boy anymore, Paul." The irritation in her voice was palpable.

"He must be somewhere. Find him. It's your job. Take care of it."

"Disappeared without a trace." She sounded defensive.

"What do you need, Ophelia?" he asked.

"You have some friends in the State Department?"

"I have friends everywhere."

"Have them check if there's a record of him leaving the country, and if so where he's landed. They should be able to trace him to an airport. I need something to work from."

"I will be in touch. And it would not hurt if once in a while you called me Papa."

"Maybe if you didn't treat me like an employee. Call when you know something."

The vow sometimes weighed quite heavily, he thought.

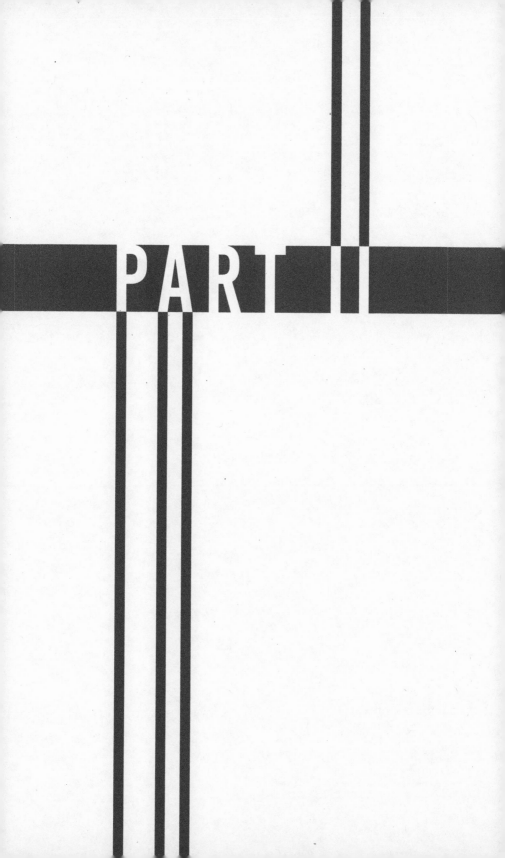

PART II

CHAPTER 20

Tal studied the slightly bent man who had just walked into the room, a huge smile plastered across his ruddy face. He was wearing a sleeveless undershirt that clung to his barrel chest. An elaborate tattoo adorned each shoulder, though Tal couldn't make out what they were. Something in cursive writing that was partially covered by the undershirt. His shoulders were thick but Tal could not yet tell whether that was from daily exertion or weight room habits cultivated in a previous life. He was handsome enough, with round cheeks and a clean-shaven face and head that were glistening, probably from a pre-dawn workout. Tal was wearing a sweater against a cooling mid-April breeze.

"G'day, mates, and for you newcomers, welcome to Serenity. Ain't Western Australia grand? You can call me Gar."

Gar paused and surveyed the twelve male faces around the semi-circle. Tal had chosen a seat at one end of the semicircle. Most of the six new members looked as if they had been dragged in off the street. Shrunken shoulders, pasty complexions, fidgety hands, wandering unfocused eyes. They had two more things in common. They all wore a red name tag, like his, and they all radiated hopelessness. They were probably looking at him thinking the same thing.

"Let me tell you a little story about a guy who ran a very successful company. It began with painkillers for my arthritic back. Eventually I was stealing from it to support my habit. I hated everything about me. Couldn't stand the way I looked, couldn't stand the way I smelled. Hated my life, I did. I tried to get off them but I continued to relapse and the pain only got worse. After a few months I started to self-medicate and before I knew it, I stopped caring who I bought from. Ended up with a five-year sentence for fraud. They shed me of my white-collar label and gave me a new one — inmate. I was no better than anyone else in that hellhole."

Tal looked around at the group. All together a baker's dozen worth of misery.

They were all dressed in the same white Serenity T-shirts and khakis.

The man sitting at the other edge across from Tal had a short stubble on his head and tattoos running up and down his bulky arms. Their eyes locked for a moment and the man smiled. Three of his front teeth were missing and the others were badly yellowed. Next to him was another man who looked to be in his late thirties. About thirty pounds overweight, all of it around his waist, head hanging. His face was much paler than his bald head. He'd probably had a beard until he arrived yesterday. Those were Gar's rules. No facial hair, no drugs, no alcohol. Cold turkey quit. Tal had shed the beard and unruly hair yesterday afternoon, a couple of hours after his arrival.

Yesterday's interview, one on one with Garson Allen, had left Tal a little shaky. He had understood that Lucinda had booked him in here for a one-year stay. Instead he discovered he was on probation. Tal had crossed the planet and it had not occurred to him that he might be returning home shortly, having failed once again.

"Tal, get through this interview and yer in. We don't have many spots so I'm very selective about who gets a bed. There's no bullshit around here. You're talking to the ex-king of bullshit. I can smell it a mile off. All of us here are addicts. Some of us are criminals."

"Which am I?" Tal asked as if he wasn't sure. Was his revenge fantasy against Red King so ingrained that he already considered himself a murderer? Was he so messed up by the voice in his head that he couldn't tell the difference between fact and fantasy?

Gar laughed. "You've arrived with a sense of humor. That'll help ya climb out from rock bottom."

He thought he'd reached rock bottom two hours and three double bourbons into the flight from New York. He couldn't be certain exactly how many days ago that was. He'd been arguing with CallMeGeri about the plan. Geri wouldn't relent. He kept insisting that the revenge had to be immediate. It couldn't wait a year. That this was a big mistake.

The woman sitting next to him in business class got up to speak to the slight female flight attendant. A moment later she was whisked to another seat. Tal was yelling, he thought just in his head. He had no recollection screaming any of it out loud.

He stared down the couple sitting across the aisle, who quickly turned their heads away.

Two minutes later the flight attendant returned. This time a bald burly man with a thick mustache, severe face, wearing a white short-sleeved shirt and a number of bars on the shoulders, followed right behind her. "If we turn this plane around, Mr. Neilson," the attendant said in a commanding tone, "you will be arrested and charged the moment we land at Kennedy." She glanced back over her shoulder at the muscle, then turned to Tal. "Is that what you want?"

Tal settled for a glass of water and reached into his pocket for the bottle of pills. He had promised himself it was only for emergencies. This was an emergency. A few minutes later he was out cold.

He had reached the bottom. Ready to deal with Serenity. Now he was sitting in front of the Australian version of Braverman. The headmaster with the power to evict him.

"I'm the kid who got thrown out of boarding school," Tal volunteered.

"Problems with authority?"

"I just wanted to live at home."

"Ya loved your parents?"

"Love, hate. Aren't all families the same?" It was a little too early to admit his mother was trying to kill him or just institutionalize him. Or that his stepfather had murdered his father. It did sound delusional. Besides, didn't everyone here have a relative who wanted them committed for ruining their lives? Or someone they would be happy to destroy given the opportunity?

"Honesty is the first step on our journey to recovery. You'll tell us more when you're good and ready. That's why we're all here."

Tal nodded.

"Understand that I was saved by embracing a higher power."

"Sounds religious."

"For some people it's religious. In all cases it's about relinquishing your delusion that will power alone will save you. It's about relying on the power of something in the universe greater than you."

He'd survived the interview and was woken, along with everyone else, by the five a.m. cowbell that morning.

Gar was pacing along the semicircle, talking about the battle between the higher power and the demonic strength of the addiction. "The drugs'll do that when they've taken over yer life. But ya can't change what ya don't understand about who is empowering you."

He went on to explain that the facility was privately funded, meaning each of them had to come up with the financing for their stay there. Minimum one year, that was the condition. But there was no guarantee Gar was going to keep you just because you had the money.

Gar stopped directly in front of Tal. "Break any of my rules and I'll boot you out on your arse so fast…" Gar pantomimed a swift kick to a rugby ball.

Was this directed at the six newcomers or just at the representative of squandered wealth and power? "I got ten guys begging for one of your seats, so don't think I need you or any of your money. It's time you get on the road of self-sufficiency."

They were sitting on wooden fold-up chairs in a white concrete garage that faced out into acres of farmland. The acrid smell of manure filled the air. The sun was beginning to rise from behind Gar and it cast an aura around him.

Everything was upside down around here. The rumor was that even the water circled down the drain in the wrong direction. The outskirts of

Perth, Australia, were about as far from his past life as Tal could possibly imagine. He felt some relief in knowing he was off Red and Trudi's radar screen. Thank God for Lucinda.

"Once you submit to your higher power, you've got to learn how to manage each day. One at a time."

"One day at a time is not going to get us what we need, Son."

The planet was obviously not big enough to avoid CallMeGeri.

"My bet is that, other than your dealers, you've had no honest contact with anyone in as long as you can remember. Those people were enablers. When you return to the world, you must cut them out of your life."

"You don't need anyone else, Tal. I didn't."

Your tune has changed, Father, Tal thought. For years it was you and Red. The brains and the marketing brawn.

"You need to remember how to love yourself if you ever want to love," Gar continued.

"This guy is getting a little preachy for me. The only two people I ever loved screwed each other and screwed me."

"Consider yourselves on a remarkable voyage that will change your lives. Trust my staff. Ask our friends sitting here who have been with the program for months. We intend to direct you where you need your life to be."

"A voyage to change your life. Did I ever tell you I almost drowned that night?"

"There will be nights coming where the only thing left in your existence will be that higher power," Gar said.

"Maybe the higher power saved me." The voice laughed. *"I saved myself. I did it all myself. So can you."*

"You'll have to do the work. And I'm not talking about getting clean. That's assumed. Look at Johnny over there. How did you manage getting clean, Johnny?"

A lanky man, all skin and bones, stood up. Young, except for his eyes. "Oh, there were some long nights, Gar. I shivered and I sweated and some of those nights felt like they was never gonna end. But I got up the next morning and I worked. Focused on the tasks for the day. Cleaned up the cow shit or repaired the pipes. Did whatever needed to be done 'round here. I finally got it. The day-to-day living is what saved me."

"Thanks, Johnny. Boys, Johnny here's been clean for a month. Like the rest of us, he's figured it out. Finding ourselves through the routine of a normal life is one of the keys. Gotta put some meat on his bones before he gets outta here. I'll throw a few extra chunks of beef on the barby for ya." Gar had a hearty laugh that rose from the bottom of his belly.

"Self-love. That's where it all begins."

"As long as you never forget where it has to end." CallMeGeri's voice felt like a smack between the shoulder blades, dislodging every thought in Tal's head.

"You've let a lot of people down, but mostly you've let yourself down. You've fallen and you've fallen and you've fallen some more. Just like I once did. Just like Johnny. But if Johnny and I could pull our arses up so can you. One day at a time, until you discover your higher power is there to help you live without the drugs."

"Now I know why MIT never had a varsity team. No patience for cheerleaders. Give this guy a couple of pompoms. If you think this will help, Son, just don't let me down."

Gar walked toward the entrance then turned back toward the semicircle. "I won't shuga coat it. The worst is coming. It'll be hell. But once you get off the drug cycle, you can begin to find ya'selves."

There was something worse? What could be worse than now? Tal had killed his brother, lost his father. Treated his girlfriend like a dishrag, fled the family business, and had to cross the world to hide out from his mother.

With the pills worn off, he felt as if he'd been run over by a truck.

"You still have no idea what hell feels like," CallMeGeri cackled.

CHAPTER 21

A blast of Mediterranean sun welcomed Ophelia to the tarmac in Tel Aviv as she stepped off the El Al flight from New York. Just as well that she was taking this vacation from her work at Danmark. The company had been turned upside down by the latest sequence of events. Red King's sensational death had been all over the news. Danmark's stock price had dipped four percent the day the photos of the fiery car crash appeared in the news across America. Since that time there had been further slippage while the company was announcing that it was working on the succession plan. That was Thomas's problem. Meanwhile the hallways of the Danmark headquarters were abuzz with rumors about who would become the next CEO. Not a stitch of work was getting done with all the distraction. It was as if Red had been found slumped over in his office chair with a gun in his hand.

Thomas had called her yesterday while she was debating whether to work from home. It had not taken Paul very long to track Tal's whereabouts. He had last touched down in Melbourne and had taken a connecting flight to Perth. From there his investigator traced the remainder of Tal's route. A route familiar to Paul and to Thomas.

"You don't expect me to track him down in Perth?" she asked, unable to mask the incredulity.

"No. It is a job for Yakov," Thomas said. "Paul agrees."

"So why are we having this conversation?" she asked. "This is between you and Yakov."

"I can't do this, Ophelia. Yakov won't listen. Not since the accident. He's divorced himself from me. Only you can get through to him. You always could."

She took a deep breath. It did not help. "What you and Paul are asking … it's … it's too much," she stuttered into the phone. "Hasn't Yakov been through enough already?" At what point did the vow have to take a back seat to their own lives, she wondered. Never, it seemed. When she'd arrived in Israel from Paris, she'd officially changed her name from Farber to Einbreier, exercising the choice so many young Jews followed when they arrived in the country to live and to serve in the military. But there was more to it for her. She had wanted no more to do with Paul, the family, or any talk of the vow. She needed to be left alone. Needed to become someone else. Like Yakov needed time and space to rebuild his own life.

"What I am asking is what is required of all of us," Thomas said evenly. "And that includes Yakov."

Pain. Endurance. Memories. Carry on. Live. Who was she to question Thomas after what he'd endured? Maybe she had no right. She had only just viewed the online testimonial Thomas had given, as a Holocaust survivor, to Spielberg's Shoah Foundation last year. He'd been no more than a thirteen-year-old walking skeleton when he was liberated in March 1945. He'd avoided the last-minute exterminations by hiding in the outhouses "like a rat living in feces." His words.

She would never forget what followed on the recording: "There was no fight left in me. I remember only lying in someone's arms as if I were already a corpse. He was substantial, dressed in green. A confused look in his eyes. After all I had suffered, had the angel of death arrived to claim me? Perhaps he was death greedily wrapping itself around me. I had expected him to be dressed in a black robe. Could I be both confused and dead? I was not certain until he screamed, 'This boy's alive! Get me a medic.' The first recognition in years that I was human. I decided to lead a life of duty to my family, in honor of those who did not have my great fortune of survival."

A life of duty. Doing what was required. The imposition of his values on her. On Yakov. Fortunately, Thomas could not see the shade of her face, which must be deep red. There was no backing away from honor. There was no arguing with an order from Paul. Thomas had to know this was a terrible idea for Yakov. The official mourning period for his wife and child had ended almost two years ago, but who could go on after such tragedy. Once again Thomas had put the vow ahead of the needs of another. This time his son.

She would not ignore the order. She would return to Israel. It had been a few years since she'd escaped the pain of her own tragedy. Perhaps the time would come, maybe even on this short trip, to face up to it. The reckoning with her fears was inevitable.

She quickly passed through security with her Israeli passport. Paul was prescient in that regard. He had wanted them to be citizens of the Western world but he also insisted that they all spend time in Israel, including military service, before continuing their lives in the West. He also thought it would impose a discipline on their lives. Just one more duty of the Farber and Leiden families.

More likely it was also a product of the family's relationship with the Holocaust. Always cautious, Paul went to extremes to make sure his children, nieces, and nephews always had a place to call home and an ability to defend themselves. Better they should know how to use an Uzi if necessary or to kill with their bare hands if the situation required it.

Ophelia left Ben Gurion terminal and headed directly to Yakov's apartment up the coast. She loved driving in Israel. Everyone was crazy, and if there were rules, it was not certain if they ever applied and if so, to whom. She wound through the tight streets and the hoarding around the new multi-level housing projects just off the ocean. Newly planted sabra trees lined the roads. The rental car sped down the narrow street and past the apartment. When she made a U-turn in the middle of the intersection, the car squealed in protest. Finally, she pulled into the parking spot and got out of the car.

She knocked at the door. He opened it and greeted her with a warm smile.

"*Ma shlomcha*, Yakov?" What is the state of your peace? Leave it to the Jews. Not "How are you?" as the Americans would meaninglessly ask.

"*B'seder.*" Everything in order. But was it? Yakov had been out of order for a very long time. "*Tutto bene.* How is it that your Hebrew has a Dutch accent?"

"You're one to talk about accents."

"You're eight minutes late," Yakov said.

"I cross the world and that's the greeting I get? No kiss for your cousin?"

Yakov stepped up and gave her a big bear hug, laughing heartily. "What's this cousin nonsense? You're a little sister to me." They had spent summers together at his parents' villa in the countryside, then months after her mother died, while Paul recovered. She occasionally wondered if Yakov knew her better than she knew herself. Her confidant, at least until he married. The only person who knew the details of her and Tal in Paris.

Ophelia's head reached the center of his chest. He smelled like fresh soap and lemons. And strength. The protective heat of his body warmed her instantly. Not the man she'd left two years ago at the end of the shiva.

"You're still a little girl, Ophelia. I could break you in half. They're not feeding you enough in America. Where's all that muscle you put on in the navy?"

He ushered her into a tiny living room with a love seat and sofa. Like everywhere else in Israel, space was at a premium. There was little adornment other than a bowl of Jaffa oranges on the tiny coffee table and beside it a tray filled with dates. Yakov reached over and offered the tray to Ophelia.

"Medjool dates direct from the Jordan Valley. Take a few. Maybe they will start fattening you up," he said.

"Thank you, brother." She popped one in her mouth. Soft and delicious. Sweet memories.

Behind Yakov was a picture window with a view of the Mediterranean. To most it would be calming, but not to her. Americans were now paying a fortune for a little real estate that overlooked the beach on this side of the world. Crazy Jewish Americans. Miami Beach in the winter wasn't nough for them? They were drawn to the mysterious attraction of Israel. She took a quick look at the whitecaps rolling in and fought back the waves of nausea. She didn't even have to dip her toes in the water to experience the symptoms.

She looked around and took a few slow breaths. Yakov's place was kept up neatly. She guessed he was not around very often and she really did not want to pry into his personal life. It was up to him to share that.

"How are you managing?" she asked.

"The move has helped. This has been a far better environment for me than Milan. The first year was awful but over the last year I've learned to take each day as it comes. Ever since I left the program. I'll never be over the guilt, but I'm learning to live with it. I'll be ready to re-enter society soon."

"Thomas and Paul are concerned about you."

"They needn't be. Look at me. I'm fine. I've adjusted… "

"It wasn't your fault, Yakov. It was an accident."

"We're not talking about this. Do you understand. The guilt of the survivors. Ask my father."

Ophelia already knew too much about the guilt of the survivors. The night off the coast of Lebanon. The struggle to get back to the Zodiac. The friends she would never speak to again.

"Thomas never talks about it to family. Just to Spielberg," she said.

"It's never easy to talk when you are the survivor."

"All behind you now."

"Yes. The miracle worker in Australia saved me."

"And that's why I'm here. Paul needs you to go back there."

"You're not serious. When I said goodbye to Gar, I was hoping it was for the last time."

"Gar knows you're coming."

"But they don't take anyone for a second tour, and besides, I am fine."

"Paul made a very generous donation that will allow Serenity to double the size of the facility."

"For what they've done for me, no amount of charity is too large. But why send me back?"

"Talem Neilson is there and they need you with him."

"Any changes I should know about since Paris?"

"The drug dependency is far more serious. His father died suddenly and he went completely nuts."

"And this time your surveillance was all business?"

She didn't answer. She didn't have to. The heat in her cheeks had given her away.

CHAPTER 22

It was finally her turn. With Geri and Red gone, there was nothing stopping her from taking over Danmark. However, she did need to follow protocol. The man across the table was the last man left to maneuver out of her way. But not until she'd gotten what she needed from him. A convenient short-term alliance.

Trudi sat across the oak coffee table from Drew Torrance. The table had probably been carved just after the Revolutionary War. Trudi knew her American antique furniture, and Drew was either an astute shopper or had a decorator with an unlimited budget. Everything in his office spoke of a man on the rise, but a man who had not quite reached the pinnacle. The photos of Drew with Kissinger, Drew with his arm around George Bush at the 9/11 Memorial, Drew shaking hands with Mandela, suggested he had an astute hand for politics. He'd risen to the twentieth floor of a steel and tinted-glass building in midtown. She knew him well enough to know Drew was not finished climbing.

Drew, the chair of the Danmark board, versus Trudi Darrow, now Danmark's largest single shareholder. A showdown she had been looking forward to for over a quarter century. They had both come a long way from the bottom of the ladder in the late sixties. He had curated his law firm, TGO, his reputation, and the appearance of his wealth quite well. His Danmark stock alone had to be worth a small fortune, even after the recent drop in price.

As a show of respect for the largest single shareholder of Danmark Pharmaceutical, Arlene, Drew's assistant, put out the bone china tea service at the rear of his office, a sitting area that had probably hosted countless dignitaries over the past ten years. Out of respect for Red, Trudi had dressed in a simple black dress and black pumps. She'd left the designer shoes at home. She would save those for the first board meeting. She had added a white scarf to make it plain that she was transitioning from grieving widow to businesswoman. Drew would probably understand that immediately. He'd known Trudi for far too long.

"My sympathies, Trudi." That was Drew. Economical with his language. Never said more than he had to. But always prepared. Always had the surgical knife ready if he needed to remove one of your organs or your board seat. Today she had packed her own scalpel, though the two were safely separated by the antique coffee table.

After Trudi had taken her seat, Arlene arrived, offering them both the Darjeeling. She poured out the tea to just past the halfway point. Drew must have warned her that the discussion might be tense. No need for spills on the Persian carpet.

She decided to wait for Arlene to disappear before taking a first sip. "Thank you for organizing Red's funeral. I appreciate the assistance."

"After so many years, Trudi, it was the least I could do."

She reached for the fragile cup and inhaled the aroma before she sipped. Expensive leaves imported from India, she guessed. "With Tal having disappeared, I don't think I could have managed this otherwise. Besides, you know how Tal felt about Red. Maybe I made an error getting remarried so quickly. Tal couldn't handle it. He never had the emotional fortitude of his father."

Drew's tea sat on the table untouched.

"And I appreciate your following my instructions to keep it simple and private," Trudi said, swirling her teacup ever so slightly. She glanced down at the residue turning in the cup. Imperceptible movement could have interesting consequences. "I didn't want the media circus of Geri's funeral repeated."

"Such a tragedy."

She took just the right amount of time to dab at her eyes. "Perhaps we can address the reason I came in today."

"Certainly."

"It's about the chairmanship of the Danmark board of directors. It's a role you have fulfilled admirably for all these years. A number of board members have reached out to me. Asking about my plans. They're wondering whether a change of blood might be a good thing for the organization right now. Particularly with all this turmoil since Red's death. I think we need to send a sign to the market that our family is back in control."

"Trudi, I serve at the pleasure of the board. We all know that. I'll abide by their decision."

There was not the slightest movement in the lines of his face. Not even a flash of anger or surprise in his pupils. She had to hand it to Drew. She had opened with a veiled threat but he was not going to give her the satisfaction of a reaction. He probably knew she had not yet approached Thomas. She could never get a read on that man. The other *lackeys*, as Geri had called them, had all taken her calls and understood the message she delivered. In the future they would serve at her pleasure. Their lucrative board fees could disappear with the snap of her fingers at the annual meeting if they did not fall into line. She had to be far more nuanced with Drew. The role of chair of Danmark was both status and power.

"To be clear, Drew, I don't give a damn what any of the board members think. As far as I'm concerned, stability at this point is more important than any other consideration."

He sat there saying nothing. Not the slightest flinch.

"Don't worry, Drew, I will continue to support you. But I had an idea."

What a particularly ironic moment. Had *she* had his support all those years ago in '69 when Drew was still in that worthless little office just off Wall Street? No elevator. She had struggled up the staircase to the second floor. The steps sagged in response to the weight she was carrying around the midsection, protesting the fetus. Four months into a marriage she did not want. A baby about to enter her world, about to kill the one she had nurtured for years.

One mistake was all it took. A mistake in the middle of cornfields. Casperton, Nebraska, almost nine months earlier. Before Danmark.

When Darrowpharm was still struggling to make it. Trudi, Geri, and Red. Business partners. The best days of her life. The business decisions, the risks, and best of all the fights that tested their beliefs, their judgment, and that reinforced their shared love for building Darrowpharm. Geri might have been intractable, but when he took charge, when his brilliance shone, then it was as if the attractive forces of the universe were pulling her toward him, despite her best efforts to resist. The ultimate goal was to build the business. Not a relationship with Geri.

She had to admit he was handsome. Red's hairline was already receding when they first met but Geri had a full scalp of unruly chestnut hair in those early days. His tresses overlapped his ear lobes and ran down over his collar. He appeared to take little interest in his appearance. Geri stood out in a crowd since everyone was wearing it military style in the early sixties. Five years later Geri fit in quite well even though by then he had allowed his hair to grow farther over his ears, almost like McCartney on the Abbey Road album cover. Geri had also grown the beard. She could never resist a man with a beard. Just like his hair, he let it run free; if Adonis had any facial hair, this is what he would look like.

They had been looking at their fourth acquisition, a mid-size company that had most of its drugs under license from the major brands. Geri had identified one drug in the portfolio as being a potential home run. The negotiations that day had gone poorly and they were all exhausted. The bar looked like what you would expect in Casperton. Turn left at the outskirts of Omaha through forty miles of cornfields. Middle of nowhere U.S.A., pictures of the local high-school football team on the wall, short efficient knotty wooden tables that had probably been there since the day Prohibition was repealed, waitresses who barely noticed you. After about an hour at the hotel bar, she and Geri got into a heated debate. Red threw up his hands in disgust.

"If the two of you are going to continue to blame one another for this stalemate, then we're wasting our time." Red picked himself up off the wooden chair, which he pushed away from the table, and headed up the staircase to his room on the second floor.

"I could close this deal tomorrow, Trudi, if you just gave me some operating room," Geri said. His eyes narrowed as he slammed his hand on the table.

"I might support you if you weren't so bloody stubborn. I keep telling you we need a concession from them about reducing their labor force before we buy," Trudi said.

"And I keep telling you to stop fussing over that. We'll fire them all after we take over. I've budgeted the severance in calculating what we're prepared to pay. Thomas has already told me he would finance this." The disgust dripped off his tongue. She needed to back off but she couldn't stop herself.

"Using the Nazi's money again? And there it is. You just don't give a damn about anyone!" she shouted. She picked up the shot glass and drained it. Was that her fifth or sixth? There was no way she was giving in on that. She'd kept pace with him shot for shot since they got to the bar.

"I'll tell you what, Geri, let's settle this dispute like men. Winner closes the deal." She stood up and raised her fists. Then she swayed. "Come outside."

"You're on."

They staggered across the driveway and into the cornfield. The ground was wet from an evening rain, the steam rising in the late summer heat, misting up the harvest moon. The corn was standing tall, bending slightly in the breeze. Ripe and sweet, ready to burst out of the husks. There was a faint scent of tractor oil. A few steps in they were swallowed up.

"Now what?" Geri said.

She threw a roundhouse toward his head that he caught just after it grazed his chin. He began to laugh. "I guess you were serious. But you punch like a girl. You forget I had to survive high school." He would not release her arm.

She began to laugh. Then she jumped at him, knocking him to the ground. "I'll bet you never made varsity wrestling," she giggled as they rolled around. He made no effort to defend himself until she perched atop his chest, her knees straddling him on each side, her arms holding down his shoulders.

"I've won," she shouted. "I get to close the deal my way."

Geri laughed. They were both laughing. "This isn't over," he said. He brought his fists up to cover his face, then exploded them outward, separating her arms. She could not resist the gravitational force, collapsing on top of him. Suddenly face to face, chest to chest, lips to lips. Neither of them could resist the force that had drawn them together. Only then did he allow her to take over. The winner. The rest was a jumble of torn clothing, then skin, and after that ... a blur.

She woke at dawn, naked in her bed. She had no idea how she'd arrived there, and her head was splitting. She could hear the shower running. Geri was whistling. A moment later he stepped out, white towel wrapped around his torso.

"Better get going, doll face, unless you want me closing this deal without you. My way."

She refused to let the hangover and the nausea spoil her win. She struggled out of bed and three hours later they closed the deal. Her way. A week later the morning sickness began to spoil her life. The beginning of the end of her dreams at Darrowpharm. Eight months later, Trudi big as a house, stumbled into Drew's office for the meeting that would change their lives.

Darrowpharm was to be no more. The three of them had come up with a plan to merge a European company three times the size into their operation. Drew called it a reverse takeover. Essentially, Conmark Pharmaceutical was buying them. The company was publicly listed on the New York Exchange, but its stock price had sagged in the past year and a half. Its drugs were no longer competitive and it had no ability to raise any debt or equity. It was a sitting duck waiting for the right savior to take them over. Geri saw a number of drugs in the development portfolio that he thought could be repurposed. If he was right, sales would go through the roof. It was a gamble, but Drew Torrance sold them on the proposition that as a public company, if they could cobble together the right story, there was money in the U.S. and Europe to fund a big expansion of the business.

Drew had explained to them at the last meeting that if the deal closed, Conmark would own Darrowpharm, but the Darrowpharm shareholder group would own enough stock of Conmark to get control of the board of directors. The name of the merged company would become Danmark. Geri would become the CEO and Red the vice chair. They were here to put the final touches on the agreement. Together they had brought Darrowpharm a long way in a short time with a unique combination of talents.

Thomas Leiden had sat through most of the meetings quietly. He was still the source of their money and owned five percent of the company with options to acquire another three. He was the one who had extended to them an operating line when the banks balked in the early years. On the last two acquisitions he'd lent the company the funds to make the deals happen and always insisted on charging a fair rate of interest. Any other risk-lender might have gouged them. He also generally kept his mouth shut in the board meetings, preferring to let his views be known to Drew in private. Even Drew admitted that Thomas spoke to him only when it became apparent that Geri and Red were at odds. They might have been fighting but they fought like brothers.

Thomas was the balance of power. Nothing could be accomplished without his mediation. If not for his fund's money, Geri and Red never could have pulled off the deal to buy Darrowpharm from Trudi's family in the first place. He spoke with an accent, difficult to place, from somewhere in Europe. Trudi was certain the money was laundered, maybe stolen from the Jews during the war. He was always going back and forth to Milan and Geneva.

Maybe he knew something about Trudi that she had not yet figured out, particularly since she had begun showing a few months ago. Or maybe he could intuit how she felt about the fetus with each successive board meeting. The baby that was about to destroy her life dream. For the first four months she continually prayed it would die within her, then she would not have to marry Geri. No such luck. He would be a useless father, but he had no inkling that Trudi would be a pathetic mother. She was born for the boardroom, for the pursuit of deals. She was born to build but not to procreate. Nine months pregnant and her dream was nearing its end.

The writing on the wall was about to be spelled out to her. Drew did not waste a moment once they had all gathered together.

"As you all know, our offer to Danmark has been accepted in principle, subject to approval of their shareholders. This should all be wrapped up in about three months. We have one critical decision to make today. Once we merge, four of their seven directors will be resigning and will be replaced by four of us." Torrance paused.

Trudi looked around the table. Not a single one of the cowards would make eye contact. Except for Thomas. He was watching her. Evaluating. Judging. Condemning.

"I don't think at this point I should be asking for a volunteer," Torrance continued, "so perhaps we can have a discussion."

Geri began by clearing his throat. "Thomas has to go on the new board. Without his financing, we would be in no position to make this offer. By virtue of our positions in the new company, Red and I will also have to sit on the board."

Trudi looked over at Torrance. *"Et tu, Brute."* She hoped the whisper smacked Brutus across the face. Hard to tell. He did not blink. Maybe he had rehearsed the entire scene in advance with the boys. She wouldn't put it past them to set her up like this without any warning.

"Look, Trudi," Red said. "I've gotten Conmark to agree to have Drew moved into the chairmanship of the board."

"This is a great coup for us," Geri said. "This is what we've all worked so hard for. And we wouldn't be here without you. But look at you. You're already big as a truck and soon you'll have a new life to care for. Something much more important than Danmark. The first heir to the empire. If I'm lucky it's a boy. We'll name him Thalem, after my father."

All eyes at the table were directed at Trudi. She smiled. After all she had done to get them the company. Then five years killing herself to build it with them. Betrayed. Her contribution and family legacy reduced to the first two letters of the corporate name.

"I guess I've drawn the short straw here. Done deal, isn't it?"

No one spoke.

"Let me remind you this was my family's company. A legacy I'm not ever turning my back on. I will take my rightful place one day. That's a promise."

"Of course," they said in chorus and on cue. The blast of relief filled the room, suffocating her.

Thomas sat quietly, watching her a little too carefully. She knew she could not hide from him what Red and Geri would never understand — that they had all better watch their backs.

■ ■ ■

And so, thirty-five years later, she sat facing Drew in the luxury office. It was not yet time to plunge the knife between his shoulder blades. That time would come if she could exercise a little patience for positioning.

"Drew. As you've probably heard from the other board members, I'm taking Red's seat on the board. I'd like that to happen at the next meeting."

Torrance nodded. His hands were resting in his lap, his legs crossed, waiting her out.

"But that's not why I came. Danmark is at a critical junction, I don't have to explain that to you. The market is waiting anxiously. Our investors are jittery. We need to send out a signal that we're in control. We need you to step up. Speaking not only for myself, but for Geri and Red, we need you to take over as CEO. I'm certain they'd agree. There's no one else. I know it's asking a lot."

"Trudi, I have a law firm to run."

"Just until the board finds a replacement. We can begin a search immediately. To make things easier on you, it would make sense that you resign as chair of the board. The load of both positions is asking too much. I've canvassed most of the members and they support the idea."

Drew nodded, as if he knew she wasn't yet finished.

Drew, always the shrewd one. He'd understood how to play Red and Geri for all those years, and she should really not ever underestimate Drew's ability to manipulate. He was smiling. Pencil thin, but still a smile. A Venus flytrap smile to the fly.

"I would like to know I have your support to succeed you as chair," she said. "That will go a long way with the other board members, particularly Thomas. I also intend to step into the role as president of Danmark, Red's job, just until things settle down a little. It will give us all time to assess what the company needs in terms of leadership."

"I will abide by the board decision on the matter. You know it's not up to me to decide." Always unflappable. Always strategic. Never admitting to have been dealt a weak hand.

"But your views carry enormous weight," she said. A show of respect that Drew would appreciate.

She could play the trump card at any point. Thirty-one percent of the stock would allow her to replace the entire board at the next annual meeting. And she knew exactly how she would punish him if he made her resort to it. And he knew it. Time to give him a graceful escape.

"The board will understand your resigning as chair to take over this important duty, Drew. Danmark needs you. It always has."

"Let me have a chat with Thomas about this. The CEO position is a lot of responsibility, even on an interim basis." Smart move, Trudi thought. Like Caesar. Don't grab for power. Allow it to be thrust on you, a lesson she would take to heart.

He smiled and offered her more tea. She smiled back and politely refused. They both understood the game. She would need his support in the weeks and months to come. Co-symbionts, the term Geri had coined all those years ago. Each of them needing the other to survive. Eventually she would move into the CEO position as well. Only then would it be time to settle old scores.

"If there is anything further I can do to help, Trudi, please let me know."

Trudi stood up to leave. "We've come a long way from your office in lower Manhattan, haven't we, Drew?"

"I'll never forget the last thing you said at the last board meeting you attended. Removing you from the board was not my call."

"Of course, Drew. That was half a lifetime ago. You know that I'm not the kind of person who holds a grudge."

She extended her hand. But I will take back what's mine, she thought. I *am* that kind of person.

CHAPTER 23

Drew Torrance removed his jacket, then loosened his tie and took his seat behind the desk. *That* was a workout! Trudi had not lost an ounce of her earlier ruthlessness. Who could have predicted the circuitous route by which she was retaking control of Danmark? The woman *was* making good on her promise — more than thirty years had passed since she'd vowed that she would be back. It took two dead husbands to get her there. Coincidence? Or was she the classic black widow? Trudi Darrow, murdering schemer? Drew laughed. Better to keep that thought where it belonged — in his imagination.

There was no escaping the fact that he was among the triumvirate that eliminated her when she was in her ninth month. "I'm not the type who holds a grudge," she had said. Why would she feel the need to tell him that? Unless … unless this was a game of high-stakes poker and Drew was sitting with a pair of deuces. When Trudi decided to move all in, he would have to gracefully fold.

Step one, strip him of the chairmanship, giving him an interim role. Maybe he had three months, maybe six as CEO. He had no intention of leaving TGO, not while he was still building the law firm. She knew that. She had to want the job herself. That's why she'd reached for the chair, where she could stand behind him and sharpen the dagger. The only question was how long it would take before she'd thrust it then push him off the board and out the door.

Leaving the board at some point had its silver linings. His stock in the company had to be worth well over thirty million, and he knew enough people in the business who would place a block trade to cash him out.

Even at a discount to market, he could walk away with a good twenty-five mill. Not a bad consolation prize for getting the boot. Were it only so simple.

The downside was that once Trudi was installed as CEO, it would not take much for her to create an excuse to get rid of Drew and with him the law firm. That would be catastrophic. Danmark was TGO's largest client, and losing it would shake the foundations of the firm. What were the immediate options? He could influence the board to deny her the path to the chair now. She would wait him out until the next annual meeting, put together her own slate of directors, and she would almost certainly have enough votes to carry the day. Her new board would install her as CEO immediately and unquestionably fire him and the firm. It was exactly what he would do in her shoes. Thwarting Trudi's ambition to reach for the Danmark crown would be a strategic error of epic proportions.

There was a better way. It was time to find out how much of this Thomas Leiden knew. If Trudi had already spoken to him, she would have dropped his name. Because he was the lead director, the other members of the board were going to take his views seriously. Together he and Thomas could smooth Trudi's return. That would have to be worth something in her books.

Thomas was a tough read at the best of times, and he had played his role as facilitator brilliantly from the start. He had the knack of knowing exactly how to assist Geri in dealing with Red. After the merger with Danmark, he became even more important in making sure that Geri maintained support of the board, even in years when their profit margins were dropping and there were cries for action. Drew had learned quite a lot about how to run a board by watching Thomas in action. He behaved like someone who had nothing to lose. How to maneuver around the worst in people's motivations. Who knew where that came from? Drew had been unsuccessful in learning anything from Leiden about his past. He was a very private man. If Trudi wanted to succeed, she had better not take Leiden lightly.

Drew could help her in that regard. Advise her. Re-establish the relationship that would make him indispensable, as he had been to Geri and Red. If worst came to worst, Drew could fall on his sword to save the firm's legal work.

Arlene broke his reverie, opening the office door and sticking her head in.

"Lucinda Horat asked to have a few minutes with you. Your schedule's open for the next half hour. Sounds important."

"Rare that one of the young partners tries to get in here," he mused out loud.

"That's because you're such an intimidating beast!" she laughed.

"Me? I've never intimidated you."

"To me you're just a beast."

Drew laughed. "You've tamed this beast," he said. "Give me two minutes then send her in."

"And do up your necktie."

This would be the second time Lucinda had insisted on meeting in the last four months. Unprecedented among all but the most senior partners. He'd never forget her first visit. She'd almost broken down in front of him, just after Geri died, certain that she had alienated Talem Neilson and had lost all his potential business.

That was the problem with the young partners. They had no sense of the bigger picture. The corporate account for Danmark had to be worth forty to eighty million dollars a year in billings, depending on how many simultaneous lawsuits Geri had going. Drew had made sure all the work stayed after Red took over, and he had stepped in to be the stabilizing and active chair after Red's sudden death. To the outside investment world he was the prudent interim leader of Danmark. To his partners he was the guardian of all the legal work coming from the company.

It would never occur to Lucinda that Talem's return to the company might spark a war between him and Trudi. If so, TGO, stuck in the middle of a shareholder fight between mother and son, would be horribly conflicted. The rules of ethics might require them to withdraw from all

Danmark work. Even if the firm's legal counsel concluded there was no ethical problem, the smallest excuse was all Trudi would need to punish him. And what better way than to embarrass him in front of his partners by losing the firm's largest and oldest client.

Drew needed to avoid that eventuality at all costs. That meant firing Talem as a client. Lucinda need not worry. She had probably done the firm a huge favor. He might as well take advantage of the opportunity and make sure she understood that.

Arlene led Lucinda into the room. She wore a well-tailored business suit over a white blouse with a short strand of white pearls around the neck, possibly real though he could never tell. Jacket buttoned at the waist and skirt hem just a notch above the knees, both some shade of green, which he guessed was her trademark color. It certainly set off her red hair, which was pulled back tightly in a knot on her neck. Plenty to distract a man from the dark circles that had gathered under her eyes. The visit was not spur of the moment.

Drew came around his desk to take her hand, offering that medium grip perfected for women, then motioned for her to take a seat before he returned to his desk chair and waited. She crossed her legs and clasped her hands tightly. Her knuckles had turned white.

She waited for Arlene to close the door and launched right into it.

"Sorry to bother you and I know your time is precious."

"No problem, Lucinda. You caught me on a window in my schedule. What's on your mind?"

"I have another problem." She sat for a moment. Probably she hadn't rehearsed the opening line enough times, although there was no sign of stage fright. Just bad news.

"Go ahead," he prodded.

"Tal Neilson has left the country." She took a deep breath.

She told him about Tal's incarceration and release from Dr. Rosen's facility and the plan to get him into rehab. "I met him at JFK. Made sure he checked in to get on the flight to Australia." Lucinda leaned forward. "He showed up at the airport half an hour late. He looked distraught. I chalked it up to leaving the country on such short notice. Then I read the newspaper reports. You know what happened to Red King." Now the floodgates had opened. Time to hand over the tissue box.

"The press called it an accident," Torrance said.

She reached up her sleeve for a tissue and took a good honk before continuing. "What the press doesn't know is that Tal was certain Red had murdered his father."

"Red killing Geri? Nonsense. They'd been at one another's throats for over thirty years. Everyone knew that."

"Everyone except Tal. Maybe it was the drugs and the effect they had on him."

"Okay, even if that's the case, so what?"

"When he arrived at the airport he was in an agitated state. He had the time to do this to Red before he met me at the airport. That might make me an accessory after the fact. I haven't slept since the night Tal left."

Right out of Criminal Law 101, the basic course all law students were obliged to take. Drew had no idea how many changes there'd been in the law since he'd taken the course at Boston U., just before his hair turned prematurely gray. Once the course was done, only the ones who specialized in criminal defense or prosecution ever looked at the provisions again. Drew never did. "Do you have any knowledge where Talem was before he met you?"

"No."

"Any evidence at all?"

"No."

A trip to the office of the firm's in-house counsel should get this off his plate. "Explain all this to Simon Lester. He'll let you know if we need to retain an outside criminal attorney to advise you. And stop worrying."

"There was no one else I could speak to. It's been eating me up inside. I'm so sorry to bother you, but I was certain you would want to know all this."

"Are you telling me Talem has left the continent?"

"He left a month ago for at least a year. I pay the monthly costs for his drug rehab program from his trust account in accordance with the provisions of Geri's will. I've done everything by the book."

. All's well that ends well, he thought. "Also ask Simon about dealing with ongoing communications with Talem. Particularly now that we are aware he might be considered a suspect at some point."

Drew stood to indicate that the meeting was over. Lucinda smiled for the first time as she left. After the door closed behind her, he walked over to his display case and poured himself a finger of his favorite scotch. Aged for thirty years.

What did this all mean? The good news was that with Talem gone, the risk diminished of an immediate dramatic shareholder fight between mother and son that would conflict Drew, with the firm caught in the middle.

All this was worthwhile only if Trudi could be managed. And that was his responsibility. Managing her was going to be a challenge. Given her track record, though, he'd better not get too close to Trudi. He had no plans to become husband number three. Maybe she really was a black widow!

CHAPTER 24

Tal had reached the midpoint of the year-long journey to recovery. The first two months of his rehab had been torture. In addition to the cold sweats at night, he was haunted by recurring nightmares of his father, blood seeping from his eyes, walking the ramparts of Kronsborg Castle. It was exactly as Father had described it when Tal was a child. Tal was two strides behind Father.

"You're not keeping pace with me, Tal."

"I'm trying." His legs, like stones, refused to respond to the simple command: keep moving.

"This isn't trying. Look at him!"

Father was pointing at the parapet, which was partially shrouded in the late-night fog. A gust of wind cleared away the fog and there stood the enemy, dressed in a flowing red robe, a gold crown resting precariously on his bald head.

"He's usurping a kingdom that is rightfully yours."

Every night the scene played out the same way with Tal thrashing wildly on the bed. The other residents took turns watching over him each night, waiting for the calm of deeper sleep to arrive predictably around three in the morning.

"Why are you doing this for me?" Tal's voice was a wisp as he asked one of the lads the question.

"Your turn to sit watch will come. It's part of your passage from who you were to what you may become."

At least the days passed quickly: mornings were spent mending fences, feeding chickens, and eventually being promoted to the team responsible for the irrigation pipes. He worked alongside the team of eight spending five hours each morning on backbreaking work, but he was bonding with a group of men who had no common background, just shared experience.

Afternoons revolved around the group sessions. There were four men in Tal's group: Tal was the Yank; beside him sat the Godfather, a gargantuan fellow with a heavy Italian accent who had arrived shortly after Tal. Across from them sat two Aussies: Digger and Greaves. It looked like Digger never missed a meal, even in the worst of times, while Greaves had probably wasted away during multiple agonizing withdrawals from his addiction. Even now, when he turned sideways, he all but disappeared; Greaves was defined by an elongated nose on a pockmarked face.

"Yer ma never beat you, did she?" Greaves asked, after Tal explained the circumstances behind his stay with Dr. Rosen.

"Just tried to lock him up foreva," Digger said. "I'd say that's a might worse than takin' the odd beating."

"Well, Digger, what would you've done if he'd called your mate a murderer?" Greaves looked at Tal, the ski-jump nose pointing straight at him. "You did tell us you hated him, didn't you?"

"Maybe your mamma did you a favor," the Godfather mused. Tal was willing to bet the Godfather knew plenty of guys doing hard time in Italian jails for taking care of unwanted relatives. But he did have a point. Given his state of mind at the time, maybe it wasn't outrageous for Mother to have locked him up.

"And why're you being so hard on your mom for remarrying so quickly? Sounds like her marriage to your da' was a bust. Maybe she was lonely," Greaves said.

"Or maybe she had always wanted to be with Red?" Digger said, his hands comfortably resting on his protruding belly.

Silence from the peanut gallery. Perhaps CallMeGeri was in an anger management program this morning.

"I never really thought about it that way," Tal finally said. Maybe Mother did need to protect me from myself, he thought. Tough love. But why not try to convince me? Why was there not even a goodbye? She dropped me into the sanatorium and threw away the key. She tricked me into making the trip. Had she done it for my sake or for her own? And nothing could explain the fact that the incarceration left barely a trace of a memory. No pain, no withdrawal, just one unending dream sequence at sea. A slow boat to oblivion, escorted by Rosen and Guilden, steering from the stern.

Gar walked into the room, peeling an orange. "There's not a one of us that hasn't faced a moment when we needed to be separated from the environment that enabled us."

The four men nodded.

"The point is, mates," said Gar, "each of us is responsible for ourself. We take what the world gives us and we deal with it. We can't blame it on others, we can't rationalize our behavior by the hate and indifference that own us. We have to find our own love and that begins by finding and loving ourselves. Yer not worth shite to anyone if you're not worth something to yerself."

■ ■ ■

A few days later Tal was out weeding the vineyard on the far end of the homestead. The hills of the national park rose up in the distance but there were no fences separating the residents from the forest to the east of the property. Gar was fond of saying that the only way to learn restraint was to find it from within. "Yer free to leave at any time," he'd tell the incoming group on arrival each month. "But take one step outta here and there's no coming back." They needed to find their place in the world before rejoining it.

Tal was on his knees, fighting with the hardened soil to loosen the unwanted yellow flowers surrounding the vines when he felt a tap on his shoulder. He turned and looked up. Where had the Godfather come from? He looked to be a few years older than Tal but probably outweighed him by about thirty pounds and was at least six inches taller. His English was quite proficient, but spoken with a heavy accent. When he smiled, his eyes narrowed in a way that sent shivers down Tal's spine. How many men understood that the Godfather's smile might be the last thing they saw in their life?

Outside of group therapy, Tal carefully avoided him — until now. They were a mile from the facility. Nothing but open space on one side and verdant forest on the other. Plenty of space to hide, assuming he could outrun the big man.

"Listen, Yank," the Godfather said, "it must have been tough watching your papa's legacy fall into the hands of others. What are you going to do about it once you leave here? If you need any help, I'm offering some assistance." He smiled.

An offer of assistance. What kind of assistance and at what cost? Since Father's funeral Tal had wanted his revenge. Everyone who had sat over his bedside knew it. Father had been screeching every night — but to put out a mob hit? Tal felt the thrill rushing through his bloodstream. Would the voices finally stop once Red was taken care of? And how much did these things cost? He could just imagine having to beg Lucinda to release the twenty-five or fifty thousand it would cost to do it properly. What was the cost of friendship with this man?

"Kind of you to offer," Tal said.

The Godfather dropped to his knees alongside Tal and picked up a weeding trowel.

"Watch me, Tal." The Godfather tapped the sharpened edge into the ground with little effort. The earth gave way immediately, and with a flick of the wrist the weed popped out. "If you're going to kill something, you've gotta use the right tool. It's all in the technique." He smiled. Tal cringed.

"Good to know, um… Godfather," Tal stammered.

"I hate that nickname, and the looks I get," the Godfather continued. "Though I have to admit it's kind of funny. Can you please call me Lorenzo. Lorenzo Lidon."

"Sure. Lorenzo." A rose by any other name? Tal picked up a trowel and mimicked Lorenzo's weeding technique. Nothing.

"Watch my wrist." Lorenzo grabbed Tal's right hand. "Like this." This time the trowel cut through the earth and Tal had no problem removing the weed.

"Teamwork," they said in unison.

Each of them now set out to weed a row of vines, side by side. After a couple of minutes of silence, Lorenzo turned to Tal.

"Looks like you haven't made any friends here. You have good friends back home?"

Tal thought about Cornelius and frowned. Always there for him as a child, but abandoned years ago. Then the three women in his life. First, Ophelia. After the dreadful way he'd treated her in Paris and New York, he owed it to her to stay away for good. Then Mother. She was probably relieved that he had disappeared; at least she was no longer a threat. But *was* she a threat? Could he ever trust her again? Finally, Lucinda. She was the one to step up to help him. The only person who knew where he was. How many people would brag about having their lawyer as their closest relationship?

"No one back home who would trust me anymore. Something I've got to work on," Tal said.

"Gar says that recovery starts with honesty. We can't really be close to anyone until we're prepared to open ourselves." Lorenzo smiled. This time a smile of warmth. Maybe Tal was jumping to the wrong conclusions about Lorenzo. Time to break the cycle of mistrust.

"I've done nothing with my life," Tal admitted. "My baby brother died just before my twelfth birthday. I've always blamed myself and it's taken me until now to admit it to anyone."

"I'm sorry. Were you responsible?"

"Does it matter?" He'd had enough of talking about himself. "What about you?"

"You asking what baggage I carry around?"

Tal nodded.

"My wife and child died in a car crash. I was driving."

"Were you responsible?"

"Does it matter? I've also missed the opportunities to do something with my life since then."

"I'm sorry. Pain," Tal said. "Something we come to terms with in group."

"That's why I'm here." Lorenzo looked upward to the sky. A fog had appeared out of nowhere, encircling them like a cone.

"The higher power," they said in unison. Then they laughed. Tal had no idea why, but for once it felt all right to laugh. They sat in the garden quietly for a few minutes. A light misty rain began to fall. The earth felt warm between Tal's fingers. The air smelled green and coppery and lush.

"Before I lost my family, I played tennis professionally in Italy." Lorenzo held up his over-sized arm. "The competition had a lot of trouble with a left-handed opponent."

He looked more like a linebacker than a tennis pro.

"I've put on about forty pounds since my playing days. I'm a financier now," he said. "I did my MBA at Wharton in finance, then returned home to join the family investment bank."

"Family bank?"

"I doubt you've heard of us."

"Everyone in the drug world knows my father and his company. Denmark. His life. He wanted me in the business, but wouldn't give me the time of day. Even when I came up with a plan for the future. For my future. He ignored me then let his partner destroy me... Not true... His partner set me up to destroy myself."

"As Gar would say, that's remarkably self-aware."

"Yes, yes, another step on the road to wellness," Tal said, noticing his tone was not sarcastic.

"Maybe I can help. I was serious when I offered assistance."

"How can you possibly help me?"

"Let's start with the guy you're always dreaming about."

Tal felt a punch to the gut. "What about him?" Tal's jaw clenched.

Lorenzo picked up the trowel and cut deep into the earth. "You keep talking about him and your revenge fantasies."

"I'm not following."

"I read an article in the *Economist* about Danmark just before I came in here. Red King, right?"

The castle, the crown, the nightmares that Tal thought were behind him. The anger that he thought he was processing, exploding in a single word. "Bastard."

Tal jumped to his feet. "What about him?"

"He died in a car accident. You really don't know?" Lorenzo stood studying him as if he was staring at a unicorn. "I have to give you credit. You're a really good actor, Tal."

Tal shook his head.

"The whole world outside this place knows it. Follow me."

Lorenzo marched at a quick clip back to the house. Tal jogged to keep pace and was out of breath by the time they'd crossed the estate. The two entered the main facility, and Tal followed Lorenzo through the kitchen and into the library, if you could call it that. A couple of laptops sat side by side on a white laminate counter built into the wall in an alcove just off the kitchen. Two bridge chairs were neatly tucked in. A stack of shelves lined with dog-eared paperbacks made up the adjacent wall. Lorenzo quickly sat down and began typing furiously. Tal studied the bowl of fruit on the kitchen counter. Kiwis, sitting on a bunch of bananas, much larger than those carried in New York grocery stores. Everything about Australia, larger than life as he knew it. Everything except the library, which was compact and out in the open. Privacy around here was not just a luxury, it was a risk.

"Pull up a chair and see for yourself," Lorenzo said.

Tal read the headline. His mouth gaped. Lorenzo stood and began pacing. He waited a couple of minutes before speaking.

Tal stared at the screen and didn't move. Three words reverberated in his head. *"Red is dead. Red is dead. Red is dead. Red is dead."*

"This really is a shock to you. Are you okay?" Lorenzo asked.

"When did this happen? How long has Red been dead?" Tal checked the date on the story. "What a minute, this happened the night I left New

York, a few hours before I met my lawyer at the airport. The news report quotes my mother openly wondering where I was that night."

Tal scrolled through the story of the car crash. It had been ruled an accident. There was a series of follow-up articles. Mother had become the new CEO of Danmark. Incredible. So much for revenge on Red, but what did it mean about Mother? Father killed by heart failure subsequent to a mild heart attack. Never made sense. Now Red in a car crash. Was it bad luck or was there something else at work? Maybe he'd been worrying about the wrong threat.

Lorenzo grabbed a banana and began to peel it. "Like this banana, you need to peel back the layers of the story and find the truth."

"What are you talking about?"

"Your father's company. It's in your mother's hands. The woman who put you away. The woman who married Red. The widow, twice over, is now in control of the company." It sounded like an Italian aria. Lorenzo was almost singing the lyrics. The right leitmotif would have the audience on their feet, while the son on stage was agonizing over his mother's treachery.

Lorenzo snapped his fingers. "Tal. Are you listening to me? Where are you?"

Tal realized his eyes were closed. "Sorry. Go ahead. I was just caught up in the past."

"The point is, Tal, that if you want to give yourself some options when you get out of here, you have to start by understanding your past so you can focus on the future."

■ ■ ■

What was the truth of the past? He'd loved every moment working at Danmark in Paris, once he had distanced from Geri and Red. He finally understood through group that referring to him as the bastard reinforced Tal's notion of himself as a victim. Ironic that Red had become the victim. Did he love the business the way Father had? He was not certain, but while in Paris, he finally felt alive while coming up with his program to change the nature of the business.

A few weeks later he approached Lorenzo after group. The leaves were swirling in a cool fall breeze, reminding him of the upside-down seasons at the bottom of the world.

"Were you serious about helping me? I'm ready to begin my comeback. I don't know how or where or when yet, but there is one business I know. Drugs. I have an inheritance coming and I could use a partner to help formulate a plan. That is, only if you were serious."

"Maybe we can begin by talking about what you might have in mind. I can help with the direction. That's a start."

"Sorry. I'm getting a little ahead of myself. That's gotten me into trouble in the past."

■ ■ ■

They spent the next few months reviewing the financial statements of the major competitors in the industry, beginning with Teva, the large Israeli drug maker, and a few international competitors. Then they started to set their sights on a number of small to midsize companies, in search of a target. When they were not attending to daily chores on the farm, the two became inseparable.

Sleet was falling outside and they were sitting at the computer table arguing over two possibilities. Lorenzo pointed at the balance sheet of one of the targets.

"It all comes down to investing in litigation strategies to get their key drugs into the market. It looks like they're short on capital."

"Shortsighted to be looking only at the supply chain. You need to consider marketing strategies too. Take a look at this. I've been meaning to show it to you. I brought it with me from America." Tal reached into a brown paper bag and pulled out a stack of papers. On top was a drawing of a church in blue-black ink. From underneath the drawing, Tal pulled out a stapled sheaf.

"Part of my legacy. Most of it, Father's notes going back thirty years. The first chapter of a memoir. One drawing that Father made. And this."

Tal withdrew a few sheets stapled together. "This is the work I completed at Danmark, then abandoned when I left the company. Strange that Father saved it, since he never read it. When Father read something, he assaulted it with his fountain pen. It would be black and blue."

"But it's marked in red."

"Those are my markings. I picked it up last week. Wanted to make sure what I thought was perfect all those years ago still made sense."

Lorenzo sat for an hour flipping back and forth between charts, grunting the way he might have when he was chasing down tennis balls. "Where in hell did you learn to do this modelling?"

"You see any errors?"

"Tal, I've been studying this stuff for years. I've never seen anything like this in my life. I'll bet no one has. Your formulas don't look like anything I learned in business school. Did they teach you this at Northwestern?"

"I developed the model in Paris, before the MBA."

"This is a whole new way of looking at foreign drug distribution. This isn't in anyone's business model that I've ever studied. If we can make this work from the right platform, we're sitting on a gold mine."

Tal reached back into the bag and withdrew a single page in Father's handwriting. Date and time at the top. "I found this glued between two pages of my spreadsheet last night."

Lorenzo laid the paper on the table. It was frayed on the sides as if torn out of a notebook. He studied the note carefully. "Except for the date and time, it's gibberish," Lorenzo said.

"It's a coded message from Father. He assumed I would figure it out. His ciphers got more and more complicated as I made my way through school. I won't give up until I solve it."

■ ■ ■

The last few months at Serenity roared by for Tal and Lorenzo. On Tal's final night, Gar and his mates threw him a small party with a cake and candles.

"I haven't had a party like this since I got thrown out of boarding school." He had shared his last piece of birthday cake with Cornelius, his only childhood friend. He'd blown the candles out and then he cried. Then the two of them went out and got stoned.

"Hey, mate, there's no crying in cricket," one of the support staff said.

"Yeah, but there's plenty of crying in rehab," Gar said. "We'll miss you, Tal. Go lead the life you were intended to lead. Are you goin' back home?"

He may have completed rehab, but there was still no home in his life. He was a man without family. A man with an inheritance that he would claim eventually. A man with a new partner. At least he could now say he was a man. That had to be worth something.

Tal raised his coffee cup. "A toast. If you look for meaning you will never find it, but if you create meaning you will never look for it."

It was time to create meaning.

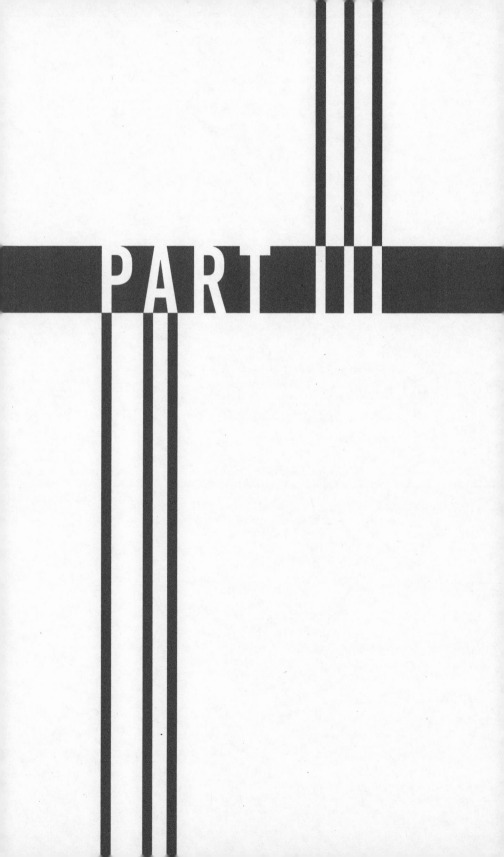

PART III

It was time for an adventure. Lucinda had never been to Montreal before, so she decided to mix business with a little pleasure. It felt like forever since she'd said goodbye to Tal at the airport. It was now almost a year and a half since that night and had become a strange measuring point for her life. Tal must have left rehab months ago, but she had heard nothing from him. She continued to wire monthly allowance checks to his account, but the amount would not have covered much more than basic existence. Was Tal so unsure of his cure that he refused to return to New York to face her, to prove he was clean of the drugs? Was he avoiding police questioning? Eventually he would make contact — Tal couldn't get at his twenty million until she was convinced.

She gave her head a shake. This trip to Montreal was supposed to be part vacation, so why was she focusing on Tal? Her sister Bea had a theory. Bea never shied away from sharing those theories. She had cornered Lucinda on her last trip to Boston for the July Fourth backyard barbecue.

"You have this fantasy he's going to come swooping in to rescue you from your drab paper-pushing life. That he's going to be this brand-new man. Your knight in rusty armor," Bea had said as they sat at the family picnic table.

"The firm is keeping me way too busy to worry about Tal, or any other man, for that matter," Lucinda had replied.

"Tick tock, tick tock, Lucy. That's your body clock talking. Get in the game, girl. Stop nursing this childish fairy tale. Take a chance. Take a vacation. Meet someone, for god's sake."

Montreal was a start. A little Latin flavor to get her blood moving again. It was rare that foreign clients came to her directly. Most files arrived on her desk as references from other TGO lawyers. This one was a little more mysterious.

A young Swiss businessman who was considering emigrating to the U.S. wanted estate planning advice. There were some complicated trust issues, and Mr. Cornelius Van Denton had been advised by his banker that she was among the best in the field. He was in Montreal on business and his assistant texted to ask if she would not mind making the trip from New York. He had paid for the flight and the accommodations. She'd decided to add a few days to the trip and make a vacation out of it.

Earlier she had spent the afternoon exploring Mount Royal, the iconic mountain that formed the northern boundary of downtown Montreal. Though it was more like meandering along the gravel roads under an overhanging canopy of maple and oak leaves. No objectives, no purpose, and no deep thoughts. Most important, no thoughts of clients. Was there a way to accomplish nothing? If there was, she wasn't any good at it. It had been longer than she could remember when she was not reading, or writing, or thinking about how to advance her law practice. Anything to distract her from thoughts of Tal.

Bea was right. She needed a spark. The same spark she'd felt when she rescued Tal from the clutches of Nurse Guilden. When she'd plotted to assist his escape from the country. A night when she'd felt alive, full of purpose, engaged in a mission to save a life. That didn't last long. She'd woken up the morning after Tal left with a sense of dread. The news media were all over the spectacular car crash. Maybe she'd made the gaffe of all gaffes. Drew Torrance and the firm's counsel had convinced her she'd done nothing wrong, but had she done right? Where was Tal?

She had decided to appreciate a summer day without the prickly heat of Manhattan, on the *montagne*, as they called it here, that dominated the city. Sunbathers reclining on a grassy knoll absorbing the afternoon glow; young lovers oblivious to the world, lying on their blankets; children running in circles chasing balls; a golden retriever lying motionless, head on the lap of its owner, a young woman in shorts and a blossoming matching pink halter. Lucinda involuntarily touched her flat stomach.

To cap off the relaxing day, she treated herself to a full body massage in the hotel spa, then returned to her room to change for the meeting. She appraised herself in the bathroom mirror, one final look before she headed out to meet the new client. Not bad for a redhead just before her thirty-fifth birthday. Her summer freckles were out, but none of them looked like age spots. Not too young and not too old. Tonight she needed to look mature, businesslike, trustworthy. The Swiss expected precision in their clocks and they must expect it in their lawyers. She drew a breath and headed to the hotel dining room, arriving six minutes early for the eight p.m. reservation.

She stood opposite the bar at the entrance to the restaurant. A few single women with dark red lips, hems hitched high, and their legs crossed hopefully were sitting at the bar, sipping on martinis. On the lookout. The glass shelving over the bar was stocked with an assortment of scotches and liquors against the mirrored wall. A waiter dressed in black passed by with drink orders for a couple of businessmen sitting at the table just inside the dining room.

Lucinda jumped when she felt a tap on the shoulder.

"*Bonsoir.* You are the guest of Monsieur Van Denton, *non?*" The hostess looked as if she might be moonlighting from her day job as a runway model.

Lucinda nodded. "*Oui.* I am. Sorry, my French is pretty rusty."

The hostess batted her eyelashes. "No problem, *madame.*"

"*Mademoiselle.*"

"Ah, very good. These days we say *madelle* in Quebec. Like the American Ms." She laughed. "Monsieur Van Denton has not yet arrived. Would you like to wait at the bar?"

She was outmatched at the bar. She was about to decline, but the hostess was a step ahead. "Allow me to exhort you to the table. That is how you Americans say it? I recently graduated from the Université de Montréal. I am working on my English at every opportunity."

"Escort."

"Ah, *pardonnez-moi*. Escort. I always thought that word had a different meaning," the hostess said, turning her attention to the women at the bar.

"It depends on which syllable you accent," Lucinda said with a smile.

The hostess led her to the rear of the dining room. A table for two in the far corner. She sat for over ten minutes. Cornelius Van Denton had not yet arrived. Perhaps he was on a business call although it was still the middle of the night in Europe. She was just beginning to make her way down the menu, trying to revive her language skills by reading the French versions of the various items, when she felt a presence behind her.

"Ms. Horat, I presume?"

A frisson passed through her. The voice was the same, yet at the same time entirely different. She turned and her jaw dropped.

"Tal, what are you doing in Montreal? What a coincidence!" It was not her voice. She was at least an octave too high. She felt like a schoolgirl gaping at Bon Jovi once again. He just stood there, handsome as ever in an open-neck dress shirt, gray jeans, tan loafers, no socks. Head-to-toe perfection. His eyes were clear and penetrating.

She finally stood up to greet him. He gave her a light hug and kiss on each cheek. "When in Montreal," he said, mimicking the local custom.

"I'm so sorry," she said. "I would love to talk and catch up but I'm expecting…"

Tal smiled warmly. "Please sit down, Lucinda." He pulled out her chair for her. She felt every ounce of preparation and professionalism spill out over the bleached hardwood floor.

This was not the same man she had escorted from the institution. Not the same person she had insulted in Central Park. He was barely a man at that time. Indecisive, self-absorbed, and slightly unhinged. This version of Tal projected confidence. And, she blushingly realized, he seemed more interested in her. But there was something else about him.

"You were expecting Cornelius," Tal said.

"You know him?"

"Intimately. We've known each other as long as I can remember. Mind if I sit down?"

She looked around awkwardly.

"I know he won't mind a bit."

How would Tal have possibly known about Van Denton? Unless... "Are you the one who referred Van Denton? Very kind of you." He just smiled. There was no nicer way to say thank you than a client referral.

"He's my oldest friend. I won't keep you long. Just until he arrives."

Lucinda turned her head slightly. No one was coming.

"I'm sure you have a thousand questions—"

"I'm so sorry, Tal. If you're staying in town, perhaps we can arrange to meet and catch up. I'm here for a few days."

"Let me just tell you one childhood story, so you can understand Cornelius," he said.

"All right." She was having trouble dealing with the rush of emotions and she would need a few minutes to settle before Van Denton arrived. Best to listen and gather her composure.

"I was an only child, but Cornelius was always around until I was shipped off to boarding school in second grade. When I returned home for summer break, he was gone. Moved away. So I was alone until my brother was born. Baby Jeffrey was a 'surprise.' A gift I never expected. Then he died unexpectedly. I was lost. Convinced Jeffrey's death was my fault—"

"I'm sorry. You've never spoken of him."

"Until Australia I couldn't. I was twelve years old. Back at home, between boarding schools. Mother had me babysitting." Tal paused as if to gather himself. His eyes were glistening. "It happened in an instant. He fell and cut himself seriously. Maybe I wasn't paying close enough attention. My memories are brief flashes. Just like that, my brother was gone." Tal dabbed at his eyes. "One thing I learned in Australia. It's okay to cry."

"It is okay, Tal." She wanted to reach out and touch his hand that was resting on the table.

"Mother couldn't deal with it and you know my father. I had no one to share my grief with. Or my guilt. Until Cornelius returned. The only person who was there whenever I reached the nadir. He knew what I was thinking without my having to speak, shared the loneliness, absorbed my guilt." He stopped and allowed her eyes to search deep into his. Allowed her to understand Cornelius: who he was and when he would be arriving.

A white-coated waiter appeared out of nowhere with a serving tray. "*Bienvenue*, Monsieur Van Denton, nice to have you back with us. I've brought your usual. Cranberry and soda, as well as a glass of champagne for you, mademoiselle, if it is to your taste."

Lucinda nodded. The waiter set down the glasses and disappeared. It was a good moment not to speak.

"So I am now Van Denton. At least as far as the hotel is concerned. Talem Neilson is not ready to admit to the world that he is back, at least not yet. I apologize for misleading you. Hopefully you don't mind?"

"Well, n-no, of course not," she stammered.

She suddenly wished her outfit was a little less businesslike. She usually tried to project good business sense, particularly in meetings with prospective clients. But this was Tal. New Tal. His shoulders were fuller, pushing out from under the shirt. His tanned face spoke of someone who had been spending plenty of time outdoors.

The biggest difference was his eyes. She had never really noticed them before. In her first few meetings with him, he had projected such uncertainty and inexperience. His head had hung low and most of the time his sunglasses hid the mess hovering behind them. This evening he was projecting a confidence and purpose. His eyes sparkled.

"Tal, before you say anything, I need to apologize. Those things I said to you in Central Park. Completely out of line and unprofessional."

"I had a lot of time to think while I was in Australia. The staff at Serenity really forced me to confront myself. What you said was harsh." He paused and sipped his soda.

"I know that and—"

"Please let me finish. What you said was also completely true. I was out of control. In such bad shape. I wasn't looking after me. You were the only person who cared enough to hold up the mirror. You were a friend. There's nothing to forgive. You saved me."

He raised his glass and waited for her to follow suit with her flute. "To you, Lucinda."

She lowered her gaze hoping he would not notice the blush that was burning her cheeks. She sipped the champagne. Talk about acting like a professional? She felt like a schoolgirl.

Tal leaned in, resting his forearms on the table. His hands were clasped. "I know I've caught you by surprise and I apologize for the cloak and dagger. I'm sure you're wondering why I asked you to come up here."

Lucinda nodded.

"I needed every day of the year I spent in Australia to turn myself around. I also met someone there who gave me new purpose. Let's order some dinner and I'll tell you all about it."

As Tal went on to tell her about Lorenzo and their work in Australia, Lucinda absorbed his passion. Tal hardly touched his dinner. She didn't eat much herself. She was having trouble handling the butterflies in her stomach.

"The point is, Lucinda, you took a risk; you gambled your career to rescue me, you found a rehab program on the other side of the planet. You cared. I owe you more than words can say. I needed to thank you in person."

He reached across the table, pushing the glassware out of the way, and touched her hand, slowly taking it in his. She felt the blood rushing up from her wrist through her heart and to her neck.

"I'm not really hungry. Judging from your plate, you're not either. Why don't we get out of here?" he finally said.

They walked the narrow *ruelles* of Vieux Montréal in the moonlight. She knew she was crossing the line once again and she no longer cared. Maybe a relationship with Tal was more valuable than managing him as a client. The well-lit streets were reminiscent of the romantic alleyways she'd strolled in Venice. Many of the buildings were one or two stories, once homes to the merchants who built Montreal as the business center of the New World centuries ago. Now the interiors had been renovated and housed an assortment of sumptuous restaurants, stationery stores, printing houses, coffee houses, jazz bars, and *boîtes à chansons*, the bars where locals gathered to sing along to their favorite folk songs or Quebec rock anthems.

The streets were teeming with tourists, and the mood was festive in Place Jacques Cartier, where couples were sitting at small white-painted metal tables in the middle of the square, nursing their drinks. Tal strolled beside her as if it was the most natural thing in the world. Her head was at his shoulder level. She noticed the six-pointed star hanging around his neck on a thin gold chain. How had she missed it in the restaurant?

"Where did you get the necklace, Tal?"

"The chain is a long story. The pendant, a parting gift from Lorenzo. He told me it belonged to his grandfather. A sign that he intended to stay close to me."

"So why Montreal? Why didn't you come back to Manhattan?" Lucinda asked.

"The deal I've been working on with Lorenzo is based here. We've assembled a team to work on a bid for a Canadian-based pharma company," Tal said. He turned his head left and right then leaned in and whispered, "Roylache is the name of the company," as if that might mean something to her.

"Following in your father's footsteps? How big is the company?"

"Four hundred million market cap. Publicly listed in Canada and New York."

Not exactly a modest dip of the toe in the water. "You're going to be competing with your mother? Does she have any idea?"

"I don't think she ever discovered I was in rehab. There was no communication from the outside world. Just a single note from Manhattan police to get in touch to answer some questions when I returned."

It would not have been difficult for Homeland to trace him. Maybe they began with a trip to Rosen's clinic. A conversation with Nurse

Guilden concerning the release a few days before Red King's death. The police never called Lucinda. She wouldn't have told them in any event. The steps she took for Tal were confidential. But how big a leap would it be to check with the airlines around the night of the death? She was no criminal law expert, but they must have their ways of getting hold of the passenger manifests.

"After what she did to me with Dr. Rosen, I'll bet she was happy enough that I had disappeared. Problem solved. I want my return to remain a secret for as long as possible. That's another reason I'm not returning to Manhattan. Not yet. I need to stay off Mother's radar."

Tal was smiling broadly now. Not at all the man she remembered. The immaturity and uncertainty had washed out of him, leaving a tall, confident warrior. Ready to do battle. Perhaps ready to do other things.

"How are you funding this? You only have the twenty million in your trust account, and your stock in Danmark isn't liquid, with all the voting trust restrictions."

"To date, Lorenzo has provided all the seed financing but I now need to reimburse him for my share of the costs. You do remember who controls the purse strings to my trust fund, right?"

"And that's why you had me come to Montreal." Her stomach dropped. The bubble of joy hissed out of the puncture in the balloon. She backed away and turned to face him. He knew she had to evaluate him in person to clear the trust funds. She was such a fool.

Lucinda nodded, hardened her voice. "You understand the conditions of your father's will. I have to review a series of expert reports confirming you're clean before I can release any funds from your legacy."

"I have the monthly test results certified by a local lab. I'll leave them for you in an envelope at the hotel."

"I invested the twenty million prudently and the income generated covered the costs of your stay in Australia. The fund is basically intact. There are a few formalities I will need to follow before funds can be transferred to your name. Shouldn't take more than a week or two."

"I trust you, Lucinda. I just need to start the process."

Tal told her about Lorenzo's investment bank and their offer to finance the entire deal.

"If I'm going to do this, I need skin in the game. My twenty million is nowhere near enough."

"You understand the voting trust, Tal. You can't trade the stock and because of that you can't use the stock as collateral for a loan. You would need your mother's agreement."

"I have no clue how to make that happen. Particularly to buy a company she wants. Lorenzo is more optimistic. His family has called on an expert to meet us tomorrow to discuss the problem. Lorenzo tells me he's a legal magician but I don't know what to believe. I want you to join me as my eyes and ears."

"At your service." Lucinda buried the sigh deep inside along with her feelings.

CHAPTER 26

The large boardroom at the law offices of Ferguson Beliveau in Montreal provided a panoramic view of Mount Royal. Tal stood at the window looking out from the forty-first floor, pondering what Samuel de Champlain must have been thinking centuries ago when his French boats made their way across the ocean and down the St. Lawrence River to carve a New World settlement out of the base of this mountain. Perhaps it was not unlike what Father and Grandfather felt when the family emigrated from their temporary abode in Sweden to a strange new world in America.

Lorenzo had arrived a few minutes earlier and was readying the boardroom table. A half dozen small binders were set out. The cover page was filled with the navy and maroon trademark for Roylache.

Lucinda entered with Tal, and Lorenzo brought them over to three men engrossed in a conversation about hockey. They looked up expectantly.

"I'd like to introduce our host, Guy Tremblay," he said to Tal, "the head of Ferguson's securities team. And this is his partner, Robert Rousseau. They're among the best in the city and will provide us the Canadian legal advice we need on buying the target."

"Pleased to meet you both," Tal said, shaking hands.

The third man, a tall African American about Tal's height and age, extended his hand to Tal. "Odell Moore," he said warmly.

"Don't let Odell's youthful appearance mislead you," Tremblay said. "He already has a reputation as one of America's leading M and A specialists. Everyone in Canada knows him."

"Probably because I played football at McGill," Odell said.

"The Canadian who made it big in New York," Rousseau added in his heavy French accent.

Lorenzo stepped over to introduce himself. "Glad you could make it up here on such short notice, Mr. Moore."

"My father was Mr. Moore." He didn't make it sound like the joke that most people used in the situation. "Please call me Odell. And your family is a legend in European investment banking. How could I refuse your uncle's request?"

They took their seats around the boardroom table. Lorenzo nodded at the five people around the table.

"I've taken the liberty of preparing a summary that outlines what we know about the target, Roylache,"

Rousseau interrupted. "The correct pronunciation is not Roy. It's more like the French word for king." He rolled the r and sounded it out. R'wah. "It loosely translates to something like the dastardly king."

"Some translate it as cowardly," Tremblay added. "There's a story behind the name, if no one minds that I digress. It will give you all some insight into the local market."

"We might as well understand the history of the company," Tal said.

Tremblay continued. "When the famous Montreal goaltender, Patrick Roy, got traded to the Colorado Avalanche, it was a national day of mourning in Quebec. Emotions ran very high. People were marching in the streets. Some were furious with management."

"Others, like me," Rousseau said, "felt Roy was a traitor. He was embarrassed the night the coach pulled him from the net in the middle of a period and demanded to be traded. Then Colorado went on to win the Stanley Cup. The company was still privately owned at the time. The owner was a passionate Canadiens fan and memorialized the day by changing the name of the company. Just a little trivia."

Lorenzo continued. "Roylache" — now properly pronounced — "trades in New York and Toronto. We're not the only ones interested. Danmark is also rumored to be a suitor."

"I did some homework on the plane," Odell said. He turned to Tal. "Don't you own ten percent of Danmark?"

"Correct," Lucinda said. "Tal and his mother hold their stock through a voting trust. The trust prohibits using the stock as collateral for a loan— "

"Sorry, Lucinda," Lorenzo interrupted. "You're getting a little ahead of our agenda."

"I don't think so," Tal said. "That is why we called you, Odell. I'm prepared to sell the stock or use it as collateral, but as Lucinda explained, right now I can't. So I have this— " Tal stopped speaking mid-sentence. He reached up and touched his nose, then closed his eyes.

"Were you going to complete that thought?" Lorenzo asked.

Father always rubbed his nose and pushed back the blue bifocals just before he expressed the epiphany. But why the sudden flash to Father, Tal wondered. Of course, it was all so obvious. He could not be sure whether he completed the formulation of the thought before the words burst out of his mouth. "So our strategy to buy Roylache requires us to convince Mother to break the trust."

Odell looked over at Lorenzo. "I know what you're probably thinking," Lorenzo said. "Why doesn't our family bank just lend Tal the money against the day when he can sell the shares? My father has offered—"

"But I won't hear of it," Tal interjected. "My father instilled in me the need to stand on my feet and do it myself. Maybe it's my time in rehab and my aversion to dependency. I might consider it, but only as a last resort." Tal turned back toward Odell. "That's why we've asked you to help."

"Getting your mother to terminate the voting trust may prove to be a challenge," Odell said.

"My family would not have called you without any ammunition," Lorenzo said. He pulled a folder from his briefcase and pushed it across the table to Odell.

Odell flipped open the folder and studied the first couple of pages. "The Turk. That's why you called me, isn't it?"

"Yes," Lorenzo said. "Sterling Yildirim, or the Turk as you call him, owns over a third of Roylache, and a few months ago he made an SEC filing confirming he now owns more than ten percent of Danmark."

"There is no buying Roylache without his approval," Tal said. "Given his holdings in Danmark, we know he's developed more than a passing interest. He is now among the three largest shareholders along with Mother and me. We also know Danmark has an interest in Roylache and may be competing with us to buy it."

"Both companies have dropped in value in the past year and a half," Lorenzo added.

Lorenzo had explained his theory to Tal a few weeks ago. It was possible that the Turk was thinking of a merger of the two companies, a move that might make him a lot of money. But he was no expert on Sterling Yildirim. They needed to hire one. Lorenzo had shown Tal the press clippings of the battles between Moore and Yildirim, which had become legendary in the print media over the last few years. They had even debated one another on CNBC.

"Merger, management shakeup. It's all right out of his playbook," Odell said. "We've opposed each other on three deals in the past four years. He's every bit as powerful as Carl Icahn, perhaps among the top five shareholder activists in America."

"At least 'activists' is what they like to call themselves," Lucinda cut in. "They're more like pirates."

Moore gave her a sharp look. "Not all of them. Even the Turk. If he finds a company badly managed, he'll replace management, though sometimes he has to go to war to displace them. A number of the CEOs in his portfolio swear up and down that he's helped them make their companies stronger. Others detest him. Sometimes he buys in low, stays in for a while and gets out for the best offer. He defines winning as making buckets of money for his investors. Sometimes it's slow and steady and in other cases it's shock attack."

Lorenzo spoke up. "We need a strategy to accomplish our two goals. Get Yildirim onside to sell us Roylache and break up the voting trust so Tal can either sell his stock or borrow against it. Are we asking too much?"

Odell sat for a long time without speaking. "One step at a time. First, we have to let the Turk convince himself that merging the two companies is not as smart as going whole hog after just Danmark. But we have to lead him to an idea that he comes up with on his own, to serve his own purpose. Breaking the voting trust has to be his idea."

Lucinda began nodding. "Brilliant. But can you pull it off, Odell?"

"Hold on," Tal said. "How does the Turk convince Mother to let me sell my shares."

Odell stroked his square jaw. "If he owns more than ten percent of Danmark, he and your mother have been talking. If we put the right idea in his head, he can figure out the rest."

"You're guessing, monsieur?" Rousseau asked.

"I don't guess." Odell's tone turned brusque. "I'm next to certain. I know Yildirim's playbook inside out. There is no question they are having discussions. We just need to come up with a plan to convince Yildirim that it's in his interest to pursue Danmark." Odell turned towards Tal. "Then we let him work his magic on your mother." Five heads around the table nodded.

"Can you do this for me? For us?" Tal asked. There was no masking his excitement.

"He won't negotiate with me," Odell said. "He considers me the enemy. The minute I walk through the door he'll assume I have an angle. There is a way of doing it, but it can't involve me." Odell stopped once more and let the silence fill the room.

Tal looked around the table. Who was going to try to open the door with the Turk? He felt a new pressure building. All eyes were on him. He'd done all the homework, studied the numbers, and had a sense of what had to be accomplished. But to go meet with Sterling Yildirim? The Turk was famous for tearing business leaders apart limb from limb. Here he was, Daniel about to agree to enter the lion's den.

No one spoke.

"If you prep me, I'll meet with him." Tal had broken the silence. The spoiled heir to the house of CallMeGeri, confronting the Turk. An epic mismatch. He took a deep breath and slowly released it. Then he smiled. If he could pull this off, he would have his financing. He didn't know how it would work, but Odell must have figured this out. If he could pull this off, the final strings by which Mother controlled him would be cut forever.

Odell outlined all of his thoughts and they spent the next hour refining the plan until Odell rose from his chair, signaling the end of the meeting.

"I get it," Tal concluded. "This is all about misdirection and manipulation."

"I have confidence in you," Lorenzo said.

"Good luck, Tal," Odell said. "Think of it as a game of high-stakes poker. When the moment comes, play the player."

How had Daniel done it? Tal wondered. *"The higher power, Son."*

CHAPTER 27

Mac Micolonides sat back in his captain's chair at the kitchen table, deep into his Sunday morning routine. He had finished the sports section of the Sunday *Times* and was sipping absently from his specially prepared coffee: two-thirds Mediterranean-ground blend that Jennifer picked up fresh for him every Saturday, one-third milk heated in the microwave for exactly twenty-five seconds, half a pack of Splenda, and his secret ingredient: exactly two teaspoons of his homemade ouzo, splashed into the mug — a reminder of why Sunday was unlike any other day of the week. A couple of hours to himself. Jennifer was puttering around at the other end of the kitchen, preparing lunch for her three "boys." The twins were out at hockey practice, building up ravenous appetites.

Mac put down the paper for a moment to watch Jennifer move. Not quite Greek goddess but close enough. She wasn't aging, just ripening into her forties. She might be a little rounder than when he first met her fifteen years ago, and she did a regular touch-up of the gray that was beginning to overrun her hair. He liked that she still wore it long, below her shoulders. She had not bothered to tie it up yet and it looked morning wild, reminding him how much he still wanted her. The kitchen was the center of Jennifer's universe, and Mac marveled at her ability to manage. She looked as comfortable as he felt at the station.

He turned back to the *Times*. Curiously, the Lifestyle section was doing another feature on the car that Red King had crashed a year and a half ago as a part of the story on his estate's specialty cars. The widow was about to auction the entire collection through Sotheby's in two sessions: one in New York and the other in Rome. The story reminded Mac of how unsatisfying the investigation had been. Everything pointed to a tragic accident, probably caused by a fainting spell behind the wheel. King's sugar level was low. He'd fainted and crashed.

It was tough to figure how it might be homicide. Had the crazy son been around, they would have checked out his alibi. Homeland had tracked Tal Neilson to a rehab facility in Western Australia, and given the timing of the flight from JFK, he had a small window of opportunity. There was no way Mac or Obie was getting a travel allowance to cross the planet for what looked like an accident. There also was not much value in having the Aussies question him. Even if he had no alibi for the two-hour window, it was almost impossible to imagine a scenario explaining how the son could have pulled it off, crazy or not.

Mac had some reservations, however. King had driven through a series of pylons and hit the concrete wall on the bridge with considerable force, possibly between sixty and eighty miles per hour. Would a fainting man be pushing up the speed on the accelerator? Besides this was a standard transmission car. The gears were shifted by way of hand paddle rather than by foot clutch and stick shift — but when he fainted his foot would be more likely to slip off the gas pedal. It was a pretty low probability that his foot would put more pressure on the gas to increase the speed to crash velocity. And how did he change gears? Why did the car crash instead of stalling? There was an answer to the riddle. The medical examiner theorized that perhaps he hadn't fainted. Maybe he was depressed, though the widow had ruled out clinical depression. The M.E. finally concluded the death was accidental. There was insufficient evidence to rule it suicide.

"A drachma for your thoughts, detective." Jennifer had appeared as if out of nowhere and was now standing behind him and had bent over to nuzzle his neck.

He leaned back in the kitchen chair, pushing the back of his head into her cheek. "Where did you come from, Jen?"

"The moussaka is in the oven. I have a few minutes before the wolves descend. I thought I'd come over and pay my husband some attention, but it looks to me like something is bothering you."

Mac was used to sharing his thoughts on cases with the only two people in his life whom he considered to be his partners. Obie and Jennifer. Obie was his partner in solving the case. Jennifer was his partner in solving himself. She never offered advice — just listened. She called him out when he was lying to himself or failing to notice something sitting right in front of his nose, but she understood that most often, Mac just needed to hear his own voice.

"It's another mystery. Case of a two-time widow in six months. One ruled natural causes. The other a car crash. And the husbands were both wealthy. Really wealthy."

"So you're ruling out that the black widow was in it for the insurance?" Jennifer laughed. "Sometimes the ones caught in that lifestyle are swimming in debt. At least in the movies."

"This one was rich as god before the first one died so I don't think that's the case. High society woman. Trudi Darrow."

"That one. She's had a run of bad luck, hasn't she? I know her name from my chapter of the Literacy Society. She's helped raise so much money to teach inner city kids to read. If I remember, she also lost a baby years ago. Tragic."

A moment later Mac heard the crash at the front door.

"The elephant herd has arrived. Shut the computer and help me fend them off until lunch is ready. I hate it when they go raiding my fridge fifteen minutes before I'm ready to serve."

"We're home," the twins shouted in unison.

They arrived in the kitchen together. The twins dropped their hockey bags at the front door, and each was sucking on a straw attached to a large red container with a green dragon emblazoned across the side.

Jennifer did not waste a moment. "How many times have I told you guys that those bags are a fire hazard! Get them out of my sight. Into the basement."

The two boys turned tail.

"Whoa, both of you. Do not take another step," Jennifer ordered. Mac smiled. The general barking out orders. This was her turf and she was the undisputed boss.

"Oh, hi, Mom. We'll get on the bags right away," Terry said. Evan nodded. "We're starved." Good attempt at deflection, Mac thought.

"What is that crap you're drinking?"

"It's the newest drink — they were giving out samples at the arena. It's got twice the caffeine boost of a Red Bull. One of the kids says it gives you way more energy on the ice."

"That poison does not enter my kitchen. Down the drain with it. Then go get rid of your bags."

"Mom, you're being unreasonable," Terry said. Clearly the more daring of the two. "It's not like it's going to kill us."

"You never know what may kill you when you put it in your body. Out now. You're eight years old, for goodness' sakes." The boys headed to the kitchen sink and began pouring the green liquid down the drain.

"You never know what might kill you when you put it in your body," Mac mumbled reflectively. That was as good a place as any to start.

■ ■ ■

Mac and Obie paid an early visit to the medical examiner on Monday morning. Mariella Cabrerra was sitting behind her desk sipping from a large coffee cup. A two-inch-thick file was sitting open and her head was down. Her gray hair was tied up in a ponytail, which probably meant she was getting ready for the next autopsy.

A single print, framed, was hanging on the wall over her desk. It looked to Mac like an Escher — a castle with a series of staircases winding around the structure. If you looked carefully enough, none of the staircases connected. Yet the brain was tricked into believing that the impossible made sense.

Mac was certain Mariella knew they were standing there waiting to be invited in. Finally he cleared his throat.

"Interesting case came up last night," she said without bothering to look up or acknowledge the guests standing in the doorway. "They dredged a body out of the East River. Pretty bloated. Must have been there for quite a while. My guess is we'll be solving someone's missing person case in the next few days."

"You have five minutes?" Obie asked.

"For you, sugar pie, any time. Not your partner, though. He's still a kid. Needs to learn how to deal with me."

Obie reached into his jacket pocket and pulled out a Three Musketeers bar. He slid it across her desk and laid it on the file she was still absorbed in. "For the only woman I love."

With that she looked up. "What can I do for you, Romeo?" she said with a wicked smile.

"It's about the autopsy you conducted over a year and a half ago. Claude King. Big-shot pharmaceutical guy," Obie said.

"Oh, yeah, the crash victim. Brooklyn Bridge. Very fancy sports car. Burned to a crisp."

"Can you gimme the report once more. It's been bugging my partner."

She pushed her way past them and headed for the cabinets down the corridor. She returned with a file with a green label for cases not ruled homicides.

"I remember now. High-speed crash. Very low levels of sugar in the blood. Diabetic. Either took too much insulin or was on a sugar low while driving. Regardless, he passed out." It looked like she was doing this from memory as she had not stopped flipping pages. Mac was becoming accustomed to Mariella's staccato approach to communication. Short shotgun blasts of information. She never let emotion or sentence structure impede her. He wondered how well that translated to her social life.

She finally found the page she wanted. She showed him a graph. "A downward spike in the sugar level."

"A diabetic, driving toward the country, who forgot to get his carbs?" Mac asked.

"I analyze the body, Mac, not the state of mind," Mariella said. "You guys and the shrinks figure that stuff out. Here, have fun." She thrust the file at him.

"I appreciate it," Mac said.

"You know, Obie," she said to his back as the two detectives were walking away, "just because there's a staircase it doesn't mean it leads anywhere."

"My life and my time, Mariella," Obie said.

■ ■ ■

They returned to their desks, facing one another as they had for years. Mac loosened his tie and sat on the edge of his desk. Obie took his seat behind the desk and leaned back.

"Don't we have enough work without taking on a case that's been ruled accidental?" Obie asked. It wasn't a question so much as a reproach. Mac had learned to read that tone. "You youngsters have all the energy in the world. Go get 'em, tiger," Obie teased.

Mac flipped open the file on his lap. "Just stay with me for a few minutes. Something has been bugging me. Red King is the CEO of a major drug company. He's been dealing with his diabetes for fifteen years." Mac finally found the page he was searching for. "Here," he said thrusting it over to Obie's desk. "The photo."

"Yeah. A burned-up remnant of a few needles. So what?"

"They found them in the charred remains of the carpet on the floor of the car. The guy's diabetic so probably an insulin needle, no?"

"Okay, so we have a needle. Suggests to me that maybe he tried to inject but not in time," Obie said.

"But he wouldn't be injecting if he felt weak. He'd be drinking a can of juice or pulling over to get some sugar. Insulin does just the opposite. It lowers the blood sugar. Maybe he got confused. Except the guy is a CEO of a drug company. Somebody like that doesn't make that kind of mistake."

"I see where you're heading. A high-class guy doesn't toss used needles on the floor of his million-dollar sports car. So how did they get there?" Obie asked. "Too many questions and not enough answers."

"And that's why I couldn't sleep last night."

"Listen, Mac, when married guys can't sleep it's cuz they haven't schtupped in a month. That slows down any man's capacity to reason. Too much testosterone buildup. You start thinking with your pecker."

"What?"

"You know what schtupping is?"

"You think because I'm Greek I don't know. Everyone knows."

"No. I think because you're married with kids, maybe you forgot how. Are you getting it?"

"I don't kiss and tell."

"You're not. That's why you can't solve this case. Your pecker's probably fallen off."

Mac slid into his chair and continued leafing through the file. One of these pages was going to trigger the key insight they were both missing. After about half an hour, he slammed the file shut and reached for his New York Giants mug sitting just out of reach on the corner of his desk.

"You and your pistachios." Obie reached out and grabbed a handful, then pushed the mug across to Mac's outstretched arm.

"There's nothing in the file." Mac was certain they had missed something. The pistachios relaxed him. Helped him think. He shucked a shell with his teeth and tongue and sucked off the salt. He enjoyed the rush, momentarily. No amount of salt was going to satisfy this craving. He spit the shells into the wastebasket.

"You and your effing nuts. How did I get you as my partner? I teach you everything I know and you spit like that?"

"Who do you think I learned from?"

"Let me see the file," Obie said. "Where's the tox report?"

"There's nothing in it."

"Where's the tox report?" Obie repeated.

"Two-thirds of the way through. But there's nothing in it, I keep telling you."

"That's my point," Obie said simultaneously, except now he was talking over him. Obie pushed the chair away from the desk. "Follow me for a moment, would you please," he said, taking off at a brisk pace. Mac followed, surprised that he had to struggle to keep up. This was double Obie's normal speed these days.

"They found the needle in the car wreckage," Obie said, breathing a little heavily. "No proof as to when it was used."

"Correct."

"We assumed the syringe was filled with insulin. He carried a small supply with him at all times."

"Correct again."

"What if the syringe was filled with something else?"

"Wouldn't that show up on the tox screen?"

"Let's find out."

Mac was beginning to understand where Obie was heading. Trudi Darrow's missing son. Could he have been in the car? Could he have injected King with some other drug that killed him? Wasn't he in a hospital before he disappeared? There was no shortage of drugs he might have had access to steal.

Obie suddenly slowed the pace, holding his stomach. "Walk slower, boychick. I got to slow this down to a schlepper's pace."

They'd taken the *schlep* countless times together.

■ ■ ■

Obie didn't bother knocking. Just stuck his head in the doorway. Mac stood just behind him. Mariella's head was covered with a hairnet, as she focused on her computer screen. She held up her left hand in a stop sign position then continued to type furiously on the keyboard. Obviously trying to catch some vitally important thought. Perhaps something that came to her after she had dictated her audio notes of the autopsy.

She looked up from her screen after two minutes.

"You're interrupting."

"Ya, so?" Obie said.

"That's why I love you so much. You're a bigger prick than me," she said.

"Better to be a prick than a schmuck," Obie said.

"Do you want us to come back?" Mac asked. Someone should show some manners.

"Would it matter if I did?"

This was a part of their shorthand that Mac still couldn't grasp after so many years. Puerto Rican versus Bronx Jew. A form of humor that escaped the Greeks. Irony, Mac could understand. But not this.

"We have a few questions," Obie said.

"So just get to them."

Obie opened the file to the toxicology report and slid it across the table.

"Is there any way Claude King could have been poisoned without it showing up on this report?"

"Sure. Injectable or oral."

"Let's go with injectable for starters," Obie said.

"One comes to mind immediately..." Mariella paused. "Succinylcholine. Anesthesiologists call it Sux. Causes short-term paralysis. Hospitals use it to intubate patients. In high enough doses, it causes paralysis."

"That sucks," Obie crowed. "Sorry, couldn't help myself."

"Yes, you could but no, you didn't. Leave your terrible puns outside my door next time you want a favor."

Mariella turned to Mac. "Let's just ignore the boor. Takes about forty-five seconds, sometimes faster. Terrible way to die. The vic is completely aware of everything going on. That is, until he can't breathe anymore. And unable to do a thing about it."

"Wouldn't that show up on a tox screen?" Obie asked.

"Probably not. The compound metabolizes quickly. Becomes succinic acid and choline. Both normally found in the body. Ever hear of Krebs cycle? They teach this stuff in high school."

"I was sick that day," Obie said.

"Maybe your partner has a little more education." Mariella looked at Mac. "It's rare that we'd find Sux in the bloodstream, though we might find slightly elevated levels of its two components, which are found naturally in the body. Really easy to miss. Especially when there's a more likely explanation for the death. In this case, low blood sugar, diabetes, faint behind the wheel, die. We don't look further."

"I just want to know if the following theory is plausible. What if King injected himself with the syringe believing it was insulin when in fact someone swapped it out for this Sux stuff?" Mac asked.

Mariella sat back in her chair and put her feet up on the desk.

"Hmm. Nope. Insulin needles are subcutaneous. Just need to get below skin level. Your average insulin needle is a twenty-four or twenty-five gauge, so thin that you can't even feel the needle going in. And it's about this long." She raised her hand and spread her thumb and forefinger to less than an inch. "To get a dose of succinylcholine to work effectively, you'd need a needle at least this big." Her fingers spread to more than double the length. "And the gauge would be around eighteen to twenty, a much thicker and longer needle. The injection would be IM," she mused.

"IM?" Mac asked.

"Intramuscular. For the appropriate dosage to work, it would have to be injected into the thigh."

Obie got up from the chair. "Sorry to waste your time."

"Humor me, Obie," Mac protested. "I just have a couple more questions. What if you were sitting in the passenger seat of a car?"

"Remember that scene in *Pulp Fiction*?" Mariella asked.

"Where Travolta jams the monster-size epinephrine needle into the heart?" Obie said. "Grossest scene in film history."

"Yeah. You need force to jam it in. Same for the IM into the thigh from a passenger seat. The driver would see it coming from a mile off... unless..." Mariella grabbed a pencil off the desk and came around and sat to Mac's right in the visitor chair that Obie had abandoned. She wrapped her left hand around the pencil and made a hammer-fist, hiding all but the tip. Then she jammed the outside of her fist with the point of the pencil into Mac's leg and pushed the eraser with her thumb.

"Ouch," he yelled.

"That's how you'd do it, Ninja style." She smirked. "Of course, it doesn't explain how the killer gets out of the car, or how the car would accelerate to 80 MPH with the driver paralyzed. Try and figure out how to write that movie scene."

Mariella made no effort to suppress the self-satisfied smile. "Besides, an injection of the drug would leave a huge welt on the victim. It would be obvious in the autopsy. No M.E. could miss it."

"Unless the victim was burned to a crisp?" Obie said.

"Forgot that part," Mariella confessed.

Mac's leg burned with pain. He wasn't limping out without some small victory.

"So maybe it's not Sux. Could it be some other drug?" Mac asked.

"It's theoretically possible. Sux was just one example."

"Then can you please humor me and take another look at your work?" Mac asked.

Mariella sighed. "Only since you asked politely. I'll go back, check the tissue samples. It'll take a couple of days. I'm backed up to my eyeballs right now."

Obie walked slowly out the door, Mac limping behind him.

"If the tox review shows nothing, I'll give up," Mac said, once they were halfway down the hall. "You'll never hear about the stupid Ferrari again."

Obie didn't bother to turn around. "You mean *when* the tox screen shows nothing. And even if some drug comes up, I can't imagine any scenario where Tal Neilson is the killer."

"I'm prepared to agree. Doesn't mean it wasn't someone else."

"Dream on partner."

CHAPTER 28

Tal Neilson stepped off the elevator into the reception area of Amygdala Investments. The furniture was understated, just three unobtrusive beige couches surrounding a glass coffee table. Not what you would expect from the offices of one of the greatest investment minds in the world, but the reason was immediately obvious. The floor-to-ceiling windows on the fifty-seventh floor looked out over the entire breadth and depth of Central Park. The autumn golds, browns, and oranges seen from above against the backdrop of a bright midafternoon sun set a breathtaking panorama. This was not just prime Manhattan real estate; it was the single most expensive office building in the city.

Odell had warned him to expect to be kept waiting for his two-thirty appointment with the chairman. Just like he had predicted that the Turk would make him wait weeks for the appointment. He imagined that ten minutes was the correct protocol for a self-absorbed billionaire who needed to show just the proper level of disrespect for the son of a deceased billionaire. He'd already made Tal wait six weeks. Less than that might suggest an eagerness to find out why Tal would have called to set up this meeting. Had Tal not been the son of CallMeGeri Neilson, he might never have gotten the meeting. The protocol of wealth required an obligatory meeting. Anything else would be a show of weakness, and Sterling Yildirim, the Turk, never revealed a hint of vulnerability.

At exactly 2:44 the receptionist ushered him into a small boardroom. The elegant mahogany table and six brown leather chairs allowed the Whistler portrait on the long wall to define the space. Not the artist's mother. Perhaps some other relative.

A moment later a tall man with slightly stooped shoulders walked into the room. His broad frame filled the doorway. He was sporting a tailored navy suit, which likely cost a small fortune, a silk dress shirt, a properly knotted tie, and his signature Yankees baseball cap. Odell had joked that he wasn't certain whether the Turk wore it as a statement about his investment philosophy or as a distraction from the large bald spot at the top of his head.

Tal stood up from the leather chair, back to the window, and they greeted one another warmly. Game on.

"I had a lot of respect for your father. He was one of my better investments. Talked circles around all my analysts. Knew the business better than anyone I ever met."

"I appreciate it. Thank you."

"But since he died, the company's been in a tailspin. Not good for either of us. Do you have any idea what your mother is up to?"

Was the question rhetorical? How much did Yildirim know about his relationship with Mother? Tal decided not to answer. He just shook his head slightly. The Turk shifted his gaze just over Tal's head and out to Central Park. As if he didn't care. Or possibly as if he already knew the answer. It had been less than five minutes and the Turk had already put him on the defensive.

The Turk refocused, then held out his hand and motioned Tal to take a seat facing the panoramic view. Odell had urged him not to rush to the point of the meeting. The Turk was the alpha male. "He won't be ready to listen until he's told you what he wants you to know about himself."

As if on cue from the voice in Tal's head, Yildirim began to speak. "You know how I came up with the name Amygdala?"

"No, sir."

"It's the part of the brain where emotion meets reason. The core center of investment behavior. As an activist investor, I have to mix fear with reason to create value. Fear. It's always at the root of power. If I can disrupt things just enough to unbalance my adversaries, and there are many, then my reason will always devastate their emotional responses."

"I guess it's working for you." Tal smiled.

The Turk laughed and switched gears again. "To what do I owe the honor?" Odell was right. The Turk had his own agenda and was going to stay in charge. Force Tal to get right to the point, so that the Turk could get to his.

It was time to play: deal the cards. "I'm assembling a group to take over Danmark. We have a detailed financial plan and I've come to begin a dialogue. I'm certain I can convince you to support my bid."

"You own how much of the company?"

"Ten percent."

"But it's tied up in that voting trust with your mother. The way I understand it, you can't do anything with your shares without her permission. And she now owns more than double your stake." The man had done his homework.

"Correct."

"So your shares are as good as useless."

Were the shares useless or was he really saying Tal was useless? Old feelings that he thought he'd put behind him in Australia.

"You can't sell them, you'll never find anyone to lend you money against them. Mama's got you by the proverbial balls."

"Not ex…act…ly." The words stammered their way out of Tal's mouth. The flop.

"Then what exactly?" The Turk did not bother to wait for an answer. He probably knew there was no answer. He was staring at the creases building on Tal's forehead. "Even if you had full control of your shares, when you add it to my stake in the company, we're still short of your mother's ownership. Do you know something I don't know, junior?"

"I figured we could mount a campaign together to buy out the shares of some of the disgruntled shareholders. Particularly the mutual funds."

"And why exactly are you qualified to run this company any better than your mother?"

Tal reached into his briefcase and pulled out a white folder. "I've studied the numbers carefully, with a detailed analysis of how we could improve sales and operating efficiency and if you'll permit me—"

"If I'll permit you? Are you kidding me? Don't you think I have a team of professionals going through these numbers every month, studying the industry, analyzing how we can improve management's performance? What's your experience in this industry other than being the son of the owner, who I might say was a great operator? Oh. I forgot, three years as a minion at the start of your career that dead-ended. You're no Geri Neilson."

"If you'll just give me a few minutes, I'll show you." Tal was using the right words, but projecting failure. The Turk had sniffed it out and was about to dismember the plan and Tal with it. About to bet his stack.

"Sure, you'll show me. Like I'm a stupid donkey." Yildirim brought his hands up to his ears and wiggled his elbows in the air. "Eee-yaw!" he blurted. Then he issued a scornful laugh. "Treat me like an ass, son, and I'll act like one. A bunch of hooey is what you'll show me. And where have you been for the last year and a half? Don't underestimate me, junior. I do my homework before I take a meeting. I have my own folder back in my office. You disappeared off the face of the earth, until I get this message that you want to meet. You think I don't know about the drug rehab? You abandoned the company even though your father probably begged you to learn the business from the bottom up. You didn't have the balls to stick it out."

"It's obvious I'm wasting my time."

Play the player. Tal closed his eyes and reached back to the moment in Red's office. The moment he'd been dismissed as less than nothing. His deepest humiliation relived in front of his eyes. The deep-set rage emerging as worthless frustration. The beginning of the end of his life. His arms began to vibrate, his eyes to mist, his face heating, his fingernails tearing into his palms on the board table. The turn.

"If you're here to talk me into some half-witted scheme because you have anger management issues with your mother, then yes, you're wasting your time. I know she locked you up. In your shoes I'd want to get even too, but don't for a moment think you're using me as a pawn in your little game of revenge. Go get some operating experience. Put in the time. Learn the business. Then maybe someone will take you seriously." Yildirim looked off into space, as if Tal was no longer in the room. Dismissed as the incompetent son.

The final play. The river. Tal hung his head, refusing to make any further eye contact. The right move at the right moment. He waited patiently until, out of the corner of his eye he caught the signal. Yildirim had fixed his gaze on Tal, hopefully ready to make his own move. Tal looked up.

"I'll tell you what, junior. You want some experience? I own a minority stake in a Canadian pharma company. Not really worth my time or effort. Ever hear of Roylache? If not, go do some homework."

"I know who they are. What about it?"

"I'll swap my stock for yours." The Turk, all in.

"How would that work? You just acknowledged I can't transfer my shares to anyone."

"I'm not anyone, junior."

"Besides what you're offering isn't close to what the stock is worth." Tal flashed an angry look.

"Take my offer, junior. It's the only one you're gonna see until mama dies. I'll deal with your mother and your voting trust problems. That has to be worth a premium."

"But—"

"Save your buts. I'll tell you what. Sleep on it." He stood up slowly as if his back had stiffened along with his temperament. "I'm withdrawing the offer at noon tomorrow. Sorry, but I have another meeting waiting for me."

Tal got up to leave, shoulders slumped, back to Yildirim, barely able to swallow back the emotion. He'd drawn the flush card on the river.

■ ■ ■

Tal stepped around the corner into the bright sunshine on Fifth Avenue and reached for his cell phone. He entered Odell's number.

"I just came out. Can you add Lorenzo to the call?"

Fifteen seconds later they were all connected.

"I played the player. He rose to the bait. How did you know it would work?"

"Nature of the beast," Odell replied. "You can't walk into the lair and ask for a favor. He has to be the one to dictate the terms. If he thinks you want Danmark then you can't have it. He needs to insult you by stripping it from you and offering the booby prize."

"The Turk has set awful economic terms," Tal said.

"But he offered to swap his stock in Roylache?" Lorenzo said.

"Exactly as Odell predicted. Except the terms are harsh."

"Now he's testing how well you stand up to insult," Odell said.

"When do I get back to him?"

"At eight a.m. tomorrow leave him a voice mail. Tell him you're not prepared to lose more than fifteen million on the swap. He'll settle off at twenty-five, but only if you close by noon."

"And you don't think Yildirim is going to be suspicious about all this?" Lorenzo asked.

"If I'm guessing correctly," Odell answered, "the Turk is focused on the prize. Control of Danmark. Tal is a means to that end. This is about focusing on his greed and presenting an opportunity for him to maneuver Tal's mother."

"And you really believe the Turk will go all-in?"

"We'll know in the morning," Odell said. "I've got a junior lawyer drafting the paperwork through the night."

CHAPTER 29

Trudi Darrow stood by the window of her suite at the Park Hyatt Hotel. The sun was peeking out over Lake Ontario to the southeast, shedding a pearly hue over the concrete monstrosity just to the west. Why build something so gaudy? A flying saucer impaled on a phallic symbol that would define Toronto forevermore. Geri probably would have loved it. And even if he hated it, he'd say at least the city's entrepreneurs had the balls to go with it. The only time she and Geri had ever visited the city together, the structure was just some frustrated builder's dream. Now, over a dozen construction cranes were perched atop various buildings, monsters sitting idle for now, getting their last few minutes of rest before the morning shift of yellow hard hats arrived.

Trudi had not been to Canada since the belated honeymoon in Niagara Falls. Just Trudi, Geri, and the growing fetus, pushing against her bladder. Toronto was only an hour and a half down the highway and they'd found a cheap hotel room in Yorkville, the hippie haven of the city. Ground zero of a new Canadian generation.

She smiled now at the recollection of having so little, being so young. At the time, however, she had not been smiling. At the time her life plan was ruined. Now, at last, she was about to recover it completely.

She had gone out for a short walk last night after she arrived, looking for the coffee houses, the grungy long-haired teenagers toking joints in the same neighborhood, and had been shocked by what awaited. Nothing was as she remembered it. The lobby of the hotel, just a block away from where they had stayed all those years ago, was crammed with women in shining necklaces and the latest in designer fashions on the arms of men in tight-fitting jackets, white T-shirts, and coordinated jeans. Tourists and locals, speaking a myriad of languages, crammed the streets. The neighborhood had been transformed into a tourist mecca, rivaling anything in Manhattan.

Toronto had also become a world financial center. By the time the bankers on Bay Street awoke tomorrow morning, they would learn why Trudi had made the trip north. She expected Wall Street would also be stunned. Sterling Yildirim had spoken to her last week, insisting that the two of them meet face to face today and it had to be in Toronto after his board meeting with the underperforming satellite company, as he dubbed it. He was headed to Europe tomorrow, so the window of opportunity might shut tonight. Sterling Yildirim — the Turk. The problem Red had left for her.

The Turk had developed a taste to acquire Danmark. All of it. Red had wanted to give it to him. The Turk must know that Trudi had blocked the sale. She could continue to fight to keep it for herself, but without control of Tal's stock, wherever the hell he was, she could not prevent the Turk from slowly amassing a big enough position to get rid of her. Particularly with the stock price not having yet recovered. The Turk was a problem for which there was only one possible solution. A negotiated peace agreement where they agreed to share power. As long as she remained as CEO with his support, she could figure out the rest.

The room service cart arrived precisely at eight. A pot of steaming mint tea; a tall glass of grapefruit juice; one perfectly poached egg, gleaming in the beam of sunlight, nestled on a slice of whole wheat toast, unbuttered. The yolk burst with the first thrust of her knife, golden perfection bleeding out slowly on to the plate. She closed her eyes and savored the morning in Toronto, the perfection of her life with the company, now her company, her first child, the only child she ever wanted, finally recovering from all those years of foster care. So much still left to accomplish. Thomas and Drew were scheduled to brief her in a couple of hours on their overnight progress in completing the most important deal of her career.

■ ■ ■

Thomas Leiden adjusted his reading glasses to review the draft agreement that Sterling Yildirim had sent over, with Drew's suggested changes. Geri would have cringed at the notion of holding a meeting with the Turk, but it was not Geri's company anymore. Would he be cringing at the fact that Trudi was in charge? Or perhaps admiring what she had pulled off?

Drew Torrance entered the meeting room in the Park Hyatt Hotel wearing his classic navy suit, powder-blue tie, and toothy grin. "Thomas, how is it that a man who understands people as well as you never shows emotion? Thirty-six years together and I can never tell what you're thinking."

Thomas laughed. "There's a first time for everything, Drew." Drew took his seat directly opposite Thomas. A waiter brought over a plate with pastries and a small pot of preserves and set it down in front of Drew.

"You're always at least one step ahead of me," Drew said.

"I don't have a big messy law firm to run. Just a few investments to manage. Besides at my age I have to get a head start. Every step hurts these days. Thank God for Danmark-naprox. Helps with the joint swelling. How's your firm's merger gone?"

"We have a few big announcements coming shortly. The pressure to continue this global law firm expansion means I put a lot of air under my wings."

"You should be proud of TGO," Thomas said. "I have a lot of respect for how far you've taken it."

"You better than anyone know how little I knew when we started. The firm has about four hundred lawyers right now. No end in sight. The two other name partners make me look like the conservative. They have this dream of taking over the world."

"We've all stretched a little from time to time."

Drew tore a strip off one of the croissants and loaded a heavy teaspoon of jam on top. "Can't curb my sweet tooth. Any word from Trudi about whether she'll accept the deal Yildirim proposed?"

"It will all be done today or it will all fall apart. Not sure which result is better."

"You know what it means for the two of us?"

"It's time."

"What about this Canadian company she wants to buy?"

"Won't matter after today. I'm sure it's off the table if she makes the deal."

Drew slowly rolled another strip of croissant into a ball and popped it in his mouth, chewed a few times with his hand covering his mouth, then swallowed hard. "Sorry. Breakfast. Have you heard anything today from Yildirim's people?"

"Not yet. I think the ball is in Trudi's court."

Thomas hoped that however it ended, the deal would finally resolve the conflict that had been raging within him ever since Tal went into rehab. The family credo: the vow always came first, superseding everything else. Which was the higher duty? His fiduciary relationship as a director of Danmark to act in the best interest of the company or his duty to Geri and now to Talem? Paul would argue the vow was holy, not simply a trans-generational duty to Geri and his progeny but a three-way pact with God. The God that had allowed Paul and his family to survive a life-threatening crossing from Denmark to Sweden, from hunted to accepted, from vermin to shining diamond.

Thomas at best doubted the existence of a god, and if he or she did exist, it was as a passive force in the universe. Another Dutchman had it all figured out. Hundreds of years ago, Spinoza postulated that very probability. The philosophy cost Spinoza his family, friends, and community as he was banished, cut off from the Jewish community that raised him and the Protestant community that tolerated all but a heretic. Thomas knew all about losing everything, being alone in the world as a child.

A week ago Lorenzo had advised him of the deal they had made with the Turk. Everything hinged on Trudi agreeing to terminate the voting trust. And that had to happen today.

Once Talem completed the sale of his stock to Yildirim, Thomas's obligations to Danmark could come to an end. Perhaps the last of his obligations under the vow. But he was getting ahead of himself. An agreement between Trudi and the Turk was by no means a certainty.

Yildirim had been stalking the company from the day Geri died, maybe even before that time. For four years, he had been slowly amassing a share interest in the company that now exceeded ten percent. That was often a signal that he was about to make some kind of move. A move that could improve the value of the company, but a move that could also take apart everything Geri had built. Perhaps he had been in secret discussions with Red. Since Trudi had moved into the CEO suite, Thomas had been wondering if and when the Turk would resurface. All the speculation ended when Yildirim called Thomas a few days ago.

"You're the lead director, Leiden," Yildirim had said. "I'm tired of sitting in the wings watching the new CEO impair my investment. The stock price has been sliding ever since Darrow took over. The son wants to sell me his stock in Danmark. I've given it some thought and I know I can help the company. I want you to help me make this happen."

Thomas had replied, "What do you want from me? This is between you and Trudi. You know very well that the son's stock is tied up in a voting trust with his mother."

"And you know I'm worth more to the company as an ally, someone with a say in the future of the company. I want you and Torrance to convince her. Once I'm on the team, I'll have the stock price turned around so fast the shareholders will all be whistling."

Thomas had two days to consider what Yildirim was proposing. While Talem's deal with the Turk was the prime objective, he wasn't so sure Yildirim could help Danmark — hence the conflict. The Turk had had some colossal successes, but one in four of his ventures flopped. Which one was Danmark destined to be? And how was Yildirim going to turn the market perception, that with Geri and Red gone, Danmark might be floundering? The business had undergone considerable change since Trudi was last involved over thirty years ago. The jury was still out as to whether she could adapt to current market conditions. Would he move to replace Trudi?

"Here's what I'm proposing," Yildirim said on the call. "First, Trudi needs to dissolve the voting trust. It's terrible governance to have any shares of a public company not freely traded. If I'm going to be a partner in building this company, there can't be a special set of rules for Trudi Darrow. I want Junior's shares outright. Second, I want two seats on the board. Her choice as to who she gets rid of. Third, there's no way I'm going to make this kind of investment to become the *second*-largest shareholder. So I have some terms for you and Drew to meet. I want us all aligned, Thomas. I know Trudi will listen to you. So will Torrance. *Make* this happen." Thomas had lost two nights of sleep over Trudi and the voting trust.

As if on cue, Trudi entered the room. She had chosen a light gray tailored blouse that downplayed her bust, buttoned to the neck, black skirt cut right at the knees, and a strand of cultured pearls. The numbed features around her mouth made her smile unreadable.

"Good morning, Thomas, Drew," she said, taking her place at the head of the table. "May we begin, gentlemen?"

"By all means," Drew answered.

Thomas did not miss a beat. "Sterling Yildirim is waiting for an answer on his proposal."

"I like it," Trudi said. "I need his support to make the changes that have to be made to Danmark. The two of us will control the company and I am prepared to be an equal shareholder with him. I will agree to Tal's transfer of his shares. I can't imagine what he's getting back in return. No doubt the Turk will screw him."

"And as part of the documentation you have to agree to terminate the voting trust," Thomas said.

"It goes without saying." Trudi shook her head slightly. "No rational buyer would allow it to stay in place. And I certainly can't allow the Turk to have any leverage on my ability to transfer shares."

Drew held up a cautioning hand. "You don't know the whole story," he said. "Late last night he asked Thomas and me to sell him half of our holdings in Danmark at a small discount to market."

"Really," Trudi said. "How much stock would that give him?"

"More than you currently own," Thomas said.

"Potentially giving him the ability to move me out any time?" Trudi drummed her fingers on the table.

Thomas had spent all last night tossing and turning over what Trudi's response might be to this turn of events. If she allowed Yildirim to become the single largest shareholder, she would be giving up her trump card. He could move her out any time. Yesterday she had probably felt herself a match for the toughest activist investor in the country. She'd just discovered she'd been outmaneuvered.

The Turk had thrown the sucker punch. She ought to walk away from the deal. But if Thomas supported that decision, Talem would not get what he wanted. Talem's desire was his prime objective. How would Trudi counter?

"Please give me some credit for brains, gentlemen. I've been expecting this from the moment he first got in touch with you, Thomas. When I left the board all those years ago, I vowed it was the last time I was ever going to let any man push me around." She took a moment to look each of them straight in the eye. A moment of irony.

"The stock price needs a boost," she said. "Yildirim's last two deals have created enormous value for his investors. I'm willing to bet the market will respond favorably to the announcement. I'm inclined to bring him on board."

"And you're prepared to allow him to hold more stock than you?" Drew asked in an even tone.

"You'll tell him, Thomas, that our shareholdings need to be equal or there is no deal."

"This last request could scuttle the deal," Thomas said, balancing on the razor edge of his conflicting duties.

"If I don't insist on it, he'll never respect me. I might as well just roll over on my stomach and let him pull my skirt up. Excuse the graphics, but that's who he is."

"So you want him to withdraw his offer to us to buy our shares?" Thomas asked.

Drew winked at him. Why?

"I'm not going to tell the Turk what to do. But I can control how I respond and I need your assistance." She looked from Thomas to Drew, who was now smiling. How could Thomas have missed what Drew had figured out minutes ago? The solution to Thomas's dilemma.

Trudi continued. "If he's buying from you two, then I'm buying from you as well. I'll match his terms."

That would leave each of them with virtually no remaining stock in Danmark. He and Drew had an immediate choice to make. For Thomas there was no choice.

"What about the two seats on the board he's asking for?" Drew asked. Only a fool would not know the answer, Thomas thought, and Drew was no fool.

Drew's mouth turned up ever so slightly.

Trudi stood. "Thomas, tell Yildirim I'll meet him at his suite in the Four Seasons at five."

"What if he refuses to accept you as an equal shareholder?" Drew asked.

"He won't," she said without hesitating.

She had nerve, Thomas thought. He nodded just as Drew said, "As you wish, Trudi."

Trudi nodded at both of them. "The way he's been stalking us, he wants this deal. I'm convening a board meeting by phone at three and I've asked our communications team to draft a press release announcing all of this. They are on hold waiting for the two of you to finish the paperwork, so I can sign. The Turk is not a patient man and I am no longer a patient woman. We want it all done by tonight." Trudi paused. She stood up and straightened her skirt. "I know I can count on both of you. We'll announce it before markets open in the morning."

Thomas nodded and looked over at Drew, whose facial expression revealed nothing. Trudi rose and headed to the door. She had figured out the game right down to the last move. But how could she be so certain that Yildirim would fall into line so easily?

She didn't say *I* want it all done by tonight, Thomas thought. She used the word *we. We'll announce it in the morning.* Trudi must have been in direct communication with the Turk and the two of them had been playing Drew and Thomas out of their stock and off the board. If they could run this con so smoothly, they might prove to be perfectly suited to one another going forward.

"And, gentlemen, I want to thank you both for your long service to the board. I'll be expecting your resignations delivered to my hotel room right after everything is signed."

CHAPTER 30

Ophelia stepped out of Centraal Station into a time warp. The red bricks of the monolith, sitting on the Amstel River harbor, looked more like a Gothic cathedral than a train station from the outside. Exactly as she remembered it as a teenager. Once again she was in blue jeans and a pink sweatshirt, hitching her carryall over her shoulder and making her way toward Dam Square and the city center, killing a little time before her appointment. She had told Paul not to send a car for her at Schiphol when her flight landed early this morning. She preferred to take some time for herself on the return home. Home was probably the wrong word. The house held memories, but the final memories were to be avoided. It was no longer home. Not since Mama died. It did not require a psychologist to explain why she had enlisted in Israel rather than return home after Paris.

Paul had summoned her. She had a duty to obey, but not a duty to stay more than a moment beyond what was necessary. She debated whether to rent a brown bicycle or walk. There was no more than the usual mist in the chilly afternoon air so she decided to make her way on foot.

She entered through the familiar front door of the canal house, which had recently been repainted the azure blue that she remembered from early childhood. This time, though, she did not race up to the second level. The wooden staircase was narrow, dark, and steep. Burnished wainscotting ran up the walls on either side to the ceiling. Each step brought her back a moment in time to the awaiting resistance of narrow thoughts. The root of obsession. Her legs felt heavy and she reached for the iron bannister, really just a hollow pipe, running up the side. Ice cold to the touch. Halfway up she stopped to gather her resolve.

Paul was waiting for her at the top of the staircase. She knew he avoided the up and down whenever possible. He limped a couple of steps down, toward her, as if the gesture might overcome her reticence of taking those final steps. He flashed the familiar smile. He probably knew better than to embrace. She still hadn't forgiven him for what he had done to Mama; she was still not ready to make the first move. He stepped backward slowly at the pace the arthritis, slowly eating away at his knee, allowed. She had taken for granted that Paul would always be here waiting for her to return. Time was passing and with it the childish notion that things remain the same.

She settled into the plush gold loveseat facing the baby grand piano. The picture of her mother was sitting comfortably in its place atop the polished ledge, frozen in time.

"You're a big girl now."

"I'll be thirty-four soon. Hardly a girl."

"Have a brandy with me." Paul handed her a short cut-crystal glass, sitting on a silver tray on top of the piano.

"*L'chaim.*" They softly clinked glasses and she took a long sip. She immediately felt the rush of alcohol to her brain and remembered she hadn't eaten anything since this morning when she'd rushed down an apple pancake from a street vendor on the Dam. Mama used to take her for pancakes and whipped cream every Sunday morning, just before they began their market shopping. *Appel gebakken mit schlag* — a child's dream.

In Ophelia's mind Mama would be perpetually young and beautiful, perhaps the only benefit of her dying while Ophelia was still a teenager. She remembered the softness of Mama's touch, the songs after story time and before bed each night. The melodies that still echoed in her head for no reason at odd times of the day or night. She wondered if Paul thought of his Alanna in the same terms. Did he see himself as the young man who had swept the nineteen-year-old girl off her feet outside the Rijksmuseum, or had she grown gnarled in his head along with him? Or maybe he was haunted with the visions that filled Ophelia's dreams: Mama's bed empty, the final snapshot no more than her bloodstained quilt, the ravages of a cancer in its merciless phase.

"She is too sick, dear. She can't see anyone," Papa had kept saying, ignoring Ophelia's wails in the final few weeks. There were so many things to tell Mama. She would have known how to mend the rift between Ophelia and Paul. Would have known the exact words to soften each of them. But Mama had not been there when the teenage anger became considerably more acute. Ophelia did not understand it at the time, when she'd acted out her aggression against Paul, who had become the enemy. The man who stole her mother's last breaths. The source of her fountain of jealousy. The person who got to embrace Mama as she passed out of this life.

Ophelia choked back the sudden rush of anger. She took a deep breath, held it for three seconds, then let it go — a gift from the Israeli army training by a therapist who focused on channeling the rage, an invaluable asset in wartime conditions. She had let the family believe that her time in naval Intelligence was a desk job. Talk about special ops was forbidden. South Lebanon was not that long ago.

"How are you, Paul?"

"For an old man with an ailing leg, not bad. How are things in America?"

"My job is actually better than I expected. They have me doing research on viruses. Denmark is no longer just a copycat. The work I'm doing in biologics may lead to some interesting finds."

"I am happy for you. And the love life? I know a father is not supposed to ask such questions of a daughter…"

"Correct. You're not supposed to ask. I'll give it to you in a nutshell. The men in my life have all been disappointments."

"The day will come when it is *b'shert*."

She sighed. "Even love is governed by God? Is that your point?"

"And with good cause." He caught himself mid-thought. Paul looked over his shoulder at the piano and then turned back to Ophelia. "I'm just sorry your mother is not here to give some advice," he said.

The two sat silent for a moment. "How's your leg?" she asked.

"Never mind my leg. How is the boy?"

"You mean Tal? He's pulled himself out of his drug dependence."

"Dependence on any one thing is not healthy."

Paul was blind to the irony. His own dependence, since Mama's death, on fulfilling the family vow, at any cost.

Paul kneaded his right leg. Working against the pain. The pain of his failures as a father? More likely the painful reminder that but for a self-less decision made by a stranger in a world gone insane, an infinitesimal moment in time, he would not be here today, she would never have been born, there would be no vow, no obligation, no life. He was right. His dependence was justified.

Yet she could not tell him that, because he never told her what she wanted to hear. The words that would ease *her* pain. She might be a woman in her thirties, but for the moment she was his child once again, yearning to climb into his lap, to benefit from his protection, his hand caressing the small of her back with approval.

She was staring at his knee.

"You are looking at the wrong organ." He pointed at the photo on the piano. "Not a day goes by that I don't ache for your mother."

As if he was the only one who had the right to ache. As if he had not stolen Mama's final moments for himself. Honor your father, honor your father, honor your father. The dam built to withstand the pressure. She began to shake. Try as she might, there was no holding back the flood.

"Do you have any idea what it's like crying yourself to sleep every night, wondering why your mother has left you without saying goodbye? You stole that from me."

Paul's face hardened. "Careful with your words. You have no idea."

"Of what?" she whispered. "Of what? Of what?" Her voice rose to a snarl. "You're hiding something from me. Like some secret that you've refused to share. Am I not entitled to know?"

Paul shook his head. "I can't."

"Don't say you can't. You won't. Don't you think that saying goodbye to Mama could have been my choice?"

"Your choice? Ha. You were a child."

"I was fifteen. I had a right!" she shrieked.

Paul did not rise to the bait, but his thumb was pressed hard into the muscle in his thigh. "You wanted to be with her? She was gone, had been for a month. From the moment I moved her. The woman in the hospital room was not your Mama." Paul closed his eyes, slumped his shoulders. Began to cry. "It was her face and her body but it was no longer her soul."

"How can that be?"

Paul dropped his head onto his wrist and began to whisper. It was more of a whimper. "It was not your Mama in the end. You would never have understood."

"But she never said goodbye to me. I came home from school and she was gone. How could you do that to me? How could you do that to her? No more excuses."

Paul didn't move. Rounded shoulders, head perched on his wrist like the man sitting atop Rodin's Gates of Hell. When he finally lifted his head she noticed black circles had formed under his eyes. Had they been there a moment ago? He opened his mouth as if to speak. No words emerged. She waited.

He continued, "I had promised she could die at home with her family. I made that promise when her pain was manageable. But I broke the promise in order to protect you from her."

The anger burned through her like a lit fuse that had picked up speed to the moment before detonation. "How could you be so selfish, Paul?" The words exploded out of her mouth. She was shaking with a rage she had been trained to control. A rage that had been buried for half her life, but had come boiling back to the surface. "You break your promises to your wife, but have no problem keeping them for strangers."

"The cancer had eaten away at her brain. She screamed at me from the moment I arrived in the morning until the moment I left in the evening. The doctors said she was in agonizing pain. Suffering bouts of confusion. Saying such things a husband should never have to hear. That a teenage daughter who idolized her would never forget."

Paul withdrew a monogrammed handkerchief from the breast pocket of his blazer and dabbed at the tears, as if he could wipe away the grief. "I know you don't think it was fair. It's the child's duty to respect," he said gathering his composure. "But it's the father's duty to protect. Even if it means you hate me. And I would rather you hate me than risk spoiling the memory of your Mama by bringing you to her in her last moments of dementia."

"Oh, Papa," she cried. Ophelia bolted across the room, traversing the ravine that had separated them. When she reached Paul, she knelt on the rug, then dropped her head in his lap. His wrinkled hand stroked her hair, the way it had in her dreams.

They sat sharing the pain for a few minutes until the wave inside her had subsided, leaving her spent.

She sighed. "I'm sorry."

Papa waited for a moment and then he smiled. "You are still my child," he said. "Sometimes being a parent requires you to make impossible choices for the benefit of your children."

Papa laid his hand on her shoulder as if to keep her close, as if he didn't want to lose her. A few minutes passed in silence. Then Paul returned.

"You recall the information you gathered from Red King's office."

"That was ages ago. Shortly after Geri died. I assumed it was of no use."

"Most of it was encrypted. All we could make out was that King had something going on in Shannon, Ireland. And there was a bank account in the Channel Islands, but other than that we couldn't get at the information. Yakov has filled us in on the background and we've finally begun to make some sense of it."

"You think King was stealing from the company?"

"We still don't have enough to come to a conclusion. That's why Thomas has never acted on what you found. It might be more serious than that. Something that could destroy the company."

"Cunzhuang?" At the root of Tal's obsessions with Red, she thought.

"Yes."

Another mission.

"There was no urgency until this morning," Paul said. "Yakov spoke to Thomas while you were in the air. Talem is on his way over to Shannon right now. Yakov is tied up with the deal, so it has to be you. I want you on the jet. It leaves from the airfield in two hours."

"You want me spying on him?"

"Geri died of a heart attack the week after his visit to Ireland. We don't want to take any chances. Go keep an eye on him. And be careful yourself."

"You need not worry about me, Paul."

CHAPTER 31

The flight attendant passed by just after takeoff with their drink orders and a couple of bowls of mixed nuts. Executive class in the overnight flight from Montreal was half full, about the state of Tal's Virgin Mary. Lucinda's gin and tonic had not yet been touched. The same was true of the novel splayed open on her tray, which had not moved from page thirty-two since takeoff.

The plane shook without warning. A rough patch of turbulence. She grabbed his arm, breaking his concentration from the picture he had been studying on the tray.

"Sorry, Tal, I'm not a very good flier. This is my first overseas flight. But I wasn't letting you go alone. Particularly after the way Lorenzo reacted."

Lorenzo's first reaction was to ask Tal if he'd lost his mind. Lucinda took a sip of her drink. "He was pretty upset that you'd pick up and leave before the Roylache deal closed."

"For the next month it's all about the lawyers, regulatory delays, and filings," Tal said. "There's nothing for me to do in Montreal. Lorenzo knows that. He's completely overreacting. You both know perfectly well that I need to get this trip to Shannon out of my system. I owe that much to my father."

He had to admit he didn't mind the company. What had begun as strictly lawyer-client had been slowly developing into he-wasn't-sure-what. Perhaps the feeling of intimacy was a function of the number of hours they'd spent putting together the deal with the Turk and then making the takeover bid offer for the company. Lucinda had been commuting back and forth from New York to Montreal and there were plenty of dead hours when they found themselves talking about anything and everything. He'd simply gotten used to Lucinda being around, in a way that he never had with Ophelia.

"What is that picture you're studying so intently?" she asked.

"My father loved to communicate with me in code. He was always sending me messages. Remember the globe he left me? This was hidden inside."

There was a crude hand-drawn crosshatch of a building, with a wide door and a cross at the top. To mark the grass outside the building he'd put three lines of y's.

"Notice how the y's are slanted in the wrong direction, as if an image in a mirror."

"Perhaps a clue having something to do with DaVinci?" she asked. "Didn't he mirror much of his writing? Though the letters on the page underneath are all gobbledygook to me."

"That's the note I have to decode. Eventually it will come to me. Father knows I never give up even if it takes months."

He turned the note over and closed his eyes. He awoke to the shuffling of flight attendants removing Lucinda's breakfast tray.

"I thought you should get as much sleep as possible," she said.

"No problem," he said drowsily, pressing his head against the oblong window. Beneath him were rolling farmland, old estates, meandering streams, and ribbons of sunlight on rivers, through intermittent patches of low-lying cloud. The bang from underneath startled Lucinda again.

"I'm okay," she whispered. "I know it's just the landing gear."

"That's Limerick below," Tal said, pointing at what looked like a city, "with its noisy pubs" — the way he remembered them from his drunken semester at Trinity College in Dublin.

"My bad old days. I don't remember much about Ireland. Mostly flashes of unreliable memory." Somewhat like the way the fragments of sunlight bounced off the clump of short office towers that led into the tarmac, just off the water.

The Shannon Airport and its Free Zone. An eyesore in the middle of heaven, serviced by a few thousand commuters attracted by employment opportunity through Ireland's bold idea: an international tax-free zone. It serviced pop-up foreign proxies, from businesses around the world. A dose of job-creating revitalization, according to the local politicians. Jobs were code for votes.

The plane taxied to a halt and Tal slid the note into his bag and reached overhead for his raincoat, about to zip the bag shut. He looked down at the crude drawing of the church that was upside down.

"Simpleton."

"You speaking to me, Tal?" Lucinda asked.

"Those aren't y's on the ground. They're upside-down lambdas, from the Greek alphabet." Finally a breakthrough.

"Lambda… Church… Not a building. Of course not. Alonzo Church and the lambda calculus. His work with Alan Turing for breaking codes."

"I barely got through high-school algebra."

"All I have to do is set up an algorithm on my computer." His own mini-Turing machine, to break Father's code. Just like the Allies broke the Nazi codes. It wouldn't take more than a few days' work.

■ ■ ■

They dropped their bags at the hotel and headed to the offices of Cunzhuang. Tal wiped the bleariness from his eyes. They threw on their coats, grabbed their bags, and stepped out of the black cab. Across the street the logos for an international diamond house and a couple of foreign airlines were barely visible through the late morning mist that had dropped like a blanket. In front of them an older brick building, two stories, looking more like a warehouse. Three concrete steps led to the front door, frosted glass, with the name Cunzhuang painted in gold with green trim. Inside the tiny welcoming area, a young woman in a turquoise blouse sat behind the reception desk, filing her nails. She stopped her work, smiled, and greeted them with a heavy Irish accent. Over the reception hung what he presumed was the logo: a shamrock surrounded by two snakes twisting around it. Beneath it was some Chinese calligraphy.

He had developed his strategy for the meeting during the first half of the flight. Perhaps if he had deciphered Father's note, he might have adopted a different approach, but he'd come too far to change course.

■ ■ ■

They were ushered into a tiny boardroom with a round cherrywood table and four black chairs on wheels. After a few minutes, a woman entered the room.

Tal stood up and extended his hand. "Stephen Leibgott. Thanks for agreeing to meet on short notice. This is Lucinda Horat, one of my partners."

"How do you do, Mr. Leibgott, Ms. Horat. I am Li Shan, manager of the office." Her accent had traces of Chinese combined with some kind of English affectation. He guessed she could be from Hong Kong.

"Some tea?"

She didn't wait for the answer and began pouring from a small red porcelain teapot on the side table into three dainty matching teacups.

"As I mentioned on the phone," Tal said, "I represent a private equity fund that believes investment in online pharmaceuticals is the wave of the future. We are about to invest half a billion in the industry and we're looking for the right partner."

"We are the dominant portal over every continent."

"And everything gets done here? I was hoping to get a tour of the facilities today," he said.

"Not much here," she said. "We process online orders. Our servers in back do most of the work. They fill the entire facility. Most of our workforce." She smiled. "Tech staff, locally hired to comply with our Shannon license." She took a sip of tea.

"What kind of volume do you process?" Lucinda asked.

"Tens of thousands of emails every day. All drug orders. Computers verify the codes. Employees thoroughly trained to double-check. A single mistake could kill." She smiled again. Tal felt a slight shiver in the back of his neck.

"But that's only the front end of the operation," Lucinda said. "Where is everyone else located? How do you deliver?"

"We use a fulfillment house in Ecuador to serve the South American market and in Romania for Europe. All subcontracted out. We handle Asia ourselves out of China. As for the U.S., we recently changed distributors. It is ramping up and growing rapidly. I don't have to tell you about U.S. drug consumption." She laughed again.

"We're big and powerful," she added. "You don't have to worry."

Big and powerful, Tal thought. Not the way a North American would describe a business. The way you might describe a military strike force.

Half an hour later he'd learned everything Li Shan was prepared to give up on Cunzhuang. But not everything. That he'd have to figure out on his own. No, not on his own, he thought. With Lucinda.

■ ■ ■

Immediately after they left, Li Shan returned to her office and hit the speed dial on her phone.

"He was here. Calls himself Leibgott. I thought Geri was naïve when he came and threatened me. The son did not fall far from the bush."

"From the tree," the woman's voice corrected. "You're certain it was the son?"

Li Shan took a careful look at the photo on her phone. "No doubt."

"He suspects, but he does not know. If he knew, we would have been visited by Interpol. I worry he is getting closer."

"Usual precautions are in place. I have eyes on him every moment."

"You will do what is required. And it will be your priority." The woman's voice was severe. An order not to be questioned. An order to be understood.

"Yes, Lingdao."

The phone disconnected and she dialed another number.

"You're watching him?" she said.

"I'm following his taxi."

"Lingdao asked me to take care of him."

"I know what to do. I don't need a fishing rod for this one."

"You leave it all to me. Understood? Just let me know when he's alone in his hotel tonight."

The son follows in the path of the father, Li Shan thought after disconnecting. A path Lingdao did not want him going down. The instructions were cryptic but precisely understood. When the opportunity presented itself tonight, Li Shan would take it. Perhaps the son had the same proclivities as the father. Alone in a hotel room. A chance for her to correct history.

■ ■ ■

The sun had already set before the clock struck five. Tal felt the grumbling in his stomach, realizing he hadn't eaten since dinner on the plane last night. They hadn't yet checked in to the hotel, but what was the rush? It would also be a chance to debrief. He leaned forward and asked the cabbie whether there was a pub near the hotel.

"O'Doule's is about a block away, sir. Should do the trick."

He looked over at Lucinda. She nodded her approval. "Good idea."

They filed into O'Doule's on the main floor of a squat office tower. The bartender waved at them from behind the long laminate bar. The place, like the building, was spanking new and sparkling modern. The glass wall held an assortment of bottles, backlit with a stark white light that shone through them. There was nothing old-fashioned about O'Doule's. The evening rush, if there were to be one, had not yet begun. A few clusters of women and men in business attire stood by the counter along the wall. They were chatting, making their animated points with their tall Guinness glasses.

"I'll grab us drinks and order something. Just a tide-over until dinner," Tal suggested.

"I'll find a table," Lucinda said, heading along the bar, toward the back. A couple of men sitting just to Tal's right gave her a careful up and down as she walked by. Tal felt a slight annoyance.

She was wearing a form-fitting green dress. Tight at the hips, cut a couple of inches above the knee. Straight confident back. Slight sashay. He hadn't really noticed how good she looked in it, though she'd been wearing it all night then all day. As if he was seeing her for the first time through the eyes of the men at the bar.

Lucinda smiled as Tal approached with the drinks. He cast a look over his shoulder until the men turned back to the bar and resumed their conversation.

He set down her Guinness glass and his tonic water, and took a seat on the wooden chair adjacent to her at the small table, his back to the bar.

"I know I resisted at first, but I'm glad you were there with me today," he began. Then he raised his glass. She tipped her glass in Tal's direction, began with a tiny sip. Then she took a couple more.

"Tastes bitter to start," Tal said with a smile, "but after a couple of sips it'll warm your belly. I may not touch it anymore, but I have to admit Guinness was always a favorite of mine." The sky had darkened outside and the din inside the bar was increasing as the gang who worked the day shift in the international offices poured in. The cacophony of multilingual conversation drew their heads closer together.

Tal broke the spell. "It was an interesting afternoon. I don't know what to think," he began. "Something is happening, but I can't figure it out."

"It will come to you eventually. Take your mind off it, let it percolate forward on its own. That's the way our brains work."

"My mind can't function anymore. I need to eat something."

The plate of wings arrived with a side of sweet potato fries and dip. Pub grub. Enough to kill the immediate hunger. They took a couple of minutes to dig in until Tal's plate had been almost picked clean, except for a single remaining wing. He was no longer hungry, but went after it anyway, almost absently, snapped it apart, eating the remaining flesh off the bone. Filled.

"Follow me, Lucinda." He broke eye contact. Looking far beyond Lucinda. Far beyond the bar.

"Follow you? Where are you going?"

"I mean figuratively. I'm thinking. The question you asked Li Shan."

"About her fulfillment operations? She talked about their world operations. Mentioned something about a new U.S. distribution deal."

"Exactly. A new U.S. deal. Maybe Father didn't come here just to cancel the Danmark agreement. Maybe he came because he figured something out about the old agreement…"

"How could we ever know that? It's not something Li Shan would ever tell us."

"But maybe Father figured out a way to tell me? Maybe it's in that coded note?"

"Take a breath, Tal. Look at me. Do you think maybe you're tilting at windmills here?"

Tal refocused. Sighed. "Don Quixote. The knight errant. Tracing the journey of CallMeGeri."

"Does that make me Sancho Panza? Your faithful liege?" Lucinda's smile warmed him. Returned him to the moment.

Perhaps Dulcinea, he thought.

She sighed and leaned in on her elbows. "You might fool yourself, Tal Neilson, but you can't fool me. You think the quest is for your father, his ghost, his secrets, but it isn't. It's about both your parents. A father who couldn't communicate with you. A mother who never gave you the time of day."

Tal studied his half-filled tonic glass.

"Look at me, Tal. You know it's true."

Tal stared into her eyes and didn't speak for what felt like a very long time. "Of course it's true. I spent hours talking about this in Australia."

"Yet here we are. You keep looking for your validation in their approval, that you can never have. Not while your father was alive, surely not now that he's dead, and more certainly never from your mother. Haven't you figured it out yet?"

Was this entire trip a backslide from the progress he'd made? A return to the old Tal who could never satisfy his parents? Or was it something entirely different?

"Leave the ghosts behind. There's only one person you need approval from. Yourself. Trust yourself. Trust your judgment. Decide what you want. Not what your father wanted for you. Not what your mother wants."

"My mother? What does my mother want?"

"Look at what you and Lorenzo chose as a target. Out of the entire world of possibilities you chose the one company your mother wants to buy. She wanted Roylache and you not only scooped it up, you manipulated the Turk to get it. She'll have to take notice, won't she?"

"I hadn't thought of it that way."

"And now you've run across the world trying to satisfy whom?"

Tal dropped his head. "I don't know anymore," he whispered.

Lucinda was cast in a completely different light. No longer just a lawyer, but as a woman. It wasn't just a thought moving forward in his head. It was a wave sweeping him along.

He stood up and reached for his coat.

"Let's get out of here," Tal said, dropping some money on the table. He draped his raincoat over her shoulders, then took her hand, escorting her through the mass of bodies that had spilled out of the doorway of the pub and into the lobby of the building. They stepped outside into a curtain of rain. Tal's arm reached around her shoulder, and they raced to the hotel and checked in. Their rooms were side by side. He stood with her outside her door.

Lucinda felt a slight dizziness. Perhaps a little bit too much Guinness. Tal opened the door for her.

"Why don't we both dry off," she said. "We can figure out dinner plans after."

"Oh," he said. "Of course… "

The door swung shut and she leaned back against it. Removed Tal's raincoat. "You fool." It was Bea's voice. Tal wasn't the only one taking instructions from voices in his head.

Lucinda stepped back into the hallway and knocked on his door. The door opened slowly.

Drenched and shivering, he invited her in.

She held out his coat. "I need to return this to the owner."

"That's not what I need," he said, pulling her close. Her head turned upward and he kissed her deeply. She heard the door close behind her. Her eyes closed. He smelled like autumn. Burnt leaves and rain. His arms were as powerful as she had dreamed. His kiss was confident, yet tender. She was warming, melting. He was shaking.

She summoned whatever was left of her reserves and pushed away. "Tal, you're shivering. Go get yourself warm. You need a hot shower."

He smiled at her and walked into the bathroom, leaving the door slightly ajar. A few moments later she heard the spray of water. She opened the bathroom door. A pile of soaked clothes lay just off to the side. Was he aware she'd entered the room? She stepped around the pile of clothing and pulled the green dress over her head. The contours of his body emerged through the cloud of steam. She hesitated, staring at the shower door, then exhaled and pulled on the handle; it opened slowly.

"What took you so long?" he asked, his hand reaching for the small of her back, guiding her to him. Her eyes closed. The last sound she remembered was the sweep of the shower door.

■ ■ ■

Ophelia sat in the darkness of her hotel room, reclined on the double bed, her legs crossed. She removed the earphones. It was no longer polite to listen to what was going on in the room next door. Had Tal and the redhead found love?

It hurt more than she expected it would.

CHAPTER 32

When it is obvious the goals cannot be reached, don't adjust the goals, adjust the action steps. The advice was far more poetic in Chinese. The words of Master Kong, one of Li Shan's heroes. The West called him Confucius, but she preferred living and thinking in her native language, without the idiotic requirement of American grammar and idioms that she would never master. Not the way Lingdao had mastered them.

Li Shan was making her way through the terminal at Kennedy Airport to the taxi stand. There were three additional transfers to be made today before she found the right motel, altered her look, and rented the right vehicle for this mission. Preparation and tactics were of supreme importance, just as they had been in her previous life.

Master Kong's advice had guided Li Shan to the apex of *wushu sanshu*, so much more than what the Westerners called kickboxing. Americans were the worst — only interested in victory and defeat, without any appreciation for the spiritual journey, the mastery of self, the pursuit of perfection. For seven years Li Shan had reigned as the best female athlete in China in a martial art that did not put any money in her pocket. For seven years she was certain the state would repay her dedication upon her retirement with a coaching job on the national team, a position that would have taken care of her needs until retirement. A state-subsidized apartment, world travel, and lifetime dignity. That was all before her father, a journalist, published an article perceived by the state as critical. Before he was arrested. Before the offer from the state fizzled. Two more years until the next world championship at which point she would retire world champion, then disappear from the national team … and starve for all they cared.

Shortly afterward she received a personal note of support, hand-delivered to her apartment, expressing dismay over the way she had been treated and offering to meet. The woman who met her at one of the finest restaurants in Shanghai appeared to have great wealth and professed to be one of her biggest fans. While they were sipping their tea after dinner, the woman set the hook. The organization she was associated with in Macao had been betting on her matches. In Macao, even amateur sports made the betting line board. Li Shan had been a very profitable investment. The woman offered to cut her in on the action. "Continue winning and by the time you retire you will be a very rich woman. No one will own you." It was as if the woman had moved into her head.

Eighteen months later she was up over a quarter of a million yuan, converted to U.S. dollars in an account in Macao, when a note was slipped under her hotel room door at the world championship. "You will win the silver medal tomorrow." It felt like a spinning roundhouse kick to the temple. Once the dizziness lifted, she ran to the toilet and vomited. The next day she lost the final match of her career. A week later another envelope arrived. Another meeting. This one in a shabby restaurant in the slums of Laoximen. This time a short, middle-aged man with a mustache, cauliflower ears, and weathered face. Perhaps a boxer in a previous life. There were all kinds of tasks that the organization could profitably use her for, he told her. When he smiled, she saw that two of his front teeth were missing. "Lingdao wants to remind you that it is in your interest to pursue this *opportunity*." A week later they arranged her travel to Macao and her apprenticeship began.

She was already an expert in submission holds and choking techniques and had honed her skills in the use of various weapons. Lingdao, the name everyone in the organization called the woman, arranged for sessions with a chemist for her education in the administration of various poisons; a stunt driver for handling an assortment of vehicles; and the makeup artist to teach her to transform her face and hair to alter her appearance. To date she had amassed half a dozen passports. One for each contract killing. Lingdao had provided a shopping list for this trip.

The plan for the son of Geri Neilson had been postponed when he had not returned alone to his hotel room on his night in Shannon. Perhaps better that way. The death of an American in Ireland surely would have created far too much attention. Same reason why she'd waited for Geri to return to America. Passport number three. Geri had arrived at the Shannon office uninvited, screaming about how "two can play this game." Something about a call he'd received two days earlier. He said he was here to issue his own ultimatum. She had no idea what he was talking about. It was not Li Shan's business to know about any of Lingdao's activities. She could only assume that the threat was delivered by another proxy.

She had to give Geri credit. How quickly he'd connected all the dots between Cunzhuang and his company. Five minutes after he stomped out, she advised Lingdao. The instructions to head to Atlantic City arrived shortly afterward. He was her toughest mission. She would be far more careful with the son. No mistakes this time.

Number five had been imaginative and technical. Red King and his red Ferrari. She had devised various alternate plans to get rid of him. Lingdao had been very specific. Make it quick, merciless, shocking. What was driving this particular order was not clear to Li Shan, but she was no fool. The husband was not repaying the debt promptly enough so the tactic was probably designed to frighten the wife. At the appropriate time, Trudi Darrow would receive the note slipped under the door, or the anonymous phone call, or the whisper in her ear from a complete stranger on Park Avenue. Lingdao had many messengers.

Fortunately Li Shan had managed it without much fuss. She had been following King in her rental car when he dropped off Darrow in Tribeca. She sped past him a couple of blocks farther on, then got out of the car, raised the hood, and waited. The red wig, matching lipstick, and tight but revealing leather jacket, gloves, and matching pants caught his attention as much as her waving arms when he drove past, slowed, and stopped. She'd leaned in through the passenger window, revealing there was nothing underneath, put on her best attempt at a British accent, and told him she had to get to Brooklyn, could he help?

Once she slid into the bucket seat, she thanked him.

"You're such a gentleman," she said. "Are you the type that would stop for any woman in distress?"

"Just the hot ones." He laughed.

"This car is hot. Does it go as fast as I think it can?"

"Faster."

"Do you go as fast as I think you can?"

"Slower." He smiled.

"You've got quite an unusual stick shift."

"Want a turn?"

"Are you sure you're ready?" She reached over and opened his belt, sliding down the zipper of his jeans. "You *are* ready! You like adventure?"

He winked.

"Ever done it on the Brooklyn Bridge?"

"I believe there's a first time for everything."

Just after he turned off Center Street, onto the bridge road, he pointed out the problem. "The signs say the bridge is closed," he said.

"Maybe I'll just offer my thanks right now for being such a gentleman."

"I'll make a U-turn up ahead then I'll find a spot to park," he offered.

"You said you wanted adventure. Keep driving." She reached into her purse. He thought he knew what was coming.

It only took a moment to slip the cover off the hypodermic in her purse and hammer-fist the paralytic into his thigh. He never saw it coming. For the first moments he was too stunned to respond. She waited until his foot slipped off the gas pedal, then in one motion she opened the door and rolled onto the pavement. She'd practiced it a hundred times in training. At ten miles an hour the key was to protect the head. The bruising would take a couple of weeks to heal. Then she removed the remote control from her jacket and pushed it full throttle until she heard the crash of Ferrari meeting unyielding concrete, the screech of the metal. Normally she had to verify the kill and report back. Tonight she could not afford to be around for the first responders. At a hundred and forty kilometers an hour, there wasn't any hope for King.

The next goal had not yet been reached. She would follow young Neilson to learn his habits, then adjust her tactics to guarantee success. He would succumb shortly.

CHAPTER 33

Ophelia was following the country road in her rented black import — a nondescript four-door sedan. Tal was a hundred meters ahead in the Jag. Out for a drive with the redhead.

"Watch him carefully," Thomas had warned on a conference call three nights ago. "He did exactly what Geri did the week before he died."

There was no way to keep an eye on him without keeping an eye on her. The redhead and Tal had been inseparable since Ireland. He had moved into her apartment. A familiar story. Not that Tal's attraction to the redhead made any sense: she was conservatively attractive, the kind of woman who would never be caught in a pair of jeans. No overt passion.

They had been driving for an hour, headed away from Manhattan. Traffic was light as they left the city and followed a route on the two-lane highway along the river, which flowed well below the road. It was a reminder of her naval service.

■ ■ ■

She'd spent a year in Intelligence followed by months of training in one of Israel's most exclusive special ops unit. A unit that professed not to accept women. Shayetet 18. Duty and missions combined with a program that would leave her with a completed university degree. There was no time for love, yet there was love. Love for country, love for comrades, love for Issar, her closest friend. He was only an inch taller than she, Mediterranean features, broad nose, brilliant tactician. The future didn't matter in covert operations. It was all about the mission. The moment.

One night they were headed to the beaches of southern Lebanon. Intelligence reported that an arms deal was taking place in one of the apartment buildings. Their job was to land the surveillance equipment in the forest just south of the beach. The sliver of the new moon was high above, lending little light to the brooding sky. Six of them bouncing in a Zodiac as they approached the drop spot.

Ophelia slipped out of the Zodiac, followed by Issar, the three others behind him swimming the final kilometer. A series of low-rise apartment buildings, set back from the beach, stood quietly to the north. Many of the windows reflected no light, wide open to catch the ocean breeze.

They emerged crouching low through the tide that lapped the shore just a few steps away. Issar was now a couple of steps ahead. It was their ninth mission together. No need to speak. Everything understood, with no more than a nod of a head or gesture of a hand.

"Complete the task and get out. Thirty minutes maximum once you land. *Ein breira*. No choice." Those were the orders.

The beach was deserted, but from the moment they landed, something felt off.

A screech of bullets. Shouts from above. "*Yehud, Yehud!*" A massive explosion of light and sound; shrapnel of sand and stone on the beach shook them. She could no longer hear. Time had slowed to nothing. She turned back to Issar, lying prone beside her, blackness seeping from his shoulder and his thigh. She looked over in the other direction. Three lifeless bodies.

Life was all about choices. So was death. Now there was no choice.

She reached down for Issar. Swearing in pain. He had to outweigh her by thirty pounds, all muscle. She grabbed him under his shoulders and flipped his body on top of hers, only thirty meters to the cover in the bush at the south end of the beach, then a swim to the Zodiac. His weight resisting every inch, squeezing the breath out of her, inching along. She was trained for swims, but a third of the way out his body went limp. She needed to assume he was still alive. She could hear the intermittent fire coming from the windows. The splashes around her in the water. Still a chance to save him. Until the moment she felt the adrenaline deplete. One more stroke, one more stroke. Until there was nothing left. The will to live abandoning her. Their bodies would wash up on the Lebanese shore where they would be dismembered and desecrated. Was Issar already dead? She would never know. She began to choke on the sea water filling her lungs, sinking her. She lost her grip.

No choice. *Ein breira*, an eye for an eye, a tooth for a tooth, a life for a life. Issar's life lost to the water so she could survive.

The nausea gripped her once again behind the wheel of the car.

■ ■ ■

A flash of lights and a blaring horn shocked her from the daydream. She had swerved toward the oncoming traffic and now pulled hard on the wheel to right the car, skidding wildly onto the gravel shoulder, fighting the wheel while the car stalled, coming to rest facing in the wrong direction. Close call. Thank God there had been no traffic. She needed a moment to catch her breath, slow her heartbeat.

A moment later a white van whizzed by traveling way over the speed limit, headlights off. She caught a glimpse of the driver. An Asian woman alone in the van. Shoot! Tal. She restarted the ignition and turned the car around, then hit the accelerator but the van had a huge head start, hundreds of meters ahead on a stretch of straight road, closing on Tal in the Jaguar, passing him, forcing his car off the road.

There was no choice but to follow the vehicle, careening down the embankment and into the water. Anything but the water.

CHAPTER 34

The icy water swirled around his head, surrounding him. His screams were swallowed by the flood that was quickly filling every inch in the vehicle. Gasping for life. Choking. A voice screaming his name. An arm reaching for his seatbelt, the back of a head submerging into the dark waters, something pulling at his leg, triggering a shock of pain that jolted his eyes open.

"Ophelia!" He heard the scream, a male voice. His breathing was greedy, gulping air, overtaken by his racing heart. What was reality and what was fiction? No car, no water, no ice, sitting on a bed in a room. Curtains drawn shut, blurred bare walls, light linen covering his torso, his clothes gone, a hospital nightshirt, alone. Twisting on the bed, the pain shot up his left leg, paralyzing his spine, sending his upper body crashing back down. A second scream. The door rustled. The outline of a woman, long hair, arm in a sling. Beside her another woman in scrubs.

"What happened?" he heard a disembodied voice say in a more measured tone.

"Mr. Neilson, do you know where you are?"

"No," he heard the male voice say, slowly realizing it was his own.

The other woman spoke. "Tal, it's me. I'm here."

A concerned voice. Familiar and intimate. He was in trouble.

"Lucinda?"

She walked over to the bed and took his hand.

"Where am I?"

Lucinda turned to the other woman. "Is it okay to talk to him about what happened, doctor?" she asked quietly.

"It will allow us to measure how much the trauma has affected his memory," the figure in scrubs said.

"Do you remember the car crash, Tal? We were run off the road," Lucinda said.

He touched the bandages on his head and right cheek. "No."

"Into the river."

That might explain the dreams. He nodded. The movement caused an explosion of pain in the back of his head. Lucinda jumped with his scream.

"Maybe that's enough for now," the doctor said calmly. "The CT showed a concussion caused by the airbag. Try not to move your head, Mr. Neilson. We've also put you in a cast for the fracture to your fibula. The break is not severe. On the whole you're very lucky."

"I need to know what happened to me," Tal insisted. "I'll be still."

Lucinda's eyes were wide and desperate. Did he really look that bad, he wondered. Or was the story that bad?

"Some crazy driver ran us off the road," Lucinda said. "You veered down an embankment. The airbags exploded when the car hit the water. You were screaming that your leg was trapped. My window splintered on impact and the water began rushing into the car. I tried to pull your leg out... I tried... You pushed me away." Lucinda was shaking.

She pulled herself together and continued. "I didn't want to leave you. The car was filling up with water. A tire iron smashed away the glass fragments in my window. Someone was grabbing my shoulders, a woman, pulling me out."

Lucinda began to pant. She drew a few deep breaths and continued.

"I was fighting the current. Wondering if... if... It felt like forever. Until I saw the bubbles. Your head broke the surface a few feet away. I grabbed for your shirt. I was never letting go."

"And the woman?"

Lucinda began to cry. "I don't... I don't know. It all happened so fast. Long dark hair is all I recall. When the paramedics arrived I told them there was a third person. They put us both on stretchers. I don't know. I'm sorry. She saved us but there was nothing I could do..." She was sobbing.

Tal reached out and let her cry on his chest. He closed his eyes and saw the face in his dream once more. Ophelia's face. He could not hold back his own tears.

"That's enough for now," the doctor said. "How is your pain, Mr. Neilson?" she asked.

"Excruciating."

"Do you recall insisting that the paramedic not administer any painkiller last night?"

"I don't remember a thing. But no opiates. No morphine. Nothing. Under no circumstances. Do you hear me?"

Lucinda sat up. He saw the admiration in her red eyes. "There must be something you can give him?" she asked the doctor.

"We can administer extra-strength Tylenol. It should give you some relief, though fairly limited. You can expect the pain to be severe for the next two to three days. Fortunately, the concussion, while not minor, is also not too severe. I want you lying in a dark room for the rest of the day. Your brain needs some quiet."

A sudden wave of nausea coursed through him. "I need to… "

He leaned over the edge of the bed and vomited on the floor.

"Can I stay with him?" Lucinda asked.

"We'll all be leaving now," the doctor ordered. "The nurses will be checking on him every twenty minutes for the next twenty-four hours."

After they left, Tal closed his eyes.

Ophelia.

CHAPTER 35

Tal lay in the darkness until day and night lost meaning. Last night the muddling clouds in his head had lifted high enough that he could follow Lucinda for more than a sentence at a time. According to the newspaper coverage, Ophelia's body had been found the morning after the accident about a half mile down from where the car had tumbled into the water. The family had posted an obituary and in accordance with the Jewish custom were sitting in mourning at Ophelia's apartment in the East Village. Today was to be the final day.

Ironic that for all Ophelia knew about his family, he knew precious little about hers. In fact, he knew nothing, other than that he had to go pay his respects. Lucinda understood enough to know there had once been something between him and Ophelia, but no more than that. She must also be wondering how an ex-girlfriend could just show up to save their lives. A question Tal needed to resolve as well.

Lucinda made him promise to wait until he was discharged, but if he kept that promise he would miss it.

"The neurologist is not convinced. He tells me the concussion may be worse than they first imagined. If he's not discharging you, it's because you need to be here," she'd argued last night. "You'll find some other way to pay your respects."

He'd gotten out of bed this morning and walked around without assistance, albeit very slowly. He'd just go for a couple of hours then return. Lucinda wasn't coming back until tonight. Easier to apologize later than beg for permission, so he discharged himself. The neurologist was pissed and told him there were no in and out privileges.

The taxi left him outside the walk-up on East Twelfth. He limped badly up the staircase to the apartment, hobbled by a walking cast, breathing heavily and resting every few stairs on his cane. Spasms of pain rocketed up his leg, the companion reminding him he was still alive. By the time he reached the front door, he was exhausted.

Nothing was going to stand in the way of Tal expressing his sympathies. But to whom?

Just part of the mystery surrounding Ophelia. What kind of coincidence brought her at exactly the right moment to exactly the wrong spot? Had she been following him? Stalking him? Was she jealous of Lucinda?

The apartment door had been left ajar and a buzz of disjointed conversation greeted him. A group of strangers who took no notice of him had gathered in the front hall, engaged in various animated discussions. He limped down the familiar hallway, which opened into the simply furnished living room with the couch on one side, the coffee table in the center of the room — all just as he remembered it. An old grey-haired woman approached and asked if he had come to see the mourner. Tal nodded.

"Yakov!" she yelled over the din. "Someone is here for you."

A large man, facing in the opposite direction, dressed in black slacks, a white shirt, and a black skullcap turned around, toward Tal. He had a thickened three-day growth with white specks highlighting the dark brown stubble, and a torn black tie. They made eye contact and he approached. His eyes were bloodshot. Tal's eyes were frozen. Like the rest of him. What the hell was Lorenzo doing here?

"You are probably looking for an explanation," Lorenzo said.

Tal stood silent, still reeling. He felt the blood rushing from his head. "I need to sit."

Lorenzo supported Tal's back and walked him into the bedroom. "Can someone please bring some juice," he yelled.

They sat beside one another on Ophelia's double bed.

"Lucinda sent me the message you were in the hospital. I'm sorry I couldn't visit. How is your head?"

"I'm too numb to respond."

"Ophelia was my sister — well, really my cousin, but she's always been more like my younger sister. I'm not technically supposed to be sitting shiva but when her father received the news he had a stroke. It practically killed him. He can't speak and the doctors are doubtful about his recovery. My own father rushed back to Amsterdam to tend to him. There's no one else to say the Kaddish for her."

"Your cousin?"

"We're both Farbers. Her grandfather and my grandmother were siblings."

"Did you know about Ophelia and me?"

"More than you know, Tal."

"More than I know," he repeated. "So much I don't know. Like her name. Why did the obituary call her Einbreier? She never mentioned a husband. Was she widowed? Divorced?"

"She never married. But she did change her name in Israel. It's not uncommon."

"Okay. Why?"

"There's a motto Israelis live by — at the core of its existence. *Ein Breira*. There is no choice. The nation must succeed against all challenges."

"And Einbreier is a derivative of *Ein Breira?*"

Lorenzo nodded.

"I still don't understand."

"It's a very long story. One that I have been forbidden from sharing up to this very moment."

Two hours later Lorenzo paused. Tal had not asked a question. Dumbstruck. It was as if the earth had shaken, collapsing beneath him, swallowing up Geri Neilson's entire life story.

Father had not gone it alone. A set of guardian angels had been sent by providence to watch over his every move. The scholarship to MIT, the first loan to fund two broke grad students looking to buy Darrowpharm. Without that funding there would have been no purchase. No Trudi. No Tal. No lifetime success stories. Father had built his dream, but without Paul and Thomas to bankroll him, there would likely have been nothing but a dream. They took the risks, but they hadn't done it out of faith in Geri. Just out of faith.

Father had feasted at a lifelong banquet, but someone else had paid the caterer. Paul Farber had tracked the family to Wisconsin, too late to help Grandfather, the true hero of Geri's life story. What incredible irony. The man who denied God had been financed by him. And the man who had earned the reward, Grandfather, didn't live long enough to benefit from any of this largesse. He died penniless. He died without even a remaining memory.

Geri's life was a deception, but where did that leave Tal?

"What about you, Lorenzo?"

"I was asked to join you in the rehab program."

"Your family didn't trust me to recover on my own?"

"Not the point, Tal. At first, I was doing my duty to my family. To our obligation. Like Ophelia's name. *Ein breira*. There was no choice. We were bound to the vow my great-uncle made."

"Were you even addicted? What in our relationship is not a lie?"

"My family insisted I go back to help you. I was doing a second tour of duty at the clinic."

"Tour of duty? Like in the army." Almost two years clean, with the help of a best friend who was not a friend at all. Just doing his duty. Glorified lifelong babysitting. "Who the hell do you think you are? All of you." Tears ran down his cheeks.

"But that was before I got to know you."

"Don't dare patronize me… Not now… And Ophelia? Was she in on this as well? Was she a pawn, like you, in this vow of yours?"

"If that was the case, then she'd be the pawn sacrifice, wouldn't she?" Lorenzo said the words quietly. As if confronting them himself for the first time. Silence hung in the air for a few moments, along with his head.

"Ophelia didn't save you out of obligation, Tal. She loved you once."

Tal stood up suddenly and teetered unevenly. Lorenzo jumped to his feet and reached out to steady him. Tal pulled away. "I don't *need* any more assistance."

"I know this is a shock. Take a few days to digest all this, then we'll figure out where we stand."

Lorenzo was right about one thing. Tal no longer knew where he stood.

CHAPTER 36

Lucinda figured she'd surprise Tal. The office was only a fifteen-minute subway ride from the hospital, so she stopped off at a sandwich shop on Forty-Seventh, picked up a picnic lunch, and headed over. They must have been switching shifts because there was no one at the nurses' station, so she let herself into Tal's room. The bed was neatly made. All the monitors removed. No sign of life. Her breath came in gasps.

"Tal!" she screamed in a voice that wasn't hers. It was two octaves higher. Had he been moved to the ICU?... Was it stroke...? Blood clot...? Or was he...? A nurse caught her as she was toppling over and moved her to the bed. After a couple of minutes, the hyperventilation eased. The nurse explained Tal had checked himself out this morning. "The doctor argued with him," the nurse said, "but Mr. Neilson is a very hard-headed man.

A rock for a brain, she thought, just as her phone rang.

"Before you say anything, I'm home." Lucinda's blood rushed to her head in anger.

"The neurologist said last night you're not ready. Are you smarter than him? Are you smarter than me? Do you think I'm an idiot?"

"I had to get to the shiva. I knew what you'd say. I'm sorry."

"Damn well you knew what I'd say. You almost killed me with worry."

"I'm not going back to the hospital. I'll be good from now on. I promise. What's the difference where I'm lying? Just come home. I'm so sorry."

"Don't you dare move again today. Get into bed. Do you hear me?" She disconnected. She'd need the half hour to calm down.

■ ■ ■

Lucinda let herself in to the apartment and called his name. No response. He must be sleeping. There was a stack of papers at one end of the kitchen table, including Geri's crudely drawn picture of the church, Tal's laptop at the other end, just the way it sat the morning of the accident. Unresolved. She had made no effort to touch it while he was gone and thankfully he'd made no attempt to tackle it after the shiva.

Tal was dozing when she tiptoed into the bedroom. Her anger rose once again. This time she let it pass, waited a moment, gently touched his shoulder.

"I know you're angry," he whispered. "But I had to pay my respects to the family."

"You almost died, Tal. It could have waited until you recovered. They're a bunch of strangers. You know nothing about Ophelia's family."

"She saved my life. She saved our lives. And they're not strangers, as it turns out. My business partner is no partner." He began to cry. Then he began to shake. She sat down on the bed beside him. Rested her good hand on top of his.

"Talk to me," she said.

Tal downloaded Lorenzo's revelations, beginning with the dramatic boat crossing in 1943 and through to his own addiction recovery. "Father's success was a lie," he said. "His theories and commandments, built on a foundation of myths."

"Your father lived an illusion. It wasn't his fault. He built something and perhaps had the Farbers not been there every step of the way, he might have convinced someone else. He had the talent. He had the determination. By sheer dint of personality he would have succeeded. Geri was an icon. But he was also self-absorbed. Inattentive. Like so many other geniuses. And your mother. Let's not even talk about her.

"You drew the straw, Tal. You have to stop looking at it as short."

"You don't understand. It's not just Father's life. It's about how I came to exist. The lessons I was taught. The false premises."

"Stop looking backwards. Stop focusing on who you were or what you were taught. That's behind you. Do I need to get a mirror to show you who you are?"

Tal made an effort to sit up. Lucinda restrained his shoulder. "You're in my hospital now," her voice now firm and steady. "*I'm* in charge of your care. Lie down. Do your deep breathing. Then listen."

He began drawing long slow breaths through his nose, releasing through his mouth, focusing intently on Lucinda's face.

"You can't change the past. Stop looking back. Instead take stock of where you are today. Over two years clean. You outfoxed your mother to get the company she wanted. You outmaneuvered the leading investment banker in the country to achieve it. You broke the voting trust. You and Lorenzo did that. You have the strength. The brains. The instincts of success. Maybe you were born with them. Maybe you've developed them. You'll never be Geri. And thank God for that.

"And for what it's worth, I don't buy for a minute that Lorenzo was acting out of duty. The two of you together are like brothers. The way you fight. The way you make peace. The way you've moved ahead. He's more than a friend."

"Like you."

"Maybe... but..."

"But what?"

"Now's not the right time."

"If something's bothering you, then it is the right time. My head hurts. But it still works. Talk to me."

"Since Ireland I've been holding back. There's something I need to know. I've been too frightened to ask."

"After everything I've been dumping on you, trust me. Ask me. Anything."

"The night you left for Australia, you arrived late at the airport. You were anxious. As if something bad had happened to you. It was more than drugs."

"It wasn't drugs."

"It was also the night of Red's car crash."

"So?"

The dam burst. "Were you somehow involved in Red's death? I have to know the truth."

"Are you asking as my girlfriend or as my lawyer?" He laughed.

She bristled. "Don't dare treat this as a joke. It's been eating away at me."

"I'm sorry. I don't mean to dismiss you. The question is just so…" Tal sighed. "I suppose it isn't as crazy as it sounds, given the drugs I was on. The thoughts in my head. The crazy things I was saying. I was very upset that night, but it had nothing to do with Red.

"I went to visit the memorial to my baby brother. I thought a final visit before I left the country might help. If babies in heaven can hear, I needed Jeffrey to forgive me. I thought I could unload the burden of guilt I'd been carrying since I was twelve. I couldn't. It took you getting me on that plane and a year of hard work to accept that Jeffrey's death was a tragic accident."

"I love you, Tal," she whispered. Silence descended on the room. She could hear his breathing but not her own. She was holding on for his response.

Tal finally broke the silence. "If I could move my head— "

"Just tell me, Tal. Use your words."

"Since I can't kiss you, I love you too."

They lay in each other's arms, entwined, like strands of a rope, braided together. Inseparable. She closed her eyes and drifted away. The first sleep in days. The start of the rest of her life.

CHAPTER 37

Mac was running five minutes late for his meeting with Obie. "Respect," Obie had drilled into him for years. "You show up on time for appointments unless someone just died." He turned off Third Avenue and dashed east on Eighteenth Street, knitting his way through the lunchtime foot traffic. Obie had mentioned something about a key revelation. From a hundred yards off, Mac could make out the silhouette on the corner of Second, Obie's stomach protruding out farther from the unbuttoned trench coat that could not possibly hold it all in, a cigar hanging out of his mouth, the *Daily News* opened at eye level. Good thing the cigar was unlit. Obie was probably checking last night's results at Belmont, though he swore he no longer had more than a hundred bucks at play on any given night. If Obie was anything like most of the witnesses he had interrogated over the years, the one hundred was more like three hundred to a thousand. "When they admit to vice, yunkl, they're only admitting the tip of the schlong. No more than the foreskin that gets removed at the Jewish *bris*." And that's why it was impossible to forget Obie's lessons.

By the time he reached the corner, Mac was out of breath.

"You're late. Not polite to keep your elders waiting. We might faint from hunger before you arrive."

"And hello to you, Obie. The dentist ran late. The left half of my mouth is still numb. What's the big deal?"

"You do look a little lopsided. I'll tell you what the big deal is. Right in here. Take a minute. Smell the roses."

A smell that defined Manhattan. The in-your-face, unmistakable, undefinable smell of pastrami. Garlic, pepper, coriander, and who knew what else? "You hauled me out of the dentist chair to have lunch at a deli?"

"Not a deli. Moishe's Deli. The best pastrami in the universe in what used to be the best location in the universe."

"Used to be?"

"Look. Two doors down where that toy store is. See it?" Mac turned back to look at the familiar Discount Billy logo. A red smiley balloon, with black dots for eyes. "That very spot used to be sacred ground. They carried the best Havanas until Bay of Pigs. Fidel that shteck dreck. Cost me the second most important thing in my life."

"The second?" Mac asked. "What's number one?"

"You'll find out in a few minutes. Look at this mob," he said, cutting the line that ran all the way from the corner of Second Avenue to Billy's smiley face. Obie then jostled through the lineup to the hostess stand. "Don't let the crowd fool you," he said, turning his head to look back over his shoulder even as he continued to press forward. "They hold a table for me whenever I show up. A favor for some work I did years ago."

Mac turned sideways and drafted in Obie's wake. The hostess met them both with a wide grin. "How's my favorite detective?" she asked and, without waiting for a response, led them to a table at the back of the restaurant. A dull roar of conversation swallowed secrets along the way.

The waiter arrived immediately and looked over at Obie. "Bring me the usual. My friend here'll have the same."

The waiter jotted the order down and took off to the next table.

"When I first came here in '58, Moishe, the owner, would kibbitz with the customers. We loved each other. 'Til he got whacked in '84."

"Were you on the case?"

"No. Just some off-duty sleuthing when the detectives closed it as a cold case. Mrs. Moishe begged me. How could I say no? Looked like a mob hit. Pillow to the head, bullet to the brain. Turns out Moishe's neighbor Tony was taking things that weren't his. One of those things was a blondie, the neglected girlfriend of a mafioso, who decided to settle it the old-fashioned way. Except the hitman showed up at the wrong address. Anyway I got the family some justice. That got me a reserved table for life."

The waiter returned remarkably quickly with two platters, with a bowl balanced precariously between them. Each platter held a pile of pastrami, freshly cut, dripping fat, stuffed between slices of rye bread. He laid down a bowl of golden french fries between the two platters in the middle of the table.

"What about the drinks?" Obie asked.

"How many hands does it look like I got?" the waiter asked. "Two Moishe specials on the way."

"What's a Moishe special?" Mac asked.

"Fancy name for cherry cola. Some secret family recipe."

Obie reached for the gold container sitting beside the silver napkin dispenser. "Needs some hot mustard." He lifted off the rye lid on each stack and poured on a swirl, then held it for another few seconds as a mound formed beside the sandwich on the plate. He put down the mustard and picked up the no-name ketchup, moving his hand across the outside of his plate, forming a retaining wall of ketchup, signaling to Mac he best not wait to dig in.

Obie bit into the pastrami and his eyes rolled back in his head. The golden paste oozed out, falling in drabs onto the plate. While he chewed, he picked up a paper napkin from the metal dispenser on the edge of the table and dabbed at the corners of his mouth. "Better than sex."

Mac struggled to get that first bite of sandwich into his mouth. He had to admit it felt really good going down, but was it going to come back and bite Obie later? Like the King case that kept nipping at him.

"That forlorn look in your eyes. The one you get whenever you're obsessing over the dead red car case."

"You mean the Red King case."

"Same difference. You're not the only one."

Obie tore off a piece of crust, dragged it through a lump of mustard on his plate, and popped it in his mouth. He probably figured there was no time to be lost, speaking while he was chewing. "Ever since the M.E. came back inconclusive on the tissue sample. We'll never know if King was poisoned. I've been doing a little work on my own. Can't help it. I can't stand messy cases." Obie stopped and pointed at Mac's face. "You got some mustard on your cheek." Mac reached for a napkin and wiped the mustard off, then Obie continued.

"So we're back to square one. Trudi Darrow gets out of the car in Tribeca and a few minutes later the Ferrari crashes into a retaining barrier at eighty miles an hour. Whack." He banged the table and knocked over the ketchup container, leaving a red streak across the table.

The woman at the table beside them screamed.

Mac looked over sheepishly. "Sorry, ma'am. My partner got a little carried away."

Mac turned back to Obie. "Which reminds me. I caught something on the wire a few days ago. Another very strange story. Tal Neilson was deliberately run off the road by a white van outside the city. No license plate on the vehicle."

"Hmmm. So what do we know for sure? Geri Neilson dies and crazy son comes in and accuses Red King. Accident, no accident, who knows?" Table thump. "Mother locks up son, 'for his own sake,' she claims." Table thump. "Son escapes and runs to the edge of the earth," Thump. "Son returns, someone tries to whack him." Thump. "Maybe the son wasn't so crazy when he insisted his father was murdered?"

"And the only common denominator right now is Trudi Darrow."

The waiter arrived with the drinks and two long straws wrapped in paper. Obie pulled off the end, stuck the straw in his mouth, and blew the paper cover in Mac's direction.

"Forget the black widow nonsense. Someone wanted King dead? They went to great lengths to get him. It was a show murder. A scene from a movie. Like a mob hit. Meant to send a message. But to who?"

"To whom?"

"Whadda you want? Good grammar or good taste? Eat. It'll help us think."

Mac grabbed a fry and dragged it through the great wall of ketchup. Crispy outside, soft center. Just the way he liked it.

"Stay with me, Mac. What if King's death was a message to Darrow?"

"A mob message? That also sounds out of a movie."

Obie continued to work his way through the pastrami pile and took a sip of his Moishe special then burped. "There are two vices at the root of most of the crimes we solve."

"I know. I know. Money and money." One of Obie's favorite jokes.

"Except I'm serious. I'll bet there's a money trail here. I spoke to one of my pals in the Southern District. He does fraud, SEC violations, manipulation of public companies. I posed the question about the two CEOs dying so quickly and the widow stepping in." Obie took a handful of fries and had an assembly line going. He didn't let the full mouth slow him down.

"He did a little homework," he said just before swallowing the remainder. "When Tal Neilson was locked up, his stock was tied up in a voting trust with his mother."

"Can I stop you for a minute, Obie? This whole Dr. Rosen clinic thing has always bothered me."

"Leave it alone, Mac. You're obsessing over nothing. The son was stoned, the mother puts him away; might sound evil, but it's not criminal. Rosen and Guilden are dead ends. Forget them. The lockup was a means to an end. While she might have claimed she was doing it for his good, if she'd managed to keep him there, she would have controlled his stock."

"Except he was released."

"My guy also said that with all these coincidences he might have enough to justify a little forensic investigation into Darrow and Danmark. He's checking financial compliance and stock trading patterns. Anything unusual. From there they move on to check for signs of money laundering. They're gonna get back to me."

"The plot sickens."

"See. You don't have to be Jewish to have a sense of humor."

■ ■ ■

Li Shan reached for the phone, assuming these were the instructions to finish the job on the son.

"*Get back here. Your work is done.*"

Li Shan felt her stomach tensing. "But—"

"*Too much exposure to continue. You've delivered the message. We'll talk when you get here. Come home.*"

"Yes, Lingdao." The phone disconnected.

One successful kill out of three. She might return to Macao only to discover she was next. The indignity of being dredged from the bottom of Van Nam Lake. Disfigured, bloated, and ugly. A message to all the others about failure.

She stood in front of the mirror, adjusted the wig, straightened the sweatshirt that made her look ordinary, then reached for the hard cover of the small blue booklet. The gold coat of arms under the word PASSPORT warmed her insides. She opened it to the photo. Li Shan was gone forever. From now on, indistinguishable Lily Wong, proud American. Her new home.

"Our greatest glory is not in never falling, it is in rising every time we fall." The words rang in her ears, just as Master Kong's words had rung just before she entered the combat ring.

CHAPTER 38

Tal limped out of the elevator onto the third floor of the nondescript six-story building on Twenty-Third Street. It had a convenience store in the back of the lobby and an iconic pizzeria next door. The receptionist smiled at him on his way past her. He made his way to the offices, just a few thousand square feet to house the accounting and management staff reviewing the activities of Roylache's operations in Montreal, Louisville, and its European plant in Oslo.

He walked past the door with his name on it. He'd asked Lorenzo to use his proper name. Thalem Neilson. Grandfather's name. That was almost a month ago: before Ophelia died, before he learned the truth about Lorenzo. When they had a business plan and what he thought was a common goal. Now it was time to confront the future of that relationship to see if his nameplate was going to remain in place or leave with him on the way out the door. He'd spent the better part of a week talking it through with Lucinda. "It's more important to listen than to speak"— her final words on his way out the door this morning.

Lorenzo was sitting behind his desk, deep in discussion on his phone, facing away from the door. At the sound of the door opening, he turned and opened his eyes wide.

"Let me call you back." He replaced the phone in its cradle and turned to face Tal. "You look a hell of a lot better."

Tal didn't respond. Just nodded.

"That was our investment banker from GS. Last quarter results exceeded the analysts' projections. The stock price shot up this morning." Lorenzo smiled.

Tal felt an unexpected spark.

"But that's not what either of us cares about right now. Is it?" Lorenzo asked.

"I'm here to listen. I'm not here to make rash decisions. So talk."

"First, sit down," Lorenzo said. "You're going to be here for a while. You want a cappuccino?"

"No stimulants and easy on the stimulus. Doctor's orders. This conversation is my quota for the day."

"Then I'll get us some water." Lorenzo got up and returned a few moments later with a couple of glasses of ice water. He set one down in front of Tal on one side of his laminate desk and resumed his seat on the other side.

"I know I shocked you at the shiva," Lorenzo said. "I'm sorry."

"Doing your duty. I remember."

"If that's what you took from our conversation, then I apologize. You walked away with a mistaken impression." Lorenzo rolled his desk chair close to the desk separating them. He leaned in on his elbows. Tal reflexively leaned back in the black cushioned chair.

Lorenzo continued. "We were born with a lifetime responsibility. Maybe the same way your father indoctrinated you with his philosophies and commandments. She and I were taught from the time we were old enough to listen. Probably even before that. The vow we were brainwashed to observe. Like a holy commandment. Paul and Thomas insisted we stay out of your personal life."

"How ironic. What could be more personal than what we went through in Australia?" The reason I'm here, Tal thought. Maybe it wasn't personal at all for Lorenzo. Just duty.

Lorenzo paused and picked up the water glass. Drew a long sip.

Tal followed suit. The ice cubes banged against the tip of his nose. He wiped it dry with the back of his hand. "Why...? Why all this secrecy?"

"Maybe it was misguided. I don't know and we weren't permitted to question."

Maybe not a lot different from my own situation with Father, Tal thought. All his rules. The lectures in the study.

"I may have arrived in Australia out of obligation. But you have to remember I was still healing as well. I might have been in control of my addiction, but I hadn't yet found the will to go on. Not since the car accident. My two dearest just snapshots on my mantle. I was only beginning to figure out who I was. No tennis. No family. No remaining ambition. I had pushed everyone away. Until I got to know you.

"I slowly realized it was no longer about keeping an eye on you. It was about my own growth. What I was learning with you. I was finding my lost ambition. But I wasn't doing it alone. You were no longer the object of a family promise. You were a friend. We were talking business. We were talking future. We saw an exciting opportunity. We reached for it together. But it's not just business."

Tal nodded. It wasn't just business for him either. It was something else. Something he could only experience after Australia. His first friendship that wasn't Cornelius. "I came to the shiva to express my condolences. I felt nothing but guilt at being alive. I couldn't say thank you but I came to say something. I wasn't sure what. I was in shock." Tal took another long sip of water. The ice was melting.

"I wasn't angry at you when I stormed out. I was angry with myself. I'm sorry for how I behaved."

"The worst kind of rage. I know it well."

"This is what I planned to tell Ophelia's family. I'm terribly sorry for your loss, Lorenzo. Ophelia deserved better than giving up her life for me. I will never forget her. I owe her my life."

"Her memory will be for a blessing. So enough with the family debts. I am proposing we stop looking at the past and build our future."

Tal smiled and extended his arm.

■ ■ ■

A week later Lorenzo walked into Tal's office. Tal's arms were crossed, but he was smiling. His self-satisfied look. A crude picture of a church lay facedown; the dark ink had bled through to the back. Underneath the church, lettering Lorenzo recalled from college math courses. In front of

Tal a row of familiar worn papers covered in a blue-black ink were lined up in an orderly progression across the desk.

"You finally figured it out?" Lorenzo asked.

"I did."

"It's still Greek to me," Lorenzo said.

"Very good. The finance major recognizes the lambda! The key to Father's final puzzle."

"I remember Australia. You were convinced it was a coded message to unlock all of your father's secrets."

"Not the secret I was expecting. Come. I'll show you."

Lorenzo walked around the desk and stood behind Tal, looking down at the page on the far end that Tal was pointing to.

"Let me read it to you.

"*Congratulations, Son.*

"*I planned to talk to you at the Danmark anniversary party but you disappeared. In case I don't get the chance to tell you face to face, I finally looked at the spreadsheet.* THE WORK IS PERFECT. *Sorry I didn't give it the time of day when it counted. When I could have told you how proud I am. You can do great things, Son. Just don't try and be me. Be your own bastard.*

"*As for the Nazi money. Did they really think I didn't know what was going on? If you don't get it, ask Thomas or his son to explain it to you.*"

"Wow. I'm speechless."

"Father lived an epic life. I guess it doesn't matter how he got there."

"Like all epics, a little fact, a little mythology, and untold hidden forces."

CHAPTER 39

The stock price had been steadily declining over the past ten days. Those damned hedge fund managers, Trudi thought. Short selling, they called it, and it was driving her mad. They were leeches, selling stock in a company they didn't even own, betting that the stock would decline in value so they could buy it back at the lower price and score huge profits.

One in particular was dogging the company. *The Sanctimonious Investor* was publishing a blog, complaining that Danmark and a number of its competitors were engaged in questionable foreign sales through a company called Cunzhuang Pharmacies. "It doesn't add up" was the daily, relentless headline, which had triggered a Senate Committee investigation into price gouging of the American public by foreign drug companies and an SEC investigation into Danmark's relationship with Cunzhuang. Rumor and speculation.

Maybe she had acted impulsively in sacking Drew and Thomas to make room for the Turk's nominees all those months ago. She could use some advice right now.

Now the regulators were digging into Cunzhuang. Reports of mail fraud. All kinds of rumors, including a link to Red. It was only a matter of time until they connected the last of the dots. If not for Red and his Macao gambling habit… the Asian "friends" who "requested" that he figure out a way for Danmark to work with Cunzhuang … not really friends … not really a request… He would set up the mechanics for them to launder their money. They would ease the debt repayment terms.

Red hadn't been smart enough to figure out the rest. Trudi had taken the ball and had run with it.

"Cunzhuang isn't making nearly the money they could if you and the Chinese were a little smarter," she began, "but there's a way for them to increase profitability, create a revenue flow for you so you can get out from under, and create an insurance policy for me. Who knows when Geri's going to tell me he's had enough. Then I'm screwed."

"What are you suggesting?"

"Go to them. Set up a fulfillment company for us, owned through a bunch of shell companies. I don't know how it's done but that's the easy part. Use one of your offshore lawyers. Cunzhuang will start taking online consumer orders from the U.S. for Chinese equivalents of Danmark's drugs. All they do is switch the labelling when the drugs arrive from Danmark and ship them back here to our new company."

"Not to New York?"

"Of course not. Far away. Colorado or something. Hire a few clerks to pack the drugs into the envelopes and mail them. No-brainer. Danmark's international sales go up and we take a rake on every pill sold back to Americans."

"Brilliant. But that means we're competing with Danmark in the U.S."

"But not enough that anyone will ever notice. Don't get too greedy. Just be careful."

■ ■ ■

Someone had finally noticed. Ella Orsic, the new head of the legal department at Danmark, had been working on this exclusively for weeks. Yesterday she'd caught Trudi up on the multiple investigations: SEC, Southern District, FBI, and even Interpol were sniffing about like bloodhounds.

She'd received four calls this morning alone from her institutional shareholders, asking what the company was planning to do to dispel all these rumors and stabilize the stock price. She could not afford to lose the faith of the key funds that had been holding Danmark stock for decades.

She closed her eyes for a moment in the solitude of her office before attending to the uninvited guests that her assistant had kept waiting for the last half hour. When they were ushered at last into her office, she recognized one familiar face. A short and stubby man in an off-the-rack suit, followed by an older, fatter fellow, fedora perched on his head, tie askew, blowing his nose into a handkerchief as he walked in. The third man's tie was properly knotted. His suit was also bargain-basement, but the look on his face suggested he wore it as a badge of honor. "Brooks. Assistant District Attorney, Southern District, ma'am."

"To what do I owe the pleasure of another visit, detective?" she asked, addressing Mac.

"Sorry to disturb you, Ms. Darrow. This is my partner, Bernard Obront."

They sat down across the desk. Obront looked bored, his eyes scanning the room, as if the walls of Geri's old office might be willing to give Trudi away.

Brooks did not waste a moment. "As your attorney knows—"

"If you're here to discuss legal technicalities, I think the company's in-house lawyer should be here with us." Trudi lifted the phone receiver. "Theresa, can you ask Orsic to join us in here immediately? And I mean immediately."

Moments later, Orsic arrived, slightly out of breath, her eyes full of surprise once the introductions were completed.

"We have it all figured out, ma'am," Brooks started. Then he stopped. As if he just wanted to get a reaction. "This is just a courtesy call," he added.

Orsic intervened. "We've been through this with your investigators, Mr. Brooks. Whatever is upsetting the regulators happened before Ms. Darrow was involved with Danmark. It relates to events from years ago."

"So we should go chase the two dead husbands?" Obront smirked.

"You don't come into *my* house and disrespect *my* family," Trudi hissed. The nerve... The disrespect... None of them interested in what she'd been building... Just in destroying it...

"This is no more than a—" Orsic's arm reached out in restraint. Trudi stopped speaking. Then she glared at Obront.

"If you're not going to be respectful, sir, this meeting is over." Orsic made a move to rise.

We're not here to offend anyone," Brooks continued evenly, staring straight at Trudi. "I just wanted you to know the roof is falling in tomorrow. Today's your last chance to make a deal. We know about your offshore account. We've already traced twenty-five million. We believe there is more and it's only a matter of time until we find it. All that's left is to put together the final pieces of the embezzlement puzzle. You can help save us some time. That will save you some prison time."

"This is preposterous," Trudi said. The world was going crazy. She was running a perfectly good company. Cunzhuang was in the rear-view mirror. The next quarter projections were improving. And she had to waste her time because of Red's gambling errors? What bearing did that have on the present? On the future? Her lawyers just had to stand tough. Call the bluff. Wait for some other news scandal to displace Danmark.

Orsic stayed in control. "Mr. Brooks, we have nothing further to offer you today. In the future I would appreciate that you advise me of any further requests or discussions. Frankly I find your pretentious behavior in hiding behind the NYPD to be unprofessional."

"Not to worry, Ms. Orsic," Brooks said. "There won't be any more talk. Just action."

Brooks turned back to Trudi as he stood to leave. "Speak to your personal attorney, Ms. Darrow. Tell him that we know what you've done. My offer of a deal for you expires at five."

CHAPTER 40

The summons from Mother arrived at the office by special courier at five this afternoon, urging him to meet her at the brownstone at nine. "A matter of life and death," she wrote in her familiar cursive hand. Not like Mother to be dramatic.

It must have to do with the drama unleashed on the world after the market closed today. Danmark and Mother's photo on every business channel. Even the mainstream networks were covering what they were calling a scandal. It was sure to be the lead story of the *WSJ* and the *New York Times* in the morning. Tal could imagine the headline. February 6, 2006. Best Before Date Expires for Danmark.

The board had announced that Trudi had taken a voluntary and indefinite leave of absence while an internal investigation was completed. A special committee had been hastily organized.

Market analysts were speculating that Danmark's stock price was going to collapse at tomorrow morning's opening bell, leaving Mother, Yildirim, and the stockholders hanging.

A sold sign greeted Tal as he stepped out of the taxi. In short order someone else would be making memories in the brownstone — hopefully better memories than those that had burdened him. He tiptoed around some patches of ice and clumps of snow that had accumulated on the steps leading to the front door, which was unlocked. As he walked up the staircase, the sense of Father lingered in the musty, haunting air.

Tal called out but there was no answer. He walked upstairs and past the grandfather clock. Triste lille ø was beating steadily once again, indicating a human presence. To the left the grand piano, a reminder of his childhood failure as a musician: the day Father had taken him into the inner sanctum of his study, explaining the theory of his life, which, as it turned out, was a complete misconception. He was still Father at that time. Not yet the CallMeGeri in Tal's head. He walked along the ornate Persian carpet to visit the silenced ghost and the scene of the baby Jeffrey accident, one last time.

The study door was wide open. The globe had been rotated so that Scandinavia faced the doorway. A message from Geri? The tiny dot on Elsinore drew his attention. Tal made a mental note to take his globe before the sale closed.

"No hello for your mother?"

Tal nearly jumped out of his skin. She was sitting in Geri's leather swivel chair, her taut face belying the stress.

"Hello, lovey. Thank you for heeding the desperate call of a lonely mother. The press is stalking the office and my house. I needed some alone time with you. I figure this is a fitting place for us to meet. Shortly, this place will be gone forever."

The desk as always was conspicuously clear of any clutter, but for two items sitting on a bed of dust that had formed on the mahogany desktop. A small empty glass vial. Beside it one of Father's philosophy books on ethics.

He took one final breath. "What is it you want, Mother?"

"The kingdom has collapsed, son. Damned Red. They've asked me to surrender at three tomorrow afternoon."

"Surrender?"

"The police. The FBI. I don't even know who else is involved." She kept her eyes fixed on Tal, refusing to show any emotion, or perhaps the face-work and the Botox made it impossible, he was not sure.

"Presumably you'll be out on bail? It's a few tough hours, Mother, then it will be over. From what I'm reading, Red is being painted as the villain here."

"It's just beginning, Tal. It will never end. The indignity of the fingerprinting, being photographed in handcuffs like a common criminal. They'll find a photo in its worst possible light, and blast it around the world."

"You may be many things, Mother, but you're not a criminal. You can afford the best lawyers in the city. The worst does eventually pass and you get your life back."

"Doesn't really matter, lovey." Her tone was matter of fact. "By tomorrow we'll be ruined."

He was ruined years ago. Not anymore. Not since he'd stepped away from his parents and their poison. "We? Did you forget that I sold my interest to your new partner?"

"So you did, good for you, lovey. Yildirim probably wants to kill me." Her right index finger drew a short line in the dust on the desk. Then she crossed the line with a second line that ended at the glass vial. The sign of the cross.

"I'm ruined. Maybe Jesus can save me."

"Don't say that. I learned in Australia that strength comes from being honest with ourselves."

"You actually believe those bromides? Good for you, lovey. You want a little honesty? I'll give you honesty. I used to think that prison might be a better alternative. There were days, the months after you were born. I could barely drag myself out of bed in the morning. The nurse took care of you at night, but I could barely look at you in the daylight hours. I just wanted to crawl away and die." She sat back in Father's swivel chair and tilted her head upward slightly, closing her eyes with effort, as if even the memory of those moments was too much to bear.

"The doctors warned me not to have another. I never intended Jeffrey. Your father caught a virus a couple of years after you were born. Doctors told him he was sterile. I relaxed. I couldn't bear the thought of another. Then I got pregnant.

"'Impossible!' your father said. But it was possible. He understood immediately. He pretended to overlook it, but he never looked at me the same way. Whatever deficiencies Geri had as a husband, until Jeffrey was conceived, he actually loved me."

She stopped speaking for a moment. Tal decided to wait her out. She drew a short breath and resumed. "Your father loved me, not in a normal way, but in the way I understood from the day I met him. Not capable of a relationship the way the rest of the world understands it. They say you can only hate someone you love, and your father hated me. Jeffrey was a daily reminder to him of my betrayal. He never trusted Red again.

"I was stuck with an infant I knew I would kill if I had the opportunity. Except *you* presented the opportunity. I did what I had to do. But I also couldn't admit it to the world. That would have been the end of my life. I kept telling you, lovey. It wasn't your fault. Just your gift to me."

Her words tightened around his neck like a noose, squeezing until he couldn't breathe. Somehow, he found his voice. "You let me believe he bled to death before you could get him help."

"Yes, but it's time you knew the truth. It wasn't you, lovey. It was me." Her voice was soft and loving. Insanely loving.

He retreated slowly, then turned his back. He wanted no more of her. No more of her truth.

"I never meant to hurt you!" she screamed, her words cascading down his back like a truckload of damp earth, slowing his pace but not stopping him. Mother was no longer in control of his life. "But the baby was destroying us. When I took Jeffrey from you, the wound on the inside of his wrist was bleeding heavily. I applied some pressure until it slowed. Then I had an idea. What if I didn't stop the bleeding? I called your father to come home. I told him I was planning to let Jeffrey bleed out." Trudi was sobbing.

"What kind of sick woman are you?" Tal shouted. He turned back toward her, closing the distance.

"That's the point, Tal." Trudi shouted back at him. "I was sick. Mentally ill. I wanted your brother out of my life so I left him in the crib. When your father got home, he took care of the rest. We never discussed Jeffrey again. He just left."

He wanted to squeeze the life out of her.

"It's time, lovey. Time for you to do what you have to do. Just like I did what I had to do." She rose and took a step toward him, offering her neck.

Just one more step. Already close enough to smell her perfume. The pungency repelled him. Nauseated him. He took a step back. Away from Mother. Away from her treachery.

Tal stood deathly still. Drew a deep breath. Then another. He was the master of only one thing. Himself. Slowly he backed away, just outside the study, beside Triste lille ø, regaining his composure.

"Why tell me all this now, Mother?" His voice was quiet. Controlled.

Trudi was just to the side of Father's desk, between Tal and the globe. "The ceiling is caving in. We embezzled." Her voice began to shake. "Tomorrow the whole world is going to know." Tears were running down her cheeks. "It's over. I'm finished."

Tal edged back toward the study door. "Did Father know?"

"He must have figured it out. He went to Ireland to confront Cunzhuang. He cancelled the agreement. He couldn't tell the difference between organized criminals and the rest of the world. He was too principled. Married to his convictions." She wiped her eyes with the sleeve of her robe. "He thought he was the master manipulator."

"Ha. You of all people."

"Grow up, Tal." Her tone was now angry. "Those people don't settle their disputes in court. They wanted him dead."

"But he had a heart attack."

"Your father, Red, and I had a deal. One your father forced on us."

"What does that have to do with anything?"

"Your grandfather's dementia. Geri swore he would never let it happen to him. He found the right drug. Hid it in the Spinoza book. There on the desk. All I had to do was bring it with me to the hospital and slip it into the I.V."

"And you killed him with it," Tal whispered. "Jeffrey and then Father." The pain in his leg was intensifying.

"Let me finish. It's what Geri would have wanted. We had a deal. It had to be his decision when to leave this world."

"But you made the decision for him." Was it the pain screaming or was it his voice?

"I couldn't do it," she said. "I wanted to but I couldn't. I slipped it in his drawer. Left the room to call you. I knew if I spoke to you, lovey, that I couldn't go back in and do it. It wasn't like Jeffrey."

"You're suggesting Father woke up, got out of bed to inject the syringe into the I.V., then got back into bed to die?"

"Come on, lovey. The rest should be obvious. I wasn't the only one in the room with your father."

"Red."

"He saw me put the vial in the drawer. I returned five minutes later. Your father was gone."

A bitterness washed over his tongue, his mouth agape, his hand on the door handle. Caught. Unable to leave the room of deceptions.

"I've told you all this because I owe you one thing. Your freedom. Mine is coming."

"The two of you. Monsters." Tal turned and stormed out. He slammed the front door and began to hyperventilate, bending over at the waist. He was weighted to the spot, emptied of emotion, void of thought. A few minutes must have passed before he could think straight.

And then the words struck him. "Mine is coming." He had a flash of the moment just before he turned away from her in the living room. Her right hand was clenched in a fist. A tip of metal stuck out from the end of the fist. Then he flashed to the empty vial on the desk.

He rushed back in the house. She was lying frozen on the floor, at the base of the grandfather clock, eyes wide open. Her gold brocade house-coat splayed open, her hand fixed in a clench, unyielding. There was a red welt on her right thigh. He felt for a pulse. Nothing. The pendulum was swinging. The clock was ticking, measuring the remaining seconds of Trudi's final act.

He reached for his cell phone and, fumbling with it, dialed 911, then he began the mouth to mouth.

■ ■ ■

The police had barricaded off the Neilson residence when Mac and Obie pulled up in front of the brownstone. An officer was stationed at the door. Tall, short blond hair, vaguely familiar. She touched the brim of her cap and nodded to him at a distance.

"Mac," she said as he climbed the stairs. "We meet again. Rachel from the car crash."

"The dead red car cop," Obie said from behind him.

"I remember," Mac said. "We meet at all the best occasions. Who do we have this time?"

"Come on. You guys already know it's the widow. Trudi Darrow. Her son called it in. Matricide, suicide, you decide."

They entered the house and made their way up the stairs and around the yellow tape cordoning off a couple of the rooms. "I like that kid," Obie said. "Got a sense of humor."

"I'll take the son's statement," Mac said. Talem Neilson was sitting on a fancy chair in the living room, bent over, head in his hands. Weird, Mac thought. He had originally sized Neilson up as not having an acting bone in his body. Darrow had locked him up in the sanatorium, yet here he was, distraught. Some things about human nature Mac would never understand.

CHAPTER 41

Tal hesitated at the entrance of the Holy Trinity Lutheran Church. Where Father's journey had ended. Where Tal's had begun. The imposing red-painted wooden doors facing the park were locked shut. The way religion had always been locked out by Father. "Your grandfather was in the business of fish and God," Father would often say when he was in a teaching mood. "I don't believe in anything other than the power of ideas and the value of science. Remember that, Son."

He made his way around to the meek side door, painted the same cheerful red, and knocked. A few small puddles of water lay on the concrete, where the final remnants of winter snow had melted. The sun was unusually warm in these first days of spring. The man who answered his knock was a little older than Tal remembered, the face a little rounder, the hair a bit thinner and grayer, the eyes searching.

"Welcome, Talem."

"Please call me Tal."

"Tal then. I'm sure you're wondering why I asked you here this morning. Please come in."

Tal followed the pastor down a few stairs along a damp, narrow hallway, then back up a couple of flights of stairs to a small room with a picture window filled with a magnificent stained glass. The sun surged through the window, reflecting reds, blues, and yellows onto the table. Almost heavenly. Tal wondered whether Father had sat here with Pastor Marcellus. What did they discuss?

The pastor offered him a seat facing the window. Marcellus sat opposite him and leaned forward slightly. "You've been through quite a lot in the past few years. I'm sorry about your mother. That was a tragedy. How have you been managing, if you don't mind my asking."

"Mother's death left me shaken. I was there when she took her life."

"It can be overwhelming. How have you coped?"

"The love of a good woman. The acceptance of a higher power. The notion that I can only control myself and my reactions to the world around me, but I can't control the world."

Marcellus nodded. "Your father was very proud," the pastor said.

"Yes, he was a proud man. One thing I could say about him."

"I mean proud of you."

The surprise must have registered all over his face, because the pastor began to laugh. "I'm not going to pretend that Geri was in line for sainthood. He rarely had anything good to say about anyone, but he had a special place in his heart for you."

"Unfortunately he had to die before it was revealed to me." Tal clasped his hands in front of him on the table.

"Revelation is often mystical." The pastor smiled. "He called me the day you worked out the square root of the speed of light to four decimal places in your head."

"Just the square root game we used to play."

"Over the years he raved to me about the quality of your brain." Lately Father had been proving to be full of surprises. "Though he was worried about your toughness. Whether you could survive in the world. I fought him on one particular issue that affects you. We finally agreed to compromise. I had to wait until I was confident you were ready. That's why I called you here today." Marcellus stood up. "Please follow me."

Marcellus led Tal briskly out the side door. Lucinda was standing off to the side, typing on her smart phone. She quickly dropped it in her purse and turned to Tal, just as he leaned in to kiss her on the cheek.

"Sorry, just checking some office emails," she said, smiling first at Tal then at the pastor.

"Am I too early? You did say to meet you here before noon?"

Tal turned to Marcellus. "Pastor, I'd like to introduce my fiancée, Lucinda Horat."

"Congratulations to you both," the pastor said.

Marcellus put his hand on Tal's shoulder. "Actually, Lucinda, your timing is perfect. I have something I was planning to show Tal but I think you will appreciate it as well. Please, follow me."

They crossed the street under a warming early spring sun and headed north to Seventy-Second Street and into Central Park. The canopy of trees lent shade over the gravel path as Marcellus's pace slowed.

The circular mosaic on the ground had partially sunk into the earth. The word *Imagine* in black tiles in the center. Strawberry Fields Memorial to John Lennon.

Just on the other side of the mosaic, a middle-aged woman nodded at them. She was standing beside a young man, round face, about Tal's height, who looked vaguely familiar. As the three of them came around, Tal noticed the radiant smile. A beam of true joy that filled the park. The man looked to be in his mid-twenties.

The pastor walked over to the man, who gave him a big hug.

"Pastor Marcellus. You've come to visit!" the man said.

Marcellus turned back to Tal and Lucinda. "I'd like to introduce you to a friend of mine. His name is Jeff. Jeff, this is Tal."

Jeff rushed over and gave Tal a hug. "So happy to meet you, Tal." A rush of love from a complete stranger. "At the home I have so many friends. I love them all. All except Edgar because he likes spinach. I hate spinach."

"So do I, Jeff."

"Well, that's good. Do you know how many leaves are on the tree behind you?"

Tal turned back to the aging oak. "I'd estimate around 18,000."

"18,242, to be precise," Jeff answered. "How about 1832 multiplied by 427?"

"782,264," Tal replied immediately. Before he had time to think. Before he had time to understand.

"That one gives most people trouble. You know my real name is Jeffrey, but everyone I like calls me Jeff."

"And my real name is Thalem. But the mean kids used to tease me, so I got rid of the 'h' and shortened it. My friends call me Tal."

Jeff rolled up his long sleeves as if he were preparing to get to tougher work. "You wanna see something special?" he asked, extending his right arm. "It's a really long scar. I got it when I was a baby and I still have it."

A thin line ran the breadth of the inside of Jeff's wrist. The tears welled up in Tal's eyes, his throat constricting until he could no longer control the flood.

Jeff showed signs of panic. "I didn't mean to hurt you. Did I hurt him, Pastor?"

"I think this is Tal's way of showing you how happy he is, Jeff."

"But he's not… " Tal started.

"He never was."

The woman finally intervened. "Jeff, why don't you give Tal another hug? Maybe he will come visit you at the home."

"Will you be my friend?" Jeff asked.

"I'd love to, Jeff," Tal said.

"Who's the lady?"

"This lady is my best friend."

"Why is she crying, Tal?"

"I think she's as happy as I am to meet you, Jeff." The tears were streaming down Tal's cheeks. He made no effort to stem the tide.

Jeffrey laughed. "The two of you have a very funny way of showing it. Don't they, Pastor?"

Marcellus nodded.

Lucinda, smiling broadly now, held out her hand. "You can call me Lucy. I'd like to be your friend, too, Jeff."

"Let's all be friends," Jeff said. "You wanna play the square root game? Everyone I play with needs a calculator."

"I should be okay without one," Tal said, "but I haven't practiced in a long time."

"Then I'll keep away from complex numbers. That way it's fair," Jeff said.

"I'm just going to watch," Lucinda said.

■ ■ ■

Marcellus linked his arm with Tal's on their walk back to the church. Lucinda walked alongside.

"Your father disowned Trudi and the fetus she was carrying during the pregnancy. He was sterile. He was certain she had slept with Red. He kept insisting to me that her eyes told him she had."

Tal nodded. He knew Father when he was certain. The unmovable object opposed to all forces. "So they thought that Jeffrey was...?"

"Red's son. Yes, your parents were certain. It was at the root of the deterioration of their marriage. He was still traveling almost every week, and your return from boarding school pushed Trudi over the edge. Her postpartum depression was unmanageable, far worse than it had been with you.

"He called me in a panic one night. Arrived at the church with a baby wrapped in a blanket. Jeffrey's wrist was crudely bandaged, but he seemed fine. Geri told me that if I couldn't help, she might finish the job in the morning. It was too big a risk. I found Jeffrey the best care available. Geri and I both did the best we could. He handled all the details including managing Trudi's delusion that Jeffrey was dead. We called it 'the project.' Jeffrey's name was never mentioned again. That is, until six months before Geri died. In the name of science, he decided to go for genetic testing. He was fascinated to discover a rare genetic marker that might explain the way his brain worked. The science of what made Geri, Geri.

"Then I remembered Jeffrey's medical records. He also had a rare marker. We checked his records, then Geri did the math and concluded he had to be the father. For a man who never experienced a moment of regret in his life, Geri was defeated.

"Geri changed his will and left me the money to take care of Jeffrey, along with our decision to share it with you, but only when I was certain you were ready."

The three of them were standing just outside the church. A heavy gust of wind blew them off balance. Instinctively Tal pulled Lucy close to him. The pastor crossed his arms and smiled.

"That would be Geri telling me to speed it up."

CHAPTER 42

One year later

———

Drew Torrance sat facing the window, rotating back and forth ever so slightly on a swiveling leather chair, admiring the view over Times Square from the forty-sixth floor of one of Sixth Avenue's prestigious towers. From the outside, green-tinted glass and cold steel defined this block of the Avenue of the Americas, such a dramatic name for this section of Sixth Avenue. Home to the professional firms that cranked out the deals that greased the wheels of the U.S. economy. Drew's firm, TGO, had joined that elite, taking over three floors of the tower last month. The smell of newly laid carpet permeated the refrigerated air.

Today Drew was playing host as chair of the board of Roylache. Four other men and one woman had taken their places around the polished oak boardroom table. Thomas had joined the board with him a little over a year ago when Tal and Lorenzo had approached them to advise the company that had been making its mark in the generic drug industry. Odell Moore was one of the original additions to the board, once their takeover of the company had been completed. Melissa Fortin-Bras, the brilliant CEO whom Tal and Lorenzo had recruited from a competitor in Quebec, was turning the industry on its ear.

Trudi's suicide had triggered a series of investigative reports into Danmark that led to a precipitous drop in its share price. It began with the SEC and quickly blossomed into a full-scale *Wall Street Journal* investigative piece. At its height, when Geri was running the company, the stock had traded as high as thirty-two dollars a share. Today the shell that was left of Danmark was trading at under two dollars. Its largest shareholder was left holding the bag.

Lorenzo had been following the news closely since the moment it broke. Tal began the financial analysis after his mother's funeral and private burial. Analysis evolved to management discussion, which was scheduled to make its way to the board next month. The schedule was advanced when Sterling Yildirim reached out to Odell last week, insisting he meet with the board this morning.

"Yildirim would not be coming unless he had something very specific in mind," Odell said.

"Tal and I have run various scenarios. We believe now is the time to go after Danmark," Lorenzo said.

"I want to make sure this isn't about ego," Thomas replied. His hairline had receded in front, and his brown eyes studied Tal and Lorenzo over the reading glasses perched on the end of his nose. His mind was still the steel trap that Drew recalled from many similar discussions over the years. "Danmark was your father's company, Tal. How much of that is motivating your decision?"

Lorenzo was quick to answer. "We've done our homework, Papa. The value of its drug patents alone are probably worth four or five times the market value of the company. Take a look at the pro formas on page four of our presentation."

The others studied the paperwork in front of them.

"Which means the impact on our stock price should be great for our investors," Tal said.

"If we're ready," Odell said, "I'll go get him."

A few moments later Yildirim swept into the boardroom. Over his pinstripe suit, Sterling Yildirim sported a red cape that flowed almost all the way to the floor, his Yankees cap perched on his head. A carved wooden cane in his right hand kept pace with his left leg until he arrived at the board table. A young woman with streaked auburn hair set down a briefcase that was straining her left shoulder, then took care of the cane and cape.

He remained standing, his shoulders slightly stooped, his back slightly humped.

"You'll excuse my posture. I am carrying the burden of Danmark investor expectations on my shoulders." The Turk laughed.

He removed the Yankees hat. "Thank you for agreeing to meet, but don't think for a moment that I come to you cap in hand." The Turk looked directly at Tal.

"Neilson. Last time we spoke was, what, a couple of years ago? Remember what I told you to do?"

"You told me to get some operating experience."

"Wise advice, if you ask me. Advice that you took to heart. I'm impressed with what you and your partner have accomplished here."

He turned his attention to the CEO. "And you, Ms. Fortin-Bras. Impressive results in the last year. Your stock price has tripled since I made the deal with Neilson. Meanwhile, I lost a fortune betting on Neilson's mother. But only on paper. The right horse but the wrong jockey. It's past time for a switch."

He turned and faced Odell. "Great operators are rare and when I find them, I back them. I've come with a proposition."

He turned to the woman beside him. "Audrey, would you give everyone a copy of the proposal I've worked out." Audrey reached into the briefcase and passed the binders around the table.

"I'll keep it very simple," the Turk continued. "I want you to lead the future of Danmark-Roylache. You may find my terms a little rich, but I have a hole that I need to climb out of." He spent the next hour outlining the terms of the merger of the two companies.

"I'm assuming your other major shareholder will fall into line?" Yildirim asked. "The owner of your late mother's stock?" The Turk stared Tal down.

Tal hadn't been the least bit surprised that there was nothing for him in Mother's will, though he had found a way to turn the tables on her ghost.

"I think I know how the Neilson Foundation feels about this," Tal said.

"You damn well ought to," the Turk boomed, "what with your wife running it." The Turk laughed hard. "I've taken the liberty of speaking to my German bankers, who have agreed to lend us a billion dollars to expand. This is going to be enormous."

Drew looked down the table at Tal and Lorenzo, both of whom were repressing the tiniest of smirks. Bad strategy when sitting across the table from America's most notorious snake charmer.

There was likely going to be a deal before anyone left this room, though it might be a very long night.

■ ■ ■

Tal dragged his exhausted bones into the apartment at five in the morning. The globe was sitting in the living room, under the window, where it fit. He felt for the axis, now smoothed to the touch. Its cutting edges had been rounded out before he'd let it into the apartment. No more accidents, especially with a baby in the house. He pressed on Elsinore and the globe opened. Then he dropped in his own coded note for the future and closed it back up.

Tal walked into the nursery. Ophelia was out cold in the crib, snoring softly. Tal leaned in to breathe in her baby smell, then softly kissed her warm forehead. He brimmed over with emotion. I'm home, he thought. A place that finally exists. A place I will never take for granted.

Lucinda murmured when he slid into bed beside her. Her arm reached back to pull him closer. Perhaps home wasn't a place at all. Just a state of mind. The place where you could go in your head to get in touch with yourself, to learn how to love yourself and to communicate that love.

Home was where you could appreciate your blessings. Where you could lie beside the person you loved more than anyone in the world. More than yourself.

EPILOGUE

Four months later, July 2007

Tal had taken a seat in one of the guest chairs in Lorenzo's office. His right leg was propped on the other chair, a habit to reduce the discomfort, long after the physio appointments had ended. Lorenzo's desk was overburdened with quarterly divisional reports. The integration of the Danmark and Roylache divisions had commenced and it would be months before the cost savings were reflected in the operating results.

The receptionist pushed the door open, holding a slip of pink paper.

"Tal, I'm sorry to interrupt but I have a message for you. The man refused to leave a voice mail. He said it was a family issue and it was important that you get back to him." She handed him the note then shut the door behind her.

"I think this is my cue to exit," Lorenzo said.

"Do I need to remind you that it's your office, Lorenzo?"

"In case you wanted some privacy. What's mine is yours."

"Believe me, you don't want what's mine. Nothing can give you a better insight into my dysfunctional family than what my cousin Steve is going to throw at me. My mother's nickname for him was Stinky. Please stay."

Tal dialed the number and put the line on speaker phone.

"Steve, how can I help you?"

"I don't know if you were told, but Walter passed away. We buried him last week. Private service."

"I'm sorry. No one reached out."

"Probably my fault. I'm calling as the executor of his estate. In short, it's a mess. Walter and I each borrowed five million dollars a couple of years ago to buy twenty million worth of stock of Danmark from your mother and her husband."

"Don't tell me."

"Yes. We thought it was a great deal at ten bucks when the stock was trading at twenty. Sure, it had dropped from the all-time high of thirty-two but we had confidence in your mother. So we held it expecting the stock price to go up. We got caught in the crash. The stock is now worth about two million in Danmark-Roylache stock after the merger. Can you believe it? We started with a claim for a hundred million and turned it into a loss of over eight million."

"Brain-dead cousins," Tal mouthed across the room to Lorenzo.

"How can I help you, Steve?"

"The bank has stepped in. Walter's life insurance covered part of the loan, but there's still a lot remaining. They insist I liquidate the position. But the block of stock is too big to trade. My broker is telling me that until all the regulatory issues relating to the merger are finalized, I've got to be patient. Except our bankers have lost their patience. They want it sold immediately. Would you buy it?"

"I've got to think about it carefully, Steve. I can't just make a rash decision because your bankers are antsy. And I've got partners to answer to." Tal winked at Lorenzo.

"First, I want to tell you I had nothing but respect for your father. Even in those years when we were fighting. Same goes for your mother."

"No hard feelings here. Whatever dispute you had with my parents is past. I'll tell you what. Because you're family, I'll offer your bank half a million for the entire lot."

"It's worth way more than that," Steve whined. "The bank will never agree."

"Leave that to me, Steve. You have sixty seconds to give me an answer. Yes or no."

NORMAN BACAL

Endless silence at the other end of the line. Tal sat quietly until he heard the utterance. "Okay."

"Pardon me, Steve?"

"I accept your terms." The words were barely audible, yet enough to signal capitulation.

"My sympathies, Steve. I know you loved your brother." Tal disconnected, then stood up to stretch his leg. The doctor had warned that arthritis would inevitably sink in to the damaged joint.

"Nice work, son."

"Thanks, Father."

"Did you say something, Tal?" Lorenzo asked.

Tal smiled.

ACKNOWLEDGMENTS AND THANKSGIVING

I am deeply indebted to my close friend, Jeff Rayman, for our two months of daily Covid-19 virtual meetings, where we fought over every line of the manuscript, to take a good draft and to make it shine.

To my story editor, Jennifer Glossop, for her advice in working through the numerous plot challenges, in what proved to be a very complicated scheme. To Wendy Thomas, for her wise suggestions in final edit.

To the wonderful team at Barlow Books, and in particular to Sarah Scott and Tracy Bordian, for their assistance in getting the book launched.

To my team of medical advisers: Dr. Norman Straker, MD, DLFAPA, Clinical Professor, Weill Cornell Department of Psychiatry, to Dr. Jane Heggie, MD, Associate Professor anesthesia, UHN, and to Dr. Sidney Croull, MD, pathologist, for their input. Any medical errors or omissions in the manuscript are strictly my own.

To my two mothers, Frances Bacal and Esther Westelman, for their encouragement along the way.

Praise for *Odell's Fall*

"A page-turning pot-boiler of a read."
—*Robert Cooper, former president, HBO Pictures*

"A powerful debut."
—*Robert Rotenberg, international bestselling author*

"A gripping rollercoaster ride of a legal thriller!"
—*Pamela Gossiaux, international bestselling author*

"Exciting, fast-paced thriller. Highly recommended!"
—*Susan Keefe, award-winning author*

"Lightning-fast pace ... a wonderful read."
—*Kimberly Love, author*

"Superbly crafted twists."
—*Grady Harp, Amazon Top 50 reviewer*

"Truly memorable. An edge-of-your-seat murder mystery."
—*John J. Kelly, Detroit Free Press*

"Bacal creates a world where the reader is held hostage."
—*Norm Goldman, Book Pleasures*

"Five stars. I was clinging to the edge of my seat throughout."
—*Olivia-Savannah Roach, book blogger*

ABOUT THE AUTHOR

Norman Bacal is the *Globe and Mail* and Amazon.ca bestselling author of *Breakdown,* a memoir about the rise and fall of Heenan Blaikie, one of Canada's most prestigious law firms (and home to two Canadian prime ministers). His debut novel, *Odell's Fall*, a modernized *Othello*, was published in 2019. Bacal was formerly managing partner of Heenan Blaikie and an expert in film and television finance (he sat on the board of directors of Lionsgate for almost ten years and advised many Hollywood studios). He writes about what he knows best: lawyers and big business. Bacal also speaks regularly to university students and professionals. Together with his life partner, Sharon, Bacal has four children and five grandchildren — all of them wonderful.

Reach Norman and check out all his books at
www.normanbacal.com